SWEETER THAN A DREAM.

"Lexi."

"Hmmm?" She kissed the corner of his mouth.

"Are you asleep?"

"I hope not." Once again she fit her mouth against his. He drank from her as if she were life itself.

"Honey, is this what you want?"

"Yes." Her soft lips roamed over his face. "Even if I'm dreaming."

"This is no dream." No middle-of-the-night fantasy had ever been as hot as this. He had never been more wide awake or more aware of the woman within his arms.

"I don't want this to end," she whispered, her breath hot against his cheek. "And, God help me, if I'm asleep, I don't want to wake up."

****

"Riveting and powerful! Sharon Mignerey blazes in her first novel. A new romantic star is on our horizon."
—*The Literary Times*

"Be on the lookout for future books from this fantastic novelist."
—*Affaire de Coeur*

ROMANCE FROM FERN MICHAELS

A SACRED TRUST

Sharon Mignerey

Zebra Books
Kensington Publishing Corp.

http://www.zebrabooks.com

ZEBRA BOOKS are published by

Kensington Publishing Corp.
850 Third Avenue
New York, NY 10022

First Printing: February, 1997
10 9 8 7 6 5 4 3 2 1

Printed in the United States of America

For Anita,
Sister of the heart,
Keeper of the faith.

ACKNOWLEDGMENTS

Though novel writing is a solitary endeavor, the completion of this, my first novel, would have been impossible without the faith and support of a lot of people.

My daughters, Yvette and Celeste, never doubted my dream of being a published author. Both heard too often my writer's admonishment: unless there is blood or fire, leave me alone for the next hour. I thank them both for giving me lots of those hours. My husband always gave me the impression the pursuit of my dream was a fair trade for frozen-food-in-a-box. I thank him for his unfailing love and faith. He is my knight, now and always.

I owe a huge debt to the members of Rocky Mountain Fiction Writers. They are fellow writers and friends whose vocations and avocations are a varied and wonderful source of expert advice. To each of you who shared your knowledge and gave your support, I thank you, most especially: Kay B., Jasmine, Maggie, Lee, Grace M., Cheryl, Colleen, Chris J., Carol R., Chris G., Jim C., Rick, Robin, Judy S., Kathee, Ann, and Steve M.

Chapter 1

"Don't think about it, just do it," Lexi Monroe muttered again to herself. She planted the toe of her left climbing boot into the next foothold. The movement was firm, confident, but a tight knot of fear climbed a little higher into her middle.

She clung to the granite face some seventy-five feet above the base of the cliff. Sweat trickled off her scalp, momentarily distracting her from her search for the handhold her instructor, Chane Callahan, had pointed out.

With sensitive fingertips, she found the handhold. A pebble dislodged and bounced down the side of the cliff. She heard each separate ping as the small stone fell. Taking a deliberate breath, she lifted herself up. The crevice felt cool and slightly sandy as she hung her weight from her fingers.

Heat seeped from the sun-warmed rock through her shirt. Endless seconds passed as she searched for the other foothold. A splotch of moisture was left where her cheek had been plastered against the unyielding granite surface. At last she sensed the depression. She balanced her right foot against it and redistributed her weight, thrusting her torso away from the cliff face, pressing her cheek against the rock until all she could see or smell was the granite. Once she had loved climbing.

That she'd ever love it again seemed, at the moment, as unlikely as loving a root canal.

"You're doing fine, Lexi," came Chane's reassuring voice five feet below her. "You've just made the three-quarter way point."

An hour ago he had reviewed the techniques they had learned both on the ropes challenge course and the twenty-foot climb done earlier in the week. He classified the hundred-foot climb as easy, then scaled the cliff in a scant ten minutes to prove it. He rappelled down, then climbed again, this time explaining each of the handholds and footholds he used. If the cliff's meager crevices would hold his six-foot five-inch frame, they would certainly hold anyone else's. The ascent was as safe as he could make it—complete with safety ropes and helmets. He climbed with each of the four students that had preceded Lexi, who had watched with growing dread.

A year ago she could have made this climb with the same finesse Chane demonstrated. She knew she had the strength and the basic knowledge to make it to the top. Today, it was all she could do to confront her fear and search for the next depression in the rock.

Lexi inhaled deeply, trying to reclaim her concentration. Do, she reminded herself. Don't think. Just do. She ventured a look up. Twenty-five feet had never seemed so far.

"Okay, Lexi, do you have your next move in mind?"

She examined the granite in front of her, locating a ledge wide enough for her foot. She took longer to find a handhold she was comfortable with.

"Here. And here." She motioned to the two places she had picked.

"Can you reach the foothold to your left? It's a longer stretch, but it looks more solid to me."

She gauged the distance, then shook her head. "I don't think so."

"Okay. Go with what feels comfortable."

She moved her foot into the crevice. It seemed to shift, almost imperceptibly. Before moving her other foot, she tested her weight. The foothold felt solid, and she lifted her other foot away from its perch and reached for the next handhold.

The unexpected pop of rock cracking sounded like thunder in her ears. The rock beneath her foot gave way suddenly. Then she was falling.

The gray face of the cliff disappeared. The deep blue September sky filled her world.

She knew she was going to die.

Now, the nightmares would finally cease, bleak dreams where orphaned children called to her. Now, the cruel icy-gray eyes that stalked her deepest fears would finally close. Now, she would finally find peace.

A scream clawed up her throat, but never escaped her mouth. Her blood chilled. Never had she been so coldly certain that she'd reached the end of her life. She should have died ten months ago in South America. Instead she had run.

Run from cruelty.

Run from her vow to the babies.

Run from her own consuming fear.

Her safety rope stretched to the end of its play and bounced her upward. An unending fall began again. Her whimper became an agonized moan ripped from her soul.

The fall abruptly ceased. Warmth curled around Lexi and she sank into it. Better, she thought vaguely. Heaven should at least be warm.

"You're okay, Lexi." The murmur was deep, reassuring, a rumbled purr against her ear. "I've got you."

She opened her eyes and found the granite cliff once again in front of her. Vertical, like it was supposed to be. She felt him shift her weight slightly, supporting her legs with his own, supporting her body with his own.

She gulped in great rasping breaths of air. Her glance fell through the open space between Chane's legs, which were braced against the rock. She moaned again, trembling violently.

"Don't look down, Lexi."

She closed her eyes and nodded her understanding, wishing she had never taken this on. She'd wanted to be in control of her life again, wanted to believe in her own judgment, her own strength. She'd wanted to banish the fear that consumed her. To do all that, she'd chosen Chane Callahan's wilderness survival course to confront and defeat the demons that had dominated her life since she'd left Central America. That choice no longer seemed reasonable or sensible. She shuddered again, opened her eyes, and stared at the rock face in front of her, the abstract patterns in the stone claiming her attention.

"You're not going to fall again," came Chane's reassuring voice as he rubbed her arms with his broad palms.

She shivered once more, hard, unaware of the goose bumps on her arms until his warm hands stroked her. She hoped his promise meant they were headed back for the bottom of the cliff. With his weight offering support, she was sure she could belay down.

"How far did I fall?"

"About five feet."

"Are you sure? It felt like—"

"A thousand. I know." His hands stroked her arms again. "We'll just rest here a couple of minutes until you're feeling better."

The taste of bile and fear rose in her throat, making her tremble. The fear was going to defeat her. Again. She'd think about that later. Just now she wanted only one thing. To be off this cliff.

"Are you okay?" Chane asked. "You're still shaking."

"For being petrified, I'm fine." The snap she had intended was lost beneath the tremor in her voice.

"I won't let you fall."

Lexi risked a glance down and immediately regretted doing so. The ground was too far away, and the white rope that snaked to the top of the cliff looked no more secure than a piece of cooked spaghetti. The sooner she was down, the better.

But she did trust Chane Callahan about one thing. He'd been picky about the equipment and he hadn't said a word when she'd checked and double-checked harnesses and ropes, a habit he encouraged in each of them, a habit she'd fostered long ago and reinforced on a hundred climbs. She might be scared out of her mind, but the rope had been there to save her life just as it was supposed to be.

Chane continued to rub his hands up and down her arms, leaving a path of warmth behind. His body easily supported hers, and for the moment, Lexi was relieved to have that security. She relaxed slightly, absorbing the novelty of having someone else to depend on, if only fleetingly.

"Ready?" he asked some moments later.

She nodded. "As ready as I'm going to be."

"Okay, kiddo. I know you're not going to like this, but we're going to finish the climb. I'll be here every step of the way."

"I'd rather go down."

Behind her, she felt him shake his head. "There's only one way off this cliff and that's up."

Another version of grit-your-teeth-and-get-back-on-the-horse. She had put that into practice more times than she cared to remember. Lexi looked up the cliff. The thirty feet or so to the top looked like a mile. She closed her eyes, her stomach churning.

"Lexi, are you listening?" Chane's imperative question penetrated her thoughts. She searched her memory, unable to remember a single thing he'd said.

His fingertips touched her cheek, forcing her to look over her shoulder at him. His dark eyes swept over her face, and his voice, no longer the soothing one of the guardian angel who had caught her, demanded she pay attention. "You're going to use this handhold here." He pointed. "And here."

"I want to go down," she said.

"Up." Steel laced his voice. "You can do it, Lexi."

I can't. The words never left her mind. Of all the words in the English language, those two had never been part of her definition of herself. "What about you?" she asked.

"I'll be right here, Lexi. You won't fall again."

His hand grasped her arm and lifted it toward the handhold he'd indicated. She slid her hand up the granite face, feeling the grit against her sensitive fingertips. She curled her fingertips into the crevice and waited for him to push her body away from him. But he didn't. Seconds passed. Gradually, she understood he'd wait until she was ready.

What's the worst that could happen? she asked herself. The consequences of falling seventy-five feet made her abandon that line of thinking fast.

Lexi took a deep breath and braced her feet against the cliff and reached for the handhold, missing instantly the warmth and support of Chane's big body as hers arched away from him. She would have given her new wide-angle lens simply to sink back into that warmth and not have to deal with getting off the cliff.

"Good girl," he murmured.

Those two words of encouragement lit a fuse to her temper.

One handhold followed by one foothold at a time, she made her way up the granite face, feeling Chane close enough to touch. His voice never lost patience, and she wished it would. Otherwise, she had no justification for being so angry at him. Abandonment. Indifference. She understood those. She knew how to react to those. But he hadn't abandoned her, and he hadn't been indifferent to her fear. She wanted to yell at him anyway.

"Just ten more feet, Lexi," he said. "You're almost there."

When she finally climbed over the top of the cliff, Lexi sat down and draped her arms over bent knees, relief seeping through her like a benediction. She sat staring at the ground as Chane hauled himself up behind her.

"You did fine, Lexi," he said, briefly touching her shoulder.

Once again his patience and reassurance tightened her tenuous hold on her temper. Being mad at him was stupid. She knew it was. But she couldn't tamp down those feelings any more than she could stop trembling.

He turned to the other four students and began talking to them about rappelling back down the cliff. Comparing the rappel to the belay techniques they had learned a couple of days earlier, he sounded as though they'd have more fun than kids playing video games at the mall.

"Like we did coming up," he concluded, "I'll rappel down with each one of you. You'll have the harness on, and I know you'll each do fine.'' His dark brown eyes were intent when his gaze rested on Lexi.

Her dread returned full force. There was no way she could launch herself into the air off the side of a cliff. She'd already experienced falling through the air a hundred feet off the ground, and she didn't want a repeat performance, thank you very much.

She folded her arms across her knees and rested her chin on them, contemplating the likelihood of jumping off the edge of the cliff. Fear—that hated companion—raced through her, and she trembled again. She closed her eyes and willed away the tears that burned for release.

''Lexi?''

She opened her eyes and met Chane's questioning glance.

''Do you have any questions?''

She shook her head, stood, and took off her climbing harness. ''I'll see you all later,'' she said.

''You're going to rappel down with the rest of the class.''

''Not me.'' She stalked over to Chane's backpack, where they had each stashed jackets and sweatshirts earlier in the day.

''You climbed up and you'll rappel down.''

''Wrong. I climbed up, and I'm walking down.''

''Like hell,'' he said, his patient instructor's voice disappearing into a sandpapery baritone.

''Like hell,'' she repeated, rummaging through the pack for her sweatshirt. ''There's no way I'm going back down that cliff.'' She stuffed the harness inside and zipped the pack shut, then tied the sweatshirt's arms around her waist.

Chane unfastened the safety rope from his climbing harness and with three long strides blocked her way. He loomed over her, unreasonably large. She was unaccustomed to tipping her head back to meet a man's gaze, and she didn't like doing so now. Those dark brown eyes that had been so reassuring and soft now glittered with tightly controlled anger. He bore down on her like a man who was used to being obeyed. She stepped backward, silently cursing her inability to stand her ground.

''There's one easy way back to Grand Lake—the road at the bottom of this cliff.'' He waved toward the pine forest that emphasized the rugged terrain. "It's at least a five-hour hike back to Grand Lake. You can't be serious that you prefer a long arduous hike to rappelling down a hundred feet where your car is parked."

Lexi nodded. "That's right exactly. I'm glad you understand."

"That's stupid."

She rounded on him, her voice low, fierce. "I'll tell you what's stupid. I fell!"

"That was an accident!"

"No kidding!"

"Is this how you deal with problems, Ms. Monroe? By running? Quitting?" Contempt laced his voice.

His accusations hurt as only the truth could. She lifted her chin and met his eyes. "That's none of your damn business, Mr. Callahan." She gave his name the same emphasis he had given hers.

"Getting back to your car is your problem."

"I understand." Her gaze never faltered.

He stared at her a moment longer, his legs spread and his arms folded across his chest, then stepped out of her way. Her blond hair framed a halo around her face, but she looked to him anything but angelic. Her chin was tipped toward him, her expression determined, her posture defiant. He figured a sunburn would be the least of her problems by the time she got home.

Students fell sometimes. That was his problem and the reason he took every effort to ensure their safety. Lexi shouldn't have fallen more than a foot or two. He knew what falling five feet and more felt like, and he could imagine how terrifying that was to her.

Worse, he blamed himself. He liked her, and he hadn't wanted to. She had listed her occupation as a news photographer on the standard application all students filled out. News photographer. Those two words had made him suspicious of her motives. News photographer. Another name for reporter.

The last time he had trusted a reporter, men had died. Good men had died, hostages hadn't been rescued, and a mission had gone all to hell because a hot-shot reporter cared more about a story than about people.

Chane had seen none of those traits in Lexi, but he hadn't been able to let go of his prejudices. She was exactly the kind of client he liked working with. Prompt to class, focused on the skills he taught, and a wry sense of humor that broke tension with other members of the class. He figured she would have turned that sharp wit on him instead of running. Why hadn't she?

She flashed him one last baleful glance with those expressive blue eyes and walked toward the trail that led across the clearing toward the timber.

He didn't doubt her fear, not now, not after feeling her tremble against him. The suspicions he'd had about her motives had been banished in that moment. He knew what it had cost her to finish the climb. The lady had gutsiness—enough to recognize she wasn't ready for the rappel—and independence enough to walk back to the village under her own steam. Grudging admiration replaced his irritation.

He rejoined the four students waiting at the edge of the cliff and made a mental note to check on Lexi later.

Five and a half hours later, the sun scant minutes away from setting, Lexi arrived home. The house was a half mile outside the small town of Grand Lake, Colorado. She'd fallen in love with her house the first time she saw it. Large expanses of glass and a hillside location gave her a panoramic view of Shadow Mountain Lake. This time of year, the surrounding mountain slopes were splashed in the yellow of aspen leaves, vivid against the dark green of the old-growth lodge pine forest. No matter the time of day or the season, she loved the view. Lately she had especially liked the early mornings. The sunshine stretching across the lake, turning it from mysteriously dark to sparkling, became a personal symbol of renewal.

A cheerful yap greeted her as a German shepherd bounded off the steps, its tail wagging. Murmuring a greeting, Lexi patted the dog's head. This, too, was one of her favorite things—having someone, even this aging dog, glad to have her home. Lexi had adopted Daisy from the animal shelter after she'd returned home last winter. Daisy had forced routine into Lexi's days and had given her companionship she hadn't known she'd missed until then.

She sat down on the bottom step of the west-facing deck that curved around her house. Sighing, she draped her arm over the dog, wishing she had Daisy's capacity to live fully in the moment. The dog had no worries about yesterday, no concerns about tomorrow.

Beyond, the lake shimmered, taking on the golden hues of late afternoon, luring Lexi to enjoy. Even so, her mind churned.

Her long, long walk had been good for one thing, she decided reluctantly. She was no longer furious with Chane Callahan for calling her a quitter. She couldn't blame the man for telling the truth, even if it wasn't something she wanted to hear. Especially when his assessment had been no worse than her own.

International News Network, INN, had given her an eighteen-month leave. She'd already used up close to a year of it, promising herself time to heal, time to soak in the simple pleasures. Only she was no more ready to return to work than she had been months ago. Sooner or later, the loyalty she'd earned with ten years of service and a Pulitzer prize would wear thin. Sooner or later, her savings would run out.

Lexi sighed and turned her face toward the jewel colors of the sunset. Beyond the lake, the brilliant autumn display of the aspen were balm to her tattered emotions.

She climbed the steps, following Daisy. Lexi unlocked the door, then waited for the dog to precede her into the house.

Inside, Lexi sat down on one of the kitchen chairs and unlaced her boots. The flexible lightweight soles were designed for climbing. The pea gravel of the road she'd walked over the last three miles had ruined the shoes. She dumped them into the wastepaper basket. She'd liked to dump her intentions to finish Chane Callahan's wilderness course in the same place.

Pulling off her socks, she examined the dilly of a blister that had formed on the little toe of one foot. Further examination revealed another on her other heel that was even larger.

For an instant, Lexi imagined what her afternoon would have been like had she rappelled down the cliff with the others. They would have sat around Cooper's Bar, a beer in hand, talking about how easy it had all been and about how much fun they had. Lexi liked the companionship that had developed with the class members. She wanted to share in that. She hated that she had walked away, hated more being so afraid of something she had once loved.

Despite her resolve not to think about those terrifying hours she had spent hanging by her hands in a musty thatched hut, the memory drew her. Once she had been convinced her own moxie and sense of presence would keep her safe. She'd been wrong.

Unbidden, another memory surfaced. One moment she had been a news photographer doing her job—objectively observing the surreal transaction of a man selling his baby daughter to El Ladron. The next she had become a woman outraged by the cold-blooded murder of the infant's mother. Joe Robertson, hot-shot reporter and Lexi's partner that fateful day, had told her she would soon forget.

Only, Lexi hadn't been able to forget, and she had sworn she would put El Ladron and his baby-smuggling ring out of business. She had spent months, putting to use every skill and every contact she had as a news photographer, toward that single quest.

Hard enough had been identifying his contacts and resources and trying to dry those up. Worse had been the realization there was a market for those babies—people, who for whatever reason, were willing to buy a baby the way they might buy a dog.

Much as she hated what El Ladron did, she hated those faceless, nameless people more. The horror that remained in Lexi's mind was a single *niña* brutally stolen from her mother and the fear that child had ended up with unscrupulous, unfit parents.

A litany filed through Lexi's mind that began and ended

with a single unanswered prayer. *If I had been able to help one child, just one, it would have been worth the cost.*

El Ladron was still in business, and he had taught her an unforgettable lesson. Fear was more powerful than honorable intentions. How she hated learning that about herself. Which brought her right back to this afternoon. She had quit, had run instead of facing the fear.

"No." Lexi stood, pushing her chair back. "This has got to stop."

Daisy jumped to her feet as well, scooting out of her mistress's way. Lexi dropped to her knees and put her arms around the dog's furry neck. "Shh. It's okay. I'm okay." She repeated her refrain of the last year. She sat on the floor, and all eighty pounds of Daisy climbed into her lap.

Lexi scratched the dog's ears, caressing their long sensitive tips, and managed a smile when the dog nuzzled her cheek with a cold black nose. "Ah, Daisy. You almost make me forget."

The dog climbed off her lap and Lexi stood. She removed the rubber band from her braid and pulled the strands of her hair free. She hobbled toward the stairs to the loft, envisioning a steamy, long soak. Bone tired, she wanted to ease her aches, maybe have a bowl of soup, and fall into bed for the next ten hours or so. Before she mounted the first step to the loft, there was a brisk knock at the door.

Visitors at this time of evening were rare. Anyone who knew Lexi came to the back door, never the front. For months Lexi had started when there had been a knock. But there had never been anyone at the door more threatening than UPS delivery. She was tempted to ignore the summons. Another series of raps followed, and this time, Daisy barked. With a sigh, Lexi went to the door and opened it.

A diminutive woman dressed in black stood on the front porch. She wasn't anyone Lexi knew, but she brought back a flood of memories from the nearly five years Lexi had spent as a news photographer in South and Central America. The woman had dark hair, liberally streaked with gray and pulled into a tight bun. Her skin was wrinkled, Lexi was certain, from

constant exposure to a tropical sun. Her nearly black, alert eyes
could have belonged to any woman in any village or town Lexi
had ever visited. A marked difference between this woman and
hundreds of others, however, was her erect, proud carriage and
her presence at Lexi's door.

Automatically, Lexi addressed the woman in Spanish.
"Hola. Como le va?"

"Me llamo Señora Ester Padilla," she answered, her pronun-
ciation crisp. "I'm looking for Alexandra Monroe."

A moment passed before Lexi answered, "I am she."

Señora Padilla's suit was old-fashioned, conservative, without a bit of ornamentation, and worn. The garb was exactly
what Lexi would have expected from a matron whose background was that of a dwindling middle class. Nothing of the
woman's accent gave a clue as to whether she was from Colom-
bia, Mexico, or any of the countries in between. Nothing in
her bearing gave a clue as to what her business with Lexi might
be.

No car was in the driveway, and though Lexi often walked
the half mile to town, few others did. Yet, this woman had
apparently walked. Courtesy, Lexi told herself, not curiosity,
made her step away from the door and motion the señora to
come in.

Señora Padilla stepped over the threshold, giving Daisy a
wide berth. Daisy's ears perked forward, and her tail lazily
wagged. The woman grasped her purse with both hands and
stopped at the doorway between the foyer and living room, her
gaze focused on the floor in front of her. Had she been an
American, Lexi would have asked immediately what she
wanted. Instead, Lexi honored the customs of the Latin American countries where she'd spent the last five years. She invited
the señora to sit down and asked if she'd like a cup of coffee
or tea.

"Tea, *por favor,*" Señora Padilla answered, crossing the
room and sitting gingerly on the edge of the sofa.

Lexi prepared a tray with a pot of tea, set out two cups, and
added cookies from an open bag in the cupboard. She sat down
on the big chair across from the sofa after setting the tray on

the coffee table between them. Pouring them both a cup, she asked in Spanish, ''Why are you looking for me?''

Señora Padilla opened her purse and brought out a photograph. The snapshot, slightly out of focus, was of a stiffly posed woman holding an infant.

''I want you to help me find my granddaughter,'' she said.

Chapter 2

Lexi forced her question past the cold lump of tension that rose in her throat. "The baby is your granddaughter?"

"*Sí.*"

"Señora, what makes you think I might know where your granddaughter is?"

"I know you worked with Señor Robertson. I know he wrote an article published in *Time* about the theft of babies from my country. I know you took photographs of the terrible things being done there. I know my granddaughter was adopted, illegally adopted, by a couple who live right here."

"Here in Grand Lake?"

Señora Padilla shook her head. "That I don't know. But in Colorado, yes."

"I still don't understand what you want from me," Lexi said as tactfully as she knew how. "I can't—"

"Your government is so complicated." The señora made a vague motion with her hand. "So many different people tell me to talk to someone else. You know how your government works—"

"I don't know the first thing about adoptions," Lexi interrupted. "And even if I did . . ."

"You must understand. I'm not an idealist, merely an old woman looking for her granddaughter. She's my grandchild. My only grandchild." Señora Padilla took another sip of her tea. "Surely you understand."

Lexi understood, all right. She understood too well that she hadn't been able to make right the injustices she'd witnessed daily for years. She understood that she'd nearly lost her life. And nothing had changed. When threatening her hadn't been enough to stop her intervention, even after he had beaten her, he had gone after friends and coworkers.

El Ladron. A sleazy, cruel American who hid behind the macho persona of an outlaw. El Ladron. The Thief. Every now and then, she thought about resuming her search to find out his real name. Fear kept her from doing anything. Fear of what he might do to people she cared about. Fear, God help her, of what he had done to her.

Lexi had come home to Colorado hoping to escape everything that reminded her of Central America. More nights than not, nightmares still reminded her that she had failed in the single most important undertaking of her life.

El Ladron was still in business. Joe Robertson's investigation hadn't stopped that. Her own intervention hadn't made a whit of difference.

She'd forsaken her role as a journalist, as an objective observer, and it hadn't helped. The words she wanted to say remained unspoken—*Señora Padilla, I cannot help you.*

Señora Padilla's expression became thoughtful. "You're a daughter, like my daughter. Maria Antoñia. You understand the bond between a mother and her daughter. Do you not?"

Lexi didn't. Her mother had been far more interested in the string of successive men in her life than in the daughter she'd born out-of-wedlock at the age of seventeen. Continually reminded that her mother would be free if she hadn't had the burden of a child, Lexi left home the week she graduated from high school and embarked on college. She hadn't spent a night under her mother's roof since, nor had her mother asked her to.

Without waiting for a reply, the señora continued. "And so

in love she was. Her husband, Juan, was older. And a good provider, but a simple man. A grocer. And then El Ladron came.''

Chills crawled through Lexi's scalp. Unwanted memories surfaced of a young woman, little more than a child herself, lying lifeless in the middle of a dusty road.

''How long ago was your granddaughter taken?'' Lexi asked, almost not wanting to know the answer.

''Nearly four years ago.''

The infant Lexi had watched being brutally stolen from her mother that momentous day could not have been Señora Padilla's granddaughter. Relief, followed closely by shame, filled Lexi. She didn't want to know, but couldn't prevent herself from confirming, ''El Ladron took your granddaughter.''

''El Ladron came.'' The señora paused, holding her cup halfway to her lips before she set it back down. ''He came for supplies for his men. This thief, this murderer, wanted Juan to hand over the supplies. He, of course, would not simply give them, so El Ladron took what he wanted. Before they were gone, Maria came into the store with the *niña*, just eight weeks old. He burned Juan's store.'' Her eyes focused unseeingly in the middle of the room. ''He took everything I loved . . .''

So few words, and so huge the images they painted, confirming everything Lexi knew about El Ladron. She touched the señora's hand, a silent communion of understanding. Señora Padilla grasped her hand tightly before letting it go.

Lexi's gaze met Señora Padilla's. Lexi knew firsthand the kind of man El Ladron was, knew with certainty that he'd killed Señora Padilla's daughter and son-in-law.

''The people who adopt these children, they're told the babies are orphans. Did you know that?'' Señora Padilla smoothed a speck of nonexistent lint from the black skirt stretched taut across her thighs.

Lexi nodded, memories skittering through her mind. She didn't even notice the silence stretch out, heard only the terrible pounding of her own heart. She remembered too clearly the musty odor of a thatched hut. She had been hung by her wrists, her shoulder dislocated by her own weight. Her toes had barely touched the dirt-packed floor—a floor that was as real to Lexi in this moment as the polished oak floor in her own living room.

"My Estella. She *is* an orphan."

The simple statement evoked more vivid images, clicking through Lexi's mind with the stark precision of the motor drive on her 35mm camera. Images she didn't want in her mind, in her life. She stood up, knocking the teacup off its saucer, splashing the rest of the tea across the coffee table.

"Señora . . . I'm sorry." *I can't help you!* Lexi wanted to shout. She hadn't been able to separate her shattered ideals from the photographer behind the camera lens. She'd wanted to change the world, to sway public opinion and national policy through photographs that revealed the truth. In the end, she had intervened and had nearly lost her life.

Señora Padilla smiled, much as one might at a child misbehaving in public.

"Estella will have her fourth birthday in November. I shall spend that day with her. *Dios mediante.*"

God willing, Lexi echoed in her thoughts. God willing, she'd be able to convince this woman she couldn't help, couldn't handle getting involved. "Your own embassy, the State Department—"

"Usted."

Lexi shook her head. "Not me. The government—"

"Your language, your customs. They are not so easy." Señora Padilla took a sip from her cup, then set it down. When she spoke, the words were this time in English. "You cared enough to put your life in danger to take photographs. They showed the world what is happening in my country. Please. Care enough now to help me find my granddaughter." When Lexi would have spoken, the señora put her hand up and continued, "I will return later." She stood up. "You can give me your answer after you have had time to think."

Lexi also rose from her seat. "Señora—"

"Lo hable luego," she said once again lapsing into Spanish and crossing the room. *"Por favor,* think about these things."

Before the señora reached the door, there was another knock

immediately followed by a warning bark from Daisy. When Lexi opened the door, the last person she expected to see was Chane Callahan. Nonetheless, he stood facing the sunset. He'd changed from his climbing garb into a wool shirt and Levis. Both emphasized his size and strength, and Lexi found herself aware of him as she hadn't been before.

At the door's opening, he turned around. "Hi. I just—"

"Hasta la vista," interrupted Señora Padilla, stepping around Lexi and brushing past Chane.

"Adios," Lexi murmured. She wished the woman had bade her goodbye instead of promising to see her again.

"I will speak with you soon." In English this time. Señora Padilla's sharp gaze punctuated her reiterated farewell.

"I won't change my mind," Lexi said as the señora started down the steps.

"Tal vez." Perhaps. And said with absolute certainty.

"Sounds important," Chane said.

"To her, it is." Lexi watched the señora walk down the driveway a moment before glancing at Chane.

"And to you?" he asked.

She forced a smile she didn't feel. "I doubt what I think matters at all." Lexi stepped back into the house, extending her arm in invitation.

"To you or to her?"

"To me." Lexi hadn't agreed to do anything—not even to think about the señora's request. That didn't prevent Lexi from feeling as though she were being swept along by an invisible current she could not escape.

Inside, Chane turned toward the expanse of glass that faced the lake and beyond, the aspen-covered mountains. "This view is great." A slow smile lit his face.

Feeling the warmth of that smile clear to the soles of her feet, Lexi responded, "It's a good thing I liked the house. I would have bought it just for the view." The only explanation for her response to his smile, she decided, was any smile would be welcome after what she'd just been though with Señora Padilla.

He took off his Stetson as his gaze swept around the room,

then focused on a photograph that hung on the wall between the entry and the stairs that led to the loft. "Did you take this?" he asked.

A surreal mist hung over a rugged black and white landscape. Within the mist were suggestions of a face here, a dwelling there, a figure, impressions of the young and the very old. This large photograph was so different than those he had seen in magazines. This was subtle, a glimpse into a private, secret place of haunted memories, confusion, and unrealized longings.

Chane lifted his eyes from the photograph to Lexi. "This is not at all like the stuff published in magazines."

"No," she agreed, her attention still on the photograph on the wall.

He wondered what she saw within the misty images.

Chane had seen the work that had won her a Pulitzer prize, a photo essay entitled "The Children of War." The piece had not had a single caption. The photographs hadn't needed them.

"The Children of War" were stark black-and-white images of children in places he never wanted his daughter to see. Bright-eyed toddlers who seemed unaware they played on a mound of garbage. Prepubescent boys dressed in fatigues, already engaged in the game of war. The image that struck him most was of a girl maybe twelve years old. Dressed in fishnet stockings, shorts, and a halter top, she leaned against the wall of a cantina, displaying herself with a come-hither smile for a couple of soldiers strolling by.

Those images were sharp, brutal, and completely unlike the photograph hanging in front of him. "It pulls you in and you don't want to look away."

His simple statement surprised her, pleasing her far more than any praise of her talent. She had spent days in the darkroom, imposing images on top of one another, adding the merest touch of an airbrush, softening the focus until the images on paper matched those in her mind. Knowing she had achieved the effect she wanted was praise enough.

Lexi lifted her eyes to Chane. On her long walk home, Lexi had rehearsed exactly what she planned to say to Chane the next time she saw him. A speech that was eloquent, to the point, and exactly expressed her feelings about continuing in his course. At the moment she couldn't remember a single word.

He was an arresting man. His attraction was more than the sum of his size, more than his sharply chiseled features or his dark penetrating eyes. Most climbers with Chane's proficiency were no taller than Lexi's five-foot-nine. Not Chane. Eight or nine inches taller than she, he had the build of a linebacker. His hands were easily twice the size of hers, and she shivered in response to the sensual memory of those hands caressing her arms.

When Lexi first met him, his smile had done nothing to warm her. He wasn't even that good-looking. Just big. Solid. With the kind of assurance few men ever achieved. An aurora of dependability that probably was the motivation for his presence in her house. She knew he had been a Marine. *Semper Fidelis* was undoubtedly his motto. He probably thought he had a duty to check on her.

The sense that she might have been an obligation triggered familiar defensiveness, especially on the heels of admitting to herself the man had a certain allure. As a small child, Lexi had simply wanted to be loved. That hadn't happened with her mother, who viewed her as an unwanted responsibility. That hadn't happened with any of the men she had dated, though she had mistaken intimacy as a source of comfort. She had learned the hard way it was far better to stand on her own two feet.

She ran a hand over the long fall of her hair, still roped into thick strands from her loosened braid. A ripple of self-consciousness about her appearance trickled through her, further annoying her.

"What can I help you with?" She had intended her voice to be sharp. Her tone fell short.

"I just wanted to make sure you made it home okay," he said. His fingers traced the edge of the brim of his hat. The German shepherd sniffed at Chane's feet. He dropped his hand and allowed the dog to smell his fingers before scratching her ears.

"As you can see, I did." So, she *had* been an obligation. For an instant, Lexi wished his motives had been something more. Mentally, she told her hormones to take a flying leap.

His gaze fell to Lexi's bare feet, which looked to him oddly vulnerable, her toes curled against the terra cotta tile of the entry way. A huge blister covered most of one toe, evoking sympathy that he pushed aside. It had been her decision to walk, he reminded himself. Nonetheless, he murmured, "And only a little worse for the wear."

"Only a little," she agreed, her glance following his to her feet. "My choice to walk. My blister."

Her verbal echo of his conclusion surprised him. A part of him had wanted to find her needing help, but she obviously didn't. She'd made it home. And based on the empty teacups and tray of cookies on her coffee table, and the woman who had just left, Lexi had been home for some time.

"What about your car?" he found himself asking.

"What about it?"

"Do you need a lift to go get it?" His eyes met hers. He hadn't noticed before, but hers were darkest blue, so much so they looked nearly black. He'd never paid any attention, either, that her skin was white beneath a sprinkling of freckles. Perhaps both were from seeing her for the first time indoors. Her dark blond hair was an unruly mass that fell down her back. He imagined easing his hands into her hair to see if those strands were as soft as they looked.

She tipped her head back, exposing the long line of her throat between her jaw and the top of a baggy sweatshirt. A full-of-the-devil smile curved her lips, a smile that didn't seem genuine to him, a smile that made him wonder what she was really thinking.

"After telling me I'm on my own. I am surprised."

"A simple yes or no, Lexi, that's all it takes."

Her smile faded, and she crossed her arms over her chest and stared at him as though weighing his answer.

"Forget it," he said. "I came to make sure you're okay. I can see that you are." He strode through the open door and across the deck.

"Chane?"

Her teasing tone was gone, her contralto voice almost husky. He paused on the step.

"Thanks," she said.

He glanced over his shoulder and found that she had followed him to the opening of the deck's stairwell. Even standing on a step above him, she still had to look up a little to meet his gaze. Her smile was apologetic. His anger dissipated as quickly as it had erupted.

"Thanks for what?" he asked.

"For being concerned enough to see that I made it home."

"No problem." He continued on down the stairs. "See you tomorrow." When she didn't answer, he stopped again. She stood, hip propped against the rail, her arms once again folded across her chest in a protective gesture. "I will see you tomorrow for the camp out, won't I?"

There was a minuscule shake to her head.

That hesitancy, so at odds with her assertiveness earlier in the day, drew him. He climbed back up the steps two at a time until his gaze was level with hers. "Think you can't hack it?"

"I know I can't," she told him.

Her answer confirmed his hunch she rarely gave herself any slack, that she expected a thousand times too much of herself. "What you did today took guts."

"I'm a quitter." She lifted her chin and met his gaze head-on. "An assessment you agreed with."

"That's true."

Her mouth tightened.

"I was mad when I said that," he said. "It takes a certain kind of courage to admit something is beyond you at the moment. The rappel was, and you had the courage to admit it."

"Courage!" She clinched her fists and her eyes became suddenly bright before she averted her gaze. "That wasn't courage. That was fear. And I ran."

"Courage, Lexi."

"Oh, please." Her voice filled with scorn.

"Okay," he agreed, altering to a new tack. "You fell. And you were scared."

"Damn right I was. I sat in your lap like a sniveling ninny—"

"And then what?" he challenged. Silence stretched tautly between them. "What happened then, Lexi?" He waited for her to look at him, then answered his own question. "You finished the climb."

"But I was so scared."

"Of course you were scared. You're supposed to be scared after you fall. It's your mind's way of protecting you from danger."

"I hate feeling like that."

"I know." He pulled one of her hands from around her body and clasped it between both of his. It felt surprisingly small. *Vulnerable,* he thought, positive she didn't see herself that way at all. A sudden urge to shelter her swept through him, surprising him. Why he thought she needed protecting, he couldn't have said. "I understood how shook you were. You finished the climb. That's more than some novices can do. You challenged me when you knew you weren't ready."

"Big deal," she answered. "I finished the climb. But I couldn't do the rappel. And instead of facing it, I ran. And I don't need you to sugar coat that or disguise it as anything else!"

With that, she turned around and hurried toward the open door. Two long steps and Chane caught up with her, bracing the door open just as she would have slammed it in his face. He took her by the elbow and stepped between her and the house.

"Yeah, you're right, Lexi. You ran. And now you have a choice. You can keep running or you can face this."

"Let me go!"

Chane released her arm, but continued to bar her way into her home. "Finishing the climb, Lexi, took guts. Telling me to take a flying leap. That took guts, too. So, you weren't ready to rappel today. We'll try it again another time."

"I don't want to," she said.

"Remember what you told me your goals were for taking this course?"

Her reply was instant and firm. "To learn to trust other people again. To overcome my fear of heights."

"This is where you have to put up or shut up." He levered himself away from her doorway, then lifted her chin with his finger. Her eyes were dark, shadowed. Beautiful. An intense need to make her feel better consumed him. Except, he didn't know how. "See you tomorrow."

He trotted down the stairs, and when he climbed into his truck, she was still standing in the doorway. He waved at her and she gave him a tiny wave back.

To learn to trust other people again. Again. What in hell happened to you, Lexi Monroe?

And why this sudden fixation? He'd talked to her as a student he cared about. He'd be lying to himself if he thought that was all there was motivating him.

He had watched her examine the ropes and climbing equipment with a familiarity that indicated she was no novice climber. She wouldn't be the first person to be afraid of heights after a climbing accident, yet he had the sense something more drove her. When they'd worked on the ropes challenge course, she'd had a mix of raw determination and raw fear that drew him. He'd come face to face with fear like that, had fought his own battles to keep from being paralyzed by it.

He'd had other students fall. But he'd never blamed himself before. This time he did. Maybe because he had a prejudice against reporter types. Maybe because he'd decided she had some ulterior motive for enrolling in his class.

She worried him as no student in his wilderness survival school ever had. He'd had students who were just as sexy, a few as intelligent, none as bullheaded. And . . . Lexi was definitely sexy. She'd felt so good against him today, high on that rock wall. Soft in all the places a woman was supposed to be soft, reminding him just how long it had been since he'd held one in his arms.

Chane drummed his fingers on the steering wheel as he drove through the evening gloom toward home. Home. Kit and Tessa waited there, the family Rose had wanted and hadn't lived to have. She'd never known that he left the Marines after his last hitch was up, that he loved the daughter she had adopted without his consent or his prior knowledge. He'd become what she had most wanted—a family man, albeit a single one.

Being an eligible bachelor in a small community, well-meaning folks kept trying to fix him up. He didn't want to be fixed up. The last thing he wanted was to be married again. His wife had turned out to be a stranger—someone he didn't know or understand. Maybe sometime down the road after his brother Kit finished high school, he'd find a woman who could share his silences. He'd settle for one he could be comfortable with. Comfortable. Like Miss Kitty and Marshal Dillon. Comfortable. Dull.

Lexi Monroe wasn't comfortable, and she was anything but dull. Being with her was more like taking an uncontrolled fall off a thousand-foot cliff. She was complex and had problems to work out. Which didn't keep her from being nice . . . pretty . . . sexy.

An image of those long legs of hers wrapped around him made powerful need surge through him. He blamed the accompanying arousal on his celibacy. Sex, he told himself, that's all it was. *So, chase her a little. Find out if she's interested. You don't have to marry the woman simply because you want to take her to bed.*

He pulled into the tree-lined drive that led to his house and shut off the engine to his pickup. He stared pensively through the windshield at his cobblestone house. *Chase her.* Yeah, right. It had been so many years, he half wondered if he remembered how. Between keeping his younger brother in line and being a full-time father to Tessa, he didn't have enough free hours in the day. Fitting a seduction in between picking Tessa up from daycare and helping Kit with algebra seemed pretty far fetched.

He missed waking in the middle of the night, his arms around a woman. Who the hell was he kidding? If he wanted a woman, any woman, all he had to do was let the matchmakers of Grand Lake fix him up. Sex wasn't that hard to find. Only, he didn't want just any woman. In fact, he didn't much like casual sex. He wanted a woman who was loyal, who'd have a sense of adventure, who'd understand his silences. And if she had Lexi Monroe's long legs, she'd be just about perfect. He sighed and got out of the truck.

"I'm home," he called as he came through the door. He hung his Stetson on a hook by the back door of the enclosed porch.

"Daddy!" came an enthusiastic squeal from the living room. "Hi!" Tessa ran through the doorway into the kitchen, her pigtails half undone. She hadn't been a child of Rose's womb, but Chane was sure no child could have looked more like her. Black hair and dark brown eyes. Tessa's round face lit with a huge smile, and she held her arms in the air as she skipped toward him.

Chane caught his nearly four-year-old daughter and lifted her over his head, delighted as always with her enthusiasm. She was sunshine, lighting all that was bleak in his life, showing him it was okay to feel good about today, proving to him he still knew how to love.

"How's my girl?" He planted a noisy kiss on her cheek, which she returned just as noisily.

"I'm a wonderful girl." She grinned. The words had been given to her by her mother from the very beginning, words Chane had repeated to her every day. "And we've been waiting for you."

"You have?"

"Hi, Chane."

He glanced over his daughter's head to his sixteen-year-old brother, who showed every promise of growing into his size thirteen feet, and who, this moment, was shrugging into a jean jacket. In the six months Kit had lived with Chane, he'd grown six inches. Chane regretted their father had never had a chance to know his youngest son, regretted their mother had died before Kit finished growing up.

"You're off somewhere?"

"Yeah. Me and Brad are going to the library. Remember? I told you."

"Brad and I," Chane corrected. "And I remember. Who's driving?"

Kit met his eyes and had the grace to blush before he held out his hand. "Me. And—"

"I am."

Kit grinned. "Nice of you to offer, but I am. I know I forgot to ask you for the truck, but I'll be back by ten. I'll even put gas in the truck. Okay?"

"Nine-thirty. Anyone going besides you two?"

"Nope." He took the keys from Chane and slapped him on the back. "Later, bro."

"Later, bro," Tessa echoed.

Kit pinched her cheek. "Catch ya on the flip side, squirt." He slammed the door, leaving behind an instant of stillness.

"He's in a hurry," Tessa announced to Chane.

"I can see that." He carried her into the kitchen. "Did he have dinner?" A stack of dishes haphazardly piled on the counter near the sink answered that question. "Never mind. Did he feed you, too?"

She shook her head.

"So. It's just you and me, squirt?"

"You and me, Daddy."

Chapter 3

The jarring ring of the telephone brought Lexi instantly awake. She groped for the receiver with one hand and the switch to the bedside lamp with the other.

"Monroe," she answered halfway through the second ring, reaching for a pencil and pad.

"Monroe, huh?" A distinct voice came over the line.

Joe Robertson. She recognized the voice. She ought to have. His phone calls had been responsible for waking her up more times than she could count in the short time they'd worked together.

"Old habits die hard if they die at all," he continued without so much as a hello. "I'll bet a bottle of Cutty Sark that you're wide awake with a pencil in your hand, ready to hit the road running for our next assignment."

She set the pencil and pad back down, resisting the urge to throw both across the room. Lexi's gaze strayed to the digital display of her clock radio. Two minutes past 5 A.M. "What do you want, Joe?"

She asked the question. But she knew. An early-morning phone call from Joe meant he was chasing down a story. She'd never worked with another reporter as single-minded. He ignored the conventions of civilization unless they suited him. Waiting until seven or eight to call wouldn't have occurred to him.

"I know you're determined to make believe you're enjoying this Bohemian life you've run off to. That you don't miss the excitement, the adrenaline high—"

"The fun?" Once it had been fun . . . a lifetime ago. A time when red had been her favorite color. Now, the only red she could tolerate was the safelight in her dark room.

"C'mon, Monroe. I can't believe you don't miss it."

"What do you want?" She pushed herself up in bed.

Joe Robertson had an uncanny sense of news, an ability to correlate unrelated pieces of rumor and fact that led to good stories, but he never did anything that didn't first serve Joe. He'd been the first to accuse her of cutting and running, even though he knew better than anyone why she had.

"You think I'd call you only because I want something. I'm wounded."

"Then call a doctor," she replied without humor. Once she would have laughed with him. That, too, was a lifetime ago. For the months since she had returned home, Joe had fed her bits and pieces of his continuing investigation of El Ladron. She hoped someday Joe would have enough information for his story, enough to identify the American behind the macho persona of El Ladron. Enough to encourage a police investigation that would put the man behind bars.

Joe Robertson was an unlikely white knight, and she hated wanting him to do something she didn't have to courage to do for herself.

As if reading her thoughts, Joe's voice sobered. "I've got a new angle on El Ladron."

Lexi shivered and gripped the telephone more tightly. *Beware of what you ask for.*

"You sent Señora Padilla to me, didn't you, Joe?"

"I thought you might be able to help her."

"You thought she might provide you with a front-page story."

"Hey," he cajoled. "You make me sound like the kind of guy who would throw that little old lady to the wolves."

"You would." Lexi closed her eyes, admitting the one thing she hadn't allowed herself to face all these months. She was afraid El Ladron would follow up on his threats. Afraid he would find her. And she had pretended she wasn't hiding, all the while making sure no one could easily find her. She had the trust department of her bank in New York pay all her bills. She had paid off her house, and her telephone number was unlisted.

"I can't believe you didn't call me before sending her here," Lexi said. "I can't believe you didn't ask me first."

"I assumed you'd tell me it was okay," he said.

"You assume a hell of a lot," she returned.

"Okay, okay. But it's all worked out. Now listen. Were any of those photos you took on that last shoot clear enough so you could do a blowup for me?"

"We've been that route, Joe," she reminded him. She had shot more than a hundred exposures that fateful morning. Not one could be used to identify El Ladron. "I made enlargements of everything I had. Every exposure had so much grain, you couldn't tell El Ladron from a thousand other men." Instead there had been sharp images of a young woman's anguish during the last moments of her life.

"What if I got you a digitizer?"

"That's hocus-pocus. You still have to have a good, clear negative. And I don't."

That wasn't strictly true. Take a reasonable image and a photographer's good eye—assuming that good eye matched an equally good memory—and you *could* do magic, generating prints that looked as though they had been taken with a Haaselblad under studio lighting. Whether you had come up with an image of the man in the negative was something else again. The tabloids loved the technology, one of the reasons Lexi hated it.

"But anything you had would be sharper than what you got last year, right?"

"Some," she agreed. "But there are no guarantees. The chances of coming up with something recognizable are—"

"Better than what we had."

"I haven't agreed to do this," she reminded him.

"But you will. You want this guy as bad as I do. You still have the negatives, don't you, Monroe?"

"Yeah, somewhere."

"Don't give me that 'somewhere' bull. Even in the middle of the bush, you knew exactly where to find the negatives of any shoot, any time."

She couldn't deny that, and she remained silent.

"Just tell me what you need to make it run, and I'll send anything you ask for. You make the prints, and I'm out of your hair."

Lexi sighed. At least helping Joe kept her working in the safety of her own darkroom. No one would know. She wouldn't have to worry about El Ladron somehow finding out. This wouldn't end up with someone being hurt because of things she did.

Helping Señora Padilla, on the other hand, required talking to people. Her search didn't involve El Ladron directly, but his presence still lurked in the background, reminding Lexi of the threats he had carried out. *Hurting people you care about. It's the same as hurting you, only better.*

With effort, Lexi refocused her attention back to Joe. This was a way to help, a way to patch back together her broken promises to herself.

"When?" she asked.

"I'm flying into Denver tomorrow. I'll bring it with me from LA and ship it to you from Denver."

"And what brings you to this neck of the woods, Robertson?"

A pause followed, during which she heard a click, probably of his lighter. She imaged him turning the engraved lighter over in his hand, his eyes focused somewhere on the ceiling.

"I'm checking out one of our South American connections."

"That sounds a little evasive, Joe. Not at all like you."

"Just being cautious."

"You?" she scoffed. If Joe Robertson was anything, he was daring, reckless, rash.

He was the reporter who'd ingratiated himself with a Marine platoon on a secret mission to rescue hostages, wrote a story that made headlines, and got himself kicked out of the Middle East so fast that he arrived in Costa Léon with dust clinging to him. He was INN's rogue reporter, a reputation he deserved.

Whatever the incident, he had gotten his hands slapped by the corporate bigwigs who shipped him off to Central America where Lexi was supposed to have kept an eye on him. Instead, she had been sucked into his intrigue, misled by her own good intentions.

Cautious? Not the Joe Robertson she knew.

"Is Lanatowski keeping you on a short leash?" she asked.

"Nah. He holds a carrot in front of my nose, and I follow."

"Keep it clean and you get to go back to Beirut."

"Something like that. What do you need to go with the digitizer, Monroe?"

Lexi gave him the list of supplies, then added, "Joe, don't give out my phone number or address again. This is my home, and I don't want to leave it. But you violate my privacy again, you'll never find me. On top of that, I'll make sure INN knows about every dirty deed you've ever been involved with. Got it?"

"Don't go ballistic on me, Monroe. You're gonna forgive me for sending Señora Padilla. She's a nice old lady. Besides, you're a sucker for babies."

"I'm serious, Joe."

He laughed. "That's your problem, Monroe. You're always so damn serious. Got a man in your life yet?"

The question was his favorite button to push to get a rise out of her. "Goodbye, Joe," she said.

"See ya in the funnies," he responded, breaking the connection.

She switched off the light. Instead of sliding down under the covers, she remained sitting, her head propped against the headboard. The hours before dawn were the hardest. The hours of vivid dreams and a remembered nightmare.

Joe was right about more than she'd ever let him know. Some days she did miss her job. Not enough to go back to it, but enough to know she'd given up an important part of her life, a part that needed to be filled with something new.

Unbidden, Chane Callahan came to mind. Warmth stole through her as she recalled his big hands on her and his dark eyes searching her own. A woman could almost believe the promise those eyes held. Almost.

With a mutter of disgust, she swung out of bed. The something new she wanted in her life was a career. Chane might be the answer to the physical longings that had lately plagued her, but he didn't have a thing to do with filling up the void in her life where work had been. Besides, for all she knew he was married and had five kids. And even if he wasn't, she had made a promise to herself a long time ago—never confuse sex with caring. What her libido wanted was the fulfillment of a man's body. What her heart wanted was a lot harder to find—someone who cared for her enough to understand her nightmares, cared enough to hold her through the endless nights without expecting sex. It had been too easy to settle for one while pretending it was the other.

She put on a robe, padded down the stairs, and made a pot of coffee before going to the basement. Daisy stretched from her usual spot in front of the darkroom door, gave a languid wag of her tail, and yawned.

"I know," Lexi murmured. "It's too early, isn't it, girl?"

She flipped on the light inside the darkroom and went to a large framed photograph of a young woman leaning negligently against a cantina wall and giving two men a come-hither smile. The photograph hid a fireproof wall safe. Without conscious thought, Lexi whirled the combination in the proper sequence and opened the door. The inside was stacked with metal index boxes. Instead of cards, the drawers contained envelopes of negatives. Over the years, Lexi had developed a kind of shorthand that gave her the date the film had been shot and whether it was the first or twenty-fifth roll she had shot that day. Cross-indexed by subject, she could usually locate a strip of negatives within minutes. The film Joe had asked about—she knew exactly where that was. The envelope lay at the front of the file.

Lexi took the envelope from the safe and closed it. She pulled the negatives out of their protective envelope and ran a sheet of contact prints. A half hour later she took the still-damp sheet to the kitchen, where she poured herself a cup of coffee, then let herself outside. Goose bumps rose on her arms, but she reveled in the cold air. She inhaled deeply and sighed. A cloud of steam formed in front of her and dissipated. This was what freedom and safety felt like, smelled like.

To the east, the sky was colorless except for an aura of yellow where the sun would momentarily stream over the horizon. She loved that exact moment light speared over the jagged rim of the mountains. She leaned against the railing, soaking it in. The early-morning song of robins filled the air, interrupted by the raucous call of a bluejay and the warning chatter of a squirrel. Lexi shivered, yet made no move to warm herself. She welcomed the sensation, the chill an antithesis to tropical heat.

At last it came, the first shaft of dazzling sunlight that chased away the shadows.

She basked in the radiant light before going back inside. Sunlight poured into the kitchen, illuminating the shelves above the table that held an eclectic collection of South American pottery. She stared at the abstract designs, her memory caught in the instant she'd opened the door to Señora Padilla yesterday. For a fleeting moment, the memories that suffused her were good ones, reminding her of forays into open-air markets in a search of a perfect pot. It seemed so long ago.

She gave herself a mental shake, then poured herself another cup of coffee and sat down at the kitchen table.

With a magnifying glass, Lexi examined the prints, as she had countless times before. She wanted to find a shot that would provide a good print with minimal correction from the digitizer. Joe must either have another photo to compare or he knew where to find El Ladron. Forget grain, forget exposure. Concentrate on features. She narrowed the hundred exposures to a half dozen.

The photographs and Joe's phone call brought her full circle to Señora Padilla. *It would have been worth it if one child had been helped.* Now was Lexi's chance. She didn't have the contacts to know where or how to begin the señora's search. But Ellen Belsen did.

The telephone rang, and Lexi crossed the kitchen to answer it.

"Lexi, good morning."

The male voice on the line wasn't Joe, but she recognized him. Chane Callahan. He identified himself, his voice deep and sounding as though he hadn't been awake long.

"Are you better this morning?" Real concern, not the phony variety that Joe peddled, filled Chane's voice. Or at least, that's what she wanted to believe.

"Actually, I am."

"Good." There was a subtle change in his tone, as though her being better mattered to him.

A flutter of anticipation teased through Lexi's stomach.

"Then you'll be coming with us this afternoon on the campout."

"Yes." She hadn't realized until then she'd made her decision.

"Good." More pleasure filled his voice.

"See you later, then?"

"Yeah."

Lexi pulled the receiver away from her ear, then put it back suddenly. "Chane?"

"Yeah?"

"Um . . . you're not married, are you?"

He laughed. "No." Still chuckling, he added, "I'm glad you're feeling better." And he broke the connection.

Lexi refilled her coffee cup, and sat back down at the sunny kitchen table. Her glance fell on the page of contact prints and she regained her train of thought. Ellen Belsen . . . an old college acquaintance and a woman who had adopted twin boys from South America. If anyone could steer Lexi in the right direction, it was Ellen.

Since Lexi's return to Grand Lake last winter, she had stopped by Ellen's day-care center numerous times, drawn by the exuberance of small children and their ability to live life to the fullest each day. Both were lessons Lexi wanted to relearn.

Impulsively, Lexi picked up the telephone and dialed the day-care center. The young lady who answered said Ellen wasn't in yet, but she'd be along later. Later.

And later, she'd be with Chane and the others on the campout.

Unlike last night, Lexi was looking forward to going. The turnaround made her laugh. Yesterday she'd run from Chane, and she hadn't even been sure she wanted to finish his course. *Voilà.* Enter Señora Padilla and Joe Robertson with their quests. Suddenly, spending time with Chane was the lesser of several evils. Not only a lesser evil, but a decided attraction.

It had been far too long since she'd felt this way about a man. She didn't want to now. Asking him if he'd been married was probably stupid. She'd hate it if he took her inquiry as an invitation she wasn't sure she was ready to extend.

He was the kind of man she'd notice in a room full of strangers, and not simply because of his size. He had that I'm-the-guy-in-charge look, which wasn't her favorite kind of man. A guy like that usually thought he knew what was best for you and didn't hesitate to tell you. She had no doubt Chane thought he knew what was best. The surprise was that he'd kept his opinions to himself until he was directly confronted. She liked that, too.

She ate breakfast, packed for the campout, and made sure Daisy's door onto the back porch was open as she locked up the house. And before Lexi headed for the rendezvous with the wilderness survival class, she went to see Ellen.

Lexi parked her car across the street from the day-care center, which was next to a park. Children played outside. Their brightly colored clothes and delighted shouts made Lexi smile as she crossed the street, answering Ellen's wave with one of her own.

Ellen met her at the gate with a half-dozen munchkins in

tow. Slender with light brown hair and vivid blue eyes, she looked more like a teenager than a woman approaching thirty.

"You're out bright and early today," Ellen said by way of greeting. "How've you been?"

"Good," Lexi replied, smiling at her and the surrounding children. She enjoyed the little ones, but teased anyway, "And how are the ankle biters?" She tousled the black hair of one small girl standing next to Ellen, watching Lexi with big black eyes and a shy smile.

"Hey, watch that kind of talk. You're in enemy territory, you know."

Lexi squatted to be eye-level with the child. "And who's this little sweetie?" Like all Hispanic children, this one had special allure for Lexi. A dimple appeared in one cheek as her smile grew bigger.

"This is Tessa," Ellen said.

"Hi, Tessa," Lexi said. "How are you?"

"I'm a wonderful girl," she announced.

Lexi laughed and held out her arms. "You sure are."

Tessa moved closer and Lexi picked her up and balanced her against one hip. "Do you like to swing?"

"Uh-huh."

"Want to swing?"

"Uh-huh."

"To the swings, then." Lexi headed toward the swings on the far side of the yard, and Ellen fell into step beside her. "It looks like your enrollment is up."

"It is," Ellen agreed. "There are a few more year-round residents, and that helps."

Lexi set Tessa down in the swing and pushed her gently, chatting with Ellen about the winter just around the corner and the tourist season just ending. Year-round residents and winter weren't the topics of interest, yet Lexi found herself relying on techniques she had used for years to manipulate the conversation.

Just ask her, Lexi mentally scolded herself. Out with it. Stop dithering and ask her. She'll either help or she won't.

"I'm trying to help out a friend," Lexi said, finally. "I hope you can steer me in the right direction." At Ellen's look of inquiry, Lexi said, "If I wanted to find out who adopted a baby from South America, how would I go about that?"

"I'm not sure you could. Those records are supposed to be sealed."

"I know." Lexi had assumed they were. "But you hear stories all the time of adoptive kids trying to find their biological family. I know a biological grandmother looking for her granddaughter."

"Does she have any proof of that?" Ellen asked.

Lexi met her friend's gaze. "I don't honestly know. We haven't gotten that far yet."

"But you're willing to put the adoptive parents through hell." The heat in Ellen's voice surprised Lexi.

Her own voice rose. "This baby was adopted illegally."

"How do you know?"

"The señora told me," Lexi responded.

"And you believe her?" Ellen asked sharply.

"Yes. My God, she's an old woman. Not a con artist, not a mother who has changed her mind. Just an old woman, looking for her grandchild."

"Maybe all that is true," Ellen said. "That doesn't mean the child's parents don't love her."

"Her parents were murdered!"

"I'm talking about her adoptive parents."

"And I'm talking about her birth parents!" Ellen's point was one Lexi had also thought about during the long hours of the previous night. No matter what happened, someone was going to be hurt if she went through with helping Señora Padilla.

Personally, Lexi thought people who would buy a baby rather than going through the normal adoption channels were only a step above pond scum. Regardless, they undoubtedly loved Señora Padilla's granddaughter, no matter how they had come to have her. And she supposed they might even rationalize their actions, might even think they had done nothing wrong. Though it was a stretch of imagination, Lexi admitted they might even have some legitimate justification for not going through legal channels. What that reason might be, she couldn't imagine.

Lexi touched Ellen's arm. "I know you're concerned about the adoptive parents. But imagine how the grandmother feels. This child is her only living relative. She needs to know where she is and how she is."

"I suppose she'd want to take the child back with her."

"I don't know," Lexi murmured. "I didn't ask her."

Ellen wasn't listening. "And for what? Take that child back to poverty and God knows what else? Break her parents' heart? Nothing good will come of this. Heartache and despair. That's all. Walk away from it, Lexi. You won't be doing this woman, whoever she is, any favors. Or yourself, either."

Ellen's voice was vehement. Lexi supposed she ought to have foreseen that Ellen would identify with the adoptive parents of Señora Padilla's granddaughter.

"I'll pass along your advice," Lexi promised. She, too, easily understood Ellen's concerns and realized how threatening all this must seem. Lexi also knew exactly how the señora felt. "I didn't realize . . ." She glanced at Ellen. "I'm not accusing you of anything."

"I didn't think you were."

"I'm sorry if I upset you," Lexi answered with a smile. "I didn't realize all this was such a touchy subject, to be honest. She hoped her unspoken message was clear. *I don't want to see anyone get hurt, either.*

Ellen nodded her understanding. "See you soon, then?"

"Sure." Lexi gave Ellen a quick hug.

Seconds later, back in her car, Lexi waved at Ellen, who stood near the gate with little Tessa in her arms. Ellen's posture was rigid and her expression pensive.

Lexi had her answer. Ellen wouldn't help.

Chapter 4

Chase her a little. This was probably his best opportunity, Chane decided as he put the finishing touches on his lean-to. The good-natured banter of the wilderness-survival students echoed around him with varying degrees of frustration as they worked on their own shelters. Students—chaperons that kept him from being alone with Lexi. He had to believe she was interested. Why else would she have asked if he was married?

Earlier in the day he had led the class several miles up North Inlet Creek to the site for their campout. The hike had been strenuous enough to push everyone, short enough to ensure their arrival by midafternoon. He'd put them to work building their shelters, recognizing they had mostly ignored his talk about the dangers of hypothermia.

If they had been a platoon being trained for a mission, Chane would have made sure they understood. More than once he'd led his men through icy streams and built shelters in timberline crevices a mountain goat would avoid. The experiences were tough, brutal, and designed to make survival second nature to men who had to be focused on a mission. Civilians were another matter. He wouldn't have many paying customers if he imposed the same standards he'd expected of the units he trained.

So he let them think they were roughing it with a forty-pound pack and down-filled sleeping bags. They'd be roughing it when they could survive a winter night carrying not much more than a Swiss army knife and a book of matches.

This group of students was the usual mix of personalities, though the class was small. A pair of students from Colorado Mountain College in Leadville—Frank Jones and Joshua Williams. Teachers from the junior high school in Granby, Brian and Julie Marconi. And Lexi.

Joshua was a bookworm who looked as though he would be more comfortable in a chemistry lab than climbing mountains. He freely admitted Frank had talked him into taking the class. Frank was brash and impatient, a young man whose dabbling was financed by his father, a bank president in Winter Park.

Both of the kids were taking the class because it had sounded like fun. Brian and Julie, newlyweds, wanted something they could do together. Only Lexi had expressed reasons for taking the class that intrigued Chane—to overcome her fear. Of what she was afraid, she hadn't said. On the surface, she was nearly as carefree as Frank, sometimes as outgoing as Julie. Chane couldn't shake the feeling—especially since her fall yesterday—there was a lot more to Lexi beneath the surface.

At the edge of the clearing, Chane could see two of the shelters taking shape. One looked like a small haystack and the other resembled a huge pile of kindling. Tucking in the last fragrant boughs from an evergreen on the outside of his lean-to, Chane watched Frank saunter toward him. Chane glanced around the clearing, spotting Joshua, Brian, and Julie. Lexi was nowhere to be seen.

"You mean you're not finished yet?" Frank asked.

"You mean you are?" Chane returned, still looking for Lexi.

"Just following your advice, man. Since we're only going to spend a night in it, don't invest a lot of time."

Chane had the feeling that applied to most things Frank did. The youngest of the group and the most impatient, he reminded Chane of his brother, Kit.

"Well, let's go see what you've got."

Chane already knew the shelter Frank and Joshua had built

would have them sweating the first half of the night and freezing the last half. He also suspected it would blow away with the first good gust of wind, but he'd need a closer look to know for sure.

Before they reached the shelter, Julie emerged from under her pile of kindling. She laughed, pointing at Josh, who had just crawled out of his shelter, bits of straw clinging to him.

"And I'll huff and puff," she said with delight, throwing her arms wide and aiming an exaggerated breath toward the shelter. "And I'll blow your house down!"

Chane grinned.

"Hey," Frank responded in kind, "that house of sticks you and Brian put together looks like a big pile of kindling. The only way you'll keep warm is to set fire to it."

"Goes to show what you know about fires," Brian retorted, winking at Julie.

"Looks more like the little pig's house of sticks," said Joshua.

Chane joined in the laughter, which he admitted was a relief. Making sure his men could survive blizzards or dust storms had been a responsibility that often prohibited humor. "You all need a little help with design, guys. Josh is right, Brian. About two o'clock tomorrow morning, you and Julie are going to be freezing. And Josh, if that hay stack hasn't blown away by two o'clock, you're going to be cold, too."

"No way."

"Trust me. The insulation all this grass provides is fine, but you've packed it so tight, you guys are going to sweat. Come the middle of the night, all that moisture from simply breathing will condense, and you'll think it's raining."

He gave the four some additional pointers, demonstrated with both shelters the kind of improvements that needed to be made, then asked, "Where's Lexi?"

"Probably building a house of bricks," Joshua answered promptly, earning a couple of chuckles.

"She went off that way," Julie said, waving toward the edge of the clearing directly across from where Chane had built his shelter.

He headed in that direction. Some fifteen feet inside the trees he stopped. If Lexi had built a shelter close by, it was invisible.

"Okay, Lexi, I give up. Where are you?" he called, on the off chance she was close enough to hear him.

"Here," she answered.

Her voice was close. He scanned the trees and underbrush around him. A blue spruce—huge and majestic—was surrounded by aspen trees, their yellow leaves fluttering in the breeze. Small lodgepole pines that would someday dominate the forest grew under the protective canopy of the aspen. He didn't see where Lexi had built her shelter and focused his attention on the undergrowth.

"You didn't have to build a blind, you know. A simple, well-constructed shelter was all you needed."

"That's what you asked for, all right." Then she recited, "Don't underestimate the importance of a good shelter."

Chane grinned. She had managed to catch his inflection almost exactly.

"In this climate keeping warm is as important as water. Don't cut down anything that takes more than a season to grow. Don't line your shelter with nettles."

If she hadn't been talking, Chane would have missed her. She had found a blue spruce under which to build a shelter. A spreading juniper encroached along the lower branches of the tree, minimizing the need to build an external structure.

"If you use a hollow log, make sure it's vacant," she continued. "I liked that one. Can't imagine a skunk putting up a 'no vacancy' sign, though."

"You've obviously never shared space with a skunk." He ducked under one of the spreading branches of the spruce, then knelt.

"True," she said.

He found her sitting, knees bent, her arms casually draped over her knees. Despite the dropping temperatures, she hadn't changed her shorts for jeans as the other students had. Those long, long tanned legs of hers were . . . nice. Better than nice. Gorgeous. He swallowed and crawled a little farther inside, forcing a casual smile that matched his chase-her-a-little mandate.

"Hi," she said with a smile. "Nice of you to drop by."

"I thought I was invited."

He forced his eyes from the glowing length of her legs to the branches above their heads. The interior of the shelter resembled a woven green basket, where she had tucked cattail leaves into the exposed branches. With the draping blue spruce branches above, he had no doubt this shelter would stay dry. The temperature inside was cozy. At the moment, though, it could have been forty below outside, and he'd still be warm.

"You were invited all right." She grinned. "If you call 'get busy—I'll be by in an hour to check on your work' an invitation."

He liked her teasing, was glad to see the return of her sense of humor. After yesterday's disaster on the rock climb, he hadn't expected her to be this relaxed. He glanced around the shelter once more. "This is okay, Lexi."

"Only okay, huh."

"Maybe a little better than okay," he conceded. "You just didn't hear what I told the rest of them."

She had somehow swept the carpet of needles out of the way and covered the bare ground with long stalks of sweet-smelling grass. Her sleeping bag was spread out, and it took no effort to imagine his next to hers. She had taken off her sweatshirt, which was folded into a pillow at the head of the dark blue sleeping bag. His gaze returned to her face, searching the depths of her eyes. She seemed to be giving him the same perusal in return. His attention fell naturally to her mouth. Her lips held a slight blush of pink and looked infinitely soft and kissable. He raised his eyes back to hers.

He cleared his throat. "You've obviously done this before."

"Building shelters?" Her voice was husky and followed after a mere pause that made him ache to know if she was as aware as he was.

He nodded.

"Once or twice," she admitted.

"So what happens if you need a fire?" Chane sat down and

spread his legs out in front of him, leaned back, and supported his weight on one shoulder and arm.

"You didn't say anything about a fire, Mr. Instructor Sir," she answered, that teasing lilt back in her voice. "I hope it's necessary to cook trout later, though."

He arched an eyebrow. "Going fishing?"

She shook her head. "Not me. You. Your trout dinners are legendary."

"I'd heard that."

"It's the only reason I came," she said.

"You wanted to go fishing."

"No. But I love fresh trout eaten around a campfire."

"What's it worth to you?" A dozen things came to his mind instantly, all of which had to do with the removal of clothes and making the most intimate use of her very inviting nest.

"Biscuits," she said.

"Biscuits?" He grinned, liking the matter-of-fact challenge in her voice. "The only good biscuit is a hot one."

"That's the way I like them."

"Too bad we're not a little closer to a modern electric oven."

"I have a better chance of giving you a hot biscuit for dinner than you do of giving me a fresh, succulent trout."

"You're on. But just in case you don't come through, what are the stakes?"

"Are you worried about losing?"

"You should be."

"I'm positive I won't lose, so there's no point . . . but if you're serious"—she paused a moment—"you can carry my pack tomorrow when we go back."

"And if you lose?"

"Chane, did you find her?" called Frank. "Chane. Lexi. Where are you?" His yell sounded as though he stood right next to the spruce tree.

"I found her," Chane answered, raising his voice only slightly.

"This is so cool. I don't even see you guys. Where are you?"

"Here." Chane glanced at Lexi, wishing he could tell Frank to go away. Instead, he shrugged his shoulders and crawled out of the shelter the way he'd come. "Want to see a good shelter, Frank? One that will keep you warm and dry?"

He scooted under the branches toward the opening, seeing Frank's feet a scant two yards away.

"If there's a shelter here—"

Chane brushed aside one of the massive branches of the blue spruce. Frank's eyes widened when he saw Chane crouched beneath the branch.

"She built a shelter in there?"

"Yeah. Do you mind another visitor, Lexi?"

"The more the merrier," she answered.

Chane hoped the note of disappointment in her voice wasn't his own wishful thinking.

"Cool," Frank said. "How'd you ever think of this?"

Chane had wanted to know the same thing, and he leaned forward far enough to see Lexi. This shelter showed skill and ingenuity and a basic understanding of how best to keep warm and dry. She hadn't spent any more time than he had, but this shelter would serve equally as well as the one he'd built, far better than the ones the other students had built. And if her boast on the biscuits was true, she was no more a novice at this than he was.

"I'm a photographer," she explained to Frank. "I learned early on that if you don't want to be seen, you'd better learn the art of blending into your surroundings. And I don't like being wet or cold."

"So, where'd you learn?" Chane asked.

"A long time ago when I was a Girl Scout."

Frank laughed. "Now why don't I believe that? When was the last time you built a shelter?"

"A year ago."

The change in her voice was subtle, Chane noted. The change in her body language was not. Her fists clinched and goose bumps rose on her arms. And those damn shadows were back in her eyes.

"A year ago," Frank repeated, apparently oblivious to the change in Lexi. "You sure haven't forgotten much in a year. I'm going to go get the others. They'll want to see this."

"Fine," Chane answered, barely acknowledging Frank as he crawled past. Chane duck-walked farther into the shelter, his eyes not leaving Lexi's face. In the space of seconds, her complexion had grown pale, and her eyes looked as though a light had been turned off. Chane touched her hands and found them cold, clammy.

He snagged her sweatshirt off the sleeping bag and held the bottom of it toward her. Automatically, she put her arms out, and he slid the garment over her head. As the shirt settled over her shoulders, he lifted her braid away from her neck, its weight soft, warm from her body.

He resisted the urge to hug her, but smoothed his hands down her arms in reassurance. He didn't understand the change, and he wanted back the teasing woman she had been moments earlier.

"C'mon," he said huskily. "Let's go catch some trout."

The bits and pieces he'd gleaned about Lexi Monroe from the local grapevine didn't touch on why she said she wanted to trust people again. His first bet would be her job. News was often ugly, doubly so in the third world, war-torn countries that had been her beat and his. The owner of the day-care center where he took Tessa told him Lexi had covered Central America and was on a year's leave of absence.

He crawled out of the shelter, then held the spruce branch back until she stood and brushed past him. He dropped the branch back into place, gently squeezing the resilient needles inside his palm, releasing the pungent scent of evergreen.

"Are you okay?" he asked.

She met his glance with a wary look. "Fine. How did the other shelters turn out?"

"You'll have to see for yourself." He smiled down at her, hoping to coax a smile. "Just keep in mind the story of the three little pigs and you'll get the picture."

"Oh." A small smile curved her lips. "As in, you huffed and puffed and blew them all down?"

"Not me, personally."

"Oh, another wolf, then?" The smile was wider.

He swung an arm at her, intending to cuff her on the back of the head. She easily ducked out of reach.

"Are you implying I'm a wolf?" Good, he thought. The smile was back. Not as bright, but enough to lessen the shadows in her eyes.

She stopped walking and looked at him from the corner of her eye before turning to face him fully. She studied him a moment as though coming to some important decision, then said, "No, Mr. Instructor Sir, I'm not implying."

He aimed another playful swat at her, which she easily deflected.

Her smile broadened to a grin. "Wolves may be endangered, misunderstood, and unnecessarily persecuted, but . . ."

"But?"

"They usually get what they deserve."

"So do people who tease them," he warned. "I think I'll go get my fishing pole."

"Good idea. I'm counting on a nice trout to go with my biscuit." She ran toward the clearing, calling to the others. Seconds later, laughter erupted from the group.

Chane headed for his own shelter, whistling under his breath. So, she thought he was a wolf, huh? A man might take that as an indication the lady was also aware. *So chase her a little.*

God, he'd forgotten how scary, how good a simple flirtation with a woman felt. Chasing her a little wasn't going to be enough. That worried him, but he couldn't stop, didn't want to stop.

By the time he pulled his waders out of his pack, he had attracted an audience.

"This doesn't look like standard survival equipment to me," said Frank.

"Maybe it's some weird kind of compass," offered Julie. "Instead of pointing north, they point to water."

"Maybe none of you want trout for dinner," Chane returned, leading the band toward a beaver pond.

"These are going to be awfully small trout if they've been growing for only a season," Lexi offered. The others laughed, and she added, "Isn't there a size requirement or you have to throw them back?"

"I wouldn't be talking size, if I were you," Chane said, pointing his fishing pole at her. "In some circles you might be considered undersize yourself. And you're not too big to be thrown in."

"You and what army?" she challenged.

He straightened. "No army. Just a few good men."

"A few good men," she muttered with a shake to her head. "Once a Marine, always a Marine."

"Semper Fi," Chane agreed.

Joshua and Brian got out their fishing poles and spaced themselves fifty feet apart on the far side of the pond. Lexi settled on the grass in a pool of sunshine near Chane. Within minutes, Brian had his arms around his bride, ostensibly teaching her the finer points of fly-fishing. Chane envied him. Talk gradually faded, leaving behind the late-afternoon quiet, punctuated with the chirp of crickets.

"We could have a hard frost tonight," Chane commented to Lexi. "Those crickets better enjoy their singing while they still have the chance."

"A little cold is good for you."

He glanced at her legs. She still hadn't changed out of her shorts, and though goose bumps covered her legs, she seemed oblivious to the chill. A fantasy of warming her within the warmth of his sleeping bag teased at the edge of his consciousness.

"After all the time that you spent in the tropics, I'd think this would feel cold," he said. "The first winter I spent here was after I'd been stationed for more than a year in the Middle East. The first time I went out ice fishing, I thought I'd freeze to death."

"There were times last spring when I felt like that, too."

"How long were you in South America?" he asked.

"Five years."

"Long time."

The occasional splash of a trout jumping and the sound of

the reel on Chane's fishing pole filled the air in the moment before Lexi answered with a soft, "Yeah."

Chane glanced at her. The pensive expression was back as she bent her knees, rested her folded arms across them, and rested her chin on her hands.

"The woman at your house yesterday. A friend visiting from South America?"

"No."

Such a long beat of silence passed that Chane wasn't certain she was going to say anything else.

"A reporter I know sent her to see me."

Lexi saw the invitation to talk in Chane's expression, and she might have said more if she could have made sense of her own jumbled thoughts. She'd spent too many years keeping her own counsel for talking to come easily. Photographs were far more eloquent, and the images within her didn't translate easily to words. With them were questions she wished she'd thought to ask. When would the señora be back? Tomorrow? Next week? Lexi didn't like the suspense of not knowing, even as she recognized the predictability she'd come to cherish in her life was one more way of staying within the safety net she'd built for herself.

All at once it seemed to be coming unraveled. Joe's lead on El Ladron ought to have pleased her instead of filling her with the sense of foreboding. The señora's request ought to have been an atonement for Lexi's inability to make things better before she left Costa Léon instead of making her want to pack up and run.

Run? Was that what she'd done, coming on the campout?

"Those look like heavy-duty thoughts," Chane said.

Lexi's gaze focused on him. "I just figured out that I came on this campout in order to avoid Señora Padilla."

He remembered the small woman promising she'd return for Lexi's answer. "And you don't want to give her whatever it is she wants."

Lexi stood up. "I'd gladly give her what she wants if that were in my power."

"But?"

"But I don't have a clue where to find her granddaughter."
Lexi shivered.

Chane glanced at Lexi's long legs, then at her face. "Better
go put on some jeans. You're on the verge of being chilled."

"Yeah." She took a couple of steps toward the camp, then
glanced back at him. "And you look like you're on the verge
of being skunked. I don't see any fish you've caught yet."

"And I don't see any biscuits, either," he returned.

"You will," she promised.

His instinct had been to accept and enjoy her company at
whatever level she wanted to give it. He'd been tempted to ask
her questions about the shadows that haunted her. And he was
positive she would have shied away if he had. Whatever was
going on with Señora Whats-her-face bothered Lexi. Once
again, the need surfaced to help Lexi, shelter her, and make
things easier for her. Another part of him wanted only the
pleasure of her body.

Chane watched her walk back toward the camp. She moved
with easy grace that drew his attention to the elliptical sway
of her hips. Despite her height, each cheek of her bottom
wasn't a lot bigger than his hand. The image of cupping her
so intimately very nearly made him miss catching the first trout
when it struck his line.

An hour and eight trout later, the group bantered with one
another as they prepared the meal. True to her word, Lexi had
made biscuits. The pit oven she'd built next to their campfire
was not the work of a novice. The flat stones warmed and
radiated more than enough heat to bake the biscuits. The other
four students were impressed. Chane was puzzled.

First that shelter. Now a makeshift oven that could have been
used by the Galloping Gourmet. He'd bet his fly rod she had
experience in wilderness survival equal to his own.

They cleaned up the camp in short order after the meal, while
Lexi teased Chane about losing the wager.

"I didn't lose," he reminded her. "You baked biscuits and
I caught fish. Even Steven. A draw. Now, if you'd like to up
the stakes and carry my pack, I could maybe interest you in a
nice game of poker."

She laughed. "I don't think so."

"Gin rummy?"

She shook her head, her dark eyes sparkling, a dimple he hadn't noticed before appearing at the corner of her mouth. She settled onto the ground next to the campfire, using a log as a backrest.

"I'd play poker with you, Chane," Julie said, holding her hands out to the fire, "if I thought you had a nice cozy tent stashed somewhere. It's getting cold."

"Yeah. Nights get real cold up here." Frank joined them around the fire. "It could even get down to zero. I heard about a miner who froze to death while panning for gold. They found him, all frozen like an icicle, at the edge of the creek."

"Oh, stop it, Frank." Julie shivered. "Do you really expect us to spend the night in those shelters? I mean, you don't have a nice tent stashed somewhere, do you?"

"Nope," Chane responded.

Julie's question echoed Lexi's thoughts. Her apprehension grew as the night became darker and the first stars popped into view. Her dark shelter hadn't smelled musty when she'd first built it. This evening, when she had gone back to it for her jeans, it had.

"I'm freezing," Julie announced.

"We'll just have to share some body heat," Brian told her, drawing her next to his side, wrapping an arm around her.

Freezing or not, Lexi knew she wouldn't be sleeping in her shelter. "You two trade shelters with me," Lexi said. "It's big enough for the two of you, and it'll be warm."

"You're not cold?" Julie asked.

Lexi shook her head, noticing Chane's puzzled gaze on her and ignoring it. If she wanted to give away her shelter, that was her business. She had been in Brian and Julie's shelter when Chane had inspected it earlier. It wasn't as cozy as the one she had built, but it was serviceable. And because it was in the open and covered with boughs from the same fallen spruce Chane had used to cover his shelter, it had a pungent aroma of pitch. That aroma was a far cry better than the musty smell of damp earth.

"Thanks, Lexi," Brian said. "That's more than generous."

"You know what it means that we don't have tents, don't you?" asked Joshua.

"Rain," Brian offered.

"Ghost stories," Frank said.

"Yeah," Julie said with breathless anticipation. "There's nothing like a good scare around a campfire."

Yeah, Lexi echoed in the deepest recesses of her mind. There's *nothing* like a good scare around a campfire.

Chapter 5

"Do you know any good stories, Chane?" Julie asked.

He stared into the flames. He knew some scary stories. Some of them weren't even ghost stories. He glanced around the campfire at each of them, his gaze resting a moment on Lexi. She stared into the flames, and he wondered what she saw.

"The Indians have been coming into these valleys for a millennium." He paused and cocked his head to the side. "Some have come and gone, and some remain. Hear them?"

The whisper of an unseen breeze brushed through the pines. Chane glanced around the campfire at the expectant faces, the only sound besides the whisper of wind the pop and crackle of the campfire.

"Ghosts," Chane said, his voice dropping in pitch, dropping in volume, "waiting to have their stories told."

Ghosts, he thought. *That was what he had seen within the misty jungle of the photograph hanging in Lexi's house. Her ghosts.*

"One day, much like this one, a band of Ute Indians were beginning to think about moving farther south for the winter. They had been hunting and fishing for the summer, and the provisions they had accumulated for the winter were plentiful.

The children were healthy, the men content, the women beautiful. Life was good, just as it was meant to be.''

"This doesn't sound like a ghost story to me," Frank said.

"Shh," commanded Julie. "What happened?"

Another breeze caught in the pine and a mournful whisper rushed toward them.

"About midday, a bloody warrior from a neighboring band of Utes stumbled into the village. Mortally wounded, he told them his band had been massacred by the Cheyenne. No one had been spared. Not children. Not women. Not the old ones. 'Protect yourselves,' he warned them. 'Save your families before it is too late.'

"The chief dispatched a scouting party to find the hated Cheyenne, then pondered how to best safeguard the women and children from the battle that was sure to come.

"The braves cut lodgepole pine and lashed them together into several large rafts. The moment the Cheyenne war party appeared, the women were to push the rafts, loaded with children and supplies, into the middle of the lake."

Lexi watched Chane as he talked. The play of light over his strong, sharply defined features teased to life her photographer's eye. Shadow and light. The taut angle of cheekbone and the deep-set eyes. Texture. The strands of razor-straight hair. His dark brown eyes reflected firelight one moment, then turned black as he gazed toward the sky, then soft as he gazed at her. For months, she had been uninterested in photographing people. Tonight she wished passionately she had her camera with her.

"Scant hours later the Cheyenne war party arrived," Chane continued, "and the most ferocious battle raged for hours. The women pushed the rafts into the lake. From the middle of the lake, the women watched helplessly, able only to offer prayers their men would be victorious. The gods answered, and victory came to the Ute warriors after a long battle that left not one Cheyenne standing.

"'The battlefield is yours,' the Cheyenne war chief said as he lay dying. Then he taunted, 'Victory belongs to the great Cheyenne. Our shaman has cursed this place, and as we die, so shall you lose what is most valuable to you.' These were his last words before the Ute chief pierced him through the heart with a lance.

"Almost at once, a wind swept down from the Never Summer Range, rushing across the lake, pushing huge turbulent waves toward the women and children. The rafts were no match for the wind, and within minutes they broke apart. The men could not swim so far to save them, and they were all too far from the shore to swim to safety. They all drowned. The old ones. The women. The children."

Chane paused, letting the wind song of the pine surround them once again. "Early in the morning, when the mist hangs low on Grand Lake, you can see them. Their spirits forever part of the lake, the lake forever part of them. Spirit Lake. And the wind song . . ." He cocked his head to the side and listened. "Even now, you can hear the warriors mourn."

"Have you ever seen them?" asked Julie. "Ghosts of the Indians in the lake?"

It was the question Lexi would have asked if she could have found her voice.

"Once you know the legend," he answered, his gaze focused on Lexi, "it's impossible not to see them."

Lexi snuggled further inside her sleeping bag, her gaze focused on the glowing embers from the campfire. Within minutes of the conclusion of Chane's story, they'd all decided to go to bed. As promised, Lexi had traded shelters with Brian and Julie. The musty smell in this one was not so strong. She would have liked it more if there had been cracks enough over her head to see a few stars. But then, the shelter wouldn't have met Chane's requirement of being rain-proof.

She was glad for the shimmering coals and the faint aroma of wood smoke in the air. That and the crisp night air reassured Lexi that she wasn't in Central America. This was no hot, sweltering night, and no ruthless hand would reach through her mosquito netting and yank her from sleep and safety.

Before Chane had headed for his shelter, he'd asked her if she was going to be okay—being alone.

"Fine," she had assured him. In the way he meant, she was.

As an only child she'd learned early how to be alone without being lonely. As the daughter of the town tramp in a too-small community, she'd been too often alone, not the proper playmate for children of more respectable parents. As an adult, she'd loved the freedom of being alone among strangers. Tonight she wished she weren't . . . alone.

Lexi sighed and stretched restlessly. Julie's soft laugh drifted through the night. Lexi too easily imagined what she and Brian were doing. Nearby, Frank regaled Josh with a tale of murder and mayhem. Judging from Josh's occasional chuckle, Frank's story failed to have the desired effect. From Chane's direction, there was no sound at all.

Alone. She slid deeper into her sleeping bag more aware than usual that she was a solitary person in a world usually made up of pairs. What would it be like to fall asleep in the arms of a man like Chane Callahan? The tactile memory of being held in his arms yesterday on the cliff made her shift restlessly. Appreciation for his strength gave way to imagining that strength wrapped around her. She was certain being held by him in so intimate an embrace would make a woman feel cherished, protected, safe. Cared for. It was an illusion that tempted her unbearably.

You're not going to fall asleep if you keep thinking about that, she scolded herself. She had never been one to moon over the guys, but tonight she'd been unable to take her eyes off him.

Once, during the tragic story of the Utes, Chane's eyes had seemed haunted. What private battles made them seem that way?

She must have slept, for some sound, some *thing*, startled her, and she opened her eyes. Her heart pounding, she peered into the night, trying to get her bearings. No stars illuminated the night sky. Beneath her, the ground was unyielding and smelled musty. She couldn't decide if she was in her cramped apartment in San Pedro or somewhere else. On a yawn, she remembered. The thatched hut near El Corcho, were she had come with Joe Robertson.

Just before dusk, they had argued. He had to meet a man, he had told her, one who could get him an interview with the captain of a local guerrilla faction. No she couldn't go. It was too dangerous. Lexi figured he wanted all the glory for himself. He could have it. He'd be back soon, he assured her. Cooling her heels while the great Joe Robertson chased down a story was her least favorite sport, and she wished she'd stayed in San Pedro. When they went back, she intended to wire New York. Corporate could find another patsy to babysit their problem reporter.

She was hot. Restless, she wiped her brow. *The noise must be Joe returning. At least now she'd get some sleep.*

Alarm flooded her, heated her.

Someone was out there. Creeping through the black interior of the hut. Someone who would reach inside the mosquito netting and grab her.

She sat up and fought her way out of the sleeping bag, feeling panicked, needing to escape.

She stood and ran outside. So black was the night, she couldn't see two feet in front of her. She gazed wildly around her. Pale cruel eyes were out there watching her. She could feel them.

She stumbled and fell, fought against crying out. Stretching her arms in front of her, she rose to her knees. Nothing in the middle of the clearing looked familiar.

Disoriented, she peered through the dark, expecting any moment to see two men separate from the shadows. She wanted to run, managed only to walk. Beneath her feet the ground was damp, the blades of grass beneath her feet feeling like shards of ice.

Cold. How could it be so cold when she'd just been so hot?

A shadow in front of her moved, and she cried out.

He was bigger, far bigger, than she remembered. And he'd hurt her so much—

"Lexi?"

The shadow moved closer.

Dear God, no!

She whirled around and ran blindly into the black maw of night.

Pounding footsteps followed her on a curse that sounded like her name. Too soon strong arms caught her, and she tumbled to the ground. Pinned beneath him, she bit her lip to keep from crying out, to keep from showing him how afraid she really was.

Unwashed, unclean, he had smothered her with his weight, and a brutal hand had clamped over her mouth, a hand smelling of . . . pine?

"Lexi? C'mon, honey. You're going to be okay."

A voice filled with concern, a voice that could have belonged to a guardian angel. Warm hands gripped her shoulders and smoothed down her arms, not clamping across her mouth and nose.

The weight smothering her was suddenly gone as he rolled off her, then lifted her to her feet.

"Honey, talk to me."

"Chane?" she whispered. She shivered hard. Beneath her feet was cold, dew-soaked grass. She wasn't in the jungle near San Pedro!

"Yes," he said.

She was safe! This time only dreams, only remembered terror. She shivered and leaned against Chane, inhaling deeply, savoring the warm skin of his chest next to her cheek and the aroma of soap and deodorant. He wrapped his arms around her, pulling her against the welcoming heat of his body.

"What are you doing?" She slid her arms around his lean waist. She ought to move, but she needed his reassurance that she was safe. Just a moment more, and she'd let go, she promised herself. Just a moment more . . . and she'd stand on her own two feet.

"That's what I'd intended to ask you."

She felt the vibration of his voice against her cheek, felt the steady beating of his heart. The shirt that covered his shoulders hung open, as though he'd put it on in a hurry. To come to her? Impossible. She had only herself to count on.

Nonetheless, she found herself answering, "I was having a nightmare." Her voice sounded small, even to her own ears.

"Ah." He ran his hands down her spine, then linked them together at the small of her back. "Are you better now?"

She nodded, her head brushing against his collarbone. She was embarrassed, but her overriding feeling was one of being safe, cherished. Protected.

"Are you ready to go back to bed?"

"Not yet."

"We're going to have to get into some more clothes. This is damn cold."

"You don't have to stay up with me," she murmured, denying her need not to be alone. She looked up, wishing she could see his eyes. A silhouette darker than the inky black of night was all she could sense. "How did you find me?"

"I heard you. And in that long white underwear, you weren't that hard to spot."

"Sure it's not ghosts?"

She decided he must have heard the trace of humor in her voice, for he chuckled.

"Nah." Once again his hands smoothed down her back. "You're too warm to be a ghost."

"That's supposed to make sense to me?"

"It's the best you're going to get on short notice. What scared you?"

She hadn't expected so direct a question, and evading it was impossible, even though she hadn't talked to anyone else about that night. "It was so black. And I was hot." Her heart began to pound again. "And I knew they were coming for me, so I ran."

A beat of silence passed before he said, "I thought you were hurt. Are you?"

"No," she whispered. *Not this time.*

He tugged on her hand. "C'mon. It's cold."

He was right. It was cold. "Yes." Relieved, she repeated, "Yes. It *is* cold, isn't it?"

"You don't have to sound so damn happy about it." He led her toward the fire ring. Letting go of her hand, he stirred through the coals, finding a few warm ones that were teased to life by his skillful addition of kindling. While he added fuel to the fire, Lexi stood shivering.

The cheerful crackle of the fire seemed so out of place, at odds with the overwhelming fear she had felt only moments earlier. Almost against her will, her gaze kept darting to the gloom at the edge of the fire's radiance. She couldn't see the danger, but she knew it was there, could sense it as surely as she sensed the pounding of her own heart. She caught Chane watching her. His eyes were dark, thoughtful . . . soft.

She concluded he knew just how frightened she had been, which left her feeling raw. Vulnerable.

He stood up and approached her slowly as though he expected her to bolt and run for the forest like a wild and wary doe. He reached for her hands when he was less than a foot away. She didn't retreat, though the urge was nearly overwhelming. He clasped both of her hands between his, raising them to his lips. He cupped her palms inside his and lightly blew into the center.

"We need to get you warm," he murmured, leading her toward the shelter she had traded for. There, he rummaged around a moment until he found her shoes. Slipping them on her bare feet, he knelt and tied the laces. Standing once again, he took her hand and led her back to the campfire.

"Be right back," he promised with a reassuring squeeze to her shoulders.

She stared into the flames a moment, found them beckoning, but not nearly warm enough to penetrate her chill. Shivering hard, she went back to her shelter and got her sleeping bag. Returning to the campfire, she smoothed the bag out next to a log that made a handy backrest and sat down.

Chane materialized out of the night a moment later, wearing a charcoal hooded sweatshirt and the wool shirt he'd been wearing earlier. In his hands was a down-filled vest. He sat down beside Lexi and stuffed her into the vest, closing all the snaps.

"Why are you doing this?" she whispered.

He took her hand and laced her fingers through his before raising his eyes to hers. "I know about nightmares, Lexi."

"They're just—"

"Shh." He placed a finger over her lips. "I know the kind that you live through. The kind that haunt your days. The kind that keep you from sleeping."

Her throat grew tight.

"Is that how it is?" he asked.

Unable to speak past the constriction in her throat, she nodded.

"Then, we'll get through this night together."

She had never been offered a more generous promise, one she was powerless to resist.

Chane leaned against the log and pulled Lexi into the circle of his arms. One end of the sleeping bag he wrapped around Lexi. Every once in a while she shivered, but gradually she stopped. Chane's big body provided blissful heat.

Streamers of warmth lengthened with each sweep of his hand down her arm, heat that curled in her belly like fine streamers of steam. His touch was without demand, which made it all the more pleasing. The sweet jolt of desire was unexpected, and she had no defense against it. She sank against him, listening to the ebb and flow of his deep voice. He told her about camping in these woods as a boy with his father and his grandfather. His voice wove reassurance and safety around her. They had been good times, he told her, full of a child's curiosity and a grandfather's wisdom, surrounded by towering mountains.

"Why is being cold a good thing?" he asked sometime later.

"It makes me know I'm not in Central America." She dragged her gaze from the flames to the chiseled outline of Chane's face.

He glanced down at her, traced the line of her jaw with one long finger.

"What happened in Central America?" His voice sounded almost as relaxed as she felt.

Wrapped securely within his arms, the old familiar panic did not rise. After a moment, she said, "It's a long story."

"It's a long night." She felt his breath warm her temple.

Her gaze returned to the hypnotizing fire. "I don't think I can talk about it," she whispered.

"Okay. We won't talk about it." He'd seen "The Children of War," and no leap of imagination at all was required to suppose those photographs were a sanitized version of what she had really encountered. He tipped her face toward him with his fingers. Her eyes shimmered. He managed a smile and forced lightness into his voice. "You're the first woman I've ever met who didn't want to talk an issue to death."

She matched his smile. "First time for everything?"

"Yeah."

"Tell me about your nightmare," she commanded in a whisper.

He cupped his palm around her arm and slid his hand down its slender length, then folded his fingers around her hand. "I served in the Marine Corps for eleven years, did you know that?"

She nodded. "You wanted it to be more?"

"The whole career."

He glanced down at her, expecting her to give voice to the questions in her eyes. When she didn't, he asked, "Have you ever had a time when you looked back on a situation and knew the exact moment that everything went all to hell?"

Lexi thought of the moment she'd decided she'd never again stand by and watch a baby being sold. Slowly, she nodded.

"Mine came the day I trusted a bastard named Joe Robertson."

Lexi felt herself grow cold. "Joe Robertson?"

"You've heard of him?"

Lexi could only nod, certain she knew where this story was going, certain she no longer wanted to hear it.

Chane swallowed. "I'd been assigned to a team that spent the better part of a year working behind the scenes to get two American hostages released. Operation Deliverance. The group holding these guys was some splinter faction no one knew much about. We spent months just trying to figure out how to talk to them before we could even confirm they were holding anyone." He sighed and raked a hand through his hair. "Anyway, we'd gotten some pretty good information about where the Americans were being held. Turned out to be as sweet a setup as you could ask for to stage a rescue. Plans were made. About four days out from the mission, Robertson showed up.''

Lexi's chill returned full force, and she shivered. ''You were at Mosul, weren't you?'' She'd known the story of the botched hostage rescue months before she ever worked with Joe. She just hadn't added up all the pieces that had been in front of her.

''Yeah.'' Chane wrapped his other arm around Lexi and rested his jaw against her temple. ''How'd you know?''

''I read about it in the papers,'' she said. ''It was awful.''

''Worse than that.'' He rubbed his cheek against Lexi's hair. ''I lost almost a dozen good men that night because that bastard had to have his story and blew our cover.''

Lexi turned, wrapping her arms around Chane. ''Watching people die . . .''

''Yeah,'' he agreed as though in tune with the awful images framed in her mind.

Lexi laid her head against his chest, hurting for him. ''I'm sorry,'' she whispered.

In answer, he squeezed her gently. She wrapped her arms around him and rested her head against his. Chane gazed into the dying embers of the fire and gathered her more closely. She relaxed against him, and one minute stretched into another.

''I was so scared,'' she whispered. ''You make me feel so safe.''

He pressed a kiss against her temple. ''I'm glad, honey.''

''You shouldn't call me that,'' she muttered sleepily.

''What?''

''Honey.'' She yawned. ''It might make a girl think you like her.''

''There's more to this than 'like,' Lexi.''

''Yes.'' Her voice was soft, barely coherent.

He slid his arms beneath her legs. Then he stood, bearing her weight as easily as a child's.

''Ready to go to bed?'' he asked softly.

She murmured something that he took as an affirmative response and nestled more fully against him. Instead of carrying her back to her shelter, Chane took her to his. In moments, he zipped the two sleeping bags together and helped her climb inside.

"This is cold," she grumbled.

He unsnapped the vest that enveloped her and took it off her, folded it, and set it inside the sleeping bag next to her. As soon as she was settled, he zipped it up. Already she was warmer, and once again drowsy.

"Thought you liked it cold," he teased.

She heard the rustle of clothing, then he settled into the sleeping bag next to her.

"I do."

A second later, she felt his arms come around her, and he hauled her closer to him. The heat of his body was inviting, and it was only natural to move closer to him. He arranged her spoon fashion against him, and she found her head pillowed on his shoulder.

His T-shirt felt soft against her cheek. She became aware of the aroma of detergent and deodorant subtly blended with him. She pressed her nose against him and inhaled.

"Better?" he whispered against her ear.

Better? This was heaven. "Yes," she whispered back.

"Good."

He pulled her closer, his hand coming to rest on her midriff, his touch as comforting as it was exciting. Gradually her shivering ceased, and she relaxed against him.

"Comfortable?" he asked.

"Hmm," was all the response she could manage. She'd been right, she decided as she drifted toward the oblivion of sleep. A woman felt safe, cherished, protected in his arms.

Her breathing became more even, and Chane sensed that she had drifted off to sleep. He, however, was wide awake.

Chase her a little.

Impossible, he decided. His body was on full alert, ready to do more than simply hold the woman within his arms. She had shown rare trust, and she had understood about Mosul. Rose had never even asked. And Lexi . . .

He'd never felt more in tune with a woman. He'd loved Rose, but she had her world and he had his. She hadn't wanted

to know what had happened on that last mission, and he hadn't
told her. Lexi had understood.

I knew they were coming to get me. Apparently, she had
cause to understand what he'd been through. His arms tightened
around her, tormented that anyone could have hurt her. Soft.
Sweet. Woman.

She sighed and relaxed more fully against him. The pressure
of her soft bottom against his lap made him imagine holding
her without layers of clothes between them. He had been this
achingly hard before, but the feeling had never been more
intense.

He closed his eyes and simply enjoyed the feel of having
her curved within his arms. She fit perfectly, just as he had
known she would. This was not a woman, however, to have a
fling with, then cast aside. The lady needed a knight to slay
her dragons. Someone to cherish her and care for her, and make
the sweetest kind of love to her.

A long time passed before he slept. Just as he drifted off,
his arms tightened around her. The woman in his arms was
his.

In his dreams, she turned in his arms, pushing her clothes
and his away. So much silky skin touching him. Her arms
wrapped around him, and she pressed herself closer. Closer.
Kisses were sprinkled against his neck, over the line of his jaw,
across his cheek. Impossibly, her lips were softer, even, than
her silky skin. On a sigh, she whispered his name.

Woman. She was his.

He drew her closer, and her lips brushed over his. Hunger
exploded through him, its ache sharp, gnawing. He opened his
mouth and drank from her. The taste of her against his tongue
. . . made him awaken.

Chapter 6

He eased his hands into her hair, the strands against his fingers as soft as he'd imagined, and anchored her head. He gave her the deep, seeking kiss he'd wanted. Her tongue brushed over his, against his, under his, a mating so perfectly exquisite he knew he had to be dreaming.

He opened his eyes and saw the faint halo of Lexi's hair against the utter black of night. Her mouth fit seamlessly against his, and the tiny catch of moan he heard was her, the sound of a woman slowly coming unraveled beneath the onslaught of her own arousal.

She rubbed sinuously against him, and it was no dream that her silky skin brushed against him. His T-shirt had ridden up, her top was bunched under her arms, and her soft, lush breasts were in full contact with his chest. His hands skimmed down her sides, up again, where he traced the rounded contour of her breasts with the heels of his hands.

Her mouth never left his. He explored deeply. Smooth serrations of her teeth. With the tip of his tongue, he touched the roof her mouth. She returned the caress exactly, feeding the wicked pressure building in his groin.

God, was he dreaming?

What if he was?

What if he *wasn't?*

Their shared kiss had no beginning, no end. Simply now. Intimate glide. Nubby texture. Aching hunger. No matter how much he took, the hunger grew. He returned to her mouth again and again, drank her taste, her texture, her sweetness. And felt as though he'd starve if he didn't have more.

God, was he dreaming?

"This is no dream," she whispered between drugging kisses. "Please . . . it's not a dream."

"Lexi?"

"More," she murmured against his mouth, touching his lower lip with the tip of her tongue. "Please."

He gave her what she wanted, what he wanted. He shifted covering her body with his. Her legs opened. Long, long . . . long legs that were somehow as bare as his most explicit fantasy. The touch of her naked thigh against his shocked him more fully awake.

"Lexi, you're not asleep?" He couldn't keep from kissing her again as he asked, tasting her, wanting nothing more than the consuming heat of her body. Her scent rose from her body, and he broke the kiss only long enough to trail his mouth down her neck, across the delicate line of bone at her shoulder. She reached for his face with slender hands that were surprisingly strong as she pulled him back where she wanted, a dark, hungry sharing of their mouths.

"Lexi."

"Hmm?" She kissed the corner of his mouth, then explored the shaped of his upper lip with the tip of her tongue.

"Are you asleep?"

"I hope not." Once again she fit her open mouth against his. He drank from her as though she were life itself.

"Honey, is this what you want?"

"God, yes." Her soft lips roamed over his face. "Even if I'm dreaming."

"This is no dream," he assured her, then wondered if he was right. No middle-of-the-night fantasy had ever been as hot as this. By definition, a dream. Yet, he had never been more wide awake or more aware of the woman within his arms.

Her hands made a brazen foray down the front of his torso, pushing his shorts down. Against his buttocks, her palms felt hot as sunlight. "I don't want this to end," she whispered, her breath hot against his neck. "And, God help me, if I'm asleep, I don't want to wake up."

Her echo of his thoughts made him anchor her head between his hands. He peered down at her, trying to see her features within the utter blackness of night. "Honey, tell me you're awake."

She arched beneath him, making room for him, inviting him closer for the most intimate embrace. He rested his forehead against hers.

"Lexi, please."

She lifted her hips toward him. "I'm awake."

He sank against her, shuddered at the first heated touch of her skin against his turgid length.

"I'm not sure I can stop, honey."

She wrapped her arms around him, then wrapped her legs around him. "Chane, I don't . . ." He pressed closer. ". . . want you to . . ." Her sensitized folds parted and he sank slowly into her. ". . . to stop."

She hadn't been sure what had been a dream and what had been real. They had been chasing her again, shadowy phantoms that could never be escaped. Then Chane was there, his arms held wide, his presence solid, comforting . . . alluring.

She felt cherished. Blessedly, beautifully, breathlessly connected, not just physically, but to the center of her dark, lonely soul. She stretched to overflowing to receive him. Nothing in her life had ever felt as perfect as this man.

"Lexi." He took her mouth with his, and with his tongue showed her what he intended to do to her. Shudders racked through her, and she lifted her hips, inviting his invasion of her body. Slowly, he moved within her, his kiss a hot counterpoint that kept pace.

She moved with him, lost in sensations that were too powerful, too needy. She wasn't like this. All heat and hunger, an open vestibule wanting him more than she'd ever wanted anything. Tension built, and she reached for it, wanting the moment it would spill over into release. But it didn't. It reach a plateau where they rode wildly, sweetly before reaching another incline. They strained together, her convulsing receipt counterpoint to his thrust, her soft femininity contrast to his hard masculinity. They climbed their wild ride toward the fire without pause, stretched on a rack of pleasure that was as endless as their awakening kiss. No beginning. No end. Simply now.

Chane didn't want it to end. Nothing had been more perfect, ever, than the feel of her tight femininity caressing him with each stroke he took. His mind emptied, and he moved within her, his total focus on the sensation of touching her. Sometimes slow, loving the catch in her voice when he brushed against her womb. Sometimes fast, enjoying her deeply whispered "Oh." Always kissing her, lost in the way she kissed him back and moved in unison with him.

He couldn't have said whether it lasted minutes or hours. It didn't matter. Nothing did except the pulses of her around him, her arms and legs hugging him tightly, her body convulsed in a climax that had begun as gradually as a sunrise. She made him feel hard, powerful, and grand as the towering mountains. The feel of her pulsing flesh sent him over the edge, and with powerful thrusts as endless as their kiss, he emptied himself inside her.

Their breathing slowed, and Chane rolled to his side, pulling Lexi with him. She relaxed bonelessly against him. He kissed her, tasted the sweetness, and between one heart beat and the next, fell asleep.

Chane woke again just as the meadow turned gray in the predawn light. Within the circle of his arms, Lexi lay trustingly against him, her face shadowed by the overhang from the lean-to that had sheltered them during the night. One arm rested on his chest, her palm over his heart.

With one hand, he brushed a strand of her hair away from her face, and as it became lighter outside, he watched her. He couldn't find it in himself to be sorry for making love to her, though God knew how that had happened. He hadn't intended it, and he'd trusted his self-discipline enough to be sure it wouldn't. All he'd wanted to do was hold her, let her know she wasn't alone.

The memory of awakening to her kisses made his body stir. For an instant, he imagined waking her the way they had in the middle of the night. For an instant only. Last night they'd shared their fear, but damn, it couldn't have been as simple as that. He'd gone to bed last night thinking about her, and when he'd seen her run into the meadow, she'd scared him to death.

When she ran from him, he knew she was asleep, but he couldn't figure out what had made her so frightened. He wondered if she had ever talked to anyone about it—whatever the hell "it" was.

Not knowing how to handle the next few hours or in the inevitable morning-after awkwardness, he eased himself out of the sleeping bag. His jeans were stiff with cold, and he hissed out a breath as he yanked them up his flanks.

He finished dressing in scant seconds and made sure the sleeping bag was tucked around Lexi before he left the lean-to. He started a fire and set a pot of water on to make coffee, then went to Lexi's shelter. He found her jeans and jacket lying on top of her pack. He folded up her jeans and stuffed them inside his vest, hoping his body heat would warm them up some. Then, he gathered up her things and took them back to his shelter.

Setting her pack at the end of the sleeping bag where she'd see it when she woke up, he stared down at her a moment. Possessiveness curled through him, and he still couldn't quite believe their heated loving in the middle of the night hadn't been a dream. The smell of her on his skin belied any dream.

* * *

Lexi shivered against the brisk air that danced over her cheek. The air had a distinct bite to it, and when she opened her eyes, a layer of frost covered the meadow with sparkling brilliance. The aroma of the campfire and coffee brought her more fully awake, and she stretched.

The nippy bite of the chill made her pull her hands back inside the sleeping bag. She nuzzled her cheek against the warmth . . . and smelled . . . Chane. She pulled a navy blue T-shirt from under her cheek, its texture soft. Again, the aroma assailed her, reminding her of the man who had worn it. Powerless against the sensual memories his scent evoked, she nuzzled her face against the soft cotton. Last night that aroma was one she had associated with safety, and he'd given her an incredible sense of being cherished.

She had been dreading the moment he'd take her back to her solitary shelter, hadn't had the courage to ask him to stay with her. He'd been too generous, by far.

This morning, she found his aroma familiar . . . full of comfort.

And her cheeks flooded with heat as she remembered. Her dreams had begun with them chasing her, just as they always did. This time, Chane stood in the clearing, his arms stretched wide. She ran into them, and he gathered her close. She was safe there, and he felt so good. She was tired, so tired, of being strong, being alone. She had leaned into him, accepting his strength, needing the comfort he so easily gave. She wondered what kissing him would be like, and so she kissed him.

Lexi opened her eyes, and she saw him squatting next to the fire, his back to her. His head was bent as though he was lost deep in thought. The plaid wool shirt was rolled partway up his arms and covered with his down vest. The one that had kept her so warm last night when they sat by the fire. She grew warm simply watching him. His jeans were taut against his buttocks. Taut as a lover's caress.

She closed her eyes. Not once, ever, had she been so bold

with a man. There had been times she'd wanted a guy, but never like last night. If she'd been aroused anytime with the only two lovers she'd ever had, last night took arousal to a whole new level. In comparison, her previous experiences were a light breeze to a hurricane-force wind.

He hadn't pressed at all when they went to bed. And she'd known the rare experience of falling asleep with a man without him expecting sex. Heat suffused her cheeks as she remembered what she had done. He hadn't expected sex, and she had been the one to initiate it. Her heated embarrassment flowed into a more profound mortification. She had done the one thing she had promised herself she would not—confuse sex with comfort. Oh, God, how could she?

But she had. And nothing in her experience compared to it.

She had thrown herself at the man. Plain and simple. Equally, she remembered he had tried to still her wandering hands, had repeatedly asked if she was awake, if she really wanted this. She was and she had, and there was no one to blame but herself.

Lexi rolled to her side, covering her face with her arm, wondering how she could face him. With that thought, she catalogued another reason why celibacy was far preferable to this—there was no easy way to get through that awkward morning after. Lexi opened her eyes and again looked toward the campfire where Chane was.

Josh and Frank crawled out of their shelter. Josh gave Chane a cheerful good morning and headed for the woods on the opposite side of the clearing. Frank disappeared back inside the shelter, grumbling about the cold, and reappeared a moment later wearing a parka that would have kept him warm at twenty-below. In spite of herself, Lexi grinned, especially when Chane's laugh at Frank's attire echoed her own opinion.

Deciding she had stayed in bed long enough, Lexi briefly wondered how she was going to make the dash between Chane's shelter and her own where her clothes were. In the next moment, she discovered her jeans, jacket, and underwear tucked into the sleeping bag next to her. They weren't as warm as her body, but they were a darn sight warmer than they would have been left outside, mute testimony to Chane's consideration. She found her backpack next to the sleeping bag, which Chane had apparently brought in while she slept. She sat up, pulling on her sweatshirt.

Somehow she had to make him understand that last night had been . . . the most special of her life. Damn, she thought. That wasn't what she wanted to tell him at all. In fact, she didn't want to say anything.

"Beam me up, Scottie," she muttered under her breath as she struggled into her jeans inside the confined warmth of the sleeping bag. Vaporized into a gazillion little particles, she wouldn't be able to do anything else as stupid as she had last night.

She put on her shoes and left the comparative warmth of the shelter. Chane glanced over his shoulder at her as she approached and smiled. Automatically, she returned the smile, seeing a wariness in his eyes that mirrored her own.

"Coffee?" he asked.

"Please." Her breath escaped in a puff of white in front of her, and she shivered. Partly from the cold and partly from remembering that she'd begged him to love her, repeating the same word over and over.

He handed her a steaming cup of coffee. She wrapped her hands around the hot cup and inhaled the steam. His eyes traveled searchingly over her face, and his wariness became something more—something she hadn't expected to see at all. Concern.

She remembered thinking that he wasn't all that good looking. She decided she must have been blind. This man was magnificent. His dark hair was brushed away from his broad forehead. The bold, straight slash of his nose and high cheekbones made his profile arrestingly masculine. No stubble shadowed his jaw and cheek, and this close she caught a faint whiff of shaving cream. He had nicked himself shaving, a tiny dot of red showing at the cleft of his chin.

"You cut yourself."

He rubbed his thumb over the scratch. "One of the risks of no mirror and cold water."

"Ah. So why do it?"

His eyes darkened, and though he didn't touch her, for a scant second she thought he would. "It just seemed like a good idea."

Silence, awkward and uncomfortable, fell between them as she sipped her coffee.

When she finally raised her eyes from the steaming coffee to his, he said, "Last night . . ."

"Changes nothing," she filled in, wishing she could look away from his penetrating stare, wishing she dared believe this one man might care as much as his eyes seemed to promise. Never once had that been the case, and she was too old to start believing in happy endings. She knew better.

The sound of Josh and Frank returning ended the moment. Seconds later, Lexi heard Julie and Brian laugh as they emerged from the forest, hand in hand.

Throughout breakfast and the cleanup afterward, Lexi was sure she'd never been more aware of another person than she was of Chane.

The group disassembled the shelters, took apart the fire ring, and scattered the water-soaked coals across the meadow. Only after they had it looking as it had when they'd arrived was Chane satisfied.

Through it all, he watched Lexi, noticing that she had a presence that indicated she was supremely at home in these surroundings. That wasn't what held his attention, though. What he sensed was her building walls around herself, walls that had crumbled during the long night. With the others around, there was no chance to find out what she was thinking. All morning, she shied away from him, finding a way to be inaccessible to him.

It wasn't until camp was broken that he got close enough to talk with her. He had a thousand things he wanted to know about her, and sensed she wasn't ready to share any of them. Helping her into her backpack, he asked, "You're not a novice climber, are you?"

She shook her head.

"But you could survive out here if you had to, without much more than a flint stone and a compass."

"Once, maybe." She fastened the webbed belt of the pack around her waist. "I used to love backpacking. This is the first time since . . ."

"You came home?"

"Yeah."

"The level of experience is something I asked about on the application, Lexi. After you fell the other day, I went back and checked, and you left those questions blank. Why?"

"To say I was inexperienced—that wasn't the truth. But I'm not competent anymore."

"Did you fall?"

She shook her head.

"What then, Lexi?"

"I . . . Listen, Chane, I needed a friend last night. You were the best one I ever had." She met his eyes, hers dark and very serious. "No one ever offered to hold me through the night before. You don't know how much it helped."

"I have a fair idea," he returned, his voice deep, husky.

"I didn't intend—"

"I know. I didn't either."

"But we . . ."

"Yeah," he agreed. "We did."

"I don't expect this to go anywhere—"

"I do," he said.

Her eyes took on a sudden shimmer. "Please don't. I'm not ready for this."

"I didn't think I was, either."

"But—"

He pressed his fingers against her lips. "No buts, Lexi." He dropped his hand. "So you've got a past that creeps a little too close sometimes. You're gonna get there, honey."

She bowed her head and shook it in mute denial.

"I know," he said, bending his head a little, trying to see her face. "I know what it's like to want back something you used to love. I know what it's like to want back the person you used to be."

"Did you find him?" she asked.

He shook his head. "And you won't, either. But the person you find, Lexi. She'll be just fine."

Lexi wished she believed him.

Chapter 7

Twenty-four hours later, Lexi opened the curtains of her living room to the bright morning sun. Her night had been restless, and her sleep fitful. For once, her dreams had not been dark and musty. Instead they had been filled with shimmering awareness and greedy need that ignored the mandates of her conscience. In the middle of the long night, she had longed for the warmth and security of Chane's arms. The longings of a foolish heart that should know better.

Even standing here on the deck, the morning air bitingly sharp with frost, when she inhaled, she smelled the man. Soap, the barest hint of a spicy aftershave, his unique masculine scent. Disgusted with her lack of discipline, she blew out a breath that condensed in front of her, once again fastening her gaze on the brilliant lake and the sheen of frost that covered the deck rails.

Gradually, the churning in her stomach abated, and her gaze became more focused on the scene in front of her. Deliberately, she mentally painted a detailed image of one of the small islands on the other side of the lake where the osprey had nested and raised their young mere weeks ago. Next year, she vowed, she would photograph them. More than that, she would plan a photo essay that encompassed a season from mating time through the fledglings being taught to hunt and leave the nest.

Movement near the stairwell captured her attention. Señora Padilla. Lexi's plans shattered around her. Who was she kidding? If she wanted to ever live with herself, she didn't have a choice between helping the señora or fantasizing about a life as *National Geographic*'s newest wildlife photographer.

Lexi padded to the edge of the deck, where Daisy was sitting, her ears perked forward, her attention focused on Señora Padilla.

"Buenas dias, señora," Lexi said. "Daisy won't hurt you, you know."

Surprisingly the señora smiled. "I think you are right. If she had wanted to bite me, she would have done so by now."

"I'm just making coffee. Would you like some?"

"Sí. Gracias." Much as she had on her prior visit, the señora held her purse in front of her as she climbed the steps and followed Lexi into the house.

"You may leave your hat and coat there." Lexi motioned to the wooden pegs on the entry wall before moving toward the kitchen. Over her shoulder, she called, "Have you had breakfast?"

"There is no need to feed me," Señora Padilla responded. "I came only for my answer."

Lexi poured two cups of coffee. She supposed the señora's response might have offended her a couple of days ago. Lexi understood direct honesty born of need. She couldn't turn her back on that. She set out milk and sugar in case the señora wanted them. An instant later, the señora came through the kitchen door, her sharp gaze taking in all the details of the room.

Chane's legend of dying women and children flitted through Lexi's mind, leaving behind the poignant realization of loss. For what she had endured. For what the señora had endured. There was no way, Lexi admitted to herself, she could say no to the señora.

"The other day, I wanted to be able to tell you that I can't— help you," Lexi said carefully in Spanish.

"Oh conscience. Silent tormenter of the soul."

Lexi had heard the proverb before, and it struck home.

"I am not without a heart." The señora's dark eyes met Lexi's. "I understand."

"I'm not promising we'll find your granddaughter."

The señora nodded. "This I also know."

"I don't know anything about adoption—"

"You tell me nothing I do not know already." Señora Padilla reached across the counter and took Lexi's hand in her own. "I am determined to find my Estella, yes. But I am no fool. I understand the search for her may be difficult. Perhaps even impossible." She squeezed Lexi's hand. "With your help, maybe a little less difficult."

"I wouldn't count on that."

"So . . . we will begin today." The merest question surfaced in the statement.

Lexi bowed her head a moment, realizing another moment of truth was at hand. One more word of agreement, and she was committed to this. No matter where it led. She lifted her head and met the señora's eyes. "Today. After breakfast."

The señora smiled, giving Lexi a glimpse of the woman she might have once been.

For the second time in as many days, Lexi itched to take pictures of a person. Last winter she had thought she'd never want to photograph people again. To have her passion back . . . Faces of the young and the old. Faces of people busy living, busy being themselves. She wanted to photograph the señora. A step. A single small step that was a far cry from accepting the challenge and risk that came with being a news photographer in a third world country.

"One more thing," Lexi said. "Perhaps I could call you something besides Señora Padilla."

The señora's smile grew even wider. "Perhaps."

"Funny name, that one. Doña Perhaps."

The señora's chuckle grew into a infectious laugh that Lexi joined.

"What might I call you?" the señora asked.

"Lexi."

"Lexi," the señora repeated. "A more suitable name is Alexandra. How your mother must despair the name she chose for her *niña* has become Lexi."

"I like Lexi."

"And you may call me *Tía* Ester. Or merely *Tía*, if you like."

Mentally, Lexi tried both out. *Tía* Ester. *Tía*. She had never had an aunt of her own, and the thought of calling this small woman from another country, another culture, "Aunt" was too tempting. Lexi couldn't afford the intimacy that came with "Aunt." Señora Padilla was safer, more distant. More objective. Lexi wished she hadn't asked. The woman would be offended if she stuck to "Señora." How could Lexi keep her distance with "Tía?"

Except, the Señora made impossible keeping any distance. She assumed *Tía* meant they were friends. And friends made themselves at home.

Ester found glasses and silverware as Lexi finished making breakfast. She told Lexi about her daughter's wedding as she poked through the kitchen, opening and closing drawers and doors, peering inside the refrigerator, touching the controls on the stove. She coaxed from Lexi that she was an only child and scolded her for not visiting her mother.

Ester gently and firmly pried. That Lexi had no marriage prospects on the horizon seemed a greater sin than neglecting her mother. Within the hour, the señora went from being a stranger to an aunt who assumed the right to meddle. *Tía*.

Lexi admitted she had lost any sense of control she might have mistakenly assumed she had.

After breakfast, she gave Lexi an assortment of papers she had collected during her search for her granddaughter. Each piece of paper came with a story. Individually, none of the sheets were significant. Added together, Ester was convinced she was closing in on her granddaughter's adoptive family. A photograph she insisted could be her granddaughter was attached to a surrender document.

"Even with a photograph as good as this one, we won't know if we've found your granddaughter unless the adoptive parents have a copy. Or maybe a picture they took about the same time that gives us a good match. What was she here? About six weeks old?''

"*Sí.*"

Ester showed Lexi the surrender document that had led her to an adoption agency—*Las Hermanas de la Esperanza.* "I went there, assuming the name belonged to a convent," Tía Ester told Lexi.

Lexi's throat tightened. She knew exactly what *Las Hermanas de La Esperanza* were. And what they weren't. They were not a charity helping orphans, despite the babies they collected.

After watching El Ladron kill a woman in cold blood, Lexi had spent weeks tracing the orphans he snatched, bought, or stole. They were funneled into a variety of orphanages, some legitimate, some shady, and some illegal by any government's standards. *Las Hermanas de la Esperanza* specialized in infants. Mostly, they sold babies, but they had done just enough adoptions the year Lexi investigated them to keep suspicion away from their operation.

The South and Central American custom of having adoptive families come to pick up their babies allowed *Las Hermanas de la Esperanza* the perfect cover for their business. Mothers and fathers arrived in the country, already "expecting" a child, their orders for a boy or a girl already placed. They spent a month to three months, "gave birth" to their child, and went home. Without the hassles of red tape and governmental interference.

Birth parents were driven by poverty, usually, and desperation to do the unthinkable—sell their baby to predators like El Ladron. Some, not many, were driven by greed.

Just when Lexi and Joe had been positive they'd catch the good "sisters" of *Las Hermanas de la Esperanza* in the act of selling babies, something or someone had tipped them off. Legitimate-looking adoptions became the norm rather than the piece of their business that gave the operation credibility.

Lexi had to give the señora credit. She had worked through an incredible maze of bureaucratic runaround and still ended up with the link of El Ladron.

"What I must find," Ester concluded, "is the name of the agency here. An official in customs told me there had to be an agency licensed in the United States. *Las Hermanas de la Esperanza* is not licensed in the United States."

Lexi knew about that as well, having discovered the same dead trail when she and Joe were working on the story.

"What do we do next?" Ester asked.

"I don't honestly know. We'll start with a trip to the library." Lexi met Tía Ester's gaze over the top of her cup.

"There should be a list of agencies somewhere that we can look up."

"And then?"

"And then we start making telephone calls."

Ester smiled. "See. I knew you would have a plan. We go to the library now, yes."

"Soon." Lexi motioned to her robe. "I have to get dressed."

"Bueno."

Lexi watched Tía Ester gather up her papers with the haste and efficiency of a New York businessman late for an important appointment. *Mañana,* too often the watch word for a more languid pace of life, was not Ester's motto.

When she glanced up and found Lexi watching her, she made a shooing motion with her hand. "You dress. I'll straighten your kitchen. Then we'll go. *Sí?"*

"Sí."

Lexi showered, dressed, and found the señora ready to go when she came back downstairs a few minutes later. Ester had a dozen questions about Grand Lake's climate that concluded with, "In winter, do you not worry about freezing?"

"Freezing?" Lexi asked. "No. My house has heat." In fact, she welcomed the chilly mornings. "The hotel where you're staying has heat—which hotel are you staying at?"

"There is no hotel."

"Where then?"

"What do you call it?" Tía Ester said. "A summer cottage."

"There should be a fireplace then. You've been cold?"

The señora shook her head. "Only in the middle of the night."

Within a few minutes they left for the library. Normally, Lexi would have walked, but not knowing where else they might go afterward, Lexi drove, answering Ester's questions about the town.

Tía Ester found the library fascinating. By most standards the library was small. Grand Lake was, after all, a small community. According to Ester, this library was magnificent.

Lexi had imagined slipping into the library, getting the references she needed, and leaving. Tía Ester was entranced with the number of books and more than a little bewildered by the system to check them out. When she discovered the computer used to locate references, she became convinced they should be able to type "Las Hermanas de la Esperanza" and find out who had adopted her Estella.

Chane dropped Tessa off at the day-care center and headed for the small office he rented from his accountant. A month's worth of bookwork was waiting, and he'd used up all his excuses to avoid it. The cleaning lady had kicked him out of the house, so he had driven up to the North Face to check out a rock climb for his intermediate students. He'd inspected the new coils of rope UPS had delivered. He'd called Lexi. Twice. She hadn't answered either time.

He'd had it all planned. Tonight, he'd take her out to a movie and dinner. Never mind he hadn't asked her yet.

He wondered if this was how it was usually done in the nineties. Take the lady to bed, then take her on a date. The whole business seemed all backwards to him, and the longer he went without talking to her, the more he worried about seeing her again. His "chase her a little" plan had become something more, and he knew he had a challenge ahead of him. A man would have to be blind not to sense her retreat or that she was shoring up her defenses. Why? And against what?

The minute he pulled out of his own driveway, he looked at every red car he passed, searching for Lexi's. Since he'd been looking for it, he wasn't surprised when he found her red Toyota Tercel parked in front of the library. A half block later he parked his truck in front of the accountant's office, then walked back to the library. Undoubtedly, more than one person in Grand Lake drove a red Toyota. Still . . .

He found her with the small woman who had been leaving her house the other day. The two of them were huddled over a microfiche reader, softly conversing in Spanish. Lexi was pointing, her attention focused wholly on the screen. She had her hair loose today, and it cascaded down her back, looking soft and touchable. As usual, her features reflected her concentration, her lower lip caught between her teeth. He imagined it caught between his, and his breath came in on a hitch.

"If you find what you're looking for in there," Chane said from over her shoulder, "you're a better person than I am."

She jumped and whirled around, her eyes wide. Her surprise softened into a smile, which relieved him. He touched her shoulder in greeting, her hair silky beneath his palm.

"Hi. I didn't mean to startle you."

Her eyebrow cocked. "Oh? What's your usual reason for sneaking up on a person?" The smile lurking at the corner of her mouth kept the question from being sharp.

"I'll have to think about that. Can't remember any, off hand." He smiled back, glad she was treating him much the way she always had. He pulled out a chair next to her and sat down, his glance encompassing her companion. He extended his hand. "I'm Chane Callahan. I saw you the other day at Lexi's house."

"This is Ester Padilla," Lexi said.

"I'm pleased to meet you," Chane said.

Lexi murmured something in Spanish to the señora, who extended her hand to him. She looked Chane up and down, then answered Lexi in a volley of Spanish accompanied by an approving glance that didn't leave his face. Twice he heard the name Alexandra. A flush of color rose in Lexi's face.

He touched her cheek with the back of one finger. "What is she saying to make you blush?"

Lexi pulled back, just far enough to let him know his touch wasn't welcome. He dropped his hand, giving her the space she seemed to need. This battle wouldn't be won by pushing too hard.

Her voice sounded faintly strangled as she said, "She thinks you're very good looking and she asked me if you're single."

He laughed. "And what did you tell her?"

The blush deepened another hue. "That you're my instructor and that your marital status is none of my business."

"Ah, Lexi. That's something we're going to have to work on." He glanced down at the señora. "Please tell her I am single. And that my intentions are entirely honorable."

"Chane!"

He'd intended to be teasing, found a note of truth beneath it, and surprised himself by admitting it was true. He couldn't think of anything better than taking Lexi to bed again. And again. And he also wanted her just as she was now.

"You're not going to tell her?" he teased gently.

"You tell her."

"I don't speak Spanish," he said. "Why does she call you Alexandra?"

"It's my name."

"Alexandra."

A little of her color faded, and her eyes took on a glint that didn't match her smile. "Callahan, I won't answer if you call me that."

He believed her. "I consider myself duly warned." He motioned toward the microfiche reader. "So, what are you two researching?"

"Adoption agencies," Lexi answered. "The señora is looking for her granddaughter. She was smuggled into the United States and illegally adopted."

Lexi's voice was so matter-of-fact, the import of her words took a moment to register. "How could such a thing happen?"

"She was an orphan." Lexi glanced at Señora Padilla. "When the child was placed for adoption, the government officials didn't recognize there were any living relatives."

Living relatives.

He feared someday, someone would show up on his doorstep claiming Tessa. He supposed every adoptive parent had such

fears. Never once had that someone remotely resembled the
tiny Señora Padilla. The depths of her black eyes carried her
sorrow for a child she loved.

During the first month after Rose had died, Chane had found
his world reduced to the two principles that had been his corner-
stones. You did your duty—no matter what. You did what was
right—no matter what. Pieces of conversation he'd had with
Rose surfaced.

*Out with it, Rose. Where did she come from and why is this
baby ours?*

I adopted her.

Just like that?

Of course not just like that. It was a private adoption.

Is the adoption final?

*It will be just as soon as the final decree is signed. With or
without you, I want this baby.*

His recollection of signing papers that Rose had given him
was far more vivid at the moment than anything else of those
last two months with his wife. In the end, he'd become what
she had wanted all along. A man who stayed at home. A father.

Somewhere along the line, duty had made way for love. A
child of his own seed would be no more his child than Tessa.

"Chane?"

Lexi had laid her hand on his arm. Chane forced his attention
away from the abyss of his memories and looked at her.

"Are you okay?" She gave him a gentle nudge.

He shook his head as if to clear it and abruptly stood. "I
. . . I've just got a lot on my mind." He took Lexi's hand, then
surprised them both by bending and brushing a kiss over her
cheek. "I'll call you."

He felt chased by phantoms as he left the library and strode
up the block toward his truck. Lexi was doing the right thing.
Helping the señora find a child she obviously loved enough to
travel thousands of miles to find.

*What if someone showed up at my doorstep claiming Tessa?
What then?* She was his daughter. He'd signed a whole raft of
papers saying she was. *Private adoption.* Why the hell should
that bother him after all these months?

He didn't recall driving home, but found himself in the driveway, the engine shut off, staring at the carpet of aspen leaves that covered the ground.

He stalked into the house. The aroma of lemon oil filled the air, and the freshly polished furniture gleamed. He shook his head and moved down the hall as though he expected an ambush. At the doorway to Tessa's room, he paused. Inside the room was a youth bed. White wallpaper covered with whimsical blue kittens covered one wall. More stuffed animals than any one child could use rested carelessly against the corner by the closet.

Only, he saw the room as it had been when he'd shared it with Rose. As it had been when he was released from the hospital after the mess in Mosul. He hadn't known anything about Tessa until he returned home. As it turned out, he hadn't known his wife, either.

"Whose baby?" he had asked that day long ago.

She had finished fastening the diaper and lifted the baby, supporting her head with an elbow. "Ours," she had answered. "Meet your daughter, Tessa Callahan."

He heard the words . . . and they failed to make sense. He sank onto the bed, stretching his braced leg out in front of him, utter surprise competing with denial, questions, and confusion. At once the baby was thrust into his arms, soft and warm and smelling of baby powder. Her solemn stare came from fathomless black eyes.

He lifted his gaze to Rose's, found her uncertain smile. She sat down next to him, her hand caressing the child's head.

"Isn't she beautiful?"

The baby tipped her head, seeking the source of Rose's voice. Rose leaned over the baby and crooned. "Hi, beautiful Tessa. You're such a wonderful girl."

The baby smiled, and Rose took her from his arms.

"Our baby?" he asked. If there had been a pregnancy—his glance fell to Rose's trim waist, and he swallowed. He'd been gone six months. And yeah, she said she wanted a baby the last time he was home. And the time before that. He didn't know what to think, but the idea that she'd taken on a decision of this magnitude without him left him confused, angry.

He'd been sure only of one thing. He'd failed his wife. All those months when all he had wanted was to come home, when he'd been worried about losing his leg, he'd just wanted to be with his wife. After he got home, he found her consumed with a child she hadn't told him about or shared with him in any way at all. With or without him, there was a baby.

He had a month's leave, and he spent the first part of it wondering if he and Rose had a life together. A week before he was scheduled to return to his post, a drunk driver ran Rose off the road near Granby. Chane was left with an infant daughter he hadn't wanted, hadn't planned for. But this was the child Rose had wanted, and he'd do what was right. He'd do his duty.

The memory of Tessa's belly laugh and sparkling eyes and fierce hugs made his throat tighten. Right or wrong, no matter how Rose had gotten Tessa, she was his.

He left Tessa's room and went back to the bedroom he had taken on as his own after Rose's death. From the top shelf of the closet, he pulled down a strong box and opened it with deft motions. He pulled out a bundle of papers he hadn't looked at since he had signed them one afternoon almost four years ago.

Carefully, he opened the papers. What he was looking for, he couldn't have said. Some clue, some reassurance no one like Señora Padilla could show up looking for his child.

A petition to adopt was dated two months before he returned home. He scanned the pages. As with any other legal document he'd ever read, the language confused him. The surprise was Ellen Belsen's signature at the bottom as a witness to Rose's.

Rose had told him Tessa's mother was a fifteen-year-old from one of the small towns in San Luis Valley. She was unmarried, had no money, and fewer options. So, why did the birth certificate list Tessa's birthplace as Costa Léon?

Chane stared at the certificate a moment longer, unable to ignore the ramifications of the documents in his hand. Tessa had not been born to some unmarried teenager in San Luis Valley.

Ellen Belsen had helped two other couples that Chane knew adopt South American babies. He could think of only one reason for Ellen to be involved with Tessa's adoption—she'd come from South America.

He riffled through the remaining documents. An affidavit of support that detailed income and assets. His and Rose's marriage certificate. A surrender document. . . . *there being no living relatives, this court hereby surrenders full custody and control of this infant female child to The Sisters of Hope.*

He searched through the papers a second time.

There was no adoption decree.

Nor any other document reassuring him that his child was legally Tessa Annmarie Callahan.

Chapter 8

"Higher!" Tessa cried, an infectious giggle filling her voice. "Push me higher!"

Lexi laughed in response as she obediently pushed the swing a little harder. Like Tessa, she loved the rush that came with swinging high. The child's enthusiasm was as brilliant as the sunshine spilling from the sky.

The day was one of those radiant autumn days full of bright colors, filled with the sounds of children's high, happy voices, the air crisp and tangy as an apple. Surrounded by children, Lexi felt whole as she hadn't in a long time. She wished she had discovered this months ago, ignoring for the moment her other reasons for being at the day-care center.

Lexi admitted what she knew about kids wouldn't fill a 35mm film canister. But she liked them. She always had. Children had often been the focus of her work—a barometer for illustrating resiliency or the pure joy of living or the too-high price of war.

The children at the day-care center were infused with life. Every time one of them held out their arms for hugging, she felt plugged into something important, something . . . more important than her own day-to-day drudgery.

"Me, too," commanded Ricky, a small boy who climbed onto the swing next to Tessa.

Lexi put his swing into motion as well, alternately giving first Tessa, then Ricky, a push. Across the playground, she watched Ellen, surrounded by another group of children. And Lexi had no doubt. Ellen enjoyed being with them.

Children scampered and skipped and laughed and jumped and ran and did all the things young carefree children were supposed to do. A yard filled with buoyant bright balloons couldn't have been any more cheerful.

She watched Ellen gently throw a big red ball to a small boy. He squealed with delight when he caught it.

"Good catch," Ellen called in encouragement, then lined up one of the other children to be his partner in a game of catch.

As she made her way toward the swings, Lexi pondered how best to get the information she needed without causing another blow up. Deception, she thought with a flash of disgust. When she had stopped working, she had readily left behind the lies and half-truths intrinsic to her job. How much easier this would all be if she could just say to Ellen, *Please help me out here. The woman is trying to find someone she loves. Where do we look first? Where does the paper trail start?*

For the better part of four days, Lexi had spent her time on the telephone tracking down leads from names she and Señora Padilla had gathered at the library. No one she had talked to had done business with Las Hermanas de la Esperanza. In fact, one agency told her they knew of no reputable agency that had done business with them. No surprise there. Frustration, though. The surprise came when one agency suggested she contact a certain Ellen Belsen and ask what she knew.

"What kind of information could she share?" Lexi had wanted to know.

A Miss Hawkins from Colorado International Adoption Agency told Lexi, "Ms. Belsen is an authority on South American adoptions. She's assisted several families in working through the red tape. If anyone has heard of Las Hermanas de la Esperanza, she will have."

Lexi hadn't been aware Ellen's interest extended beyond her own twin boys. More than ever, Lexi wanted to talk to her. It had been a stroke of luck yesterday afternoon that she heard Ellen's helper was out with the flu. When Lexi called to volunteer to help for the duration, Ellen had seemed relieved their spat was over and forgotten.

Now that Lexi was here, she felt like a traitor, knowing she wanted something from Ellen and being too chicken to ask for it. Even so, Lexi had coaxed from Ellen how she had come to be involved with helping six or seven other couples.

"I had to," Ellen told her. "After going down to get my boys and seeing how bad the conditions are and how many babies there are. Everyone of those children deserves love. A home."

Lexi recognized Ellen was campaigning for the position she had taken the other day—that finding the adoptive parents couldn't be done. The records were so well sealed, the chances of finding a specific child were slim and none.

Lexi gave Tessa another push, smiling as the child looked over her shoulder and gave her a cheeky grin.

"I'm higher than you," Tessa bragged to the little boy next to her.

"No, you're not."

"I am, too. I'm higher than the moon!"

Ellen joined her at the swings, a couple of children trailing behind her.

"Tessa's snagged you for swing duty, I see," Ellen said.

"She told me I'm the best. Find a job and learn to do it well. That's always been my motto," Lexi responded, giving the swings another gentle push.

Ellen smiled. "And just when I had you pegged as a paste and construction paper supervisor."

"Paste and little kids, huh? Sounds dangerous."

"Pasting?" Tessa asked as she swung past Lexi. "I love to paste."

"See?" Ellen said to Lexi. "Tessa loves to paste. Another thing you could learn."

"Me, too," said Tessa's companion on the swing.

"Which we'll do right after snack," Ellen added.

"I'm game," Lexi said. "You're the boss."

The comment earned a laugh from Ellen. Companionable silence surrounded them before she spoke. "Are you still looking for that woman's granddaughter?"

"Yes." Lexi met Ellen's gaze, relieved to have it in the open. "She's determined, and I think she has a right to know what happened to the child."

"How's it going?"

"Slow," Lexi said, analyzing the edge she heard in Ellen's voice. Lexi wished she could promise everything would turn out all right. But for whom? "I haven't been able to track down the agency that handled the adoption."

"Who have you talked to?"

Lexi recited the list of a half-dozen agencies she had spoken with, and Ellen nodded.

"Those are the major ones," she confirmed. "They probably handle ninety- or ninety-five percent of the international adoptions in the state."

"If I just find one that has done business with *Las Hermanas de la Esperanza,* we'll be closer."

"*Las Hermanas . . .*" Ellen frowned. "What was the rest?"

"*De la Esperanza,*" Lexi supplied. "The group the child was surrendered to in San Pedro. Have you heard of them?"

Ellen stuffed her hands into the pockets of her sweater and stared at the ground a moment. "If I've heard the name," she said finally, "it's been a long time ago."

Lexi knew hedging when she heard it. "Are they reputable?"

"What did the other agencies tell you?" Ellen asked.

"Most hadn't heard of them and the ones that had wouldn't do business with them."

"You have your answer, then."

"Yeah," Lexi agreed. "I'll just keep talking to people until I find someone who's done business with them."

"If they're dishonest, no one is likely to admit it," Ellen said.

That was one statement Lexi was in complete agreement with.

"Is it time yet?" one of the children asked, tugging on Ellen's pant leg.

"Time for what, Jonathan?"

He grinned. "For snack."

"Can I help make the apple juice?" Tessa asked, slowing her swing. Lexi automatically wrapped her hand around Tessa's small one as she got out of the swing.

"I don't see why not," Ellen answered. "Think you can show Lexi how?"

"Uh-huh. It's easy."

Ellen told Lexi where to find the supplies in the kitchen, and she followed the energetic Tessa, who wanted to know if she could put the pieces of fruit for the midmorning snack on a plate after they made juice.

"Sure," Lexi answered. "You'll have to wash your hands first."

"No sweat," Tessa said.

Lexi laughed and held the door open. The child's inflection was exactly that of a teenager. "No sweat?"

"That's what Kit says. 'No sweat.' Daddy says to him, 'You're not leaving this house until that room is clean.' And then Kit says, 'No sweat.' "

Inside the kitchen, Tessa pulled a chair toward the sink. Lexi lifted her up and turned on the water, handing the child a bar of soap. Lexi got the can of concentrated juice that had been thawing in the refrigerator and a pitcher out of the cupboard.

"Why do I have to wash my hands and you don't have to wash yours?" Tessa wanted to know, as she diligently soaped her little hands.

"Good point." Lexi took the soap from Tessa and washed her own hands. Kids kept you on your toes, she thought, another thing she liked about them. No telling what might happen to civilization if you didn't have kids to set a good example for.

They had the drinks and fruit prepared in no time, and Tessa ran back outside to let Ellen know they were ready.

Lexi didn't think the children would ever run out of energy, and by the end of the day she concluded running a day-care center was a far more difficult job than most people knew.

Somehow, Ellen still looked nearly as fresh as she had earlier in the day. Lexi felt as though she'd been on a twenty-mile hike.

When a bunch of the kids asked for a story, Lexi thankfully settled into a huge bean-bag chair to read. Tessa, who had been following her around for the day, curled up in Lexi's lap. Two other kids perched almost as close.

That was how Chane found them when he arrived a scant half hour later to pick up Tessa. He'd put a couple of calls into Lexi since he last saw her at the library. He either got a busy signal or her answering machine. He left a message the first time, decided against it the second and third, figuring he'd sound like a love-sick fifteen-year-old. When he had decided to follow his chase-her-a-little program, he hadn't anticipated it becoming so important to him or that she would be building walls around herself.

And since seeing her at the library the other day, he had an additional motive, every bit as important. He wanted to know more about what she was doing with Señora Padilla.

After reading and rereading every piece of paper he could find in the house having to do with Tessa's adoption, he had more questions than answers. So, he had gathered up the whole lot and taken them to an attorney. The attorney asked a few terse questions and promised to call Chane back.

This afternoon he had, and Chane didn't like the answer a bit. Unless the final decree had taken place in some other state, there was no record of Tessa's adoption. No final decree had been issued by a court in the State of Colorado. There was no record of a petition having been filed. No home study had been done.

Chane's first impulse had been to come get his daughter and go home, or better yet, pack her and Kit up and leave for parts unknown. If running would solve the problem, he'd do it. But past experience had taught him running was the worst choice he could make.

He paused in the doorway of the day-care center, the late-afternoon sun slanting across the floor. Dead center in that cataract of light was an immense bean-bag chair where Lexi sat with Tessa and two other children. Lexi had her arms around Tessa and another little boy. Her cheek was pressed against Tessa's glossy hair.

Lexi read, inflection in her voice carrying the part of an ever-so-curious elephant from a Rudyard Kipling tale. In spite of the turmoil tearing at him, Chane smiled.

He leaned against the doorjamb, liking the look of her with her arms all full of children. A jumble of impressions competed for his attention. Lexi's hair fell across her shoulder, caught in a barrette that held it away from her face. Most arresting was Lexi's expression, all soft, just a hint of a smile at her mouth and in her eyes. *Soft.*

Yeah, she did look soft. Her sweater was pale pink, knitted with fuzzy fine yarn, and until now, not a color he would have associated with her.

He had mostly spent the last several nights remembering how good she had felt in his arms and wondering if she'd lost any sleep thinking about them. He hoped so.

He knew the instant she saw him. Her gaze left the page she was reading and traveled up his legs. By the time her eyes reached his face, hers had taken on the more guarded expression familiar to him. Recognition came, and she smiled, as radiant as he had ever seen her.

"Hi," he said, smiling back, ridiculously glad to see her, wondering why she was here. He levered himself away from the doorjamb and sauntered across the room.

"Hi, Daddy," Tessa responded. "This is a good story. Can we stay to hear the end? Please?"

Lexi's smile dissolved into shock. "Daddy?"

"This is my daddy," Tessa announced.

"You are Tessa's father? You're . . . you said you were—"

"Widowed." Chane met her gaze full on. "My wife died almost four years ago."

"Oh."

Lexi's gaze dropped to the pages of the forgotten storybook. She fingered the last few pages. "We shouldn't be more than a few minutes."

"Okay. Sure."

Tessa patted the edge of the red bean-bag chair that looked as though it might swallow Lexi and the children. "You'll like this, too, Daddy. It's about cur-os-ity. Sit here."

Chane lowered himself to the floor next to Lexi and his daughter. Tessa gave him a brilliant smile before her attention returned to the story.

Chane listened to Lexi as she finished reading, liking the lilt in her voice. This was a softer, more animated side of her. The contrast between her blond hair and Tessa's shiny black tresses was night and day. He'd never been drawn much to fair-haired women, generally found their coloring too bland for his tastes. Somehow Lexi defied all that, from her creamy skin to the blush at her cheeks, to the deeper pink of her lips.

He'd touched her intimately in the dark, and he wanted to know just as intimately how those shades of pink were repeated on her body. The speculation brought to life the ache that had been with him since he'd found out what she felt like. His gaze shifted to her lashes and eyebrows, both smoky shades of blond, darker than the sun-streaked strands of her hair.

"The end," Lexi announced some minutes later.

"I liked that story," Tessa said, peering up at Lexi.

Chane agreed, but he admitted to himself, listening to Lexi lured him more than the story. She was terrific with the kids, which surprised him. Not once in all the times he'd thought about her had he imagined her surrounded by children. Tessa, who was affectionate with almost anyone, seemed most especially taken with her.

"I liked it, too," one of Ellen's twin boys said.

Lexi tousled his head. "I'm glad, sweetie."

"I thought I was 'sweetie,'" Tessa said, twisting in Lexi's lap.

"You are. And so is Andrew." Lexi reach over to help another child struggling to escape from the enveloping bean-bag chair. "Stephie is my sweetie, too, aren't you?"

"I am," Stephie said.

"That's too many," Tessa said earnestly. She turned her father. "You can have just one sweetie, huh, Daddy?"

Chane scooped Tessa into his arms. "You're my little girl. My sweetie, and that is what counts."

Lexi smiled, drawn to Chane's enjoyment of his child and his reassurance that she was special to him. Tessa giggled as Chane tossed her into the air and deftly caught her.

"I'm a wonderful girl." She laughed again, a deep delighted belly laugh as he rubbed his nose into her tummy.

Lexi stood up and briefly touched Tessa's hair. "You're my extraspecial sweetie."

Tessa leaned out of Chane's arms and wrapped her little chubby ones around Lexi's neck. Tessa planted a noisy kiss on Lexi's cheek. "I like you." She turned guileless eyes on her dad. "Do you like her, Daddy?"

Lexi met Chane's teasing eyes, and the air seeped out of her lungs on a sigh.

"Yeah, I like her." His voice as deep, full of promise.

An unfamiliar sensation of elation swelled within Lexi. *He likes me.* The refrain was stupid given what they had shared. Still, the chorus inside her head made her think of junior high school and all the exciting uncertainty that accompanied young love. Only she was no adolescent, and this shimmering hope stretched taut on desire was no crush. Chane had told her the other night he liked her, and he'd urged her to trust him.

She had. To the embarrassing point of seducing him out of a sound sleep. Her mortification about that hadn't abated, even after several days. Sure, he had called since then, and he had left a couple of messages on her answering machine. But then he'd done that before, reminding her about this or that with his class. The message yesterday had been a reminder about tomorrow's class, which wasn't an invitation to a date, Lexi told herself, even if he had asked if she was okay and had requested that she call him back. A week ago, she would have. Now? Well, that was a whole other thing. Don't read anything into his attentions, she silently chided herself.

"I see you've met Tessa's dad," Ellen said from the doorway of the playroom.

Somehow Lexi wrenched her eyes away from Chane and watched Ellen approach them.

"I've known Chane for a while," Lexi said. "I just didn't know he had a daughter."

Ellen's gaze was speculative. "There must have been a lot of other things on your mind, Chane."

"Carabiniers, nuts, rope, harnesses," he agreed easily.

"Ah. Climbing. I still think you're both crazy. Heights scare me," Ellen returned.

Lexi chuckled. "Me too."

Ellen rolled her eyes. "Logical answer, Lexi. Very."

"Makes sense to me," Chane said. He poked Tessa in her tummy with a long finger. "Ready to go, squirt?"

"I've got to be getting home, too," Lexi said, following them toward the door.

"Lexi. What I came to tell you," Ellen said. "That reporter you told me about. The one you worked with. Joe Robertson."

Chane stopped dead in his tracks. *Joe Robertson? Lexi had worked with Joe Robertson?*

"He was shot," Ellen said. "I just heard it on the news."

"Shot?" Lexi licked her lips as though they were suddenly dry.

"Shot?" Chane echoed, his attention torn between Lexi's reaction and his own certainty Robertson had probably deserved whatever happened to him.

Ellen nodded. "Apparently a drive-by shooting somewhere in Denver. The newscaster said he had just flown in from Los Angeles—"

"Is he—"

"Dead?" Ellen interrupted. "No. Anyway, I don't think so."

The color drained out of Lexi's face. "Oh, God."

"So the bastard finally got his," Chane said.

Lexi turned on him, giving vent to shock and fear for the one person in her life who had stood by her, even if it had been for his own selfish reasons. "That bastard saved my life."

She swept past him, picking up her purse on the way, and automatically searching the bottom of the bag for her keys. She had to call, had to find out which hospital he'd been taken to. Joe shot? No!

"Ellen, what hospital?" she asked, her mind racing, her heart pounding right up her throat. "Do you remember?"

"Denver General, maybe." Ellen shrugged. "I don't remember."

Chane, carrying Tessa, followed Lexi outside. "Why didn't you tell me you worked with Robertson?" he demanded.

The question caught her by surprise, as much as his following her had. She faced him with the open door of her car between them. She stared at Chane and his daughter without really seeing him, fractured images of Joe competing for her attention.

"Well?" Chane repeated.

Lexi met his gaze, though focusing her thoughts enough to answer his question was beyond her. "I intended to," she answered finally. She touched Tessa's cheek. "I've gotta go."

She slid behind the wheel of her Toyota Tercel and started the engine. Chane watched her drive out of the parking lot, then turn the corner at the end of the street and head toward her house. *That bastard saved my life.* Why hadn't she told him the other night when he was spilling his guts?

"She seemed pretty upset, didn't she?" Ellen asked from Chane's side.

"Yeah."

"Surprising, isn't it? After what he did to her, I sure didn't think she'd respond like that. I half expected she'd think he deserved it."

Chane glanced down at Ellen. "What did Robertson do to her?"

Ellen shrugged. "I'm not too clear on the details, but he was apparently responsible for her being kidnapped and held by a gang of outlaws."

"While she still worked in Central America?"

"Yes."

They were coming to get me. The spectral image of Lexi running through a black night returned full force. No wonder she had sounded so certain they were in danger. He had actually looked around the meadow for the unseen assailants.

"Oh, he came back for her," Ellen added. "But not before they beat her." She wrapped her sweater more firmly around her. "I know you want to go home. Besides, I doubt you really want to hear this."

Yeah, I do want to hear this, he thought, shifting Tessa in his arms. Other questions, though, were crowding to the surface. "I didn't know you two were such good friends."

Ellen shrugged. "Actually, we've never been that close. We knew each other in college. I saw her off and on after she bought her place. In fact, she was the one who got me interested in orphans. I have her to thank for adopting the twins."

Chane frowned, the knot in his stomach tighter than ever. "Was she involved when you helped Rose get Tessa?"

"Why would you ask such a thing?" Ellen raised her eyes to Chane's.

"Because of that woman she's helping. Señora Padilla." He couldn't keep the worry out of his voice or ignore the suspicion that had formed. "How long has Lexi been working for you?"

"She doesn't."

"What was she doing here, then?"

"Helping out. One of my teachers has the flu. I needed help, and Lexi volunteered." Ellen punched Chane lightly on the arm. "Lighten up, fella. You'd think it was this little tyke that Lexi's friend was looking for."

Chane would have settled for an ironclad guarantee that Tessa wasn't.

Ellen smiled and smoothed her palm over Tessa's cheek. "This was the sweetest little baby you could imagine."

"I'm trying to find a phone number for the agency that was used and—"

"There was no agency," Ellen told him. "It was a private adoption. There was no need—"

"Then who are The Sisters of Hope?"

Ellen met his gaze. "What do you mean?"

"I found a surrender document turning Tessa over to a group called The Sisters of Hope. Is that your agency?"

"No. Heavens, no. Chane, why do you want to go into all this now?"

"Because I can't find the adoption decree."

"It probably has just been misplaced." Ellen smiled. "You

know how Rose was. I'm sure you'll find it.'' She glanced down at her watch. ''My word, it's late. Listen, I've got to go.''

''What about The Sisters of Hope?'' he persisted.

''Chane, there's nothing much I can tell you.''

''Ellen—'' Surprising anger surfaced, leaving him feeling raw and exposed. Ellen had answers to Rose's secrets. He was sure of it.

''Give me a call in the morning. I'll go through my stuff and see what I can find. Okay?'' She took a couple of steps backwards and waved at Tessa. ''See you later, little love.''

Ellen went inside and locked the door behind her. From the window, she watched Chane fasten the seatbelt around Tessa, then drive away. Automatically, she straightened chairs and gathered toys to be put away as she worked her way toward her office.

There she pulled her Rolodex toward her, flipped through the cards, and found a number she had never used. She dialed, and when a voice on the other end of the line answered, Ellen said, ''You promised me no one—*no one* would ever ask about The Sisters of Hope. Today, I was asked. Not once, but twice.''

Chapter 9

Less than an hour later, Chane pulled into Lexi's driveway and killed the engine to his truck. Night had grown dark enough so the light inside her house spilled across the deck. He hadn't been sure he'd even find her at home.

Given her reaction to the news about Joe Robertson, Chane figured she might have already been on her way to Denver. He could see her inside, though. The telephone receiver was tucked between her head and shoulder as she paced back and forth, occasionally raking her hand through her hair. She had been upset this afternoon. She looked more disturbed now. Why the hell was she so upset about a guy responsible for her being kidnapped? Worse, why did he care?

Chane's frustration simmered to the surface. The attorney had been real straight with his answers. Chane hadn't liked them a bit. Ellen Belsen had been anything but straight. He didn't like that either. And then, there was Lexi Monroe.

Chane had never believed in coincidences. It was just a little too pat that Lexi should be enrolled in his class, helping a Hispanic woman find her stolen granddaughter, have ties to the one man in his life he considered an enemy, and be the catalyst for Ellen Belsen to adopt babies from South America.

But damn! Lexi had been so convincing. Her fear up on the rock had been absolutely real. He was convinced the nightmare that drove her into the meadow the other night was just as real. So, what the hell was she up to?

He hadn't planned on coming to see her, but the minute he got home and stashed Tessa with Kit, he headed here. He didn't know if she'd be any more forthcoming than Ellen had been, but he had to know if Lexi had been connected with Tessa's adoption. And he wasn't leaving until he had the answers he wanted.

When Lexi hung up the phone and disappeared into the kitchen, Chane got out of the truck and climbed the stairs two at a time. He knocked—pounded—on the door and heard her footfalls inside.

She opened the door, and Chane pushed it open farther and stepped over the threshold, forcing himself to ignore how drained she looked. The door closed behind him with a click.

"We have to talk," he said without preamble. The remembered sensation of her wrapped around him flowed over him, followed by an icy speculation that he hated. Had she and Joe Robertson been lovers? With everything else on his mind, that was the last thing that ought to have mattered to him.

For a second, raw anguish chased through her eyes, bloodshot and red-rimmed from crying. She had changed her clothes, and the black sweater she wore made her look pale, made her eyes even darker. A brilliant silver and turquoise pendant hung between her breasts, drawing his attention to them, an aching reminder of their sweet weight filling his hands. When she noticed the direction of his gaze, she straightened and fingered the heavy chain. It was her only outward indication of nerves.

Her vulnerability and her discipline to pull herself together beckoned to him. To keep from touching her, he took off his Stetson.

"I know we do, Chane," she agreed with a nod. "But not now."

"Now." He fingered the brim of his hat, frowned, and stared at her, seeing a woman he wanted to comfort. His lack of focus annoyed him as much as his jealousy did. He didn't want to feel sympathy for her, but he couldn't banish it. Any more than he could banish the thought that she had somehow betrayed him.

"I'm leaving in just—"

"Why the hell are you enrolled in the wilderness survival class?" He ground out the question, ignoring all the things she made him feel except the one that mattered. Betrayed.

"What?" The bafflement in her voice was reflected in her expression.

"What are you trying to find out?"

Bewilderment creased her brow. "What are you talking about?"

"There's a story in it, isn't there? That's why you're in the class."

"Ah." Understanding dawned in her eyes and she held his gaze a moment, her eyes losing their sheen. "A story. Show up, be part of the scenery, use people." She snapped her fingers. "And write an exposé."

"You sound familiar with the tactics. I'm not quite as trusting as I used to be."

"With justification," she agreed evenly. "Only, I'm not after a story."

"No?"

"No."

"Then maybe you'll tell me what you are after." He made no attempt to keep the sarcasm out of his voice.

She raised an eyebrow, her glance never faltering. "What I'm after. That is supposed to make sense to me?" She went to the hall closet and took a jacket off a hanger. "I don't have time for Twenty Questions, Chane. Get to the point."

"Does Ellen Belsen have anything to do with your friend, Señora Padilla? That's her name, right?"

"Not a thing. I had hoped Ellen could help point her in the direction of contacts or agencies that could help."

"You asked her?"

"Of course I asked her. Listen—"

"Did you ever help Ellen place kids for adoption?"

"No."

As with his other questions, her answer was quick, the tone of her voice revealing surprise and growing impatience.

"And you weren't her contact with any orphanages in Central America."

"No. I didn't even know she had helped other couples wrangle through the red tape to adopt babies until a couple of days ago." Lexi dropped the jacket on the back of the couch and moved toward him. "What's this all about? I'm not looking for a story. I enrolled in your class for the reasons I told you. I don't want anything from you." Her glance faltered for a second, then she added, "In fact, I'm not sure I even know you."

"You know me," he stated gruffly.

She shook her head. "I don't think so." She glanced up, an odd glint of challenge in her eyes. "At least you've set me straight on something." She made a point of glancing at her watch. "I've got to go."

"Set you straight on what?"

A slow flush crawled across her cheeks. She pressed her lips together, then nodded as though coming to some sort of decision. "Never confuse sex with friendship."

His own mouth tightened, and his temper, barely under control, flared. "Sex? You think this is about the other night?"

"If I were in your shoes, I'd be thinking the same things. You hate Joe Robertson. I worked with him, and I didn't tell you. Worse, you and I . . . we had sex—"

"Made love," he ground out, hating the way she put it.

She looked away, her color still high. "Anyway, I should have told you I knew him, and I didn't. You want me to say I'm sorry?" She looked at him and swallowed. "Well, I'm sorry."

With the last statement, her voice lost its defensiveness, and he believed her.

Her eyes grew bright with unshed tears. "I know I probably deserve whatever you're thinking, but I'm not the enemy."

"You were hiding things from me."

"Not the way you seem to think." She closed the distance between them and laid a hand on his arm. "You asked me why I hadn't told you I knew him." Her eyes misted and she swallowed. "I don't honestly know. I didn't want to interrupt you when you were telling me your story. And later . . . Talking about the last months I was in Costa Léon is hard. But what happened to me isn't a secret."

"Ellen told me what happened."

"All I kept thinking was that Joe had been at the center of the worst experience of your life." She met Chane's gaze. "He was at the center of mine, too."

"But you're on your way to Denver anyway."

She nodded. "I owe him my life."

"He's a bastard."

She smiled sadly. "I know."

"If he saved your life, he had some other motive."

"That's right." A tear escaped from the corner of her eye. "There's nothing you can tell me about Joe Robertson that I don't already know."

He caught the tear with his thumb. "Are you in love with him?" He hadn't intended to ask that, but he searched her face, needing to see the truth of her answer.

Lexi shook her head. "No. Not now, not ever. I'd be lying if I said he was even a good friend. But . . ."

He believed her. God help him, right or wrong, he believed her. She said she hadn't been involved with Ellen Belsen, and he believed her. Chane turned his hand over, brought their palms together, and laced their fingers. "I want to understand. I came here thinking the worse, you know."

"That I'm a user like Joe Robertson. That I enrolled in your class for some ulterior motive."

Chane traced a vein down the back of her hand with his index finger. "Yeah."

She bowed her head, then looked back at him. "You're right about one thing." At his raised eyebrow, she continued. "Just like Joe, I've used people to get information."

"Couldn't be just like Robertson," Chane interrupted. "People died because of him."

A spasm of pain crossed her features. "And because of me."

Chane grasped her by the shoulders. "Stop it!" He lifted

her chin with his knuckle. "I came here wanting to prove to myself that you're just like Robertson. I was wrong."

Lexi's eyes closed and a tear slipped from beneath the lid. He caught that one, too. She shook her head and tried to step away from him, but he folded his arms around her.

"I was wrong," he repeated.

Held within his embrace, Lexi felt his voice rumble against her ear, the sound touching her soul. She didn't begin to understand Chane Callahan. He had been angry, and now he held her, offering . . . comfort. She didn't know what motivated one any more than the other. Only, being in his arms felt so good. So many times over the last year she had wanted to be able to rely on someone else's strength when her own wasn't enough. She wrapped her arms around his waist and rested her head against his shoulder, knowing she shouldn't, knowing that she had only her own two feet to stand on, no matter what.

"How long are you going to be gone?" he asked.

"I don't know." In just a minute, she would lift her head, she told herself, listening to the reassuring beat of his heart beneath her ear. In just a minute. "I guess it all depends on how Joe is doing."

"We have a lot to talk about when you get back."

She tipped her head back so she could see his face. Those dark eyes had gone all soft. Whatever had been driving him earlier was gone. He brushed her nose with his own.

The small, innocent caress shimmered through her. She focused on his mouth. His lower lip was full and slightly chapped, utterly masculine. She tipped her head farther back and stood on tiptoe, inviting his kiss.

His breath feathered her temple as he whispered, "I haven't been able to think about anything but making love to you again. Now is not the time for that."

"It's not," she agreed, wanting him to kiss her. She was going to regret this later, but just now, she needed what he was offering.

"Are you sure you want this?"

Her chuckle was soft and she pulled his head toward her. "You've got to be kidding."

He kissed her with the same assurance he did everything. Full out with complete confidence, a possession that was sweeter than she remembered. Coherent thought vanished. She felt as though she had come home, as though everything she had ever wanted could be found in his caress if she could simply get close enough. His lips brushed gently against hers until they parted. He deepened the caress, encouraging her to offer the sensitive interior of her mouth. On a sigh, she parted her lips.

The touch of his tongue against hers made her tremble. A moment of morning sunshine spearing through darkness, she thought. She opened her mouth wider, drinking from him as though she were dying of thirst. And she was. She filled herself with the taste of him, with the scent of him, with the texture of his wool shirt and resilient muscles beneath her palms. Filled herself until her heart, too long empty, was filled, too. One kiss became another, then another until she could no longer tell where one ended and another began. As if she cared.

He wrapped his big palms around her face, holding her immobile as he slowly brought the kiss back under control.

When the contact broke, Lexi couldn't help her small groan of protest.

"See," he whispered against her lips. "There's lots more for us to talk about. Right?"

"Just as soon as I get back," she promised. She had loved having Chane as a friend. Equally, she had loved having him as a lover. Friendships lasted. Sex didn't. How could she choose when she wanted—needed—both so badly.

Joe Robertson lay motionless on the hospital bed, tubes and wires connecting him to monitors, a respirator, and IV units. A huge white bandage covered his head and one ear. His color was pasty. He didn't much resemble the dynamic, cocky Joe Robertson she both admired and despised.

She'd had to persuade a receptionist, two nurses, and a tired resident that she just wanted to sit with Joe for a while. Visitors in the intensive care unit during the middle of the night were frowned upon, but Lexi had been insistent. The young doctor explained to Lexi that Joe had been shot in the head, that he was on life support, and that they were waiting for a final recommendation from the neurologist.

Lexi interpreted that to mean they were waiting to get the okay to turn off the machines that were keeping Joe alive. After being told Joe would never know she'd even been there, she was allowed in.

Seeing him like this was worse than she had imagined. Lexi didn't like hospitals, especially not big, high-tech ones like this one. The machines seemed to have their own life and purpose, somehow more important in the scheme of things than the patients they were hooked to. Unfortunately, none of that energy seemed transferred to Joe, despite the respirator doing the work to keep him alive.

Lexi sat down in a chair next to the bed and took one of Joe's hands in hers. It felt lifeless, which alarmed her more than the machines and tubes and bandages.

"Ah, Joe," she whispered, and recited his favorite quote from the old Laurel and Hardy movies. "Here's another fine mess you've gotten us into." She caressed the back of his hand, absently noticing the dry skin and the skeletal structure beneath. "You're creating an uproar, you know. If you want to enjoy all this furor, you're going to have to start breathing on your own and wake up."

He'd had a restless energy, a vitality that she supposed came from living on the edge. Lexi had never known anyone with a quicker mind. She found him exasperating and thoroughly irritating. He'd been brilliant, anyway.

He should be posting his most recent story or regaling an audience at a bar with his latest escapades. He should have been shot while pursuing a story, not because of some senseless drive-by shooting where he was an innocent victim in the wrong spot at the wrong time.

She found believing that impossible. Joe had stumbled onto something. If she had been told he had been shot by an informant or had been set up by someone he had exposed, this whole thing would have made sense. But a drive-by shooting?

The duty nurse Lexi had spoken with earlier came into the cubicle. Lexi stepped away from the bed while she checked monitors and IV, making notes in the chart. She listened to his heart, then checked his pupils.

"Is there any change?" Lexi asked.

The nurse shook her head and gave Lexi a sympathetic smile. She left and Lexi sat back down.

Lexi had called the managing editor she and Joe reported to before leaving Grand Lake. Mike Lanatowski had been as shocked as Lexi.

"My first thought was that it had something to do with his story," Mike had told her.

His statement echoed Lexi's suspicions. "El Ladron has connections in Denver? When Joe and I were working on the story, we were suspicious, but—"

"I told Robertson to drop that months ago. He's been working on a feature about the nuclear arms race in our newer, less dangerous world—from a nuclear point of view, anyway. He was supposed to be talking to some officials at Rocky Flats and a spokesman for Green Peace."

So Joe had been pulled off the El Ladron story. She listened to Mike, comparing his narration to her last conversation with Joe. If he wasn't working on El Ladron, why the hell was he stringing her along? Even half dead, Joe spun intricate webs that only he understood. Did he have something he was working up, so he could give Mike the finished piece as a *fait accompli?* Or had he been covering his butt after sending Señora Padilla to Grand Lake? Either way, Lexi wouldn't be surprised. And since Joe couldn't defend himself, she hadn't said anything further to Mike about El Ladron.

She had promised to call Mike when she found out more. Now that she was here, surrounded by the impersonal machines keeping Joe alive, she put off calling. Staring down at Joe, she remembered his telling her he wanted to grow old enough to be a 'pompous bastard.' At the time, she had told him he didn't have to grow any older. He'd already achieved that status.

"You won't make it to eighty years old this way, Joe. Keep

fighting.'' Lexi blinked away the tears that burned at the back of her eyes. She closed her eyes and squeezed his hand.

She couldn't have said how long she sat with him before she felt a hand touch her shoulder.

Lexi looked up to see the nurse. ''There's a man who wants to talk to you.''

''The neurologist?'' Lexi asked.

The nurse shook her head. ''We don't expect him until morning.''

Lexi glanced over her shoulder at the silhouette of a big man through the cubicle window. For an instant she thought it was Chane, and she stood up and hurried to the door.

The man waiting for her in the hall was big, but several inches shy of Chane's height. Disappointed, Lexi paused in the doorway. This man wore a dark rumpled suit. His shoulder braced against the wall and his legs crossed, he watched Lexi approach with alert eyes that stared at her from an otherwise ordinary face. Everything about him telegraphed he was a cop.

''You wanted to see me?'' Lexi asked.

''The nurse says that you're a friend of his,'' he said, nodding in the direction of Joe's room.

''That's right. And you're . . .''

''Darren Burke.'' He pulled a wallet from his inside breast pocket and held it open in front of Lexi, revealing a badge on one side and a photo ID on the other.

So, she was right about his being a cop. Her glance returned to his face.

''FBI. We're investigating this shooting.'' He snapped the wallet closed and put it back in his pocket.

''I didn't know the FBI got involved with drive-by shootings,'' Lexi said.

''Normally, we don't.'' He straightened. ''Normally victims aren't world-famous reporters, either. What's your connection to Robertson?''

''I'm just a friend.''

''What's your name?''

''Alexandra Monroe,'' she answered. His blunt questions had a certain edge Lexi didn't like. The man looked dog tired.

But neither that nor this middle-of-the-night hour excused bad manners.

"Do you know what he might have been doing at the Pike Place apartments?"

Lexi recognized the name from the newscast as the address where Joe had been shot. She shook her head.

"Mr. Robertson doesn't normally work in Denver, is that right?"

"He works out of L.A.," Lexi confirmed.

"Do you know why he was in Denver?"

Lexi wasn't likely to forget that Joe had come to Denver on a nuclear arms story rather than the lead on El Ladron. Maybe that had been a ruse all these months. Maybe he'd just wanted her to think he was still working on that story to make her feel better.

Whether the agent already knew what Joe had been working on or was finishing, Lexi didn't know. Either way, the question struck her as odd in the context of the assault on Joe. "You don't think this was a simple drive-by shooting, do you?"

"We don't know yet."

Lexi crossed the hall and sat down in one of the chairs. Her earlier suspicions returned. This would make sense if someone with a grudge had shot Joe. In that context, the anonymous cover of a drive-by shooting made sense.

The agent followed her and sat down across from her.

"Joe was on assignment," she finally said. "But you'll have to talk to his managing editor, Mike Lanatowski."

"What was he working on?" Burke asked.

"I don't know," Lexi answered truthfully. "Ask Lanatowski."

Burke snorted. "You worked with him for months. Sure you know what he's working on."

Lexi raised an eyebrow, both her temper and her suspicions rising. "I speak with a lot of my former coworkers. That doesn't mean I know what stories they're working on. Joe Robertson included."

"What else can you tell me?"

"Nothing," Lexi said. "I haven't worked with Joe in a long time, so I'm kind of out of the game."

"Did he have enemies?"

Lexi stared at the agent, again struck by the incongruency of his questions. On one hand, he acted as though he knew exactly what Joe had been doing. On the other, he acted like a green cop straight out of the academy. "Read any story he's ever done, and you'll have your answer."

"You don't like cops much, do you, Ms. Monroe?" The question held something more than idle curiosity.

"Your point, Mr. Burke?" Lexi mentally ran over his question again, wondering what it was that struck her so odd. During her years as a news photographer, she'd had dealings with all sorts of law enforcement officers—DEA agents, immigration officers, local detectives, and FBI agents.

He smiled—one that seemed as phony to Lexi as the front-page photos on the tabloids. "If you think of anything, you'll keep us posted, right?"

"As I said, I don't know anything."

He stood. "Thanks for your help, Ms. Monroe."

What help? she wondered, watching him walk down the dimly lit hallway to the elevator where he punched the call button. Seconds later the doors opened, and he stepped inside. As the doors closed behind him, her unease clicked into place. Not once had she ever heard an FBI agent refer to himself as a cop.

She glanced toward Joe's bed inside the cubicle. The nurse was checking on him once again. Lexi headed for the pay telephone at the end of the hall. Dialing the number for Mike Lanatowski's home, she counted off the rings.

He answered on the fourth one, sounding wide awake. Lexi identified herself, and Mike said, "I knew it had to be you. How's he doing?"

"Not good," she replied. "The nurses haven't said, but I don't think he's responding at all. They're waiting for a recommendation from the neurologist who operated on him."

"Think they're gonna pull the plug?"

How like Mike to be to the point, Lexi thought, knowing his direct gruffness was his way of dealing with stress.

"Yes," she answered. Taking a breath, she added, "Listen, I just had an FBI agent ask me some questions. A guy named Burke. He wants to know what Joe was working on. I told him to call you."

"What the hell is the FBI doing on a drive-by shooting?" Mike demanded.

"That's the same question I asked him." She glanced down the hall and saw the nurse leave Joe's cubicle. "I just wanted you to know in case he calls. And speaking of that, you did call Joe's parents, right?"

"They're on their way from Norwich, New York. They should be there sometime in the morning." He cleared his throat, then asked, "You okay, kid?"

It was the most emotion she had ever heard in Mike.

"So far, so good," she told him. "I'll talk to you tomorrow, Mike."

Lexi hung up the phone, the sensation that something was terribly wrong nagging at her. Piece by piece, she analyzed the conversation with Darren Burke. And realized she had never told him she had worked with Joe. But somehow, he had known. *You worked with him for months. What else can you tell me?*

"She's here." Darren Burke slid into a booth at an all-night café a few blocks from the hospital.

"Good. It's about time a plan came together." George Moody had waited a year for this moment. Alexandra Monroe's meddling had cost him close to a million dollars. Those were losses he couldn't tolerate.

She was going back to Costa Léon, according to Robertson, and ready to resume her fight. Moody wasn't going to let that happen. Pressure and surveillance from law enforcement in the U.S. and Canada had just recently let up enough to get operations back in full swing.

This time, he'd finish the job with Alexandra Monroe.

Last year, he had been determined she wouldn't leave Costa

Léon alive, but she had been cagey, moving into a high-security
building after she got out of the hospital. INN had even provided
some muscle for her. He hadn't been able to get to her personally, but he'd made sure everyone around her knew they could
not afford to be her friend. After her housekeeper's son gave
an eye in payment for her continued meddling, Monroe had
finally left Costa Léon.

George Moody smiled to himself. Killing Robertson served
a number of quite useful purposes. It had gotten rid of a double-
crosser. It had flushed out Monroe. And it would remind Monroe, before she died, of the high cost she exacted from her
friends.

"I don't even have to get you," he had told her on the
telephone in the middle of the night a year ago after he had
released her housekeeper's son. "That boy. Hurting him was
the same as hurting you. Only better. How long will you expect
others to pay the price for your actions?"

He smiled, remembering the way she had slammed the phone
down.

After Alexandra Monroe left Costa Léon, she had spent a
month in New York City, and he'd almost had her then. Then,
she'd disappeared. The damn woman had been nearly impossible to track down, but he had eventually discovered she was
living somewhere in Colorado and that, with Robertson's help,
she was continuing her investigation and her attempts to shut
him down.

He'd bided his time and been patient. Señora Padilla had
been his ace. Moody had carefully set the stage, positive the
woman would lead him to Alexandra Monroe. Only there had
been a slipup after she went to see Robertson, and they had
lost her.

Providing Robertson with enough leads to make him think
he was closing in on El Ladron's identity had been easy. Using
Robertson to draw out Monroe wasn't as fail safe as using the
old woman, but it had worked.

Sooner or later, everyone made mistakes. And Alexandra
Monroe had just made a big one.

A waitress came with a coffee carafe and a cup for Burke. She poured it and left.

"What about Robertson?"

Burke shrugged. "He's on life support. I heard one of the nurses say they'll turn him off as soon as the doc gives the okay."

Good, Moody thought, mentally tying up one more loose end. "And Alexandra Monroe?"

"She won't be leaving the hospital until they shut down Robertson's life support. We'll pick her up when she leaves the hospital."

Moody nodded in anticipation. Hurting her, making her afraid—that's what he wanted. He had done so once before. And before he killed her, she'd know the outer limits of fear. He smiled.

Dead was dead, and Robertson wasn't a problem anymore. One down. One to go.

Chapter 10

The alarm on the clock radio in the bookcase headboard above Chane's head went off at six-thirty that same morning. Wide awake, he punched it off, got out of bed, and began his morning routine of calisthenics. By rote, he went through the exercises, his mind focused on the day ahead, reviewing the conclusions he had reached during a long sleepless night.

During the weeks after Rose's death, sleeping the night through had been nearly impossible. "Give yourself time," his mother had told him with age-old wisdom. And time had eased the hurt. Gradually, he learned to sleep at night again instead of being ridden with overwhelming guilt.

Last night was the first time in months he had spent the long hours of the night mostly staring at the ceiling. Anger, not guilt, consumed him. Oh, he'd been angry with Rose about adopting a baby without including him in that decision. That emotion paled in comparison to being furious because the adoption hadn't been completed. Not knowing who to be mad at, not knowing exactly what had to be done to fix the problem, made him feel impotent. That was most infuriating of all.

He'd thought about the last weeks before Rose died. He'd thought about his daughter. He'd thought about his conversation with Ellen Belsen. He'd thought about Lexi Monroe. A lot.

Admitting to himself that a night's perspective wasn't enough, he was still clear on several points.

He trusted Lexi Monroe. In some ways, that one had been easiest. Distrusting her because she was a news photographer and because she had worked with Robertson was easy. But it was also stupid. In his gut, where his decisions mattered, Chane believed her and believed in her. If he had learned one thing in thirty plus years, it was to trust his instincts. His mental list of decisions he regretted all had in common one thing. In every one, he had gone with his head instead of trusting his gut instincts.

He also trusted body language way more than he trusted words. Body language didn't lie. Lexi hadn't been lying when she told him she hadn't helped Ellen place babies for adoption. Her body radiated longing and intent when she told him she wanted back the person she used to be. He liked the person she was now just fine, but he respected her need to defeat the demons that haunted her. Whatever loyalty she had for Señora Padilla or even Joe Robertson, for that matter, didn't have a damn thing to do with Tessa.

In fact, Lexi hadn't picked up on his questions about Ellen Belsen and Señora Padilla and adoptions. Lexi had thought he was mad solely because of Joe Robertson. That single realization had done a lot toward reassuring him.

The second conclusion he had reaching during the long hours of the night had been far more difficult. He didn't trust Ellen Belsen. Never mind he had known her for years. Never mind that she had been one of Rose's closest friends. Never mind that her credentials were impeccable and her day-care center was terrific. Body language didn't lie. Ellen, even after all this time, was still protecting Rose, still keeping her secrets.

Nearly four years had passed, and Chane still remembered the shock of arriving home to a baby. The feeling was nearly as vivid now as it had been then. Guilt rode him for months for not realizing just how much Rose had wanted a child or to what lengths she had been willing to go.

So long as he lived, he'd never forget that first instant when he gazed down at Tessa. So tiny, with bottomless dark eyes and equally dark hair. She looked enough like Rose to have been her child. His heart had softened in that instant—at least toward the baby. Tessa was an innocent, and he had made damn sure his confusion and disappointment and anger didn't touch her. Every so often since then, he was gripped with a terrible sense of loss of what might have been. A child that looked like Rose. However uncertain Rose's legacy, Tessa was his child.

The list of reasons he had come up with for there being no adoption decree was short—extremely short. Rose had died before it could be issued. That didn't explain why there was none of the usual paperwork that came with an international adoption. There had to be thousands of international adoptions every year, he reasoned. The missing papers were nothing more than a snafu. And now that he knew there was a problem, he'd take care of it.

The first order of business was to have his attorney do whatever was necessary to ensure no one could ever take Tessa away from him. Missing decree or not. The second was to see Ellen Belsen. His third was to make sure Lexi was okay. In fact, he decided, that should be the first.

He sat down on the bed and made the calls to get the hospital's telephone number, then dialed Denver General Hospital. Yes, Joe Robertson was a patient, a polite female voice told him. Visiting hours didn't start until eleven. Since he was listed in critical condition in intensive care, he wouldn't be having visitors. The operator paged Lexi for him, but she didn't answer. Since he wasn't family, his call wouldn't be transferred to intensive care. Frustrated, Chane hung up the telephone.

He had just finished showering and giving Kit his third wake-up call when Tessa came into the bathroom. Chane lifted her up, hugged her, and set her on the counter next to the sink.

"Did you have a good sleepy time?" he asked her.

"Uh-huh."

Most mornings she arrived just before he finished shaving. The faces she made in imitation of him as he pulled the razor blade across his jaw made him feel warm inside, always, especially so this morning. Chane rinsed the blade and reached for the aftershave in the cabinet.

"I want to do it," Tessa said, as she did every morning.

Chane poured a couple of drops into her hands, then squatted in front of her. Tessa patted his face, her small features pursed in concentration.

"Mmmmm. Smells better when you put it on." He kissed her cheek with a loud smack.

He screwed the cap back on the bottle and put it away, then picked her up and carried her into the bedroom, where he opened the closet door. "Blue shirt or brown shirt?" he asked, holding both up for her inspection.

"Blue shirt," she answered promptly.

"Blue shirt it is. Then, we have to get you dressed."

"I'm hungry first."

"Then I guess we'll have to rustle up some grub first." Setting her down, he put on the dark blue flannel shirt.

"I don't want to eat grubs," she informed him, climbing onto the bed. "Ricky says grubs are bugs. Yuck."

Chane grinned. "Maybe soft boiled eggs, then."

"Yucky more. How 'bout Fruit Loops?"

"Not for breakfast." Chane glanced at his watch. "I think Kit is going to be late."

Tessa slid off the bed. "I'll go wake him up, Daddy. He'll look at me like this." She moved one eyebrow up and down with her finger. "Then he'll tickle me."

She skipped out the room and down the hall. Chane watched her go, a smile on his face. This was another of those ordinary details so ordinary he'd forget too soon, so special. He never wanted to forget. Life . . . Which brought him full circle to Lexi and Joe Robertson. Chane's smile faded.

He tucked in his shirt and headed down the hall. "Up and at 'em," he called to Kit. "You've got a half hour before the school bus comes."

Kit appeared in the doorway, Tessa sitting on his shoulders. "I think I'll drop out," he said with a yawn. "Then I could sleep 'til noon."

"Last I heard, reveille was at five A.M., not noon," Chane said. At least once a week Kit told him he was going to drop out, and just as often Chane replied that was fine. He'd sign the consent forms for Kit to enlist in the Marines.

"Keep it up, bro," Kit said, "and someday I'm going to think you're serious."

Chane lifted his daughter off Kit's shoulders and headed toward the kitchen. "Breakfast in ten minutes, ready or not."

Lexi spent part of the night pacing the hallway outside the ICU, part of it sitting next to Joe, and all of it remembering bits and pieces of the time she'd been on assignment with him. Whatever his faults had been, Joe didn't deserve this. No one deserved this. As the night dragged on, she had less and less doubt about the outcome. The nurses and the resident all spoke in hushed tones that translated to a simple, devastating truth: Joe was brain dead.

Morning arrived without a sunrise. Lexi could smell rain in the air, and during one of her sojourns to the front window, rain began to fall in a steady drizzle. The day shift replaced the night shift, and the pace of activity around her subtly picked up. The neurologist was due soon. Lexi hoped Joe's parents arrived first.

A nurse and orderly efficiently changed the bed beneath Joe. When they were finished, Lexi sat back down next to him. Just as she had every other time during the long night, she took his hand. As before, she was infused with memories of those last weeks in Costa Léon.

She hadn't wanted Joe to come to the airport to see her off that last morning nearly a year ago. He had come anyway, ignoring her anger.

"I don't want you here, Joe."

"Tough." He sat down in a chair next to hers. *"You can't keep avoiding me just because you're pissed."*

"I am not—"

"Yeah, you are." He grinned. *"Mad as a hatter, Monroe."*

He stretched an arm across the back of her chair. "But it's okay because you're gonna forgive me."

"Not in this life. I was there, remember?"

For the first time his voice revealed a trace of irritation. "I hightailed it back to San Pedro when I found out what had happened to you. And I came back with the police who, by the way, weren't all that anxious to cross El Ladron and his cronies. You were pretty damned happy to see me then."

"I would have been happy to see Godzilla."

"Yeah? And maybe you would have stopped being so damn self-righteous long enough to say thank you."

"For what?" *she demanded.* "Using me to get your story?"

"I didn't mean for you to get hurt—"

"You never mean for bad things to happen, Joe. They just do."

"You're not so lily white, you know," *he said.* "You wanted El Ladron just as much as I did. Whatever it took. And if it meant paying off corrupt officials, risking my hide, or selling your mother's soul, you would have done it. You sure told me often enough that you'd do what it took—from going after the well-meaning bastards who took a shortcut to adoption to the corrupt system that turned a blind eye to El Ladron. So don't be giving me that crap that I used you."

Lexi dropped her gaze, unable to bear the intensity of his any longer.

"The problem is, Monroe, you want it both ways. An ivory tower where your ideals can be taken out and polished. Where you're in control. Well, baby, this is the real world. And you can't get slime like El Ladron without crawling under the rock with him."

"I did that," *she whispered.*

"Yeah, you did. And now that the going has gotten a little tough—"

"A lot tough," *she interrupted, hating the searing memories of the beating she took at El Ladron's hands. Worse—far worse—was the deliberate cruelty and the pleasure he got from exploiting her fears. One by one, he had ripped them from her, then acted them out.*

"Okay," Joe agreed with a shrug. *"A lot tough. Now, you're running. Worse, you're sealing off the entrance to your ivory tower. Nothing is ever going to hurt you again, Monroe."*

"That's right," she agreed.

"And nothing as important as these babies is ever going to touch you again. A sacred trust that you're giving up."

"You don't know what you're talking about, Joe."

"Think about it, Monroe. I'm going to be alive—you've got that? Alive—doing what I love to do. And you're going to be an empty shell that won't even recognize the woman who once had the passion to do work good enough to win a Pulitzer prize."

"You don't understand," Lexi said, knowing there was nothing she could say to make him understand. He'd been there—and if he hadn't understood what had happened to her then, he certainly wouldn't now.

Lexi's flight was called, and Joe stood up with her.

"There's nothing wrong with you, Monroe, that the right man couldn't fix."

She felt her face heat. *"The day I need a man—"*

Joe grinned. *"You rise to the bait every time."*

"You don't get it."

"Oh, I get it," he said. *"I just don't take life as seriously as you do, Monroe."* He picked up her totebag and carried it as they strolled toward the jetway. *"For a watchdog, Monroe, you've been okay."*

"And you've been—"

"Ah, ah," he chided, pressing a finger against her lips. He slipped the totebag over her shoulder. *"You might slip and say something nice."*

"Goodbye, Joe."

She was ten paces away from him when he called, *"Monroe."*

Lexi turned around and Joe closed the space between them. *"About that story . . ."* His hazel eyes grew dark. *"Getting you out instead was a more than even trade."* He dropped a kiss on her cheek. As he walked away, he called over his shoulder, *"And like I said, you're gonna forgive me."*

The conversation replayed inside Lexi's mind, bringing with

it insights she hadn't had at the time. A year ago she had been so sure things would have turned out differently if Joe hadn't used her as bait to lure out El Ladron. And today, she had to admit she would have gladly gone if it meant catching him, putting him out of business. It was a risk that should have worked. And it wasn't Joe's fault she had been caught.

And Joe had been uncannily right about the ivory tower, Lexi thought. She was safe. Lexi could rage all she wanted at the unfairness of the world and wait for Joe to do her dirty work. Until he sent her Señora Padilla, nobody had gotten in. No cause beyond Lexi's personal survival had been important—until she had joined a quest to find a child.

Fresh tears seeped from beneath Lexi's eyelids. Joe had given her something important to focus on. She owed him that. She had left her convictions in Costa Léon. But she still had a chance to make a difference. At least for Señora Padilla and her granddaughter.

"Your son is right here," a nurse said from outside the cubicle.

Lexi looked up as a couple was ushered inside, the woman maternally round, and the man an older, more distinguished version of Joe. Worry and fatigue etched both of their faces.

Unobtrusively as she could, Lexi stood up and moved out of the way. Mr. and Mrs. Robertson converged on the bed. Silence reigned except for the repetitive mechanical noise of the respirator.

At last Mr. Robertson looked up from his son, caught Lexi's glance before his slid past her to the nurse. "What's the doctor's name again?"

"Steinbrenner," the nurse supplied. "He should be along soon."

Mrs. Robertson sat down in the chair Lexi had vacated, and as Lexi had done countless times during the endless night, took Joe's limp hand.

"You must be Alexandra Monroe," Mr. Robertson said.

Lexi nodded and had to clear her throat before her answer was audible. "Yes."

"Mike Lanatowski told us you'd be here."

There didn't seem to be anything to say to that, so Lexi nodded.

Mrs. Robertson raised her head and looked across the hospital bed to Lexi. "Joe had a lot to say about you the last time he was home."

She nodded. "I . . . Joe . . . we worked together about a year and a half ago."

"He admired your work," Mr. Robertson said.

"It was good of you to come," Mrs. Robertson said. "The nurse told us she thought you had been here all night."

"Yes. Most of it."

"I'm glad he wasn't alone." Her glance fell back to her son. "When we spoke with the doctor yesterday, we weren't sure he'd still be . . ."

Alive. Her voice faded, but Lexi heard the next word echo through her mind.

Silence surged around them awkward and uncomfortable, interrupted by Dr. Steinbrenner's arrival.

Lexi slipped away, unwilling to intrude on Joe's parents, already sure what the neurologist was going to tell them.

"Miss Monroe?" a nurse at the nurse's station called.

"Yes?"

She held up a telephone receiver. "Phone call for you."

Lexi crossed to the counter. "This is Lexi Monroe," she said into the receiver.

"Hi," came Chane's baritone voice over the line. "I just called to make sure you're okay and to see if there is anything I can do for you."

Pleasure seeped through Lexi and she leaned against the counter. "Hi."

"You sound tired."

"Yeah."

"How's Robertson?"

Lexi closed her eyes. "He's not going to make it, Chane."

An instant of silence filled the line. "I'm sorry, Lexi."

If one man had ever had a reason to wish another ill will, Chane did. Yet he was sorry. He'd been stealing her heart one little piece at a time with concern and compassion. Those three simple words earned him another major chunk.

"What can I do for you?" he asked.

"Nothing." She raised her head. In Joe's cubicle, the doctor and Joe's parents were still talking. "Joe's parents just got here. I don't have any idea what they may need."

"He's on life support?"

"Yeah."

"I can come to Denver."

The offer surprised her more than his telephone call had.

"It's a long drive just to sit around and wait," she said, instead of giving him the outright refusal she knew she should.

"I don't mind."

"You don't know how much your offer means to me," she said. "That's enough—just knowing you'd come if I wanted you to."

"Do you?"

"Want you to come?" She sighed. Honesty forced her to admit she wanted him to, and she added, "Yes. No! I understand that doesn't make any sense."

"More than you think." A pause followed. "Tell you what. Give me a call in a couple of hours. Or at least call me before you leave Denver. We can decide what to do then. I'm just worried about you. And I don't want you on the road driving a hundred plus miles on no sleep when you're upset. I could meet you at Empire. That way, you won't have to drive over Berthoud pass by yourself."

"I'll be okay."

"Or you could get a motel room and get some sleep before you head home."

"No. I want to come home. I imagine I'll be on my way in three or four hours."

"Promise me you'll call me before you leave. Do you have the telephone numbers?"

She didn't, so he gave them to her, one for the house and one for his office.

"Anything you want, Lexi. Anything. I'm here for you. You call me."

"I will," she promised, then remembered a promise she had made to Señora Padilla. "Chane?"

"Yeah."

"There is one thing."

"Name it."

"It's raining down here, and if this storm does its usual, it's raining at home, too."

"It is," he confirmed.

"I was supposed to get Señora Padilla today. She's been staying in a little tent trailer that some guy rented her. It's back behind the summer cottages just before you come into town. You know where I mean?"

"The road behind Helen's Grocery."

"Yeah."

"I'll take care of it, Lexi. She'll be fine."

"Thanks."

"If you need anything else, you let me know."

"Anything?" Her voice didn't quite tease, but she was filled with sensual memories of his loving the other night.

His chuckle came over the line. "That, too, Lexi. Most especially that."

"I'll call you before I leave," she told him, and hung up the telephone. *Anything.* That single word sang through her mind in the cadence of Chane's deep voice.

His call revealed one more layer of him. Lexi found him increasingly complex. At odd times during the night, the memory of his kiss and his lovemaking surfaced. Equally alluring were his strength and his enveloping empathy.

Friend or lover?

It wasn't a choice she wanted to make.

And the man had promised her anything. *Anything.* No one had ever offered her *anything* before. Not once in her whole life.

Chapter 11

Anything. His own words echoed through his mind as Chane hung up the telephone after talking to Lexi. With a muttered curse, he surged to his feet. He had given his word, and he'd live by that. But damn, he hadn't anticipated *anything* would include Señora Padilla. If anyone held the key to his own Pandora's box, she did.

The likelihood she was in any way connected with Tessa was slim. So slim as to be a near impossibility. And even if she was, she wasn't likely to have any conclusive proof that Tessa was hers. Chane caught the inside of his cheek between his teeth, looking for the flaws in his reasoning that would invalidate his gut reaction. More than one person in town had commented how much his daughter looked like Rose. He'd just have to make sure the señora thought so, too.

Presuming he took her home. He could leave her off at a motel. That's what he'd do, he decided. Likelihood and gut instinct weren't the same thing, and his instinct was to keep the good señora as far away from his daughter as he could.

Except that he had promised Lexi *anything.* He had an equally strong gut reaction that Lexi seldom asked favors, large or small, of anyone.

The trust between them was new, fragile. To ignore her request would breach that. He'd promised. And he was a man who kept his promises.

He stared outside at the mist that hung low over the lake, reminded of the photograph in Lexi's house. He'd recognized the ghosts within those images, so different from the photographs that had won her a Pulitzer prize. One of those would haunt him forever—a picture of a naked child not much more than two on a pile of garbage. The image was so sharp a fly on the baby's cheek was in focus. Dark, bright eyes framed by long lashes stared at him from the photograph—eyes too much like Tessa's.

He hated not knowing why he couldn't find the adoption decree. He still figured Ellen Belsen would know, had to know. She had been Rose's best friend, and she had been involved in the adoption. If she didn't know where to find the papers, no one would. If sheer will could make the phone ring, Ellen would have called hours ago.

She hadn't been at the day-care center when he took Tessa there, and one of her helpers told him Ellen wasn't expected until much later in the day. That information surprised Chane since he thought Ellen had been shorthanded—at least that was the reason he'd been given for Lexi being there yesterday. He had called Ellen at home, but no one had answered. Not even the answering machine.

Since he had to go out that way to find Señora Padilla, he'd stop by Ellen's.

Chane locked his office and headed for his truck. The rain that had threatened all morning fell in a fine mist, soaking the ground. On afternoons like this, he liked to build a fire, make a big bowl of popcorn, and put on a movie. Old Clint Eastwood movies were the best, where right was right—always—and where the bad guys always paid the price for their evil deeds.

Even better would be to spend the afternoon making love with Lexi. Arousal accompanied the thought. They had passion and hunger enough to burn each other alive. Even kissing her, just kissing her, felt wonderful. The shape of her mouth fascinated him, and its texture and contour required as much study and examination as the rock face of a cliff he was planning to climb.

"You've lost it, Callahan," he muttered to himself. How he could be this aroused when he had sixteen other things on his mind baffled him. Thinking about sex hadn't been this uncomfortable or all-consuming since he was a teenager. "Get a grip."

He glanced at the clock on the dash of his truck. He and Lexi hadn't set a time when she would call, but he doubted he'd hear from her for a couple of hours yet. Even knowing the answering machine was on, he didn't want to miss her call.

The road to Ellen's house was beyond the summer cottages, some little more than canvas tents or camper trailers, that lined the highway. The lots were small, and Chane supposed they represented escape from the city for the folks who owned them, but their proximity one to another didn't appeal to him. Most of the units had been abandoned for the season. With snow on the way, only the very hardy would be sticking around. No wonder Lexi was worried about the señora.

He drove past the seasonal cabins, toward the lake front properties that were a lot more expensive.

Ellen's house, a massive A-frame, took advantage of the view. On the opposite shore of Shadow Mountain Lake, Chane could see a dull glint off the windows of Lexi's house. In between, the lake stretched, gray and misty. He pulled into the circle drive in front of Ellen's house and parked. There was no sign of activity. He'd be surprised if anyone was home, but he got out of the truck anyway.

Turning up the collar of his denim jacket against the fine drizzle, he climbed the flagstone steps and approached the front door. Wall-size windows faced the lake, their bronzed surfacing casting back his own reflection. An ornate brass plate surrounded the doorbell. The chimes echoed through the deserted entryway. Around him, the air was quiet except for the sound of the softly falling rain and the occasional forlorn call of a crow.

Chane peered through the sidelight, thinking he heard the patter of approaching footsteps. No one came to the door.

His attorney's advice not to advertise his business surfaced as he walked across the front porch to the side of the house. Chane agreed, except talking to Ellen was no advertisement. He just wanted to know what Ellen knew. Where the devil was the woman?

Chane went around to the back of the house. The yard there looked as deserted as the front of the house. Peeking in the garage window, he saw one of the cars parked inside.

A big deck stretched from the back of the house, strewn with trucks and balls and a couple of tricycles. At the patio doors, a fluffy tabby cat stood on the other side of the glass and watched him with unblinking intensity.

Obviously no one was home.

Chane slogged back through the mist to his truck and found it blocked in the driveway by a sheriff's car. Inside was a deputy, one of his oldest friends. Hank Warner. He got out of the vehicle, zipping up his uniform jacket.

"So, Callahan, you're the prowler one of the neighbors reported. I wondered when I saw it was your truck." Hank jammed his hands in the pockets of his jacket as he approached. "Haven't seen you in a couple of weeks. How've you been?"

"Busy," Chane answered. "It will be cold enough soon for some serious ice fishing."

"I hope." Hank turned with Chane to face the lake. "I imagine it will still be December before she's frozen solid enough to go out on."

"Yeah."

"Looking for Ellen?"

"Yeah."

"The call I got from one of the neighbors indicated she wasn't home."

Chane noted the trees shielded the house from the neighbors on both sides. "You must have been in the neighborhood if the call just came in."

"That's the way it works. Get a call like this one, and you're two minutes out. Get a call where some slob really needs help, and you can't get there for fifteen or twenty minutes."

Hank surveyed the ground on either side of the house much

as Chane had. "Guess I better earn my keep and take a look around."

Chane followed Hank back around the house, curious. The only houses with much visibility to this one were across the lake. Had the call really come from a neighbor, or had someone inside Ellen's house made the call? Chane didn't question his instincts or his suspicions.

"How's that little charmer of yours?" Hank asked.

"Tessa's growing like a weed."

While Hank made a check of the yard and garage, he and Chane caught up on the news of their families. Chane wasn't fooled by the casual conversation and knew if anything was amiss, Hank would see it. While Chane had been off in the Marines, Hank had been a Ranger. They arrived home within six months of one another, and their friendship had taken up about where it had left off when they were still teenagers.

Hank flashed his light inside one of the windows of the house as they walked back around. "I see you've got a flier posted for an alpine course next month. Got any takers yet?"

"A couple. I've been saving room for you."

Hank chuckled and Chane joined him. Hank's survival skills were equal to his own.

He glanced at his watch. "I might as well call dispatch back and let them know everything is secure."

Chane glanced back at the house, unable to shake the feeling something wasn't quite right. His instincts focused on some incongruency just beyond his recognition.

"Later," Hank said.

"Sure thing." Chane climbed into his truck and started the engine. He followed Hank out of the driveway, went down to the end of the road. Hank disappeared around a bend, and Chane slowed his truck, then pulled off to the side of the road.

Something about that whole phone call to the sheriff didn't fit—and Chane trusted his gut instinct that Ellen had put in the call. She was home, he'd bet on it.

Turning around, he headed slowly back toward Ellen's house. Irritated that Ellen seemed to be avoiding him and irritated at his own vivid imagination about her reasons, he came to a stop at the bottom of her driveway. The house looked just as deserted as before.

Then, the front door opened. Ellen hurried across the entryway to the garage and went inside. A moment later, she raised the garage door.

Chane drove the few feet farther to the driveway just as Ellen backed the car out of the garage. When she caught sight of his truck in the rearview mirror, she stepped on the brakes, their light casting a red glow.

Chane got out of the truck and strolled up to the car. She stretched her fingers from around the steering wheel, then met his gaze with a smile brittle as hard candy.

Rolling down the window, she said, "Chane, hi."

The forced warmth in her voice didn't fit.

"I was hoping to talk to you this afternoon," he said.

"Gee, I—" She glanced at her watch. "I'm on my way to—"

"This isn't that big a deal," Chane said. "Ten minutes, Ellen. All I want is for you to tell me what you remember about Tessa's adoption."

"Chane—"

The sound of another car approaching caught his attention and Ellen's. Glancing back to the road, Chane saw that Hank Warner had returned.

"I just remembered something," he said by way of greeting when he got out of the car. "Hey, Ellen, you're here after all. Looked like the place was deserted when Chane and I were here before."

"You were here?" she asked.

Hank nodded, catching Chane's eye. "Everything okay?"

"Fine," she answered, her forced smile back. "You need anything from me, Hank?"

"Nope. I just came back to ask Chane something."

"Well, then, I'll leave you two alone. I've got an appointment in town and I've gotta run." She wiggled her fingers and drove out the opposite side of the circle driveway.

Chane watched her go. If the woman wanted to placate him,

she'd tell him what had happened. Even if she lied. But all this evasiveness . . . he didn't understand.

Hank strolled over to Chane. "I was beginning to think I'd missed you," he said. "Remember that group of Explorer Boy Scouts I told you about? They still want to spend a weekend up here before the weather gets too bad."

Chane forced himself to concentrate on what Hank was saying, all the while pondering how to make Ellen talk to him when she obviously didn't want to.

In response to Hank's request, Chane promised he'd help set up a ropes challenge course for the Boy Scouts and participate in a campout they had planned for early November. By the time Hank climbed back into his car, Chane figured Ellen was long gone.

He headed back toward the summer cottages and began looking for the tent trailer Lexi had described. He was almost to the highway when he found Señora Padilla. Beneath a lean-to that offered meager protection, she was bent over something, but darned if he could figure out what she was doing.

Behind her stood the tent trailer, its dark green canvas streaked where the rain slid down the sides. Beyond was an outhouse with a quarter moon cut out of the door.

Chane assessed the cold weather, the unsuitability of her accommodations, especially assuming she was used to a tropical climate, and wondered why she was staying here. She didn't even look up when he got out of his truck and the door slammed behind him. A picnic table sat under the lean-to. Closer inspection revealed she was leaning over a hibachi, coaxing heat from a couple of charcoal briquettes by blowing softly on them.

"Hola, señora," he said, exhausting almost his entire vocabulary of Spanish.

She looked up and smiled at him. *"Hola, Señor Callahan."*

A volley of Spanish followed. Chane didn't understand a bit of it. She waved at the hibachi and the gray sky dripping rain and the tent trailer behind her. Judging from the tone of her voice, she was cold, and she was disgusted with the day and the weather. He heard Lexi's name a couple of times. And each time he tried to interrupt to tell the señora he couldn't understand her, she rushed on with another torrent of Spanish. Chane could have sworn Lexi told him the lady spoke English. The señora hadn't given him any indication that was true. She finally ran out of things to say and tipped her head back to meet his gaze. He looked down close to a foot and a half to meet her eyes.

"Señora, do you speak English?"

"*Sí.*"

"Lexi sent me."

Señora Padilla smiled, the wrinkles around her eyes nearly hiding them. "Alexandra. Yes."

"She was called away unexpectedly, and she asked me to come check on you."

The señora nodded. "I am fine."

"You look cold." Chane glanced around the clearing. The tent trailer might be a fine summer retreat for a few days at a time. Not this time of year. Not with the first snowstorm of the season on the way. "Why are you living here?"

She thought a moment, clearly trying to make sure she understood his questions. "I made an agreement and paid money." She smiled suddenly and held up a finger. "Rent. I rent this cottage."

A tent sure as hell wasn't a cottage. "Why aren't you staying with Lexi?"

"She did not invite me to."

That struck Chane as odd. Though he'd never asked, he had presumed they had known one another when Lexi lived in Costa Léon.

He waved a hand toward the hibachi. "It's a little cold for a barbecue."

"Bar be que?"

"Cookout," he explained. "Don't you have a stove?"

She pointed at the hibachi. "Stove."

"I don't suppose you have any heat, either."

"I am very warm, Señor Callahan," she said.

He recognized her statement for the blatant lie it was. She was shivering.

"I will brew coffee for us," she told him.

Chane took another look at the smoldering charcoal and the

pot of ice cold water next to it. They could wait all night and that water still wouldn't be warm enough to make coffee. Without asking her permission, he strode to the camper, opened the door, and peered inside.

The gloomy interior was laid out as he had expected. Double-bed-size bunks on both wings. A camp table and benches in the center. A canvas satchel and an old-fashioned suitcase were on one bed, and a couple of blankets were neatly folded on the other one. A small sauce pan, a chipped earthenware mug, and a plate occupied the middle of the table. Next to the door, a box held a few cans of food. He stepped back out and let the door, held onto the canvas by Velcro strips, close. No heat, inadequate blankets to stay warm, and a hibachi to cook on. He shook his head with disgust at the thoughtlessness of the person who'd rented her the camper.

Sympathy he hadn't wanted to feel for the señora surfaced.

"You can't stay here," he said, his voice a good deal more gentle than he felt. "It's going to snow and be very cold."

"I am not cold." The denial didn't keep her from rubbing her hands up and down her arms.

"And tonight it's going to be even colder. You can't stay here. You'll freeze."

Maternal style, she patted his hand and smiled. "You are worried for me, no? There is no need. The rain will pass. Tomorrow the sun will shine. I will be fine."

Chane's gaze encompassed the sky above him. She was right. Tomorrow the sun would shine. Just now, the temperature had dropped enough to make the rain gradually turn to snow. The first giant snowflakes floated to the ground as if in response to his prediction. The señora's frown returned for a moment as she focused on the falling snow as though she had never before seen it.

With her dawning recognition came a brilliant smile that lit her face.

"Está nevando." Her voice held all the wonder of a child. She turned to him, her eyes dancing and her smile encompassing her face. "I have never seen this. *Está nevando."* She stepped out from under the shelter and held her hands out, a surprising

giggle of delight bubbling from her when the first flake hit her hand.

Chane rubbed the back of his neck, even as he returned her smile. Her laughter reminded him of Tessa's delight in snow. Damn, but he didn't want to like the señora. And he did.

"Get your things," he said. "And I'll take you to town. We'll figure something out."

"I will go to Alexandra's. When she returns—"

"I don't know for sure when she'll be back," Chane said, finding something new to worry about. If Lexi drove home tonight, she'd have a snowstorm to cope with coming over Berthoud Pass. He followed the señora to the entry of the tent trailer. "She went to Denver."

"A long trip. It took me some hours to get here from there." The señora went inside and returned a moment later, thrusting the satchel and small suitcase into Chane's hands. He put them inside the cab, then helped her up.

Once they were on their way, she asked, "When did Alexandra go to Denver?"

"Last night."

The señora murmured a response he didn't understand, then asked, "This trip. It was sudden, no?"

"Yes. A friend of hers, Joe Robertson, was shot. She's gone to the hospital to see him."

"Señor Robertson! Oh, no!"

Another person who knew the exalted Joe Robertson. Great, Chane thought with a trace of irritation.

The señora touched his arm. "Shot, you say?

Chane nodded curtly. "With a gun."

"Balazo. Por Dios. The American doctors and American hospitals, they are good. He will be O.K., no?"

Chane briefly met her gaze, registered the concern there, then gently shook his head. "No. I spoke with Lexi. She told me the doctors don't think he's going to live."

The señora murmured something else in Spanish, her tone distraught.

"Is Robertson your friend?"

She shook her head. "I have talked to him once only. He gave me the money to travel to here."

"I don't understand."

"In San Pedro, when I was looking for my Estella. I talked to many people. To all the adoption agencies. A man at one of them told me Alexandra could help me, but he didn't know how to contact her. He told me that Señor Robertson is a good man who would help, and he gave me Señor Robertson's address in Los Angeles. So, when I arrived in Los Angeles, I talked to him. In the beginning, he was reluctant to give me Alexandra's address. He told me he thought my search was . . . How do you say it? . . . futile. He does not believe I will find my granddaughter."

A grandmother who loved a grandchild. Just as it should be, Chane thought.

Chane's own mother had loved Tessa, but she had died shortly before Tessa's first birthday. Rose's parents hadn't expressed any interest in Tessa after Rose died, which surprised him. They blamed him for Rose's death, and as her dad had bluntly put it, the child was Rose's by adoption, not by blood. Tessa Callahan was no concern of theirs. She was Chane's problem, which suited him just fine. His baby deserved a grandmother who loved her the way Señora Padilla loved her granddaughter.

As a boy he had explored the Never Summer Range with his grandfather and eaten cinnamon pie his grandmother had made especially for him. Chane regretted Tessa wouldn't know those same joys. She needed a grandmother.

He spared the señora a glance.

Just not this woman. Especially not this woman.

Chapter 12

"Were you and Joe close?" Mrs. Robertson asked Lexi.

Lexi turned from the window where raindrops spattered against the glass.

"Not in the usual sense. When you work together under the kind of conditions we did, there's an immediacy, an intimacy that develops almost at once." Lexi paused, searching for the right words. "After you move to the next assignment, it usually goes away."

"So why are you keeping vigil over my son?"

"He saved my life," Lexi replied simply. "I owe him at least this."

A smile briefly lit Mrs. Robertson's face. "That's good for a mother to hear. I love my son, but I know he has a reputation for being . . . difficult." She stared at her hands a moment as she twisted her wedding ring round and round on her finger. "We've decided to take him off life support."

Lexi sat down next to her. "I can imagine how difficult that decision was."

"Yes. Well."

Lexi touched her hand. "It's the right thing. Joe wouldn't want this."

"We've asked for a priest to come for Last Rites. And we've decided to donate his organs."

A lump grew and stuck in Lexi's throat. "That's generous. I think . . . Joe would think so, too."

Mrs. Robertson afforded a small smile. "Joe's an atheist, you know. So, he probably wouldn't want Last Rites."

Lexi remembered Joe's surprising compassion the last time she had seen him. "If it's what you need, I think he'll understand."

The rest of the day passed at a lethargic pace. The priest came and performed the simple ceremony. Nurses and doctors spoke at length with Mr. and Mrs. Robertson, explaining they might have a long number of hours before they took him off life support. Tissue and blood had to be cross-matched, and donor recipients had to be contacted.

Lexi found all the details and conferences more wearing and tiring than it had been to sit with Joe through the night. Joe's parents urged her to go home.

"There's nothing more you can do," Mr. Robertson told her. "You've been a good friend to stay this long."

Lexi didn't know what to say. Leave, though? She wasn't sure she could do that, either. She turned down their invitation to accompany them for dinner, sensing they needed time together to absorb all that had happened. The way they spoke, Lexi knew they didn't expect her to still be there when they returned.

After they left, she wandered back into Joe's cubicle and stared down at him. Ah, Joe, she thought. How can it end like this?

It's okay because you're gonna forgive me.

"I do," she whispered. She squeezed his hand and turned blindly from the cubicle.

She made her way to the lobby of the hospital, then had to rummage through her purse to find her car keys. Outside she could see rain still fell in a steady drizzle, the kind of rain that could mean snow in the mountains. A perfect end for a perfect day, she thought wearily.

She looked up to see the FBI agent approach.

"How is Robertson?" he asked.

"You can go full steam ahead on your murder investigation," she replied.

"He's dead?"

There was no curiosity in the man's question, only a certain cold-blooded calculation. In a way, he sounded like Joe when he was tying together the pieces of a story.

"For all practical purposes." She pulled her keys out of her purse. "Tell me again why the FBI is interested in this."

"Since Mr. Robertson is a man of some celebrity, we're interested."

She recognized stonewalling when she saw it. "Was this or wasn't it a drive-by shooting?"

"We don't know yet. But I do have some questions I wanted to ask you."

Lexi sighed. "Like what?"

"What was he working on?"

What I wouldn't give to know, she thought. "We already talked about that, Mr. . . . ."

"Burke," he supplied. "Darren Burke."

"Mr. Burke. I told you. Call Joe's managing editor, Mike Lanatowski. He can tell you. I can't."

"Or won't."

Lexi raised her chin and leveled the man a disdainful stare. "What do you mean?"

"You worked with him. We have cause to think you were working with him on a story."

She met Burke's gaze and managed a smile. "I don't know who your sources are, Mr. Burke. Anyone can tell you I haven't worked in a year—"

"Which is also suspicious."

"I haven't had more than a few telephone conversations with Joe in all those months," she continued, ignoring his accusation. The man's manners hadn't improved any since their last visit. "I can't be more plain. I don't know anything." She settled the strap of her purse over her shoulder. "Now. I'm tired. I'm hungry. Ask me something I know the answer to, and I'll tell you if I can."

He met her gaze without saying anything.

Lexi shrugged. "This is stupid, Mr. Burke. You don't want to tip your hand by telling me why you think this wasn't a simple drive-by shooting. I can't be more specific until I know what you're getting at. So . . . I'm leaving."

"I don't recommend that, Ms. Monroe."

"Unless you're ready to charge me with a crime and arrest me, Mr. Burke, you can't stop me." She stepped around him. "Please excuse me."

She marched through the double doors. The FBI agent needed to call Mike Lanatowski. Then he'd know the same thing she did. That for once in his life, Joe had been doing what he was told. And look where it got him.

Outside, she sidestepped to avoid a man rushing toward the building, his head down. He jostled her as he came past her, and Lexi had a fleeting impression of familiarity.

"Lexi. Lexi Monroe," someone called.

She turned toward the voice and saw Joe's father striding toward her. When he reached her, he snapped open an umbrella, protecting them both from the rain.

"My wife told me she had encouraged you to go home," he said.

Lexi nodded. "I wish there was something more I could do."

"You've done all a friend could do," he assured her. "Where's your car parked?"

Lexi motioned toward the parking lot.

"I appreciate your coming," he said.

Lexi stole a glance at him, seeing Joe in his father—in the narrow face and the sharp hazel eyes.

He glanced down and met her gaze. "At a time like this, it's good to know he had a friend."

Not knowing what to say, and feeling a bit like a fraud because she hadn't considered Joe a friend, she simply nodded. They walked the rest of the way to her car without saying anything further, the patter of rain on the umbrella and the splashing sounds of their footsteps on the pavement echoing around them.

At the car, Joe's father waited while Lexi unlocked the door, then thanked her again as she got into the car. She started the engine, and he didn't walk away until she pulled away from the parking spot. At the street, she stopped, waiting for traffic to pass, noticing that Darren Burke stood in front of the hospital with another man.

She turned onto the street, aware he watched her. If she was lucky, she wouldn't be talking to him again. The routine tasks of filling her car with gas and getting something quick to eat occupied her attention, failing to keep at bay an overwhelming realization. Joe Robertson, nemesis . . . and friend, was dead.

Chane had read about birth mothers changing their minds and setting out to find their child. He had heard about natural fathers who sued for custody, feeling their rights had been violated. He even remembered a case where grandparents had come forward, seeking the reversal of an adoption. The stuff of nightmares, each one a variation on that theme. In Chane's nightmares, the stranger laying claim to his daughter had never been a benevolent-looking grandmother with soul-deep, sorrowful eyes.

Drop the woman off at a motel. You can afford it. Let her fend for herself.

"You are a good man, señor," the señora said.

Chane flushed. A good man wouldn't be plotting how to dump a little old lady whose determination had led her to a strange country. He would have done no less if he had been in her shoes.

"Señor Robertson is not such a good man, I think," she continued. "It is true he gave me money to come here, but I believe it was for his own purpose. Not an act of generosity."

Chane grunted. That sounded just like the bastard he had known.

"Alexandra has not said," the señora continued, "but I believe she thinks you are a good man."

"I hope so." Chane bit back a silent curse. He wasn't a good man, simply one who saw the world in black and white, who knew his duty and did it. He couldn't leave this woman in the middle of a snowstorm without adequate shelter. Simple.

"*Ya lo se!*" she said, another of those delighted smiles erasing the worry from her face.

"Pardon?"

"Alexandra explained to me you are merely friends," the señora explained, waving her hands expressively. "I watched her. I watch you. I see more than friends. Much more. *Querencia.*" She frowned. "The word . . . Not so much as love, but a caring." She glanced at Chane and snapped her fingers. "Fondness. Yes, that is what I see in Alexandra when she speaks of you."

Fondness, huh, Chane thought. He would bet the señora's assessment would surprise Lexi.

"I hear the same in your voice," the señora added.

"We're not—" Memories of holding Lexi intimately made him break off the sentence. "We're . . ." To his irritation, the señora laughed, and he felt his neck heat. Hell, he thought. How could he promise Lexi *anything,* then be embarrassed when someone else hinted they were lovers?

"When did you last see Robertson?" Chane asked, telling himself he really wanted to know, that he was not asking to change the subject.

"Before I came here. In Los Angeles. Señor Robertson was in a hurry the day we spoke. A very busy man he is. He had no time for an old woman." She reached across the width of the truck to pat Chane's arm. "I am a stranger to you, but you've been very kind. *Gracias.*"

"You're welcome." Dammit all to hell, Chane thought. Kind. Good. Thoughtful, courteous, clean, reverent, and helpful to little old ladies. Great for a Boy Scout, but he didn't want to be cast in this light. He wanted to drop her off, and he didn't want to feel responsible for making sure she was okay until Lexi returned.

He intended to take her to a hotel. He really did. He'd grown

up here, but he'd never before paid that much attention to them.
Most closed for the winter—and those that had remained open
were filled with hunters. The good señora's cheerfulness and
acceptance at every NO VACANCY sign fueled his irritation and
his frustration. She was so damn nice about his trying to dump
her, suggesting that he could leave her at the gas station or the
library or the café until Lexi could come get her. Every suggestion made him feel worse.

The snow fell harder. Chane hadn't wanted to take the señora
home, didn't plan to take her home. That's where they ended
up anyway. When push came to shove, he couldn't just leave
her hanging around someplace until Lexi got back. A single
refrain played through his head—he had promised Lexi *anything*.

Chane retrieved Señora Padilla's satchel and suitcase from
the truck, helped her get out, and led her onto the back porch
and into the kitchen. The house was quiet. Kit hadn't arrived
home from school yet, and Tessa was at the day-care center.

Chane showed the señora to the guest bedroom, setting her
satchel on the bed and her suitcase on the floor next to it.
Figuring she felt cold since she was shivering, he made a pot
of coffee. He waited until she sat down at the kitchen table
and wrapped her hands around the warm mug before he said,
"You can stay here until Lexi gets back."

"Alexandra. Yes."

"I think she'll be home by tomorrow at the latest."

"You are worried for her," the señora stated.

Chane nodded, and she smiled as though satisfied somehow.

"Since you have given me the hospitality of your home, I
will cook you dinner," she said.

"That's not necessary. Really."

"Are you a good cook, señor?"

Her serious question broke through his reserve and worry,
and he laughed. He'd had dozens of conversations with Kit
about his very lack of cooking ability. "You'll have to ask my
brother."

"And how old is he?"

"Sixteen."

The señora returned his smile. "Ah. The age where a boy is hollow. He eats much, no?"

"Yes." Chane sat down across from her. Black and white issues aside, he liked Señora Padilla. "Your offer to cook dinner is nice. Thank you."

"De nada," she said.

"You didn't know Lexi before you came here?"

"No. And she was not pleased at first."

"Why not?"

The señora stared into her coffee cup a moment. "This I do not know. Señor Robertson, perhaps. He did not tell her he had sent me." She smiled briefly. "You know how a surprise, one that you do not want, feels."

"Yes."

"Señor Robertson told me she would know about *Las Hermanas de la Esperanza.* Only—"

"That name," Chane interrupted. *"Las Her ..."*

"Las Hermanas, the sisters of—"

"Hope?" Chane finished, a new flood of dread washing over him.

The señora nodded. "I have the papers. They sold away my Estella."

"I don't understand," Chane said. "Sold. Please explain."

"The family that adopted her. They paid a large sum of money."

"Do you know the name of the family who adopted her?" Never in his life had he forced more casualness into his voice, as though nothing more than idle curiosity drove his question.

She shook her head. "This I do not know. I must keep looking, though. I must discover what happened to my precious Estella." The señora took a sip of her coffee and met his gaze. "We can do nothing about these things today. Enough. We will talk of other things. You have a brother. And you have a child."

Chane followed the señora's glance to Tessa's high chair. "Yes. A daughter. Her name is Tessa."

The señora smiled. "I hear in your voice a father's pride. Where is your daughter?"

"While I work, she stays at a day-care center."

"You have pictures, no?"

He wanted to say that he didn't. There was no point in prolonging the inevitable, so he stood up. The señora trailed after him into the living room. The mantle was covered with photographs, not because he wanted them, however. The memories they evoked were better avoided. But he'd been told by a psychologist that Kit and Tessa needed the connection to family, so Chane kept the photographs out for them.

Chane took down a picture of Rose with Tessa and handed it to the señora. His daughter and wife were entranced with one another, oblivious to the camera. They were smiling at each other, their shared dark eyes alight with laughter and joy.

The señora stared at the photograph a long time before handing it back to him. "Your child looks like her mother, no? My Estella looked like my Maria Antoñia. Your wife, what happened to her?"

"Rose was killed in a car accident," Chane replied, breathing a sigh of relief at the señora's conclusion, feeling annoyed that the deception bothered him.

The señora's eyes softened even more. "I feel so much for you. Inside. You are kind because you understand how precious is this life."

He turned away from her. He had lied by omission, and he wasn't kind. But then, he'd lie to St. Peter himself to protect Tessa, to keep her with him. The señora thought his daughter looked like her mother. And she had. Plenty of other people had said so, as well. Even so, the knot in his stomach didn't feel like relief.

"Hey, bro, what are you doing home?" Kit called from the kitchen. An instant later the door slammed, and Chane heard the refrigerator door open. Continuing to shout, Kit added, "Time to get out the ski wax. It's snow time in the Rockies."

"I'm in the living room," Chane called.

Kit appeared in the doorway a moment later, a glass of milk in one hand and a peanut butter sandwich in the other. Chane made the introductions, saying the señora would be spending the night.

Then he made his escape, saying he had to get Tessa. Kit said he'd help the señora cook, since she seemed determined to do that. Chane didn't want to like the woman, but he did. He didn't want to take Tessa home, and he didn't want the señora in his house. No matter how much he liked her. And he was the damn fool who had brought her there. All because he had made a promise.

Lexi and the señora knew about the Sisters of Hope. Chane wished he had known that last night when he'd talked to Lexi. He would have asked her better questions. He wanted to know everything he could about that organization, and he wanted that information yesterday.

"Of all the damn rotten luck," George Moody said, watching Lexi Monroe's car weave through Denver's traffic. "We nearly had her." As soon as she had left the parking lot at the hospital, they got into their own vehicle, following her at a discreet distance.

"We'll have her again," Darren Burke replied. At a stoplight he braked the truck, three vehicles behind Lexi's red Toyota. "I've been thinking."

"You think too much."

"Maybe," he agreed, "but it's kept your butt out of a sling. I think your plan to abduct her is too risky—too many things can go wrong. Why not just shoot her and be done with it?" The light changed color, and he put the truck into gear, signaling for a turn when he saw the direction she was headed.

Moody stared at him. "Simple. She needs to know what she's done. She needs to know she's paying me back."

"After she's dead, what's it going to matter?"

Moody laughed. "That is one way of looking at it." He turned in his seat to face Burke. "Have you ever looked into a person's eyes as you're killing them?"

Burke glanced from the traffic to Moody, feeling an unwanted chill crawl across his scalp. "No."

"I have." He faced forward again, then nodded as if having come to a conclusion. "A deal. If you can kill her before she reaches her home, then we'll do it your way. A simple shooting or an accident—whatever you want."

"And if I don't succeed?"

Moody smiled. "We'll do it my way."

Chapter 13

Lexi left Denver, her thoughts as gray as the rain-laden sky. So many unanswered questions with Joe. She couldn't decide if he had been playing one of his elaborate games with her or if he had really been on to something with El Ladron.

She found herself thinking about their last conversation. Why would he have promised to send her a digitizer if he hadn't been working on something? Or maybe it was one more ploy.

Just suppose, she thought, Joe really had a lead on El Ladron. What then? And Joe had said he was being cautious. Of course, he wouldn't want Lanatowski to know what he was doing. That would account for his evasiveness.

She pondered as she drove up Interstate 70 past Idaho Springs. Less than fifteen minutes later, she turned off the interstate onto US 40 that led her over Berthoud Pass. It wasn't until after she was beyond Empire that she remembered she was supposed to have called Chane.

Too late now, she thought. She'd call him when she got home. Chane had proven to be surprisingly good company, and having him with her on this last stretch home would have been welcome. She regretted she had forgotten to call him.

The rain continued to fall at a steady pace. The gloom became ever more dark, and Lexi switched on her headlights. She was accustomed to the traffic over the pass being heavy. Summertime visitors on their way to Rocky Mountain National Park, wintertime skiers headed for Mary Jane or Winter Park. This evening, the road was nearly deserted. She glanced in the rearview mirror. Tonight, the only travelers across Berthoud Pass were herself and one other lone vehicle a half mile behind her.

The radio station she had been listening to faded into static interference. She turned off the radio, wishing for the company it provided, knowing from experience she wouldn't have decent reception until she was closer to Winter Park.

A short distance outside of Empire, the rain turned to snow as Lexi had anticipated. As she followed the road steadily up the mountain, the snow began to stick to the road and to the windshield.

Lexi turned the wipers up a notch and turned on the defroster. Her little car slowed as the incline became steeper, and she down-shifted. The oncoming snow beat against the windshield in a mesmerizing pattern. Visibility reduced to yards in front of her car. Her headlights speared through the darkness. Snow and an enveloping darkness demanded her attention.

She rounded a bend. Caught within the beam of her headlights stood three deer, as if frozen in place. Lexi hit the brake. Instead of slowing down, her car slid. She took her foot off the brake. At the last moment, the deer bounded to safety and disappeared into the snowy night. Cautiously, she put her foot back on the accelerator, her heart pounding. She had never come so close to hitting a deer though she had seen them along the highway many times.

The car behind her came closer, but made no move to pass as she slowly climbed the winding road. Lexi envied the car behind her. He had a set of tracks to follow. She had to watch for the reflective signal posts that marked the road's passage. At the summit, she gave a sigh of relief. Home was downhill from here, literally. Even with the snow, it shouldn't take her more than another hour to get home.

Suddenly, the other car appeared right behind her, its bright headlights catching in the mirror and momentarily blinding her.

Lexi moved to the outside of the narrow lane. To pick up that kind of speed, the driver either wasn't familiar with the pass or was having trouble with the slick highway. Whatever his problem, she didn't like him riding her rear bumper.

She slowed to let the car pass. It didn't move around her, though, but rode directly behind her as she navigated the narrow hairpin turn, this one on the inside of the steep mountain.

On the straightaway, visibility improved, and the snow didn't seem to be falling quite so fast. Lexi sped up, but the car stayed right with her. She didn't want to play bumper car on the slick pass with some yo-yo this night or any other. The big vehicle weaved behind her, and she wished it would pass her. She slowed even more, giving the other driver all the encouragement needed to pass her.

"What in the world?" she muttered, cursing the driver. The next hairpin curve loomed closer. She didn't see any oncoming headlights. The other car came beside her, and she thought it was going to pass. She edged over to the right of the lane and touched the brakes. Her car slid, and she took her foot off the brake, her attention divided between the car next to her and the precipice on the other side.

A loud pop startled her and echoed like thunder. Lexi's car pulled hard to the left. She kept the car on the pavement with difficulty. She cursed. Of all the times for a tire to blow, this wasn't it. Not with some maniac riding her tail and not with the edge of the mountain in front of her. Not in the middle of a blinding snowstorm.

Just when she thought things couldn't get worse, the other car bumped her. Its larger size and weight forced her off the highway into the soft muddy shoulder of the hairpin turn.

The headlights of her car glanced off the tops of trees against the steep slope below her.

Lexi slammed on the brakes and cranked the steering wheel hard to the left, toward pavement, toward safety. The other car—a big pickup with oversize tires—passed her and sped on down the mountain, leaving a trail of wide parallel tracks.

Her own car fish-tailed wildly as she fought to get it back on the road. Tires screeching and spinning, her car bounced as it left the mud. She expected the road to be slick and took her foot off the brake so the car wouldn't slide. Instead, the tires grabbed, and she careened down the highway, the car still pulling hard to the left.

She braked, fighting to keep the car inside her own lane. A hundred yards later, she brought it to a stop. Lexi rested her head against the steering wheel, breathing hard. She drove the car a few yards farther, edging as close to the side of the road and the steep dropoff as she dared.

Her hands and legs shaking, she set the hazard light on, snagged a flashlight out of the glove box, and climbed out of the car. The front left tire was flat. She walked around the car and found no other discernible damage. Not that she could see much. Mud and slush caked the undercarriage and the sides of the car, huge spatters covering even the windows. The slush showed every promise of turning into ice.

She glanced back up the road, feeling panicked as she realized just how close she had come to plunging over the side of the mountain. Just below timberline, the lodgepole pine grew in thick abundance, shrouded by the night and the streamers of clouds illuminated by her headlights. It would surely have been hours before anyone found her car, if at all.

That thought made her scalp prickle.

She rubbed her arms and for a moment wished she were the kind of woman who played the damsel-in-distress role, who could get her tire changed without getting soaked. Only, Lexi knew better. She had only herself to depend on. As always.

With a muttered curse directed at the driver who had forced her off the road, she opened the trunk of her car in search of the tire-changing kit and the spare tire. Too bad she hadn't gotten a look at the license plates. Otherwise, as soon as she got to Granby, she'd stop at the sheriff's office and file a complaint. She was tempted, anyway.

Right, she mentally scoffed at herself, visualizing the vehicle. It was a big pickup with a shell on the back. Or maybe a four-by-four. Tall, because the headlights had shown through her back window. The description fit dozens of cars. Hundreds. Undoubtedly the sheriff would want a little more to go on.

A flash of headlights from an oncoming car made her peer over the top of the trunk. Two cars, actually, that slowed as they drove past. The first was a van, and it looked to Lexi as though there were seven or eight children inside.

The second was a big, dark four-by-four, looking enough like the one that had forced her off the road that she gave it her full attention. Unlike the van, glass tinted nearly as dark as the paint hid the occupants of the truck. Both vehicles drove past. She watched the second one for long moments before returning her attention to the task of finding the tools she needed.

The sound of the cars changed somehow. Lexi scanned the road behind her, watching the lights mark the progress of one car going to the top of the mountain and another coming down. A third set of lights were at the curve where she had been forced off the road. The lights of another car coming down the mountain shone on the vehicle at the curve. The big four-by-four. It pulled onto the highway behind the other car, again headed in her direction.

For the second time in minutes, Lexi's scalp crawled. Two dark-colored cars like that one on this stretch of highway this time of night was no coincidence. Maybe a kind stranger felt contrite for forcing her off the road. Maybe. She didn't think so.

She slammed the trunk lid down and ran back to the driver's side. She flung open the door and scooted inside. A flick to the ignition and the car started. She threw it into gear and pressed the accelerator. Her car continued to pull to the left, but she urged more speed out of it, going as fast as she dared. The car in front of the four-by-four passed her on the next straightaway. In her rearview mirror, she watched the four-by-four loom closer, looking like an immense menacing shadow behind its bright headlights.

Those headlights flashed onto its bright beams. The white light illuminated the inside of her car. The glare in the rearview mirror nearly blinded her. Her hands grew slick with sweat, and she felt cold. She flipped up the rearview mirror, which brought only marginal relief from the glare.

Snow beat against the windshield. Icy trails of melting snow slid down her face and neck. She gripped the steering wheel so hard her hands hurt. Every so often her car fishtailed on the road. She tried to drive faster anyway.

Her thoughts were frantic, chaotic. Maybe the driver of the four-by-four didn't know how to drive in this kind of weather. Maybe the bright lights were simply a rude way of telling her to move it or milk it.

Maybe pigs could fly.

Two more hairpin curves and the road would straighten. Then she wouldn't have to fight quite so hard to stay on the road, presuming the tire held together a little longer. She smelled hot rubber. It was only a matter of time before the tire fell off the wheel.

She slowed as she approached the first curve. The four-by-four behind her rammed into her, and her head snapped forward.

Her last doubts vanished.

Someone was trying to kill her.

Anxious to hear from Lexi and worried he might have missed her call, Chane stopped by his office. Only one message was left on the machine. When he pressed the PLAY button, Ellen's voice, not Lexi's, filled the air. "I've got some papers for you, Chane. Rose would have wanted . . . Well, never mind about that. Anyway, the papers I have answer your questions. When you bring Tessa tomorrow to the day-care center, I'll give them to you." According to the time stamp on the machine, she had left the call about a half hour after he had talked to her in her driveway.

When he picked Tessa up from the day-care center, she was excited about the snow, chattering to him all the way home. Instead of being focused on Tessa, though, he found himself wondering how the road conditions were going over Berthoud Pass. Interspersed with that worry, he kept thinking about the señora and Tessa and his attorney's advice not to borrow trouble.

"Can we make a snowman?" Tessa asked when they got out of the truck at home. She skipped through the snow, her bright red coat a beacon of color in the falling snow, her dark eyes dancing with excitement.

"There's not enough snow yet, squirt."

"Tomorrow?" She clapped her hands together and looked up at him.

"Maybe." He scooped her up to carry her into the house.

"I like the snow, Daddy."

"I know you do," he replied, thinking again of the señora. She believed Tessa was Rose's child by blood. He wanted to keep it that way. But somewhere out there, Tessa could have grandparents who wondered what her fate had been.

"When you stick your tongue out like this." Tessa demonstrated, her face tipped toward the sky and her eyes closed. "The snow feels cold. And it tastes good." She opened her eyes. "You try it, Daddy."

He closed his eyes and obligingly stuck out his tongue. The melting snowflakes tingled. A simple pleasure. Too bad his life wasn't equally simple. He wanted to have nothing more urgent on his mind than enjoying Tessa's enthusiasm for the taste of a snowflake.

"Do you like it?" With small cold hands, she touched his cheek.

"Yep." He opened the back door and carried Tessa inside.

The first thing Chane noticed was the aroma of frying potatoes and onions, which made his mouth water. He knew the cooking had to be Señora Padilla's doing because Kit's idea of cooking went only so far as popping popcorn in the microwave.

She and Kit weren't in the kitchen or living room. Chane found them in Kit's bedroom. He was standing on his snowboard, his legs bent, and his arms extended to the side. The colorful terms Kit used to explain the sport made the señora look perplexed, and her glance traveled from Kit to the bright posters of snowboarders above his bed and back again.

"This looks very dangerous," was her only comment.

"Hi," Chane said from the doorway. He moved into the room, carrying Tessa. He felt like Daniel facing the lions, even as he silently told himself that he had nothing to fear from the diminutive Señora Padilla.

"Señora, this is my daughter, Tessa."

The señora smiled and held her arms out to Tessa. *"Me llamo Tía Ester."* As she took the child from Chane, she murmured, *"Estás muy hermosa. Ya es tan bonita como su madre."*

"I understood that," Kit said with a laugh. "Tessa is beautiful. As pretty as her mother."

"Ah," Chane responded with a smile, relieved to hear the translation. "Glad to know you've learned something in school."

Kit touched the señora's arm. "Tía Ester, this is *so* cool. I can practice my Spanish with you." He flushed, then repeated the sentence in Spanish. She beamed at him, and he grinned in return, following her into the kitchen.

Tía Ester! Chane watched them, not quite sure when or how things had gotten so out of hand. He hadn't anticipated that Kit would make a friend of the woman in something less than an hour.

Chane followed them into the kitchen. The señora raised an eyebrow when Chane got the chicken out of the refrigerator. She fussed at him, and he had the feeling he was just as glad he didn't understand what she had said. There was no mistaking her intentions, however, when she pushed him into a chair and put the daily newspaper in his hand. Kit laughed.

"I can't just sit here," Chane said.

"No?" Tía Ester said. "That was my understanding, señor. You would allow me to stay. I would cook."

"I didn't mean—"

"Then, you want I should leave?"

"No. Of course, not. I just want to help—"

"Ah," she said with sudden understanding. "I have read about this thing. In the home, a man is equal."

"Yes."

"Then you can cut onions. We must have many onions."

"Fine." Chane suspected the task to be a ploy to shut him up and keep him out of the way. The señora confirmed his suspicions when she put the freshly chopped onions in the refrigerator. Without a cover. If he didn't want onion-flavored milk in the morning, he'd have to remember to do something about that.

By the time they sat down to dinner, Chane was sure every pot he owned had been used to cook. He figured he'd be until midnight getting things cleaned up. Everything smelled and looked wonderful from the browned potatoes and homemade tortillas to the baked chicken.

"If this tastes half as good as it smells," Kit said. He took a bit of his chicken and sighed. "It's worth the mess, bro."

"Remember that after we've eaten," Chane admonished. "You're on the cleanup crew, remember?"

He agreed with Kit. The kitchen may be a disaster area, but the señora was a good cook. The baked chicken was like nothing he had ever eaten before, a combination of flavors he wouldn't have thought could come from anything in his pantry.

Delicious as the food was, Chane kept watching the clock. He expected Lexi's call hours ago. As soon as he was finished eating, he pushed away from the table and went to the window. The snow still fell, though not as hard as before. Even so, by morning several inches to a foot would be on the ground.

Unable to stand the suspense any longer, he phoned the hospital. When his call was transferred to the intensive care unit, he asked to speak with Ms. Monroe.

"She's not here," a nurse told him. "She left hours ago."

"Do you expect her back?"

"I don't think so."

He ended the connection, then dialed Lexi's house. Her answering machine came on, and he left a message that she was to call him the instant she got home. Worried that she had been caught in the storm, a couple of dozen images chased through his mind. She'd had car trouble. Worse, she'd had an accident.

He returned to the kitchen and helped his brother with the dishes. They had no more than gotten started when another attack of anxiety hit him. He headed for the back door, following his instincts. "I'm going out," he told Kit. "I'll check back with you in a while."

"Where are you going?"

"To see if Lexi Monroe made it home." He fished his keys out of his pocket and put on a fleece-lined leather coat. "You'll put Tessa to bed?"

"Sure," Kit replied. "Only who is Lexi Monroe?"

Lexi pressed on the accelerator as she swerved around the corner, praying her car would stay on the road. The big pickup behind her pulled along side again and rammed her.

Stupid things swam through her mind. That dark truck was going to have red paint all over its bumper. Her insurance rates would probably be raised when she filed the claim on this. Her mother had always told her, "Wear clean underwear in case you're run over by a truck. You wouldn't want to arrive at the hospital in dirty underwear."

Lexi slammed hard on the brakes, then pumped them to keep from sliding. The truck shot ahead of her like a cannon ball. It barreled on down the highway, tires sliding. The truck went into a spin just as it approached the next hairpin curve. The truck came to a stop just beyond Lexi's line of sight, but she could see the beam from its headlights aimed toward the curve.

She came to a complete stop just shy of the hairpin curve, figuring if she couldn't see the truck, it couldn't see her. She knew she couldn't just sit here in the middle of the road, but damned if she was going to drive down there and wait for the truck to ram her again.

As she pondered how to best handle the situation, she decided the pickup's driver didn't have much experience driving in snow. He had ridden the brake through the spin around the curve. A reflexive action, one that could be taken advantage of, if she could just figure out how.

In her rearview mirror, Lexi saw another vehicle coming down the mountain. She waited until it was close behind her before she put her car into gear.

Her car still pulled hard to the left. Somehow she had to make that be an advantage.

The truck sat in the uphill lane just beyond the next curve.

Waiting like a patient predator, its headlights cutting through the falling snow.

She inched around the turn, going no faster than she had to. The truck lurched forward. Lexi didn't speed up a bit. The truck came toward her, taking up most of her lane. The driver of the truck gave the vehicle too much gas, and the rear wheels fishtailed. It was the break Lexi had been looking for. At the last possible moment, she let her car bear left into the oncoming lane. She prayed the truck's driver didn't want a head-on collision any more than she did.

Her car swerved in front of the truck, and for an instant she thought it would broadside her. Instead, it veered, scraping against the passenger side of her car as it passed her. She watched it in her rearview mirror, wondering how long she'd have before it chased her again.

To keep from hitting the car behind Lexi, the truck swerved back into its own lane. Once again, the driver failed to compensate for the road conditions. The pickup slid into an embankment, burying the front axle in mud and slush. She couldn't be sure, but the truck looked stuck.

"Thank God," she whispered. Tears threatened and her hands shook from the adrenaline storm rushing through her. She couldn't give in to that yet. She still had a tire to change. Just as soon as she got more distance between her and that pickup.

She drove on down the highway. After negotiating the last hairpin turn, the road straightened. A half mile ahead, the highway was lit bright as a mall parking lot, complete with blue and red blinking lights. As Lexi approached, she saw a barricade across the highway and knew the pass had either been closed or the chain law was being enforced. Seconds later she passed a huge blinking sign that warned, "Chain law in effect." Closer, she could see that cars were being stopped. She steered her car into the well-lit parking lane and got out.

A state patrolman manned the gate that barred the way back up the pass. Lexi could have vouched firsthand how slick the road was. She put on her jacket, then walked around her car. The damage was as extensive as she had expected. The rear fender on the driver's side was all caved in, and the passenger side looked like a piece of red crumpled aluminum foil.

"Damn!" This was her first brand new car. Not expensive as cars went, but special to her. The damage to the body was so extensive, she suspected fixing it would be far more expensive than replacing it. How dare anyone do this to her!

She thrust her hands in her pockets and strode toward the officer.

"Evenin', ma'am," he told her as she approached.

"I'd like to file a complaint," she said.

"You mean accident report, right?"

"No, I mean a complaint." She pointed to her car. "An hour ago that car didn't have a scratch on it. Someone hit me. Deliberately."

"How can you be so sure?" he asked. "It's slick up there."

"Yeah, it is that." Then she told him what had happened.

"You're not exaggerating?"

"Of course not," she snapped, her temper fraying. "Bumping into me once might be an accident. Turning around to come back and get me again is deliberate."

"Do you have a license plate number?"

"No." She frowned, trying to remember the truck as it had passed her. "In fact, I couldn't tell you if it even had Colorado plates. The truck is big, with one of those tall bodies and oversize tires. You shouldn't have any trouble finding it. It's stuck up to its axle a couple of miles back up the pass. It'll have red paint that matches my car all over it."

"I can take a complaint. Without a license plate or better description, the chances of anything coming of this are nil."

"You don't understand," Lexi said. "The truck is stuck up there in the mud. All you have to do is go get it."

The patrolman gave her a placating smile, one that grated at her already frayed temper. "And we'll do that. Just as soon as we can."

Lexi interpreted that to mean that he didn't really believe her. And in an hour or two or ten, someone would look for the vehicle that had rammed her. Only by then, it would be gone. An exercise in futility. She filed the report anyway.

In the middle of giving the officer the information, a big Suburban filled with hunters parked next to her. Chivalrous to the core, they had her tire changed by the time she was finished talking to the patrolman. Though she didn't need chains for the balance of her trip home, they put those on her tires, as well.

Before she reached Granby, the snow had almost stopped falling, which meant the highway wasn't so slick. Lexi drove most of the miles with her attention half on the set of headlights shining in her rearview mirror. Each one was sinister. After she turned onto Highway 34 for the last leg of her journey home, the road behind her was black.

It should have been reassuring that no one followed her.

It wasn't.

Chapter 14

Lexi arrived at home, chilled and drenched in a cold sweat. Turning the car into the driveway, she pressed the remote control button on the garage door. It went up, and a welcoming light came on inside. Daisy bounded out the door, and Lexi breathed a sigh of relief.

Behind her a pair of headlights from a big vehicle appeared suddenly, blindingly bright in her rearview mirror. A truck drove into the driveway. Fear clawed up her throat with the intensity of a scream. She turned around and looked at the truck.

She had been followed.

She was so tempted to drive inside and close the door.

But then she'd be trapped. She knew it. *And they knew it.*

"No!" She didn't realize she had shouted until the sound of her own voice reverberated through her car.

She slammed the gear into reverse and floored the accelerator pedal. She veered to circle around the truck. It swerved to avoid her. Her car collided with the truck and came to a neck-jarring halt with the sound of crunching metal and shattering glass.

Lexi changed the gear to low and stepped on the gas. Her car rocked, but didn't move forward. "No. No . . . no."

She heard a car door slam. She stepped on the gas again, but her car remained locked with the truck.

An instant later, her door was wrenched open. It crashed against the hinges, letting in a blast of cold air and a familiar furious voice.

"Lexi, what the hell are you doing?" He leaned inside the car, unsnapped her seat belt, and hauled her out in one fluid motion.

She stared dumbly up at him, then at his pickup. Slow dawning recognition flowed through her. This was Chane. Not some faceless monster chasing her down an endless ribbon of highway. "Oh, God. I thought you were . . ."

Tears that had burned the back of her eyes blinded her, streaming down her face. She threw her arms around him, holding him as though he were a lifeline. Warm and solid and familiar. She inhaled deeply, absorbing his scent, then shook beneath the force of her relief. *She was safe!* Somehow, the realization was worse to bear than her fear had been.

"You thought I was what?" Chane asked.

His arms came around her, and she burrowed closer, unable to answer, all her pent-up emotion released in a flood of tears she was powerless to stem.

A barrage of impressions filled Chane as he held Lexi. She was trembling so badly she would have fallen if he hadn't held her upright. And she was cold and clammy. As though she was in shock.

"Who did you think I was?" he asked, only a trace of anger left in his voice.

She took a deep shuddering sigh, her sobs subsiding. If anything, she held him even tighter.

Chane tipped her face toward him. "Lexi?"

He watched her struggle for the composure she had so often summoned before. This time, it seemed beyond her. The two inches of snow covering the ground had just about as much color as her face. She looked beat, like a woman who needed twenty-four hours of uninterrupted sleep.

He leaned inside her car and snagged her purse. "Go on in," he told her. "I'll put your car away and be right up."

She went inside and climbed the stairs to the main level of the house, the German shepherd at her heels. Chane's attention returned to the two vehicles locked together. He couldn't have been more relieved to see that she was home when he pulled into the driveway or more shocked that she had backed up when she saw him, like a trapped animal bent on escape.

Chane's eyes narrowed.

One of the headlights on his truck was broken, and one of her taillights was shattered. Her bumper was caught under his, which a couple of good jiggles released. The whole rear fender of her car was battered. Running his fingers over the metal, he crouched to take a closer look. Her car hadn't had a dent in it when she left yesterday. Now, it looked as though something had repeatedly rammed it.

He parked her car in the basement garage. Absently Chane noticed it was spotless—painted white and well lit. Beneath the light, the damage looked even worse. Frowning, he went back outside and parked his pickup closer to the house, shutting off the engine and lights. Going back inside, he closed the garage door behind him. A couple of closed doors were at the rear of the garage. Chane opened the first and turned on the light. The laundry room, again well lit and clean. Beyond the second door, he found her darkroom. He stood at the doorway a moment, examining the equipment. On the far wall hung a photograph he recognized from her Pulitzer prize–winning magazine spread. Like everything else he had seen, the room was spotless. Chane closed the door.

He took the stairs two at a time. At the landing in front of another door, he looked back down into the garage at Lexi's battered car. *What the hell had happened to her?* He opened the door and went into the house.

Glancing at his muddy boots, he yanked them off rather than tracking across the immaculate floor. Then he peeled off his coat and hat, which he set on the kitchen counter.

Lexi stood in the middle of the kitchen, her jacket still on, her gaze unfocused. Daisy sat at her feet, and Lexi scratched the dog's ears. Chane would have bet her actions were pure reflex.

He pulled the strap of her purse off her shoulder and set it on the kitchen table.

"You were supposed to call me. I didn't want you driving alone." His voice was far more surly than he had intended, but his hands were gentle as he unzipped her jacket and pulled the sleeves down her arms.

"I'm sorry about running into your truck."

"Screw the truck." He threw the jacket on top of her purse. "Why didn't you call me? My God, woman, do you know how worried I've been? You could have gotten yourself killed."

Her eyes suddenly filled with tears and Chane wanted to kick himself. He was worried. And her car had been battered. He gathered her close, holding her next to him with one arm, brushing her tears away with his hand. "I didn't mean that. It was a stupid thing for me to say. With Robertson and all. Oh, c'mon, honey. Don't cry because—"

"Someone . . . tried to kill me." Her voice was all muffled against his shirt.

He held her away from him and tipped her face toward him. "Honey, say it again. I didn't understand you." Someone was trying to kill her was what he had heard. That couldn't be right.

"Someone tried to kill me," she repeated with a new flood of tears. Words tumbled out one after another as though she couldn't tell him fast enough, couldn't wait to get her thoughts organized. A big truck chased her down the pass, repeatedly hitting her. At first she thought it was an accident, but then, after her tire blew out, the truck came back and hit her again. And again.

"And . . . when you came into the driveway I thought—"

"Shh." He wiped her tears away with the pads of his thumbs. "It's okay. You're safe."

A swift look of his dark eyes was all she had before he enveloped her in another hug. Chane style, she thought. All warm, strong, comforting, and feeling like the answer to her deepest longings. He worried about her, she thought with a touch of wonder. Not because she was a reporter on a job and an asset valuable to the organization. But about her. Lexi. She couldn't stop crying.

"You'll feel better after you have a bath and something to eat and some sleep." He swept her into his arms and carried her up the stairs to the loft as though she weighed no more than Tessa.

Lexi intended to protest, to tell him she could walk. Except, being carried felt so good. Once again, being held by him suffused her with a feeling of being cherished, being kept safe the way home was supposed to feel and never had.

He set her down at the bathroom door. "While you take a bath, I'll see what there is to eat."

"I'm not hungry."

He lifted her face with his finger and stared deeply into her eyes.

So warm, she thought. Eyes that were dark, compassionate, and so, so warm. He bent and kissed her, cherishing her mouth. His big hands cupped both sides of her face, his long fingers easing into her hair. When he lifted his head, he touched a finger to her lips.

"Fixing you something to eat . . ." He paused and cleared his throat. "That's mostly for me. To keep me busy while you're in here." He nodded toward the bath. "I'm going to be thinking about it anyway. You. Naked." He bent and kissed her again, caressing her lips as though they were fragile, savoring them as though nothing was more special. "But that's not what you need right now. So, I'm going to go figure out what there is to eat in your kitchen."

Gently, he pushed her through the bathroom door and closed it behind her. He stood a moment, staring at the door, filled with the image of her undressing. Moments later he heard the water running. Turning his back to the door, he left her bedroom. There was a time for sex. This wasn't it.

Chane went back down the stairs to the kitchen, which was spotlessly clean and uncluttered. Uncluttered, anyway, until he opened cupboards. Lexi was a pack rat, and not a neat one. He grinned, pleased with this new aspect of her personality. She kept cans of soup and cereal in the same cupboard with bowls. Containers of rice and pasta were with the saucepans. It all made sense at a certain level, he decided.

He eventually chose a frozen potpie, which he put in the microwave oven to cook. Then he found a tray, plate, napkin, and silverware. All the while he kept thinking some bastard had tried to kill her. Who? Why?

Chane hung up Lexi's jacket in the hall closet and wandered into the living room. He liked the open floor plan of her house, but a fish in an aquarium couldn't be any more exposed. His assessment was quick and experienced. The house couldn't be defended. The one place he wished there was a window, there was none—overlooking the driveway. The flap in the kitchen door where Daisy went in and out was probably advertised as "people proof." In Chane's view, it was an open invitation to every burglar in the county.

As for someone trying to kill her, Robertson had to be the connection. Chane trusted his instinct on that one enough to take it to the bank. Whoever it was, he gathered Lexi had left stuck up on the pass. Did they know where she lived? He mulled that over a moment, finally deciding they might not. Otherwise, why try to run her off the pass? His pacing took him back to the broad expanse of glass. Outside, it had started to snow again, huge flakes evident only a few feet beyond the window.

He called home, told Kit he wouldn't be back for a long while yet, and gave him Lexi's telephone number. Then he called Hank Warner's house. When he answered, Chane explained what had happened to Lexi and asked Hank to do whatever was required to keep a closer eye on Lexi's house. Hank told him it was as good as done.

The potpie finished cooking two minutes after Chane heard the shower water stop running. He dumped the pie onto a plate and poured a glass of milk.

At the top of the stairs he paused. "Are you decent?"

"Only when required," Lexi responded, a trace of humor in her voice.

Chane was beginning to recognize that tone of voice, and he wasn't sure he liked it. This was her I'm-fine,-don't-give-me-a-second-thought voice behind which she hid. She'd call him Callahan instead of Chane, putting even more distance between them if he analyzed their situation intellectually. At the instinctive level where he paid close attention, he didn't want distance. He hoped she didn't either. No matter what messages she put out.

"I'm coming in anyway." He nudged the door open with his shoulder. She sat on the end of her bed. Her flash of humor should have been reflected in her posture, but it wasn't. An ivory towel was wrapped turban style around her head and she was wearing a long, tailored, satiny-looking shirt, deep burgundy. Her nipples were puckered, beautifully evident beneath the fabric. He imagined unbuttoning the shirt and looking his fill of her body.

She smiled at him, which only emphasized the tired lines around her eyes. Her expression was pure weary. Only a rat of a man would think about making love to a woman in Lexi's condition. Which made him a rat.

"You look like you're feeling a little better." He set the tray down on the end of the bed next to her.

"Some. And you obviously found something to keep you busy, Callahan."

He hated being right.

She unwrapped the towel from around her head and shook out her hair, which was only slightly damp. He took the towel from her hands and brushed his hand over her silky tresses.

"Eat," he ordered gruffly, taking the towel into the bathroom.

It was steamy and redolent with her clean, floral fragrance. He hung up the towel and returned to the bedroom. She still hadn't touched the food.

Sitting down next to her, he lifted the tray onto his lap and faced her. "You have to eat something."

"I've been thinking about that truck," she said.

That didn't surprise him. He'd like to keep her from thinking about it, though, until she had a good night's sleep. He loaded the fork with a bite of food and held it toward her. "There's plenty of time to think about that tomorrow. We can't do anything tonight."

She pulled the bit of food off the fork and chewed it slowly. "This has to be connected with Joe's death."

"Let it go, Lexi," Chane murmured.

She chewed a moment, then said, "And I kept thinking I should have noticed something. Maybe at the hospital. Or maybe when I got gas. Or . . ."

He offered her another bite.

She ignored the offered food, staring into space. ". . . There wasn't a damn thing. Nothing. I didn't talk to anyone except the FBI agent assigned to Joe's case." Her gaze became even more unfocused as her thoughts turned inward. She shuddered.

"What is it?" he asked, needing to know the cause of her anxiety, needing equally to protect her from her racing thoughts.

"I've got to call the sheriff. If that truck followed me from Denver—"

"I already called Hank Warner, a buddy of mine who is one of the deputies," Chane said. Whoever said blondes were dumb obviously hadn't met Lexi, he thought. He gave her points for thinking coherently at all, much less coming to the same conclusion he had.

Another flash of anger raced through him at the thought of anyone trying to hurt her.

The realization surprised him, made him admit to himself he was half in love with her. His gaze focused on her face. A crumb from the crust of the potpie was on her lower lip. He brushed it away with his thumb. Against his callused hand, her skin felt like warmed velvet. *And some bastard had tried to kill her.* He swallowed.

Offering her another bite, he asked, "Do you have to go back to Denver?"

"No." She chewed slowly and washed the food down with a long drink of milk. "There's only one thing left to do."

"Which is?"

She set the glass on the tray, and looked at him directly. "Send you home."

Of all the things she might have said, he wasn't expecting that one. Carefully, he set the tray on the nightstand. "You want me to leave?'' He had been so positive she didn't want to be alone. Yet here she was, asking him to leave.

She nodded. ''I'll be fine.''

''You don't look fine,'' he replied, his voice gruff.

''Gee, thanks, Callahan.''

He raked a hand through his hair. ''That's not what I meant.''

''You don't have to stay,'' she said.

Her eyes told him something altogether different.

''I know. You're such a tough guy you can fight your demons without any help from me.'' He figured if her nightmares had been bad the other night, Joe's death and the attempt on her life would make them even worse. If she managed to fall asleep.

''Damn you, Callahan.'' Her whisper was at odds with the vehement words. She dropped her head, and her hair fell forward, shielding her expression.

Chane stood and pulled down the bedspread, then patted the sheet, inviting her to lie down.

She met his gaze. Within her eyes were questions and confusion and exhaustion. And the knowledge of what had happened the last time she had fallen asleep in his arms.

Keep it light, he told himself. Smiling, he said, ''I'll tuck you in and read you a bedtime story.''

''What kind of come-on is this, Callahan?''

''No come-on. Not tonight. All I want to do is hold you.''

She sat stock-still for a long moment. Watching the play of expressions over her face, Chane wondered which side was winning the argument she was having with herself. Regardless, he wasn't leaving. The sooner she figured that out, the better.

Finally, she scooted over to the turned-back sheet, her long legs gleaming in the lamplight. Despite his assertion he wasn't interested in making love, arousal that would not be denied surged heavily through him, pooling into a painful ache that demanded attention.

''This bedtime story,'' she said, as if deciding to play along with his suggestion. ''What did you have in mind?''

Wariness and something else he couldn't quite pin down laced her voice. Her words were teasing, but nothing in her body language was. The lady had asked him to leave. He absolutely trusted his gut instinct she wanted him—needed him—to stay. And maybe she thought the price for simply being held through the night was sex. Maybe that was the source of her wariness.

"I'm keeping my clothes on," he informed her. Nothing sounded better than stripping his clothes off and sliding into the sheets with her. But he wouldn't.

She arched an eyebrow.

"There's more between us than sex, Lexi."

Her eyes met his, then skittered away. She closed her eyes, and her eyelashes cast a shadow on her cheeks. A slow flush climbed slowly from her neck to her hairline.

"Lexi?" He brushed some strands of hair away from her face. She turned her head and looked back at him.

"You never make things easy, do you, Callahan?"

He smiled. "You'll have to explain that one. I don't understand."

She worried her lower lip between her teeth then met his gaze again. "I . . . can't."

"You figured if I stayed, we'd make love."

She gave an embarrassed-sounding cough, but didn't deny his assumption.

He patted the sheet again, and she lay down. He covered her with the blanket.

"I'll stay with you. No strings. No hidden agendas." He eased down beside her staying on top of the covers. She scooted toward the middle of the bed to make room for him. "I want to make love to you just about more than I want to breathe. But not tonight."

She watched him with wide eyes, but didn't fill in the silence when his voice faded away.

He cleared his throat. "Like it or not, Lexi, tonight I'm your friend. I'm not leaving you, and I'm sure as hell not seducing you."

She was so still, so silent. Gently, he traced the satin curve of her cheek with sensitive fingertips. When he encountered the unmistakable wetness of tears, he turned her head toward him. Her eyes shimmered and she slid her hand along his waist, bringing herself closer to him.

"What is it, honey?"

She bent her head enough to press a kiss into his palm, and lifted her own hand to his face. "You're pretty amazing, Callahan."

"So are you," he returned, his voice as husky as hers.

He turned off the bedside lamp, leaving the room illuminated only from the lights left on downstairs. He wrapped both his arms around her and pressed a kiss against her temple. She turned toward him more fully. He couldn't ignore her soft breasts pressed against his chest or the firm pressure of her mound against him. He didn't try. Holding her was the sweetest kind of torture. He wouldn't have changed that, either.

"If I had an ounce of willpower, I'd make you go home," she whispered.

"Go to sleep, Lexi."

Between one heart beat and the next, she did just that.

He remembered her telling him that she had trouble trusting. Twice now, she had fallen asleep in his arms. With trust.

A man couldn't ask for more than that.

Chapter 15

Chane came awake a few minutes before five, his arms tightening around Lexi. Spoon style, his lap cradled her bottom, and her head rested against his shoulder. He wanted her, just as he had wanted her every time he awoke during the night. He hadn't intended to stay. The first time she clung to him, her sleep interrupted by a nightmare, and he'd wanted to shelter her, even from her dreams.

All night her sleep had been fitful, punctuated by restless dreams and anxious murmurs of protest. Through it all, she held on to him, sometimes fiercely, as though she'd be lost without his touch. Few things had ever been as satisfying as holding her, feeling needed by her, knowing that he had the experience to understand what she felt. No other connection in his life—that as father to Tessa or that as brother to Kit—touched him to his soul the way Lexi did.

Despite being gritty from having slept in his clothes and having been awake at different times during the night, he felt surprisingly alert. This time, there was no putting off the inevitable. He had to go home. He needed to get Kit up for school. He needed his morning rituals with Tessa. What he needed—he gazed down at Lexi and swallowed—what he needed was to make her part of his life, sharing with her the morning rituals, the mundane tasks of everyday life.

Gently he disentangled himself from Lexi's warm body and slipped out of her bed. He didn't feel good about leaving her and thought about waking her to take her with him. For the first time all night, she seemed to be resting more deeply, and he decided against waking her.

Asleep like this, she looked completely vulnerable. Soft. Like this, he'd never suspect she had an iron will or unwavering directness. The need to shield her returned. He wanted to keep her away from harm and ugliness and hurt.

He bent over her and pressed a kiss against her brow. She smiled in her sleep. Chaste as a monk, he'd kept his word to himself and to her. Next time, he promised himself, would be different.

He turned off the lights downstairs, and murmured quietly to Daisy to take good care of her mistress. Despite a German shepherd heritage that should have made her a good watchdog, Daisy was worthless in that department, Chane figured. Watchdogs had names like Killer or Duke, not Daisy. On first glance, the dog might give an intruder a moment's pause. By the second, anyone would figure out Daisy was more interested in having her ears scratched than in protecting her mistress.

Chane pulled on his cold boots. More inviting and warmer by far were Lexi's arms. After checking to make sure the front and back doors were locked, he left the house through the garage, stopping long enough to pocket the garage door opener so he could get back in later. He retrieved the flat tire from the trunk of Lexi's car. Getting it fixed was only one of his motives. Discovering why it had blown out was another.

Sometime during the night a suspicion lodged and wouldn't go away. Tires blew out under stress—high speeds, hot temperatures, or heavy loads. They didn't blow out in the middle of a cold storm on a hairpin curve. Not without help. The only explanation he could think of, he didn't like a bit. The tire had been shot out.

Joe Robertson, according to the news, had been shot while sitting in his rental car in front of an apartment building. For

Lexi to have been shot at in her car after visiting Joe kept bothering Chane. Hank Warner could get answers, and Chane intended to talk to him first thing.

Chane opened the garage door with the opener, then closed the door behind him. During the night the snow had stopped falling and the sky was full of brilliant stars and the sliver of a setting moon. The air had a crisp bite to it and the snow crunched under his feet as he walked to his pickup. His breath clouded in steamy puffs in front of him. He set the tire in the back of the truck and climbed into the cab.

The road back into the village was completely deserted. Quietly, he let himself into his own house. The last thing he expected to find was his younger brother leaning negligently against the doorway between the kitchen and back porch, his arms folded across his chest. Kit, despite his youth, looked just as stern as a father waiting for a wayward son who had broken curfew.

"You're late," Kit said.

"Or early, depending on your point of view." Chane hung his coat on a peg and put his Stetson next to it.

"Was she good?" Kit asked.

A flash of anger surfaced, and Chane reacted without thought. He grabbed the front of Kit's navy T-shirt and hauled him close. "You get one thing straight, Kit. You never talk about a woman like that. Not ever. And especially not about Lexi Monroe."

His words echoed back to him as he glared into his brother's topaz eyes. Lexi wasn't just a woman he wanted to bed, though God knew that need hadn't left him for days. She wasn't just a person with ghosts he recognized. She wasn't just a woman of unwavering directness that drew him. She was . . . the woman he had fallen in love with. The abyss he'd faced last night, unwilling to name, was this.

Love.

He stared into his brother's eyes, the truth washing over him. Chane gave Kit's shirt a little shake. His brother didn't resist, but he didn't back down either.

"I hope she was worth it."

Chane's other hand clinched into a big fist. "Don't push me."

Kit met his angry gaze without a flinch. "You don't know what you've gotten yourself into."

"And you don't know what the hell you're talking about."

Kit nodded curtly. "Damn right, I do, bro." He pulled his shirt out of Chane's grasp. "I wouldn't be trusting Lexi Monroe too much, if I were you."

If there was one thing Chane instinctively knew, it was that he could trust Lexi. He shouldered his way past his brother and headed for the coffeepot. "If you're going to tell me that she's helping Señora Padilla find her granddaughter, I already know that." He yanked the cupboard door open and got out a can of coffee.

"Did you know Tía Ester's granddaughter was illegally adopted?"

"The señora told me." Chane spooned coffee into the filter and filling the reservoir with water. He turned on the coffeemaker and faced his brother.

"And it was through The Sisters of Hope. Did you know that?"

"Yes." That was the one piece Chane wished he knew more about. A whole hell of a lot more. "And I know that Lexi Monroe lived in Costa Léon for most of the past five years. I even know her photo essay about South American orphans is the reason Ellen Belsen adopted her little boys." He folded his arms over his chest. "Is there anything else we need to cover?"

"What about Tessa?"

"What about her?"

"Tía Ester is looking for a little girl about Tessa's age," Kit said as if he were explaining simple arithmetic to a first grader. "A little girl who was adopted about the same time Tessa was."

"Tessa was *not* illegally adopted." Chane winced, wishing he were as positive as he sounded.

Kit frowned. "I know, but that is all pretty weird. Too many coincidences. All the sudden you start hanging around a woman—" He punctuated that with a poke to Chane's chest—

"that you don't even tell me about. Then an old lady shows up looking for a child just about the same time. This is too strange, bro."

"You're right," Chane agreed, giving his brother credit for having figured all this out on his own.

"Don't get me wrong," Kit added. "Tía Ester is a nice lady. I like her. But we don't know anything about her. What if she got weird or something and took Tessa?"

"Over my dead body," Chane said quietly.

The objections Kit voiced, Chane understood perfectly. The señora *was* an engaging woman who blossomed when she had others to care for. She obviously liked feeling useful. Or maybe it was something else. He didn't know what the señora intended to do if she found her granddaughter, but he refused to consider her anything other than the obvious—she was an old woman with a quest. Nothing more.

"People see what they want to see, Kit. Sometimes, even, what they are led to see. The señora sees Tessa. A child who looks like Rose." Chane moved the coffeepot from under the drip filter and held a coffee cup under the stream, then replaced the pot. "She doesn't know Tessa was adopted. I intend to keep it that way."

"So. You're telling me you're not worried?"

"Hell, yes, I'm worried," Chane said. "About some things more than others."

"About Lexi Monroe? Where'd you meet her?"

"She's taking a class from me." Chane took a sip of the steaming coffee.

"And this is a little more serious than a simple date with Suzanne Whats-her-face."

"Yeah."

"Is she pretty?"

Chane stared into the dark liquid in the coffee cup, thinking about Lexi's equally dark eyes. "Yeah."

"And you're not going to tell me any more about it." Kit's voice lost its serious note.

Chane glanced at his brother over the rim of his cup. "Go take your shower."

Kit grinned. "Don't go away mad. Just go away. Is that it, bro?"

"Something like that."

Kit headed toward the back hallway, then stopped. "I'm sorry about that crack—"

"I don't remember any cracks," Chane answered, the last of his irritation with Kit dissolving. He strolled across the kitchen and snagged his brother around the neck with his elbow. "All I saw was my kid brother worrying." He dropped his forehead against Kit's hair.

"Worried? Nah, I wasn't worried." Kit ducked his head and stepped away from Chane. "She's pretty cool, huh?"

"Yeah."

"So. When am I gonna meet her?"

"Soon." Chane's tone turned gruff again. "Go take your shower."

"I'm going." Kit backed down the hall. "Nag, nag, nag."

Chane poured another cup of coffee, then headed for his bedroom and a morning routine that began with his calisthenics. By the time he got out of his shower, he smelled the aroma of breakfast cooking and knew the señora had taken over the kitchen again. Kit arrived in the bedroom moments later dressed for school and with Tessa on his shoulders.

"Forget what I said earlier," he told Chane with a grin. "What we've needed the past year is a woman who cooks breakfast and dinner. And she cleans up, too. I think I've died and gone to heaven."

"You make a few choice comments like that to the girls at school, and they'll call you a male chauvinist pig."

"What does a show van pig look like?" Tessa asked.

Chane laughed. "Exactly like Kit."

The señora greeted Chane warmly when he came into the kitchen, which made him feel guilty for all the suspicions he harbored. She had made enough oatmeal to feed a platoon. Of course, as far as Chane was concerned, a single bowl was enough to feed a platoon. He only kept the stuff in the house to make oatmeal cookies. Kit and Tessa ate their oatmeal as if it were ice cream. Chane forced his down, each bite sticking like glue to his throat.

For the first time in Chane's recent memory, Kit was out the door in time to catch his school bus without being reminded six different times. Chane was ready to take Tessa to the day-care center, but the señora, broken English or not, made it plain she would take care of Tessa today.

Without saying yes or no, Chane decided he'd think about that while he inspected Lexi's tire. In bright daylight, the damage to the tire was clearly revealed. He couldn't imagine how Lexi had kept control of her car driving on the tire. Strands of steel and rubber barely hung on to the wheel. Chane rotated the tire slowly, looking at every inch of the outside surface. One spot looked suspicious to him, but he was no ballistics expert, and he needed Hank's expertise to prove his suspicions.

Before he was finished checking over the tire, he'd decided to take Tessa to the day-care center and Señora Padilla with him. It was one thing to tell Kit he wasn't worried about the señora and another to come face to face with leaving Tessa in her care. When push came to shove, he couldn't do it. Logically, he knew the señora thought Tessa was his daughter by birth. Logic didn't help, and faced with the choice between his gut instinct and logic, he'd choose instinct every time.

In addition to that, he had an envelope to pick up from Ellen. Any luck at all, and it would have the adoption decree, though why Ellen would have it, he couldn't begin to fathom.

He bundled up Tessa, found one of Kit's outgrown jackets for the señora, and put them in the truck. Since it was on the way to the day-care center, his first stop was the sheriff's office. He carried the tire into the office, and Tessa and the señora tagged in behind him. Chane introduced Hank to the señora, telling her they had some things to discuss. Hank gave her a cup of coffee, and she sat down stiffly in one of the chairs as though expecting a long wait. Tessa climbed onto a chair next to her, playing her version of twenty questions.

Eyeing the tire, Hank Warner said, "The garage is a couple of doors down the street."

"Don't be cute," Chane told him. "It's early and I don't

have time." He set the tire down and took the cup of coffee Hank held toward him. "Think you'd be able to tell if this was shot out?"

"This is the tire you told me about last night?"

"Yeah."

Hank took the tire from Chane and took it to the front window where the daylight streamed through, searching the surface in much the same way Chane had. Moments later, Hank said, "A two-year-old could tell this tire was shot out." He turned back to Chane, and between his thumb and forefinger, he held up a slug. "This was lodged under the rim." He poked the spot Chane had been suspicious of. "Looks like right here is where it hit the tire."

A cold chill snaked down Chane's spine, and he took the slug from Hank.

"Do you think this can be traced?"

"If you get the gun." Hank took the slug back and turned it over in his palm. "If the slug is not too beat up from rattling around inside this tire. It's probably a thirty-eight, which we can prove easily enough. The caliber is common as cornflakes, though. Without a suspect and a weapon, we barely have physical evidence much less a case."

"She filed a report with the state patrol," Chane said.

"I'll get a copy from them," Hank promised. "And I'll hang on to this. I want to keep the tire for a while, too."

"Thanks, bud." Chane set the cup of coffee down and headed toward the door.

"Don't thank me yet. Your lady is in a lot of trouble if she's got someone shooting at her. I'm going to want to talk to her."

"I'll tell her," Chane promised. "I'm on my way there now. You'll be here later?"

"Yeah."

"I'll be back with her."

That thought foremost on his mind as they left the sheriff's office gave Chane a sense of urgency. He had been too damn complacent, leaving her alone in a secluded house, knowing someone had tried to kill her. The señora brightened when she figured out they were headed for Lexi's house, chatting to Tessa in Spanish, who listened as though she understood. The cheerful conversation grated on Chane, and he pressed harder on the accelerator.

The snow was already beginning to melt beneath the bright sun. Ahead of them, Shadow Mountain Lake was brilliant, deep blue beneath an equally brilliant sky.

At barely nine o'clock in the morning, Chane figured Lexi would still be sleeping. He parked in her driveway, pressing on the garage door opener he had taken from her car. Lexi's car was parked inside, looking just as bad this morning as it had last night.

Carrying Tessa, he climbed the stairs to the kitchen after the señora. The kitchen was deserted, and Chane wondered where Daisy was. They hadn't seen her outside, and she didn't appear to be in the house.

"I like this house, Daddy," Tessa said, stretching over his shoulder and looking around.

"Shh," he commanded softly, setting her down, then said to the señora, "Wait here."

"Wait," she mimicked. "This is something you say too much, Señor Chane."

He ignored her and silently climbed the stairs to the loft two at a time and gently pushed open the door to Lexi's room, expecting to find her still asleep.

Her unmade bed was empty.

His heart lodged in his throat, pounding, as he glanced around the room. The bathroom door was open, so he knew she wasn't in there. His imagination ran riot and a dozen possibilities flitted through his mind, none of them pleasant. Damn, he knew he shouldn't have left her.

He turned around and descended the stairs in a rushed clatter. The señora stood in front of the windows, murmuring to Tessa. The two of them waved, and Chane's glance strayed outside. Lexi was walking along the path from the lake.

"Thank God," he muttered to himself.

"Has Alexandra eaten breakfast?" the señora asked.

"I don't know," Chane answered on his way to the door.

"I'll cook," she announced.

"Fine." Long, hurried strides carried him across the deck, down the stairs, and toward the lake. Lexi was still closer to the lake than to her house when he reached her. A quarter mile away, Daisy loped along the water's edge.

Lexi still didn't look rested, Chane thought as he approached her. She wasn't as pale as last night, but her welcoming smile didn't quite reach her eyes.

"Where's the fire, Callahan?"

He recognized her tart question and the use of his last name for the distancing techniques they were. She didn't want to talk about what had happened last night or how she was feeling. Which was too bad, because they were going to have to talk and seriously. He didn't have to be a detective to figure the bullet that hit Joe Robertson and the one in Lexi's tire came from the same gun. Supposition, sure, but he'd bet a new set of carabiniers on it.

"Right here," he said, answering her question about fire, and pressing a hand to the center of his chest.

"Ah." The corners of her eyes crinkled as she gazed up at him. "That's too high for an ulcer. It must be heartburn."

He took her hand. "Probably. I got it from being fed oatmeal for breakfast."

"If you don't like it, why make it?"

"I didn't. Señora Padilla did."

Lexi frowned. "Why is she making oatmeal at your house?"

"Hell if I know why she's making oatmeal."

"Chane." Lexi poked him in the stomach.

He took her finger in his hand and pulled her palm flush against his. "I went to get her—remember?"

Lexi blanched. "Oh, God, I'd forgotten. I can't believe—"

"You've only had a couple other things on your mind. Don't worry about it."

Chane explained about bringing the señora to his house and how she had taken over his household and kitchen before he quite realized what had happened.

"I didn't mean for her to stay with you," Lexi said. "I know I wasn't too clear about things yesterday afternoon, but I didn't really expect you to take her home. Why didn't you bring her with you last night?''

Chane shrugged. "To tell you the truth, I didn't think about it." He glanced back toward Lexi's house. "She's here now. But since you've got only one bedroom and a fish bowl for a living room downstairs, I wondered where you planned to put her."

"I hadn't thought ahead about things," Lexi confessed.

"She's fine with me," Chane murmured, surprising himself. Maybe this was the way to keep an eye on her, he decided. Better to have her underfoot than not know what her search was turning up. "I was surprised to find you awake."

"I've been up for a couple of hours." Lexi dipped her head. Her hair, which she had left loose this morning, fell forward and hid her face. "Thanks to you I got a decent night's sleep."

"You look like you could use some more."

She pushed her hair back and studied Chane's face. "And you look surprisingly rested, Callahan."

"What's this with using my last name, Lexi?" he asked, deliberately using her first name.

She didn't answer.

He knew she used his last name to put distance between them. What he didn't understand was why, and he was hoping she would tell him. When one minute stretched into two, he decided maybe he should let her have the distance she seemed to want.

He wrapped a companionable arm across her shoulder and steered her back down the path toward the lake.

"So why are you up so early?"

"It's not early, Chane."

"Okay," he agreed, noticing her use of his first name, applauding it. "Why are you down here at the lake instead of enjoying the view from your deck with a hot cup of coffee?"

The question was innocent enough. When she didn't answer right away, Chane stopped walking and made her face him. "I'm not asking for all your secrets, honey."

"They aren't secrets, exactly."

"Then what?"

"I'm just . . . this is all pretty new to me, Callahan."

"What?"

"Having someone who really wants to know. Who isn't just making polite noises."

"I'm not being polite, Lexi. And I really want to know what's on your mind."

She searched his face. "Most people can't handle what's happened to me."

His expression became grave. "I'm not most people. I've watched people die violently. You're never the same after seeing that. And I was betrayed by a bastard named Joe Robertson. Ellen Belsen told me you were, too."

"He called me." Lexi faced the lake and wrapped her arms around herself. "Just before he was shot, he called."

Chane took one of her hands and squeezed it reassuringly.

"I woke up, and I was hungry," she said. "So I was rummaging through the refrigerator. And I noticed the light on the answering machine blinking. The time stamp on it said the message had been left a couple of days ago, and at first I couldn't remember why I hadn't picked it up. He called only an hour or two before he was shot."

"He. You mean Robertson?"

"Yeah. He said he thought he was close to figuring out who El Ladron was."

"El Ladron?" Chane questioned.

Lexi stared across the surface of the lake a moment, wanting to answer honestly, wanting equally to make sure she said nothing to increase Chane's worry. His behavior made it plain he had cast himself in the role of protector. Alluring as that was, she wasn't about to say or do anything that would put him or his daughter in danger. Which meant she had to put some distance between them until she knew for sure what was going on.

Joe's message had been his usual cryptic shorthand, telling her enough to make her worry, not enough to give her anything solid to work with. Except for Señora Padilla, the woman who had so easily become Tía Ester. *Lexi, I'm worried that Señora Padilla may have been followed. Don't ask me how I know. It would take too long to explain. But I have reason to think she was a plant to lead El Ladron from me to you. Watch your backside, Monroe.*

And Tía Ester was at Chane's house.

What if her instincts were wrong? Lexi wondered. She had been so sure Tía Ester was exactly what she portrayed herself as—a woman searching her for grandchild. Could she be working for El Ladron? Lexi didn't think so.

Too easily, she imagined El Ladron using Tía Ester, filling her with hope.

Lexi's throat tightened. Hope, when there was none.

If Tía Ester had been used to find Lexi, the trail from the *Las Hermanas de la Esperanza* was bogus. There would be no reunion between grandmother and grandchild. And that would break Tía Ester's heart.

And if El Ladron had finally found Lexi . . .

She had been telling herself for months she wasn't hiding, wasn't pretending to live a normal life while waiting for something awful to happen. But buried in her nightmares with El Ladron's pale eyes were his threats. *I'll find you. It's only a matter of time. And if I find someone you love first* . . . Admit it, she thought, you have been hiding.

Joe had been right about her ivory tower in too many ways. She had been safe. Nobody could get in. Nothing happened there, and nothing was important. And now, things were important. People. Chane.

Lexi glanced at him, wishing she had said nothing about El Ladron. Now that she had, what could she say, she wondered, that would worry Chane least?

Lexi kicked a pebble ahead of her. For the first time in her life, she had a man she cared about. And the mess she thought she'd had when she came home a year ago was nothing compared to this.

"Lexi, who is El Ladron? The guy who kidnapped you?"

She met Chane's glance, then nodded. "When I was still in Costa Léon, Joe and I uncovered a baby-smuggling ring, a noble-sounding group called *Las Hermanas de la Esperanza.*"

"The people that took Señora Padilla's granddaughter," Chane said.

Lexi nodded. "A perfect scam. American or Canadian couples with enough money to buy a baby would come into the country for a visit or on business—the wife pretending to be pregnant. They'd stay a few weeks, sometimes a few months. When they returned home, they'd have their baby."

"Sounds like people desperate to have a child," Chane said.

Lexi turned to face him. "What's it called when one human being buys another?"

"Slavery."

She nodded. "And who cares what kind of people these are if you've got enough cash to make the purchase? As long as there are people out there willing to buy, there will be bastards like El Ladron willing to fill the demand."

"So what else did Robertson have to say?" Chane asked.

Surprised at his abrupt change in subject, she met his gaze. "That Señora Padilla has been duped. It's going to break her heart when I tell her the search has been for nothing. That her granddaughter could be anywhere." Lexi paused. "I think the whole purpose was for her to lead El Ladron to Robertson."

"His whereabouts was known to just about anybody. That doesn't make sense."

"You're right," Lexi agreed, wishing she had never told Chane last night that someone had tried to kill her on Berthoud Pass. Someone. El Ladron or a hired hand. All she could do now was minimize the conclusion anyone with two brain cells to rub together would come to.

"I took your tire to the sheriff's office, and I had Hank Warner take a look at it," Chane said. He held her glance and added, "Your tire didn't blow out on its own, Lexi. Someone shot it out."

Lexi felt the blood drain out of her face, and a rush of pure fear sliced through her stomach. She shouldn't have been surprised, she thought. But she was.

"This El Ladron character. You're the one he's really after."

Lexi shook her head, giving voice to a blatant lie. "If he's the one who got Joe—if it wasn't a drive-by shooting, he has nothing to gain by coming after me.''

"Don't give me that crap, Lexi. By your own account, someone tried to drive you off the pass last night. Someone shot out your tire.''

"I don't know that it was El Ladron.''

Chane doubled his hand into a fist and hit his own chest. ''I do. Are you willing to bet your life—''

"No.'' Lexi touched his fist, and repeated. "No. You've already talked to a deputy. I'll go talk to him, too. We'll let them handle it.''

"That's the first sensible thing you've said,'' Chane muttered, taking her hand within his.

Lexi focused on Chane's hand wrapped so tightly around hers. She didn't doubt his concern—he had proven it in more ways than a man should have to. And nothing could be a bigger mistake than letting him any closer. She wouldn't, couldn't endanger him. If anything happened to him, Tessa would be an orphan.

Yesterday he had offered her *anything*. In her heart, she hadn't thought he really meant it. But when she'd arrived home, he'd been there for her. No anger that she ran into his truck. No questions or snide remarks about her assertion that someone was trying to kill her. He'd stayed with her last night and he was back.

Yesterday had been a lifetime ago, when all she had to sort out was figuring out if she could have a friend *and* lover within the same man. Today, things weren't that simple.

All her life she had dreamed of someone caring for her like this. As a child, she had wanted it passionately and had made promises to herself that she'd have a family like those she saw around her. By the time she reached college, she had filed away those fantasies for the idealized childhood dreams they were.

She had poured all she had into her career. Once, she had searched for the intimacy she craved in sex. She had never felt emptier after giving herself to a man who shared sexual satisfaction, who wanted nothing more from her.

Lexi wanted more. And at last she had found that something

more in Chane Callahan. She had wanted to make love with
him as much as he had professed wanting her. His restraint,
his giving her intimacy without sex—had shattered the last of
her defenses. No one had ever touched her more deeply.

"Honey?" Chane lifted her face for his inspection with
gentle fingers. "A penny for your thoughts."

"Just . . ." She sighed. "Trying to figure all this out."

"We'll have Hank track it down."

That part was good advice. Only two other things she had
to figure out. How to put some distance between herself and
Chane until El Ladron was caught. How to break the news of
El Ladron's deception to Tía Ester. "Let's go get it done,
then."

Chapter 16

They arrived at the kitchen door of her house just as Daisy backed outside through it, her tail between her legs. The clattering of a pan and Tía Ester's angry voice followed her through the door.

Lexi pushed open the kitchen door and found Tía Ester standing with her hands on her hips. Daisy poked her head around Lexi's legs, wanting to go back into the house.

"¡Salga de aquí!" Tía Ester commanded.

Daisy ducked back out.

"Daisy vive en las casa," Lexi said.

The señora turned around to face Lexi and the cowering Daisy. *"El perro no limpio."*

Lexi let Daisy into the kitchen. She glided past Lexi, heading for refuge under the kitchen table. Lexi said to Tía Ester, "I put the little door in so Daisy can come inside and go outside as she wants. She lives inside. *Aquí.* And I don't care if you think she's dirty." Lexi smiled. "I'm sorry that she frightens you, Tía Ester, but she's used to living inside."

"A dog inside the house is not a good thing," Tía Ester said.

"I like having her in the house," Lexi returned. "And it is *my* house."

"Perhaps I was hasty," Tía Ester returned after an instant of silence. "And you are right. It is your house. If you want a filthy beast inside, you can do what you wish."

Lexi grinned at the grudging apology. "Thank you."

Tessa skipped across the floor and crawled under the table where Daisy was and put her arms around the dog's neck. "Pretty Daisy." To her father, she said, "I like this dog. Can we take her home?"

"She belongs to Lexi."

"Oh."

Lexi smiled. "She can come visit you, okay?"

"Okay!" Tessa smiled and stroked the tips of Daisy's ears. The dog closed her eyes as though in bliss, her tail wagging.

"You eat breakfast?" Tía Ester asked.

Lexi eyed the pot of oatmeal on the stove. She supposed there were things that looked worse. Offhand, she couldn't think of any. "Do I eat breakfast? Well, yes."

"Liar," Chane whispered in her ear.

"Perhaps you'd like some." She gave him a saccharin smile.

He backed away, his palms raised. "Not me. If I had ever thought you could make anything besides oatmeal cookies with it, I wouldn't have bought it."

Lexi put an arm across Tía Ester's shoulder, determined to avoid eating the oatmeal, loath to hurt her feelings. In Spanish, she said, "I appreciate your kindness in making me breakfast. It's my custom to eat very lightly in the morning. Oatmeal is a bit—"

"Señor Callahan does not care for oatmeal, either." She patted Lexi's hand. "Next time I will know better."

Lexi smiled. "I'm curious, Tía. Why oatmeal? A tortilla, some beans, and perhaps some fruit is more traditional."

"I watched it on the television last night with Señor Chane's brother. The man, he says oatmeal . . ." She paused as though thinking of exactly the right words, then continued, the cadence of her voice awkward, "Is a hot and hearty breakfast that lasts the whole day through."

"Ah." Lexi glanced at Chance. A brother? Another important facet of his life he hadn't mentioned. "Television commercials really work. So you have a brother who lives with you. Do you have any more relatives I don't know about?"

"Dozens."

"That live with you?"

"God, no."

"Just a brother?"

Chane frowned. "I didn't tell you about Kit?"

She shook her head. "This is getting to be a habit, Callahan. You're a man with a lot of secrets. Makes a woman wonder if you've got any really big skeletons hanging in the closet."

"Not many," Chane said. "Kit is my brother. He's half my age and twice as smart."

"Sounds like a typical teenager."

"He's that, all right."

"His mommy went to heaven," Tessa said from the vicinity of Lexi's knees. "And his daddy, too. Just like my mommy."

Lexi raised her eyes to Chane's. "You've taken on a lot lately, haven't you, Callahan?"

He shrugged, released her hand, and moved toward the expanse of windows.

"Daddy's not going to heaven," Tessa added. "He told me."

"He did, huh?" Lexi picked up Tessa and joined Chane at the window. She easily imagined him reassuring his daughter that he'd be there for her forever. Tessa deserved no less. "All this, and you have time for my puny problems?"

"Your problems aren't puny."

"Not to me. But—"

"Is it that hard to accept that I'm worried about you?"

"Yes."

Tessa squirmed to get out of Lexi's arms, and she set her down. Lexi watched the child run back into the kitchen and crawl under the table to pet Daisy. Lexi cleared her throat and met Chane's penetrating gaze. When she had promised herself no more deceptions, she hadn't known honesty was going to be this hard. The last of Joe's advice kept echoing through her

head in counterpoint to Tessa's *Daddy's not going to heaven.*
Watch your backside, Monroe. Equally strong this morning
was another remembered threat, one from El Ladron. *I'll find
you, Monroe. And if I happen to find someone you love first,
well . . .*

He wouldn't, Lexi silently vowed. Not her or Chane or
Chane's family.

"Do you have any other family besides Kit and Tessa?"
Lexi asked.

"What does that have to do with me being worried about
you?"

She shrugged.

"Two sisters," he said. "One is in college and the other is
married to a seaman stationed in San Diego. She teaches junior
high school."

"I was an only child," Lexi said, adding bare honesty she
had never given anyone. "My mother was the town tramp in
a community small enough where that means something. I bet
you were the kind of big brother that looked out for his little
sisters."

"Maybe, but that still doesn't have anything to do with you,"
he said.

"It does from the standpoint that you're used to taking care
of people. Me? I'm used to standing on my own two feet.
Alone." That sounded more defensive than she'd intended, but
maybe it was a beginning. Maybe picking a fight with him
was the way to get him to leave. She couldn't live with the
consequences of putting him—or his family—in danger. "You
probably grew up being the responsible one and you've never
outgrown—"

"Not hardly," he interrupted. "I felt pressured. And then I
spent thirteen years pretending I didn't have any responsibilities
though I had a wife, parents, a brother, and sisters. I wasn't
there when my dad died. I wasn't there when Tessa—"

The raw pain reflected in Chane's eyes made Lexi press her
fingers against his mouth. Driving him away was one thing.
Hurting him deliberately was another.

You have to, came the persistent voice of her conscience.

Tessa needs her father. Kit needs his brother, and he's already lost both parents.

Chane's arms came around Lexi. Softly he said, "I learned that I couldn't ignore my family. I learned, but it was too late." His arms tightened. "I don't want to make the same mistake again. I'm not blind, Lexi. I see that you're used to going it alone. You don't have to be." He tried to smile. "You're more than I bargained for, you know."

She shook her head.

"I started chasing you because I'm mad about your body."

She swallowed the lump in her throat. "Must be why you've ravished me every opportunity you got."

"I don't ravish bone-tired women."

"Ah. I'm on notice, then."

"Yeah. Only there's a slight problem."

"Which is?"

"Ravish says that you love 'em and leave 'em. That's not quite what I have in mind for you." He bent and kissed her.

Pent-up longing and promises were conveyed in that kiss. She returned it in kind, knowing she had lost this battle with herself. She should send him away, but she couldn't.

Chane lifted his head and smiled. "I've been thinking."

"Yeah?"

The smile faded and his dark eyes grew serious. "You said you talked to the FBI agent as you were leaving the hospital last night." Chane nodded his head toward the phone. "I think you should call him."

Chane's suggestion echoed her own conclusions, and she went to the phone. Picking up the receiver, she called information for the number.

"He didn't give you a card with his number on it?"

Lexi shook her head. After she got a number from the operator, she put the call through.

"I'd like to speak to Darren Burke," she said.

"There's no one here by that name."

Lexi frowned, sure she had the name right. "He's the agent investigating Joe Robertson's murder."

"One moment, please."

Lexi faced Chane.

"Problem?" he asked.

"I must have the name wrong. No Darren Burke is there."

"Maybe he works out of a different office. L.A., maybe."

While she listened to the music coming through the receiver while she was on hold, Chane made plans for the day. She knew exactly why he was being so nonchalant—to keep her from thinking about last night.

"This afternoon, we have wilderness survival class." He caught her glance. "I'd cancel it, but with Josh and Frank coming from Leadville and Julie and Brian coming from Granby—"

"It's okay." Lexi met Chane's glance, again surprised by the man. She hadn't considered that he'd adjust his schedule because something was going on with her—even though he had made the offer before. "I suppose since it's snowed, you'll want to build igloos, or something."

"Good idea," he agreed. "And you're having dinner at my house tonight."

"A busy day." Lexi admitted that she liked his plans even as she made plans of her own—plans to separate herself as far as possible from him and his family. Plans she kept to herself because she knew he wouldn't agree with them.

"Maybe I'll let Tía Ester cook again."

"*¿Come se dice?*" the señora called from the kitchen.

"Chane says you're going to cook dinner tonight," Lexi told her. Long before then, Lexi intended to take Tía Ester aside and find out just exactly how she came to be here. If she was an accomplice . . . she wouldn't be cooking dinner for Chane. In fact, she'd be as far away from Chane and his family as Lexi could manage.

"*Bueno,*" Tía Ester said. "I will need to purchase groceries."

"Daddy will take you," Tessa said. "Isn't that right, Daddy?"

"I just went a couple of days ago."

A surprising dimple appeared in Tía Ester's cheek. "Perhaps I could make oatmeal again."

Chane lifted his hands in surrender. "I'll take you."

Lexi chuckled at the exchange, finding it nearly impossible to believe Tía Ester was El Ladron's accomplice. If she had been, Lexi thought, he would have already been here. Days ago. He would have known where to find her before she went on Chane's campout.

"*Bueno,*" Tessa echoed. "I like it when Tía Ester cooks."

"You don't like your daddy's cooking?" Lexi teased, giving Chane a wink.

"I do. But Tía Ester makes the kitchen smell good."

The music on the telephone receiver abruptly ended, reminding Lexi she had been on hold for quite a while. Over the line came a voice that introduced himself as Agent Parkins and asked what he could do for her. Lexi explained that she was trying to locate Darren Burke, the agent investigating Joe Robertson's murder.

"To the best of my knowledge, that's a local matter. We have no one assigned to that case," he said.

A fist of ice formed in Lexi's stomach. "Could he be from somewhere else?"

"It's possible, of course, but not likely."

Lexi caught her lower lip between her teeth and wrapped her free arm around her waist. "I'd appreciate your checking. Last night a man identified himself as an FBI agent and asked me a whole raft of questions about—"

"You're sure it was the FBI? Could it have been the CBI—the Colorado Bureau of Investigation?"

"I'm sure it was the FBI. His name was Darren Burke."

Agent Parkins asked a few other questions, which Lexi answered before hanging up the telephone.

"The FBI isn't working on this," she said, meeting Chane's gaze. "God—"

The front doorbell rang. Lexi started. Someone, only hours ago, had followed her and tried to run her off the highway. Someone who could have followed her home. Someone . . .

She watched Chane approach the open expanse of window like a man approaching a mine field. In that instant, Lexi had a glimpse of the Marine in him, the warrior trained to do battle. Warriors protected those weaker than themselves.

They also frequently got themselves killed.

Lexi's glance went to Tessa.

And this warrior was a father.

He glanced outside, and his posture relaxed.

"It's the UPS truck, and the usual driver," he said, going to the door.

Throwaway comment though it was, Lexi latched on to his reference about the driver. Chane wasn't the sort of man to be worried simply because she was—like her, he really thought she was in danger.

Chane opened the door, chatted a moment with the driver as he signed for the package. He took the box from the driver and closed the door.

Lexi met him halfway across the room. As soon as she saw the address label, she bit her lip, took the box from Chane, and carried it to the kitchen.

"What is it?" he asked.

"A digitizer," she answered, removing the packing from the box. "It's a way to computer-enhance fuzzy negatives. Instead of blowing them up in an enlarger, you scan them, then use the computer and the software to make them sharper."

"That sounds like an expensive piece of equipment," Chane said.

"Not as much as it used to be. Joe Robertson sent it."

Chane scowled. "Then you were helping him with a story." He didn't like the way this was going at all. Not a single thing he had learned this morning reassured him. Not the bullet in her tire. Not the identity of a thug on her trail. Not Lexi's connection to The Sisters of Hope. Not even the possibility that Señora Padilla had been sent on a wild-goose chase.

"Yes," she answered, her gaze direct, her tone, however, without any challenge.

Chane passed a hand over his forehead, glanced at her, then shoveled his hand through his hair. "I should have known better," he muttered. He raised his head. "And you should know better, too. After what he did to you—"

"You don't know—"

"I know you were kidnapped because of him. How the hell could you be helping him?"

"He came back for me. I owe him!"

"He's dead!" Chane's voice grew rough, and he leaned toward Lexi, his gaze nearly level with hers. "And goddammit, you're going to pay with your life, too, if you don't get smart about this!"

An instant of silence dropped like a stone between them.

Tessa whimpered.

Lexi had forgotten she and Chane weren't alone. She had the opportunity to finish it. To send him packing. Damn the man for caring about her! Nothing in her life had ever been more alluring. Even as she fought another battle with her conscience, she wrenched her gaze from Chane's and dropped to her knees. Tessa sat on the floor, her whimpers one more piece of Lexi's undoing. Chane was already reaching under the table for his daughter.

"It's okay," he crooned, picking her up.

Tessa leaned her cheek against his massive chest, tears streaming down her face.

Lexi glanced at Tía Ester, who was wringing her hands. "*Lo lamento,*" she said.

"There's nothing for you to be sorry about," Lexi told her. Instead of taking advantage of the breach as she knew she ought to do, she found herself mending the argument, needing to soothe Chane, Tessa, and Tía Ester. "Chane and I . . ." She glanced at him. "It was a simple quarrel. *Nada mas.*" In English, she added, "A quarrel. That's all."

Chane nodded in agreement, his dark eyes intent. "Are you ready to go talk to Hank?"

"I can drive myself," she answered. "You don't have to take me."

"The hell I don't," he said. "Get your coat."

* * *

In a motel in Winter Park, George Moody let himself into a room where Darren Burke sat next to the telephone and an overflowing ashtray.

"We just got a break," Moody said.

"We need one." Burke crossed off another of the towns in northwestern Colorado on his handwritten list. "From Berthoud Pass she could have been on her way anywhere. Not many towns, but a whole lot of geography. And if she doesn't have a listed telephone number, I've been wasting my time."

"I found her. She's in Grand Lake."

"How do you know?"

Moody shrugged. "The old woman is with Monroe." He shook a cigarette out of a pack. "It turns out a certain Lexi Monroe has been asking about the Sisters of Hope on behalf of a woman looking for her stolen grandchild." He smiled and held out a sheet of paper with an address written on it. "It makes people very nervous when you go around asking the wrong questions."

Burke raised an eyebrow.

"A woman named Ellen Belsen has done business with the good sisters. She got scared when Monroe started asking questions. The good Mrs. Belsen needs to be reminded how very precarious her position could be if she shared secrets with the wrong people."

"And Monroe?" Burke asked.

Moody brought the cigarette to his lips, struck a match, and lit it, inhaling deeply. He stared at the flame of the match as it burned toward his fingers. "She lives outside of town. Alone."

Chapter 17

They all piled into the cab of the pickup, and Chane drove into Grand Lake, his thoughts in turmoil. He didn't begin to understand her loyalty to the likes of Joe Robertson, though he grudgingly admitted he might feel the same had the man saved his life. At least she had agreed to talk to Hank.

Chane kept feeling as though he was missing something important. To figure what, he needed a little space—more precisely, time to think about all this. Time—a commodity in short supply this day. Class was scheduled for this afternoon, and he was tempted to cancel it. Except that was something he never did at the last minute—getting hold of students was always a problem—especially when none of them except Lexi lived in Grand Lake. And this morning . . . he racked his memory a moment, trying to remember what he needed to be doing this morning.

Suddenly, he remembered he was supposed to have met with Ellen Belsen when he dropped Tessa by the day-care center.

Since Lexi would be safely tucked away with Hank, now was as good a time as any. Chane spared her a glance. She seemed lost within her own thoughts as he was within his. As usual, the señora and Tessa were busy amusing one another.

"I'm going to drop Tessa off at day-care," Chane said a few minutes later after he had introduced Lexi to Hank.

Something close to relief chased over her expression. "Fine," she said.

"Don't go anywhere. I'll pick you up after you've finished here."

Hank winked at him. "I can put her under house arrest."

Chane allowed a smile, though he didn't find the situation funny at all. "Whatever it takes, man." He picked Tessa up and ushered the señora outside.

Back in the pickup again, Señora Padilla said to him, "This day-care where you are taking Tessa. It is a good place?"

"Yes."

"A place where strangers care for your child?"

He glanced at her, hearing the censure within her tone.

"The woman who runs the place was my wife's best friend," he explained. "So, she's not exactly a stranger. And it's good for Tessa to be around other children."

"You can come inside with me," Tessa said. "And you can meet Stephie and Ricky and Michael and Joanie. But you can't stay all day," Tessa added, " 'cause it's a kid place. Grown-ups are too big for the chairs."

Chane turned into the parking lot in front of the day-care center, pulling his truck into an empty parking space next to Ellen's Wagoneer. As soon as he opened the car door for her, Tessa skipped up the sidewalk, the señora in tow. Chane followed them into the building and made his way to Ellen's office.

He rapped on the door and, at her summons to enter, opened it. Her automatic smile of welcome faded when she recognized him.

"You said you had an envelope for me," he said without preamble.

"And good morning to you, too," she said.

"Will the pleasantries make this any better?" he asked.

"Probably," she said.

"Well, then, Ellen. Good morning. I trust that when we're

done dancing around one another, you'll be able to tell me where I can find the adoption decree. The envelope?"

"You won't find the decree in it," Ellen said.

"Why the hell not?"

Ellen looked at him a moment, then asked, "Why now, Chane? Why dig all this up now?"

"I wasn't digging," he said tightly. "All I wanted to do was find the damn decree—"

"And what if it never turns up? What then? Do you send Tessa back to Costa Léon?"

"Of course not," he said, his temper fraying. "She's my daughter."

"That, at least, would make Rose happy to know."

Chane sat down in a chair across from Ellen. "I suppose you have reason to be mad at me. But I don't have time for this. Just give me the envelope, and I'll be out of your hair."

She opened the lap drawer of her desk and pulled out a large manila envelope. "When Rose decided to go to Costa Léon, I had no—"

"Rose went to Central America?" Chane stood, knocking his chair over. Travel was something Rose had hated, and flying most of all. "She wouldn't have gotten on a plane to save her life."

"Maybe not. But she did fly to Central America to get the one thing she wanted."

"No."

"You can deny things all you want, Chane. God knows you certainly were never around to listen to her or take care of things while you were married. Why would she have told you when you made it plain what you wanted was the only thing that mattered."

"That makes me sound like a selfish bastard."

"She'd be glad to know you recognized yourself."

"I don't have to stand here and listen to this."

"Then leave!"

He held his hand out. "The envelope."

Ellen handed it to him. "Beware of what you ask for, Chane

Callahan. You may decide Rose's secrets would have been better off buried with her.''

Without a word, he turned and made his way through the big playroom outside Ellen's office. He was outside and almost to the truck when he heard someone call his name. The señora hurried after him, and he helped her into the pickup.

"I think you forgot me, Señor Chane," she said a little breathlessly.

His glance fell to the envelope he had thrown in the seat between them. She was right, but he wasn't about to admit that to her.

"And you are correct," she added.

"About what?" he asked, his attention still mostly on his conversation with Ellen.

The señora waved toward the building. "This place. It is a good place for little Tessa. No strangers." She smiled. "No stern *monjas.*"

"No what?"

"*Monjas.* In the Catholic Church. The women—"

"Nuns?"

"*Sí.*" In spite of his preoccupation, Chane chuckled. Evidently nuns were much the same world over.

"You will take me to the grocery store now," she announced.

"Later," he said.

"Now," she insisted. "If I cook, I must have ..." She paused, then said, "Supplies."

"Supplies?"

"*Sí.* Rice. Fish. Chilis. You are worried for Alexandra. I go to the store. You go to Alexandra. You come back for me. Everybody is happy."

Chane's glance fell to the envelope. Happy. Not if there was a grain of truth in Ellen's warning. Not bloody likely.

"Okay, Señor Chane."

"Okay."

Only there was no way she was going into the store alone. Not while there was a possibility she could be meeting with one of El Ladron's henchmen. Chane parked the pickup in the parking lot in front of the grocery store, and followed the señora inside. Dutifully, he followed her up and down the aisles, translating labels she didn't understand and picking items off the top shelves.

All the while his attention was focused on the envelope and Ellen's dire warning. Equal measures of dread at what the envelope might or might not contain and a desire to deep-six the damn thing tore through him. Until a few short weeks ago, he had considered himself a man without secrets. No longer.

At last, the señora seemed to have everything she needed, and they stood in line to pay. Through it all, she seemed to have nothing more urgent on her mind than finding exactly the ingredients she wanted. That relieved Chane, though none of the supposition surrounding the woman brought any comfort. If she was the nice, little old lady she seemed to be, she had been lied to and used. And she'd probably never know what happened to her granddaughter. And if she wasn't—if she had led El Ladron's henchmen to Lexi, Chane wouldn't be above locking her up himself and throwing away the key.

Feeling both surprised and relieved, Lexi watched Chane leave with his daughter and Tía Ester. The way he had been hovering over her, she assumed he would stay. She was glad she didn't have to figure out a ruse to make him leave.

Her only hope of getting Chane out of this was to lay her cards on the table and hope Grand Lake's small police department could provide the kind of expertise needed to protect her and grab El Ladron or his thugs when he showed up.

Lexi told Hank everything she knew and everything she suspected. That a bogus FBI agent had interviewed her at the hospital and her discovery this morning that the FBI wasn't working on the case. That whoever had tried to run her down last night was connected to El Ladron.

As she talked, Hank interrupted her, asking more questions than a seasoned reporter, even a few she hadn't thought of herself. He made notes in an abbreviated shorthand that reminded her of a big-city detective.

She concluded by telling him that Señora Padilla had connections to both The Sisters of Hope and to Joe Robertson. "She got my address from Joe."

"And he was working on a story about El Ladron?"

"He wasn't supposed to be," Lexi answered. "But when we talked a couple days ago, he told me that he had a lead, and he wanted to know if I had any negatives that could be run through a digitizer." She swallowed. "The digitizer arrived this morning."

"This El Ladron guy," Hank said. "Does he have another name? I can put out a John Doe APB. Chances are, we won't get anything."

Lexi shook her head. "That was the one piece of the puzzle Joe and I never found. He's an American, I know that. But I could never turn up a name."

"But you could get me a picture?"

Lexi nodded. "Now that I have the digitizer, I should be able to get to a good one."

"When?" Hank asked. "The sooner, the better."

"Not until later," Chane said from the doorway. He stepped into the room, and the door slammed behind him. His expression was implacable. "I don't want her anywhere near her house. In fact, I'd like to see a stakeout. We all know that's where her assailant is eventually headed."

"I don't have a listed telephone number, and my license plates list my address in New York, not here. Whoever this is, he's going to have to work hard to figure out I'm here."

"Not that hard," Chane said. "He'll work his way up US 40. You can hope he'll head for Steamboat instead of coming to Grand Lake. But I wouldn't count on it."

"Even if I agree with you," Hank interrupted, "we don't have the manpower for a stakeout. For that matter, I'm not sure we even have enough motive to warrant it. My boss is going to call all this supposition. The most I can do is add extra patrols."

"If Señora Padilla can find you here," Chane added, "anyone can."

"But Joe sent her."

"Somehow, I don't find that real damn reassuring," Chane said.

"Do you think she's involved with El Ladron?" Hank asked.

"I don't know," Lexi answered, meeting his gaze. "I intend to find out. I really believe she's been duped. I think—I hope—she's exactly what she seems to be—an old woman looking for her granddaughter. If what she told me is true, she has as much reason to hate El Ladron as anyone. He killed her daughter and son-in-law."

"Get me a photograph," Hank said. "That and a description of the vehicle isn't as good as a name, but it might help."

"Consider it done," she promised. Maybe, she thought, just maybe all this would work out. One more chance to make a difference for the babies. One more chance to get El Ladron. And this time, she would succeed.

"You're not going back to your house," Chane said.

"We'll talk about that later," Lexi said, taking him by the arm and steering him toward the door. On the way out, she told Hank she'd see him in a few hours. "Now. I'm starved. What's for lunch?"

"If you think you're going to sidetrack me, you're wrong."

She stopped walking and turned to face him. "And if you think I can drop this, you're wrong."

The fierceness in his expression didn't lighten a bit, but he reached out and cupped her cheek with his big hand. "You always this stubborn, or is it just me?" he asked in a voice gravelly with suppressed emotion.

She put her hand over his and gripped his fingers hard. "I'm stubborn."

"Then we'll go do this together later. I'll take you back to your house and you can make the damn pictures. After class, okay?"

Lexi nodded, even as she admitted to herself she had no intention of doing this Chane's way. El Ladron was a killer, a man who viewed people as disposable things. This was her battle to finish alone.

They got in the truck, where Tía Ester waited.

The three of them rode back to Chane's house, only a few

blocks from the center of town and high enough on the hillside to have a view of Grand Lake. Noticing Chane's mail on the dash, Lexi picked it up and put it in one of the sacks of groceries she helped carry inside. In the kitchen, she emptied the sacks as Chane put things away. Tía Ester fussed at the two of them, gathering up the ingredients for whatever it was she planned to make for lunch. Finally, the señora shooed the two of them out of the kitchen.

"I put your mail by the phone," Lexi said, motioning toward the manila envelope she had carried into the house.

He glanced briefly in that direction, then nodded. "Thanks."

"I like your house," Lexi said, following him into the living room. Throughout, the dark woodwork and polished oak floors gleamed. The house had a cozy, lived-in feel that she found inviting. She wandered toward the fireplace, drawn by the assortment of photographs on the mantel. Eyes stared out from formal and informal portraits. Chane followed her without offering any commentary on the pictures. There was a picture of him, looking much younger. He wore a military dress uniform and was standing next to a Hispanic woman in a wedding dress who looked petite in comparison to him.

"Your wife?" she asked.

"Yes."

"How long were you married?"

"Almost twelve years," he answered shortly.

"A long time."

"Yeah."

The reality of his being married struck Lexi for the first time, a topic apparently as uncomfortable for him as it was her. A woman who would forever be a part of Chane's life, Lexi realized. Knowing the kind of man Chane was, he undoubtedly had loved her deeply—probably still did.

And no children except Tessa, Lexi thought, her attention moving on to a photograph of Tessa and her mother. Whoever had shot the picture had captured the joy and love that flowed between mother and daughter.

"It must have been hard for you when she died," Lexi

said and instantly wished she could take back the words. The comment sounded stupid. She added, "Of course it was hard."

Chane nodded.

"Was she ill?"

"Rose died in a car accident," Chane said, "less than two months after I got out of the hospital and came home. Tessa was maybe seven months old then."

"So you're the only parent she's ever known."

"She's my daughter," he said. Laced within his voice was pride, love, and a father's claiming of his responsibility to protect.

All things Lexi thought a father should be. "And she's a sweetie." Her voice grew wistful. "There are so many babies I photographed. Hungry babies and babies from families so poor . . ." Her voice trailed off. "You wouldn't believe the things I saw."

"I know what you saw. Anyone who has seen your magazine spread knows." Chane smoothed a speck of dust off one of the photographs of Tessa. "But for the grace of God, Tessa could have been one of those children."

"She's lucky, then, she has a daddy like you," Lexi said, reminding herself why she needed to be someplace else—anyplace else.

"Lucky." His voice sounded gravelly, and he cleared his throat. "I have to tell you . . ." He stared at another photograph a long moment, the one of his wife and his daughter. When he faced Lexi, his eyes were troubled. "Tessa's adopted."

Lexi stared at him, absorbing the words, wondering why he looked so grim about it.

"Ellen Belsen helped."

"Tessa's from South America?" Lexi asked, still not comprehending the source of Chane's obvious tension.

Chane nodded. "Yeah."

A river of dread ran through her stomach. "What's the rest of it?"

"In the research you've been doing about The Sisters of Hope—"

''Tessa came from them?'' Even as she asked the question, that river widened and flowed coldly through her.

''They did have legitimate adoptions, didn't they?''

''Enough to give their operation some credibility. Enough to keep the State Police from looking too closely at their activities. Is that where she came from, Chane?''

He nodded.

Lexi closed her eyes, remembering that she had asked Ellen about *Las Hermanas de la Esperanza*—The Sister of Hope— and that Ellen hadn't seemed to know who they were. Why lie? Why?

''If you have all of Tessa's adoption papers, you shouldn't have any problems,'' Lexi said, remembering how upstanding the operation had become for those few months after she turned over everything she had to the State Police. ''Though only an attorney could tell you for sure.'' She paused. ''Would you have told me about this if Señora Padilla was on a legitimate quest?''

Chane's gaze dropped to the floor for a long moment. ''I don't know,'' he said finally. ''I have to admit, she's given me a lot to think about the last few days. You wonder, of course, what happened to your baby's family—wonder if there are people who loved her and worried for her. But I never imagined someone like the señora.''

Lexi glanced toward the kitchen. The aroma of tortillas and peppers cooking wafted through the air. The sizzling sounds of something cooking accompanied a song on the radio and Tía Ester's humming. ''I still have to talk to her about that.'' She moved toward the kitchen.

''Lexi?''

Chane's voice stopped her, and she turned around.

Slowly he walked toward her, stopping when he was a scant foot away. His expression was so controlled his features might have been carved from stone. He took one of her hands. ''There's no point in telling her about Tessa.''

Lexi searched his face, remembering Ellen's assertion Tía Ester's quest would lead only to heartbreak. ''No,'' Lexi agreed. ''There's no reason to tell her.''

He squeezed her hand and let it go. "Thank you."

Lexi came to a stop at the kitchen door. Tía Ester glanced up from her preparations.

"*Arroz y pescado*," she said with a smile. "I am nearly finished."

"Why is the rice green?" Chane asked, standing behind Lexi.

She glanced over her shoulder and grinned. "Pureed chilis are added to it. Trust me, you'll like it."

"I have no doubt, but you have to admit, it does look different."

Lexi noted only two places had been set at the table. Without saying a word, she searched through the cupboards and drawers, finding plates and silverware, and adding another place setting to the table.

"You and Señor Chane have much to talk about," Tía Ester said. "You do not need the presence of an old woman."

"Actually we do," Lexi responded. "You cooked. You get to eat with us."

"I don't—"

"I agree with Lexi," Chane interrupted. "Two against one."

Tía Ester glanced from one to the other, and finally smiled. "You would court Alexandra," she said to Chane. "When I was a young girl, a chaperon was required. That is no longer the custom."

"It no longer is," he agreed easily. "But right now, we want to share lunch with you."

"I will serve you," she said, motioning toward the chairs.

"And you'll join us," Lexi said.

"If you insist."

"I insist," Chane said, sitting down.

"I did not take the time to tell you how troubled I am by Señor Robertson," Tía Ester said. She patted Lexi's hand. "He was a good friend, no?"

Lexi managed a smile. "A friend, Tía."

She clucked her tongue. "Such a wasteful thing. These guns and these shootings."

"Yes," Lexi murmured.

"You said Robertson told you how to find Lexi," Chane said. "How did that come to pass?"

"I had been to the agency many times—"

"The Sisters of Hope?" Chane questioned.

She nodded, handing Lexi another plate she had just dished up. "Each time I go there, I talk to a different person. Each one tells me they cannot help. I must talk to someone else. Then one day, there is a young man working there. Very helpful, very eager, very polite. He tells me he will search through the records and for me to come back to see him in two days."

"And then," Lexi prompted.

Tía Ester sat down and spread a napkin over her lap. "And then I go back. He has papers for me. Dates when three little girls were sent to the United States—to Colorado. One of these, he tells me, is my Estella. I want to come to the United States, but I know nothing of the customs, nothing of the legalities. I need a guide. The young man told me Señor Robertson could help. So, I fly to Los Angeles and see him, and I ask for help." She paused and patted Lexi's hand. "And the rest you know. I am here."

"You must love your grandchild very much to do all this," Chane said.

The señora's gaze was direct when she looked at him. "Is not little Tessa your heart?"

"Yes."

"My Estella. She is my heart, just as her mother was." The señora made the sign of the Cross. "Safe and cherished, God willing."

"What will you do if you find her?" Lexi asked gently.

Tía Ester stared at her plate a moment. "Once I knew how it would be. She is my granddaughter, after all. And the ties of blood—they are strong. The ties of love—these, too, are strong." She glanced at Chane. "I see you with your daughter, and know how much you love her. My Estella, perhaps she is blessed with a father and a mother who love her as much. If this is true, how can I break that tie?" Her voice trembled. "And yet, how can I leave her? Never to know of her heritage, her mother. Never to be her true *abuela*?"

The anguished question dropped like a stone into the silence. Lexi reached for Tía Ester's hand, squeezing it gently.

Tía Ester lifted her head, her eyes bright with emotion. "With your help, Alexandra, I know we will find Estella."

"We might not," Lexi said, gently. "I told you when we began this, the odds were not with us."

"I have faith," Tía stated firmly, as though her declaration settled the matter.

Lexi caught Chane's glance, all her distrust vanquished.

As they finished lunch, Chane related anecdotes about Kit and Tessa and coaxed from Tía Ester tidbits about her home and her family that further dissolved Lexi's doubts. Everything Tía Ester revealed about her life in Costa Léon seemed to confirm the story she had told Lexi. The years of warfare in the country had robbed her family of everything, beginning with her husband's death more than a decade ago and ending with her daughter's death and the abduction of her granddaughter. No one person should have had to endure so much. The least she should have been granted to know was that her only living relative—her granddaughter—was well and happy and cared for. And even that would be denied her.

As Lexi listened, her heart broke that such a determined, lonely old woman had been so callously used. To tell Tía Ester her journey was a hoax would simply heap an additional layer of cruelty upon the old woman. Lexi didn't know how she could do it.

She caught Chane's eye, seeking some assurance, some indication of what she could say—what she should say. When he finally glanced at her, he gave his head a negligible shake, and she let the moment pass, plagued by her conscience. What was the right thing to do?

Chapter 18

Chane stood up from the table, picking up his plate and carrying it to the sink. "Will you be ready to go in about fifteen minutes?" he asked her.

She followed him to the sink, carrying her own plate. "You know, I've been thinking about the class and—"

"You're going," he said, laying a finger across Lexi's lips. "I've already figured out that if I leave you safe and sound here with Tía Ester, you'll head for home."

"But—"

"Don't try to deny it."

"You're exasperating," she said.

"What I am," he countered, "is right." He dropped a quick kiss on her mouth. "I've got a couple of things to gather up for the class, and then I'll be ready to go. And you are going with me. Agreed?"

"Ah, a benevolent dictator who seeks my agreement. Amazing." Lexi smiled at him, hating his perception. No matter how nice the last hour had been, she didn't dare believe this was more than a passing moment. It couldn't be until this whole business with El Ladron was taken care of.

He grinned. "Glad you understand the situation. I'll be back in a jiffy."

Lexi watched him leave the kitchen with a mixture of frustration and amusement. Nothing would keep her from leaving right now, except that he would catch up with her and she'd again be back to square one.

Facing Tía Ester, Lexi asked, "Are you going to be okay here alone?"

"Of course," she said simply. A sudden frown furrowed her brow. "Is there some reason you ask?"

Avoiding Tía Ester's gaze, Lexi returned to the table, gathering up miscellaneous silverware and glasses.

"When you began your search for your granddaughter, and you were still in Costa Léon, did anyone suggest you talk to me?" She lifted her eyes and met Tía Ester's gaze.

"No comprendo," she said, lapsing into Spanish.

"Who gave you my name?" Lexi asked in Spanish, wishing she had asked the question days ago.

"Señor Robertson," Tía Ester said after a moment's thought. Continuing to speak in her native tongue, she added, "I had seen the magazine with the pictures of the children, but I didn't know you would be able to help."

"So nobody mentioned my name—nobody but Joe."

"Sí."

Lexi searched Tía Ester's face. "Do you remember who told you to find Joe?"

She nodded. *"El chico en Las Hermanas de la Esperanza."* She brightened suddenly. "He was American. I remember his name sounded strange."

"Do you have it?"

"Sí." Without another word, Tía Ester bustled out of the kitchen.

While she waited, Lexi finished clearing and wiping down the table and loaded the dishwasher. Moving the mail she had set down earlier to the clean table, she washed the counters as well. A few minutes later Tía Ester returned to the kitchen with several manila envelopes.

"I have the name," she said. "In one of these."

She set them down, and they spread across the table.

Lexi sat down and opened one of the envelopes. "What are we looking for?"

"A note. On it are the names of three *niñas.* I asked his name, and I wrote it on the paper." She sat down, opening one of the envelopes, and began fingering through the papers.

Lexi scanned through the documents, searching through each piece of paper. The name would put her one step closer to discovering El Ladron's identity. Whatever name Tía Ester had was undoubtedly not El Ladron himself, but one of his henchmen. If they were lucky, he'd have some known associates, one of whom might be El Ladron's real identity. The illusive sheet wasn't in the first envelope Lexi searched through.

Nor the second.

She set it aside and reached for another manila envelope, opening the clasp and pulling out the papers.

"Was the note handwritten?" Lexi asked.

"*Sí.*" Lexi glanced at the faded copy of a plane ticket and was on the verge of setting it aside when a name at the top caught her eye. *Rose Callahan.* Lexi turned it over, then set it aside.

Underneath was a birth certificate. For Tessa.

Puzzled, Lexi thumbed through the documents in her hands, finding paperwork for certificates of deposit that had been cashed in and stock that had been sold, and a faded copy of a cashier's check. Payable to The Sisters of Hope. For thousands of dollars more than a legitimate adoption cost.

Her hands shaking, Lexi stared at the check, noting the date, seeing Chane's name and his wife's listed as the payees.

Tessa's adopted. Adopted.

In a rush, Lexi turned over the empty envelope, finding only a single word written on the outside. Chane.

Chilly fingers of dread slithered down her back as she realized this was the mail she had brought into the house. Only, it wasn't mail. And somehow, it had been mixed up with Tía Ester's papers.

Horrible suspicions lodged in her mind. She looked through the papers again. A copy of plane tickets, the itinerary still

attached. A flight to Costa Léon. Six weeks later a return flight
to the United States. Feeling her heart begin to pound, Lexi
picked up the birth certificate.

Tessa Callahan. Born on the fourteenth of November to
Chane and Rose Callahan, citizens of the United States of
America. Not quite four years ago.

Oh, God, she thought, feeling the blood drain out of her
face, pooling into a cold lump in the pit of her stomach. This
can't mean what I think it means. It can't.

Wordlessly, Lexi gathered up the documents, wishing she
had never seen them. *Tessa's adopted.* Her head pounding,
Lexi closed her eyes, remembering Chane's troubled expression
as he told her. Why lie? Why?

In that blinding instant, she remembered she had asked herself the same question about Ellen Belsen. *Heartache and
despair,* Ellen had warned Lexi, were all that would come of
Tía Ester's search. And Ellen had lied about *Las Hermanas de
la Esperanza.*

And Chane . . . Lexi closed her eyes against a stab of pain
. . . had asked her if the group did legitimate business. As if
he didn't know. Bile rose in her throat, and she dropped her
chin to her chest.

"Ah-ha," Tía Ester exclaimed, holding up a sheet of paper.
"I knew it was here." She extended it toward Lexi.

Reflexively, Lexi took the sheet, staring at the handwritten
notes, her vision blurred.

"Alexandra?" Tía Ester questioned. *"¿Estás bien? Tienes
mal aspecto."*

Lexi glanced up and shook her head. "I'm not ill, Tía."
With effort she returned her attention to the handwritten note.
Three infant girls born in November four years ago. And a
man's name. George Moody. An ordinary-sounding name that
was one more link in identifying the illusive El Ladron.

Lexi's gaze strayed back to the birth certificate. And Tessa
was born in November four years ago. Again, Chane's voice
echoed through her head. *The Sisters of Hope.*

Tía Ester stood and came around the table. "This is the name
you wanted. Yes?"

Lexi handed her back the sheet. "George Moody. Yes."

"This name. It means something to you?"

"No." Gathering the papers back together, Lexi slid them back in the envelope. Fastening the metal tab, she discarded one possibility after another, wanting to believe anything but the damning truth. Chane and his wife had bought Tessa from The Sisters of Hope. And Chane's voice pounded through her head. *You wonder, of course, what happened to your baby's family—wonder if there are people who loved her and worried for her. But I never imagined someone like the señora. . . . There's no point in telling her about Tessa.*

And Lexi had agreed. Had, in effect, promised.

The sound of the back door opening interrupted her thoughts. Chane came through the door.

"Ready?" he asked. "We've got to get going if we don't want to be late."

Lexi searched his face, seeking some clue, some indication, . . . some *thing* that would help her understand. This man— this decent, caring man—had bought a baby. How could he? One part of her wanted to rant at him, to demand answers for the unthinkable. Another part of her wanted to run. And yet one last part wanted explanations, wanted him to deny the truth of the papers she had just seen.

"We found the name of the young man at *Las Hermanas de la Esperanza,*" Tía Ester said. "George Moody."

The pleased sound in her voice was in mocking contrast to the cold reality of fear that wound through Lexi, making her hands cold. Her feet cold. Her heart . . . cold.

"The name mean anything to you, Lexi?" Chane moved toward her, holding her jacket in his hands. He held it up for her, and she slipped into it.

"No." Nothing in his manner was any different. And why should it be, Lexi thought. He hadn't changed in the last fifteen minutes. Only her knowledge was different.

"Think it's this El Ladron character? Or maybe one of his hired hands?"

"I don't know." Feeling oddly disjointed, she headed toward the door.

"Hasta luego," Tía Ester said.

"Kit will probably be home before we get back," Chane said. "We're going to Lexi's house after class." He ushered Lexi toward the door. "Did you want to come with us?" he asked, pausing at the door.

Tía Ester shook her head.

Lexi absently waved at the other woman and preceded Chane out of the house. Halfway to the truck she turned to face him.

"We have to talk," she said.

He took her by the elbow and continued steering her toward the vehicle. "So, George Moody *is* a name you recognize."

"I never heard of him. About our conversation earlier—"

"You'll have to remind me which one," he interrupted, opening the door. "C'mon. We're gonna be late."

Lexi climbed into the truck and waited while he came around to the other side.

"Now," he said, putting it in gear and backing out of the driveway. "If this is about your going home instead of going to class, forget it. You and I are joined at the hip for the duration. Got it?"

"Chane—"

"Got it?"

"I need—"

"Agree that you're not going to run off during class, Lexi."

"Another promise?" she asked, her voice sharp.

"Yeah," he agreed. "Another promise. In case you hadn't noticed, it would kind of upset me if you got yourself killed."

"A steamroller has nothing on you, Callahan."

"Thanks for the compliment."

Frustration and fear flowed through her, one burning her, one chilling her, both leaving her seething. She and Chane made the balance of the trip in silence.

A scant five-minute drive from Lexi's house, the site for the class was a clearing with tall lodgepole pines on one side and a beach and Shadow Mountain Lake on the other. Around the cove not quite two miles away, Lexi could see the gleaming reflection of the windows of her house.

"We'll have plenty of time to talk after class, Lexi," he said, parking the truck. "You okay?"

She met his eyes and swallowed. She was anything but okay.

"Everything is going to be fine," he added when she didn't answer.

"Easy for you to say," she muttered, pushing open the door.

He grabbed her hand before she slid from the truck. "If you're trying to pick a fight with me, it's not going to work." He let go of her. "I told you I'd go with you to make the prints after class."

"And I heard you," she snapped.

"Then let go of whatever the hell is ridin' you until after class." He got out of the truck and slammed the door.

She sat there a moment longer, staring through the windshield. All day she had wanted to get away, to separate herself from Chane and anything that could hurt him. And now? She simply wanted to get away, wanted to deny the reality of what she had found.

With the same finesse Chane always exhibited when teaching, he had the class cooperating with each other in no time, bolting together a platform from which they would do trust falls.

More than once, Lexi slid to the back of the small group, wanting time and space and, most of all, an escape. Each time, Chane unobtrusively noticed and brought her back into the fold, the warning glint in his eyes reminding her she had promised to wait until after class to go back to her house.

And she had promised not to tell Tía Ester about Tessa.

"This is something most courses do first thing," Chane said after explaining how the trust falls were to be done. "The theory is it helps break down the barriers when you're strangers. In lots of ways, it's easier to trust a stranger. You haven't had time to develop dislikes or prejudices. For many folks, it's a matter of pride to prove to themselves they can do it. Sheer grit isn't the same thing as trust."

His glance passed over Lexi, and she realized again how very perceptive he was. Bravado and trust were light-years away from one another.

"Now you know each other better. And some of the annoying little habits get on your nerves. Now you're more exposed, and for some of you, the trust fall is going to be harder than it would have been a few weeks ago."

He didn't look at Lexi this time, but she knew he was still talking to her. He was right. She did feel exposed, and she wished she'd never written on her application that she wanted to learn to trust again. She had lied when she had said *trust again. Again* had never been part of the equation. To trust, to believe that someone else would care for you the way they cared for themselves. Chane had shown her glimpses of what that could be like, and the depth with which she wanted it shook her.

Trust. A glimpse into a world that was all illusion. Filled with lies. The slow burning fuse to her temper flared as she mentally ticked off how very little Chane had shared of himself while encouraging—demanding—her trust. He hadn't told her he was a father. Hadn't shared he was raising his brother. Had lied about Tessa.

Had . . . kept her nightmares at bay, not just once, but twice. Had taken in Tía Ester. Had expressed nothing but concern since the whole ugly business with El Ladron had come up.

Had been a man she could love.

Had bought a baby.

"Okay," Chane finished, "who besides Frank wants to be first?"

Joshua and Brian chuckled. Frank always wanted to be first. No one else volunteered.

"Okay," Chane said. "Back to the straws, which it just so happens, I have ready." He held out a selection of toothpicks in his palm, each one a different length. "And just to make it interesting, the longest one goes first this time. In that order to the shortest." He closed his palm and arranged them so they extended the same height from his fist.

Lexi drew the shortest one, which suited her just fine.

They all laughed when Frank drew the longest one. He climbed the platform and stepped to the edge with his back to the class members who lined up in two parallel lines beneath him. They barely had time to get prepared before Frank fell backwards, his body stiff and his eyes closed, into their arms.

"You're not trusting," Brian said to Frank as they set him up upright. "You're stupid. You didn't even look to see if we were ready."

Unabashed, Frank grinned. "That's the whole point of trust. Knowing you wouldn't let me crash to the ground."

"Who's next?" Chane asked.

Julie climbed the platform.

Lexi chafed for the class to be done. Each word of encouragement from Chane warred with her new knowledge. The shadows of the pines stretching across the clearing were only slightly less dark than those stretching across her heart. The musty smell of melting snow seeping into the earth renewed Lexi's memories of hurt and betrayal. Again, she was reminded that she had only herself to depend on. No matter what Chane said.

After a moment's coaxing, Julie fell into the waiting arms of her classmates. Brian and Josh followed.

"Your turn, Lexi," Chane told her.

She climbed the platform, her steps dragging. She recognized Chane had chosen this exercise for her. To make her come face to face with her deepest longing. Trust that someone else would look out for her. What a goddamn lie.

She approached the edge of the platform, turned around, and folded her arms against her chest, her fists clenched around the fabric of her shirt.

"You can do it," Julie encouraged.

"Don't think about it," Frank said. "Just close your eyes and step off. Callahan would kill us if we didn't catch you. And me? I like my life."

Lexi closed her eyes. Intellectually, she knew they were waiting, that they would catch her. Emotionally, she kept seeing a black void. One that could have been—should have been— filled with Chane.

"Lexi?" came his deep voice.

"In a minute," she whispered.

"Lexi, turn around and look at us," he commanded.

She opened her eyes and looked down.

"We're all right here. See?"

She started to nod, then shook her head. "I don't think I can do this," she told him.

"If you think you can, you're right. And if you think you can't, you're still right. Which do you want to do?"

She closed her eyes again and backed toward the edge of the platform. She took a deep breath and closed her eyes. Instead of being certain she'd be caught, other images raced through her mind. An endless night of terror and pain. Her car careening crazily toward an abyss at the top of Berthoud Pass. An innocuous sheet of paper with Tessa's name on it.

"Lexi," Chane said, his voice warm, reassuring. "I'm here. I'll catch you, babe. You can trust me."

Trust me.

She had almost believed she could.

She let her body fall backward. Gravity claimed her and she fell . . . and fell . . . into the arms waiting for her. The only ones she felt were Chane's. She trembled so badly she had trouble standing when they put her upright. Stupid tears burned at the back of her eyes, and she wanted to believe the promise she felt in his arms.

"Great job, you guys. Let's call it a day, gang," Chane said without releasing her. "See you next week."

"All right!" exclaimed Frank, a sentiment echoed by the others as they said goodbye and made their way toward the parking lot.

After they were gone, Chane said to Lexi, "You did it, honey." He gave her a reassuring squeeze. "And you keep trying to tell me you're afraid—"

She wrenched herself out of his grasp and put a couple of feet between them. "And you keep telling me—"

"What? Why are you so mad?"

"You made me promise," she said.

"It was for your own good—"

"Knowing that you had lied to me."

"Lied to you?" He closed this distance between them, looming over her. "What the hell are you talking about?"

"Tessa."

A look of sheer astonishment flashed across his face. "This is about Tessa?"

"Trust me," Lexi mocked, turning on him, pushing him away from her. "And you don't tell me—"

"That she's adopted. This is what's got you so upset?" His voice held a note of genuine puzzlement she almost believed. Almost.

"Adopted?" Lexi returned. "It is a nice, clean, sanitized word, isn't it?"

His face blanched, and his hand snaked out to grab her arm. "You've been talking to the good señora, haven't you? You told her Tessa came from—"

"I did no such thing," she replied, pointedly glancing at his hand. "But believe me, I thought about it."

He let go of her arm, raking his hand through his hair.

"You know what month Tía Ester's granddaughter was born?" Lexi paused, waiting for him to look at her. "November."

He shook his head as if in denial.

"It's just a little too pat that Tessa was born November fourteenth four years ago and Tía Ester—"

"But you thought she was sent here as a plant—"

"She believes she's on a genuine quest. And I'm this close?"—Lexi held her thumb and index finger a scant quarter inch apart—"to having proof I know where her granddaughter is."

"You'll take my daughter only over my dead body." Chane took a threatening step toward Lexi. "And you gave your word you wouldn't tell her."

"That's right. I did. And I'll keep it—she won't find out from me. Maybe you can live with the secrets and the lies, but I'll be fighting my conscience about that for a long time."

His stance relaxed slightly.

"You know how *Las Hermanas de la Esperanza* get their babies, Callahan? They buy them. They steal them." Her voice caught, the image filling her mind of a young woman lying dead in the middle of a dusty road, a dark blossom of blood spread over her back. "They murder for them."

"Lexi." He reached for her.

"And then they sell sweet little baby girls like Tessa to bastards like you." She slapped his hand away and stepped back. "And as long as there are unscrupulous people willing to buy—"

"I didn't—"

"You did. Goddamn you, you did!" Tears sprang to her eyes. "And I don't ever want to see you again."

She turned her back on him and began walking toward home.

Chapter 19

Chane watched Lexi walk away from him, disjointed pieces of their conversation ringing in his ears. Her stinging accusations had a conviction of truth. Besides looking for the name of the man who had sent Señora Padilla on her quest, what had the two of them discussed? Legally his or not, Tessa was more closely tied to his heart than his own life.

And he had harbored the hope Lexi would be, as well.

He climbed into the truck and slammed it into gear, his thoughts reeling as he spun out of the parking lot, throwing gravel up behind his tires.

By her own admission, The Sisters of Hope did legitimate adoptions. Why tell him now they bought and sold babies, stole them, murdered for them?

He arrived at the day-care center to pick up Tessa, unanswerable questions swirling through his mind. His mood surly and his thoughts disjoined, he pulled his truck to an empty parking space between Ellen's Wagoneer and a pickup even dirtier than his own. His long strides carried him inside. He paused just inside the doorway, glancing toward Ellen's office.

The glass door was closed, preventing him from hearing the conversation, but not hiding her tense posture. Chane's glance slid to her visitors—two men, neither of them looking like the parents of toddlers. Chane looked away, deciding his frame of mind had him reading into things sinister overtones where there were none.

Tessa ran across the playroom, and Chane scooped her up, gave her a kiss, and held her until she squirmed to be put down. His daughter, he thought fiercely.

"Can we go feed the geese today, Daddy?" she asked a few minutes later as he strapped her into the seat. "You said the next time you came early, we could." She patted his hand and the dimple in her cheek flashed as she smiled at him, and her voice lowered to a conspiratorial whisper. "And it's early."

"It is?" he whispered back. Today of all days, he didn't want to honor the promise. Today of all days, a promise had never held more importance.

She giggled. "It is."

"We have to go buy bread."

"Okay."

They stopped for the loaf of bread, then headed for the canal that separated Shadow Mountain Lake from Lake Granby, one of Tessa's favorite places. Instead of the flocks of Canadian geese they normally saw, today there were only a pair of mallards, too shy to approach any of the pieces of bread that Tessa threw at them. Their lack of response did nothing to diminish her enjoyment of the moment.

Chane envied her for that. It was an afternoon to do nothing more than enjoy the sunshine and crisp air. But for the life of him, he couldn't banish the echo of Lexi's voice taunting him that he was one of the bastards who had bought a baby. Said as though she knew. Really knew.

She couldn't have known how shaken he was at her revelation the señora's granddaughter had been born the same month as Tessa. Lexi was right about one thing—that was stretching the limits of coincidence too far.

Though his heart wasn't in it, he played with Tessa, reminding himself all he had to do was walk the walk until he really felt the feeling. Just as he had done many times since

Rose's death. The sun had slipped closed to the western horizon before Tessa was ready to head for home.

Kit and the señora were in the kitchen when Chane came through the back door carrying Tessa on his shoulders.

"*¿Donde está Alexandra?*" the señora asked as soon as he set Tessa down.

"Where's—" Kit asked. "Good question. When am I going to get to meet this woman?"

"She decided to go home," Chane answered shortly.

"She should not be alone," the señora said.

"It's what she wanted."

"And you will not bring her here?"

"No."

The señora clucked her tongue, then said, "*La comida está servida en unos minutos.*"

"Soup's on," Kit said. "Better wash up, bro, or we'll start without you."

Eating was the last thing Chane wanted to do, but he joined his family at the table a few minutes later anyway. The last time he had sat down to one of the señora's meals, he had hoped it would be the first of many he shared with Lexi. He hadn't anticipated it would be the only . . . the last.

He still couldn't figure out what had set her off. During lunch she had been fine. Before class she had been agitated, and after . . . He stared across the kitchen, sure there was some piece of this he wasn't seeing, wasn't understanding. His gaze lit on the manila envelope Ellen had given him this morning. An envelope Lexi had told him she put next to the phone. Which was now propped against the phone books at the opposite end of the counter.

Without conscious thought, Chane stood and crossed the kitchen. "Where did this come from?" he asked.

"Don't ask me, bro. I found it on the table when I was setting it."

"I saw it there after you and Alexandra left."

Chane glanced at the señora. "Did you open it?"

She gasped and placed her open hand against her breast.

"Señor Chane, I am not a . . ." She paused, searching for the right word.

"Snoop?" Kit prompted.

The señora's obvious shock at his accusation shamed Chane. "That was out of line," he said. "Sorry." He turned the envelope over, examining the clasp. Without another word, he left the kitchen.

"Hey, bro, everything okay?" Kit called after him.

"Fine." But it wasn't. A terrible, sick feeling of premonition washed through him. Lexi had spoken as though she knew—really knew—the truth of her accusations. And the envelope hadn't been sealed.

"There's a rock concert in Denver on Tuesday night," Kit said. "Can I go?"

"Hell, no," Chane responded.

Kit laughed. "Gosh, he had me goin' there for a minute, Tía."

Chane walked down the hall toward his bedroom and shut the door behind him. Wondering what final surprises Rose had in store for him, he spilled the contents of the envelope onto the bed. He expected to find the adoption decree, prayed he would.

The last thing he expected to find was a birth certificate. Tessa's name. And Rose's and his. Born to Rose and Chane Callahan, citizens of the United States of America.

If Chane had been pushed over a cliff without a lifeline, he could not have been more shocked.

There was no way Tessa was biologically his child. Nor Rose's for that matter. He'd been gone seven months. When he arrived home, Tessa was five months old. For Tessa to have been theirs, Rose would have to have been eight months pregnant when he left for the fateful mission to Mosul.

And what about the other birth certificate? The one he had given to his attorney.

Chane riffled through the papers. A passport issued to Rose within two weeks of his departure for Mosul. Plane tickets to Costa Léon and an itinerary. A week after he had flown to the Mddle East, Rose had gone to Costa Léon. She apparently had stayed about six weeks, then returned home. The last two items in the envelope were a certificate of deposit she had cashed in and for some stock she had sold. When Rose had told him how much the adoption cost, he had thought the fees exorbitant. The amount of cash she'd taken from savings was more than four times the amount she'd told him.

Conclusions that couldn't be right pushed through Chane's chaotic thoughts. Conclusions that wouldn't be dispelled. Conclusions that make him sick at heart.

Rose had gone to Central America and bought a baby.

Lexi arrived at home feeling numb, which she eventually decided was just fine. When this afternoon's numbness wore off, she was going to hurt as she never had before. Analytically, she planned what she had to do, reminding herself the basic things she had to accomplish hadn't changed.

El Ladron still had to be stopped, and she still needed to make sure his vendetta against her didn't put others in danger. Equally obvious, sooner or later he would find her if she stayed in Grand Lake. And, Lord knew, she had no reason to stay.

Every time her mind veered toward Chane Callahan, she hauled it back with ruthless discipline. He didn't matter. Stopping El Ladron did. This time her stake was more personal than ever. This time she knew a grieving grandmother, a sweet little girl, and a buyer. This time, she would finish it, even if she had to return to Costa Léon to do it.

Lexi picked up the phone and called an airline for reservations to New York City, making arrangements for a flight out the following morning. The plan set into motion, she made a quick list of the things she needed to take care of. At the top of that list was making a recognizable print of El Ladron and delivering it to Hank Warner.

She installed the digitizer software in her computer, then hooked it to her enlarger, remembering she had thought the technology both curse and marvel when she had first used it. Images could be altered, people could be put into places they had never been with people they had never met. Gone were the old days of cut and paste. Lexi hoped simply to sharpen one of the images into the face of El Ladron.

The one time she had met him, his face had been in shadows—a deliberate attempt to intimidate her and manipulate her—but she remembered the eyes.

Putting a negative into a holder, she returned to the computer. Following the instructions in the accompanying manual, she began working on the first negative. She had a few false starts before she got the rhythm down, comparing the image on the computer screen with the one in her memory. Methodically, she worked, sharpening the lines that poor lighting had blurred.

Several hours later she came face to face with El Ladron. She had expected an evil, menacing face. Except for his eyes, he was average looking. Those eyes had stalked through her nightmares for a year. Those eyes . . . she'd never forget.

She had pinned her hopes on recognizing a man beyond the person, one known as Bill Smith or John Jones or Archibald Hinklestein. Anything she could have taken to the police and said, *Here he is. This is the man. Arrest him.* She wanted that for herself. She wanted it for Joe.

Instead she'd have to pass on to Hank Warner a photograph that matched her memory, but had no name associated to it. Unless, of course, they hit the lottery and El Ladron was George Moody. Lexi doubted it. More likely, George Moody was a minion.

She transferred the image to a negative, then saved it on disk. Turning off the computer, she made a series of enlargements and left them hanging to dry in the darkroom.

When she went upstairs, she was surprised to see that the sun had gone down, even more surprised that it was nine o'clock. Stretching the kinks out of her back, she took a frozen dinner out of the freezer and put it in the microwave without paying attention to what it was. Then she went to the phone to call Hank Warner, the deputy.

"I've got a face for you," she said when she got him on the line.

"Want me to come get it?" he asked.

"That's not necessary," Lexi said. "I've got a couple of things to do here. I'll drop the prints by the station."

"Good," he replied. "I've been thinking. Have you given any thought to leaving town until this blows over?"

"Great minds travel on the same track," she said. "I'm flying back to New York tomorrow morning."

"Good," he said.

"And," she added, "I've got a name for you, but I doubt if it's El Ladron."

"Anything but Jim Smith will be good."

"George Moody," Lexi said, relating how Tía Ester had met him. "He's probably nothing more than a cog in the organization, but since he's an American, maybe knowing who he is will lead somewhere."

"Maybe," Hank agreed. "It's better than we had."

"I hope this works," she said. She gave him INN's and Mike Lanatowski's phone number and ended the call. Lexi didn't like the idea of driving to Denver in the middle of the night, but it beat staying here and remembering.

The bell on the microwave oven rang. Lexi took the dinner out and pulled the cover off the tray. She wrinkled her nose. Noodles and something. She pulled a fork from the drawer and took an experimental bite wondering if this would stay down any better than the hamburger she had bought as she left Denver or taste any better than the potpie Chane had made for her after she arrived home.

Chane.

Despite her resolve not to think about him, he'd been there at the back of her mind. Oh, how she had wanted to believe his shock and his confusion. How she had wanted him to prove he hadn't bought Tessa. How she wanted to believe this was some horrible mistake. But it wasn't.

Tonight's dinner tasted like cardboard. Unlike the rice and fish Tía Ester had made for lunch. Lexi closed her eyes, willing her mind in another direction.

With a sigh, she set her fork down and put the meal on the floor for Daisy to eat. The dog looked from the meal to Lexi, then rested her head on Lexi's lap. She scratched the dog's ears, fighting memories that swamped her, both new and old. She climbed the stairs to her bedroom, Daisy following her like a silent shadow.

"I can't leave you here to fend for yourself," Lexi told the dog as she dragged a suitcase from under her bed. "And New York City isn't such a great place for you, either. What are we going to do, girl?"

Daisy sat down and rested her muzzle on top of the bed, watching Lexi with dark eyes. Lexi opened the closet door and sorted through her clothes. Methodically, she filled the suitcase. She'd take Daisy to the station with her, she finally decided, and she'd have Hank take her to Chane's. Daisy and little Tessa would be a fine pair.

A lump rose in Lexi's throat at that thought. Daisy would be wonderful for the little girl. The image of Chane holding his daughter close, his hands huge around her small body, his expression filled with gentleness and possessiveness and joy when he held her.

The images of a loving father didn't match those of an unfit parent that had always filled her mind when she thought of people who purchased the lucrative goods offered by *Las Hermanas de la Esperanza*. Lexi had no doubt he meant what he'd said—anyone who took Tessa would do it over his dead body. However Chane Callahan had come to be Tessa's father, Lexi had to admit he was a good one. The kind any little girl should have.

Lexi returned to the darkroom, where she took down the now-dry prints. She put them in an envelope with the computer disk. From the bottom of a cabinet, she retrieved her camera case and set it down on the top of the counter.

Opening the case, she surveyed the tools of her trade that she hadn't used in months. Three camera bodies and an assortment of lenses were nestled within their foam cutouts. She hadn't used the new wide-angle lens yet, but the rest of the equipment was as familiar to her as the back of her hand. Various filters and two flash units completed the case's contents. She set the envelope on top of the cameras, closed the case, locked it, carried it to her car, and set it in the back seat.

Climbing the stairs once again, she wondered how long she'd be gone. A few days? Weeks? Longer?

Much as she hated to admit it, fatigue was catching up with her. She hoped taking a shower would help. In the bathroom, Lexi stripped down and turned on the water. She stepped inside the steamy shower and tried to lose all the thoughts that tormented her.

As soon as Lexi turned off the shower, she heard Daisy barking. Furiously. Alarmed, Lexi threw open the bathroom door and smelled smoke. It billowed into her bedroom. Grabbing a thick chenille robe en route, she headed for the bedroom door.

Below her, a sinuous orange glow illuminated the living room, accompanied by the crackling, moving roar of fire.

Lexi pulled the robe on and tied the belt into a knot as she ran back into the bedroom. She picked up the receiver to dial the fire department.

The line was dead.

The line was dead.

Chane carefully returned the papers to the envelope. Opening the drawer of his nightstand, he set the envelope inside.

In stocking feet, he left his bedroom and checked on Tessa. The night light cast the only illumination in her room. She had thrown off her blanket, and she was asleep with her thumb in her mouth and her little rump in the air. He covered her with the blanket, then touched the silky black hair. More precious than life to him, this child.

Face to face with a possibility he hadn't ever imagined, he left her room and silently glided down the dark hallway to the living room. What Rose had done was wrong. Pure and simple and undeniable. But now. Now, today, this minute. What was right?

Just as pure and simple and undeniable—Tessa was his daughter.

Had he been so blind, Chane wondered. He remembered Rose telling him that she wanted a child. He'd wanted to wait.

What kind of life would it have been to be gone months at a time and not see his children grow? Being with Tessa now, he understood his motivations exactly. Each day with her was a gift. Knowing how precious Tessa was to him, he had an inkling it must have been that way for Rose, too. But my God—to buy a baby?

He prowled through the dark house, needing an outlet for all the pent-up emotions churning inside him.

His mistakes with Rose had been many, mistakes he was determined not to repeat. They had been married, but they hadn't shared a life. She hadn't wanted to be part of his, and he'd paid her back by refusing to be part of hers.

Then Lexi Monroe had come into his life. He'd started off by wanting her body, but that hadn't been enough. He wanted her heart, too. Had it been only this morning he'd stood in the kitchen thinking he had fallen in love with her?

And this afternoon she had thrown all that back at him like so much dirty laundry. Accusing him of the unthinkable, so sure of herself in her fury. He might try explaining to her that he hadn't known.

And what would you have done if you had known?

Chane found himself in front of the living room window, staring into the night. Not a damn thing differently, he finally concluded. A man did his duty, did what was right. He hadn't set any of this in motion, but once it was, he honestly didn't know what he could have done differently.

And Lexi—how could he blame her for doing her duty as she saw it, for doing what was right. She, of all people, had paid a high price for following her conscience. The hell of it was, he believed she was right. Babies shouldn't be bought and sold. How had Rose decided to follow that particular path to get a baby, he wondered. If anyone knew, it was Ellen Belsen.

With the sudden clarity of a photograph being shoved in front of him, Chane saw the vehicle he had parked next to this afternoon at the day-care center. A big, dark-colored pickup. And Ellen, looking pale and strained as she spoke with two men—two strangers.

"God, no," he muttered, racing to a phone. He dialed Lexi's number. There was no answer even after fifteen rings. He hung up and dialed the sheriff's office and said he wanted to report a disturbance, giving Lexi's address and a description of the pickup.

He hung up the telephone, pulled on his boots, grabbed his hat and coat on the way out the door, and within sixty seconds was on his way to Lexi's house.

Blind stupid was what he had been. Every hurtful thing she had said contradicted her body language. Her body had been taut, her eyes filled with anguish. She had said the most hurtful things she could to drive him away. And then she had nearly run from him.

If he had believed what her body was telling him instead of hearing her with his mind, he would have never left her.

Lexi's house was a bit more than two miles from his. The drive felt like ten. He rounded the last curve and came to a skidding halt in front of her driveway. His glance was first drawn to an odd reflection in the dark waters of the lake. Dancing, orange, eerie.

He barreled into the driveway and followed the reflection to its source. Dancing, orange, eerie flames shone through the big windows of Lexi's house.

Chapter 20

The ghastly glow of the fire transfixed Lexi, its reflection bright in the huge windows of her house. For an instant, she was so shocked, so horrified she couldn't move.

She rushed down the stairs. Panic clawed through her. She ran toward the front door. Fire blocked her way. Get out. She had to get out. She ran toward the kitchen, stumbling falling picking herself upright in her haste. Toward the back door.

More fire.

She cried out.

Flames licked up the walls.

At the top of the stairs, Daisy barked.

Lexi went back to the bottom of the stairs. *Think. You'll never get out of this alive if you don't think.*

Alive. That's what the fire was. The ravenous sound of a beast eating. Clicking, crunching, belching. Teasing her as though sensing her fear. And in that instant she knew the fire had been started by El Ladron—a man who fed on fear. He was out there somewhere. Watching.

Think!

Fire licked up the walls and across the floor, devouring

everything in its path. Furniture, rugs, curtains. At the top of
the stairs Daisy whined, then barked again.

"Come on, girl," Lexi coaxed.

Daisy refused to come down the stairs, so Lexi ran back up,
grabbed her by the collar, and dragged her down the stairs.
"It's okay," she panted. "It's okay."

A wall of fire prevented her escape at both the front and
back doors. Thick smoke choked her, and she coughed. Eyes
watering, she dropped to her knees. Wasn't there supposed to
be less smoke near the floor?

"Think, Lexi," she muttered. "You can get out."

Damned if she was going to die like this in her own house!

Keeping hold of Daisy's collar, Lexi crawled toward the
basement door. Wondering if fire raged on the other side, she
pressed a hand against the door.

Thankfully, it felt cool.

She put her hand on the knob, turned it, and pushed. The
door didn't budge.

She let go of the dog and put her shoulder against the door
and pushed hard. It did not open. Lexi coughed and pushed
one last time with all her might.

Still, nothing.

Maybe I'm simply disoriented, she thought. Maybe it opens
the other way. Grabbing hold of the doorknob again, she pulled.
The doorknob snapped off in her hand.

Fire roiled toward her from the back of the kitchen. Individual
flames danced across the ceiling, blistering the paint ahead of
them.

Lexi shook her head, burying her nose in the collar of her
robe. She crawled back into the living room and peered through
the smoke toward the windows. Without conscious thought,
she grabbed one of the heavy beanpot lamps and moved toward
the window.

She lifted the lamp above her head and heaved it toward the
glass. The ceramic base bounced against the glass, cracking
the window.

Inanely, she remembered the realtor assuring her the glass

in the windows was double-paned safety glass and unlikely to break except in extreme circumstances.

Circumstances couldn't be much more extreme than these, Lexi thought.

Smoke burned her throat. She was running out of time.

She swept magazines and bric-a-brac off the coffee table and heaved that toward the window. Once again, it did not break.

Coughing hard, Lexi sank on the floor and looked around her. The undulating flames surrounded her, each competing for her attention, each lurking closer. The fire reflected in the windows, the eerie scene changing from second to second, a kaleidoscope of terror.

Daisy crawled toward her, whining. When she reached Lexi, she licked her face. Lexi put her arms around the dog and peered over the dog's head.

Images swam in front of her. She spotted another lamp she could bash into the window. Her legs felt weighted down as she crawled toward the lamp. Finally, she reached it. She stood up and lifted it off the table. The lamp couldn't have weighed more than a few pounds. It felt like a hundred.

Drunkenly, she staggered back to the cracked pane. Please, God, she prayed. I don't want to die in a fire. She lifted the lamp and threw it toward the window.

On the other side, the menacing outline of a man appeared and rushed toward her, his arms over his head.

Lexi screamed.

From the outside of the house, Chane saw Lexi flinch away from the window. Her eyes were wide with terror. Her dog stood next to her. Fire surrounded them, blocking every avenue of escape. He lifted the tire iron over his head and bashed the window again and again until the glass shattered.

Unbearable heat rushed past him. Beyond Lexi, he saw the fire surge forward toward the open window and a new source of oxygen.

"Lexi, run!" he shouted.

She stood motionless, mesmerized by the fire surrounding her. He vaulted over the window sill and reached for her.

"Lexi!"

Daisy barked at him.

Chane pushed Lexi toward the window, picked up Daisy, and threw her toward their escape route. Reaching Lexi, he lifted her in front of him and ran. Heat penetrated his clothes, burning his back.

Daisy jumped through the window. A millisecond later, Chane followed. Behind him, unbearable heat pursued him. He followed the dog across the deck and ran down the stairs, scarcely aware of Lexi's weight in his arms. A hundred feet away from the house, he stopped. He knelt and set Lexi down. Like him, she gulped in great rasping breaths of air.

"You're all right." He cupped his hands around her face and lifted it toward him. "Oh, thank God. You're all right." Relief flowing through him, his lips moved over her face in a hundred soft kisses.

She touched his face in return, questions forming in her eyes.

An explosion split the night. The house groaned. A ball of fire reached for the sky through the window Chane had broken. Orange light undulated behind the rest of the windows.

The house looked like a specter from hell, the upstairs windows demonic, orange eyes that stared into the night. A portion of the roof caved in and a second later fire appeared on the roof. The fire, awful to behold, lit up the night.

Next to him, Lexi sobbed, heaving wrenching sounds that tore at his soul. She began to shiver. Chane put his arm around her and pulled her close. In the distance, he heard sirens, their wailing approaching from the village.

A fire engine sped into the driveway a few minutes later. It wouldn't have mattered if they had been hours later, Chane thought. The house and everything in it were gone. Men ran a hose down to the lake and someone started up the pumper on the fire truck. The first streamers of water against the house evaporated into steam.

Lexi watched her whole world go up in flame. Inside, she had never been colder. How could it be so cold, she wondered, when her world was burning?

She sagged against Chane, transfixed by the fire. Rafters and beams outlined against the night sky sank, one by one, to the ground like giant pickup sticks.

Later she became aware that Chane was talking to someone. She struggled to focus on the voices, focus on the faces. She needed to remember something important . . . if she only could. Her nightmare beckoned, tempting her to close her eyes and let it consume her.

"C'mon, Lexi, let's go," Chane said to her. He lifted her into his arms and carried her to his truck. Someone opened the door for him, and Chane set her inside.

Lexi rested her head against the seat back. Her mind eased into a fog. She felt Daisy next to her, knew Chane drove the truck, but couldn't have said why or where they were going.

The truck stopped and Chane lifted her out once again. The fire was gone. All gone. Overhead, a canopy of brilliant stars sprinkled light across the sky, the same as always. Her world had burned up, but nothing had changed. Lexi shivered.

Chane paused at the back door, opened it, and carried her inside. After Daisy followed them through the door, he pushed it shut with his foot.

The house was dark, silent, just as he had left it.

He carried Lexi down the hall to his bedroom. There, he shut the door and stood her in the middle of the room. Making sure she wouldn't fall before he let her go, he turned on the lamp next to the bed.

Clad only in a bathrobe that looked as though it had once been white, Lexi watched him from eyes that were uncomprehending. He touched her cheek gently, tracing a long red scratch to her jaw.

"Honey, it's okay. You're safe now." The words sounded so familiar, and he knew he had said them to her before. This time, though, the danger had been real and present, not some foe chasing her through her own mind.

"Was it only last night when I got back from Denver?" she whispered, her voice so soft he had to bend to hear her.

"Seems like a lifetime, doesn't it? Do you hurt anywhere?"

Her chin quivered. "I hurt . . . everywhere."

"Oh, God, honey. I know." He gathered her into his arms. "I know."

Giant sobs racked her body, their sound muffled against his chest. He held her close as a single thought echoed through his mind. *She could have died.*

The soft click of the bedroom door sounded like thunder to him. He lifted his head. Kit poked his head around the door, his eyes wide, his expression filled with surprise and concern.

"I thought I heard someone crying," he said. "I got up to check on Tessa, but she's sound asleep. Is everything okay?"

"As good as they're gonna get tonight."

"What happened?" Kit asked.

"Her house burned down."

"This is Lexi?"

"Yeah."

Lexi stirred against Chane's chest, and she turned far enough to see Kit standing at the doorway.

"This is my brother, Kit," Chane said, sitting her down on the edge of the bed. "Will you be okay for a minute?"

She nodded.

Chane guided Kit out of the bedroom. "I want you to park the pickup in the garage."

"Sure, but why?"

"I just want it in the garage." Chane had watched every vehicle between Lexi's house and his on the drive home. He hadn't seen the big pickup, didn't have any reason to think it was still around, but he believed in being cautious.

"Okay."

Chane followed his brother to the kitchen, picked up the telephone, and dialed Hank Warner's home. When Hank answered, Chane told him about the fire, then asked, "What the hell is going on? I called to get someone out there. The first emergency vehicle there was the fire truck."

"It shouldn't have happened," Hank admitted. "Damn, but we had a busy night. There was a report of prowlers up at the Grand Lake Lodge. Then, we had a car full of teenagers to fish out of Lake Granby. And someone reported a wild party going on and they'd heard shots were fired. Damnedest thing. The only call we had tonight that wasn't bogus was a domestic disturbance.''

"It sounds to me like our boy wanted you guys too busy to keep an eye on Lexi."

"She was supposed to have dropped the package of photographs by the station," Hank said. "Do you know if she made it?"

"I'll have to ask her."

"She's there?"

"Yeah."

"She said she intended to fly to New York tomorrow morning. I thought she was on her way—she was still in the house when the fire broke out?"

"Oh, yeah," Chane confirmed. "What do you mean she was going to New York?"

Hank cleared his throat. "When she and I talked this evening, she told me she was leaving town for a few days, which I encouraged."

Chane closed his eyes. "Why?"

But he knew why. Knew to the depths of his soul how betrayed she felt. Even as he listened to Hank's explanation, the why was obvious. She intended to put as much distance between them as she could.

"Hell, man, it's the smartest thing for her to leave town. I had intended to put some extra surveillance on her house. With the description of the vehicle and a photograph of the guy, I figured we'd be able to find him."

Anger crept through Chane. "Only you didn't. He found her first. She wasn't supposed to get out, Hank. The door to the basement had been nailed shut. I know. That's how I tried to get into the house."

"I'll make sure we get someone to keep an eye on your house if I have to come do it myself," Hank said.

"Thanks. One more thing. Talk to Ellen Belsen. A guy driving a big pickup like the one you're looking for was in to see her today. She looked real upset, and I'm betting he put the strong arm on her.''

''About what, do you know?''

''You'll have to ask her. She isn't talking to me.''

''It's done.''

Kit came back into the house as Chane hung up the telephone. ''Anything else I can do, bro?''

Daisy came into the kitchen. Chane got a dish out of the cupboard, filled it with water, and set it on the floor. The dog sniffed at the water, then lapped it up.

Briefly, Chane explained about the fire at Lexi's house, including the supposition an arsonist set the fire. ''I'm not expecting any trouble, but . . .''

''Keep a close eye out?'' Kit offered. He locked the back door.

''Yeah. And take Daisy with you.''

''Daisy, huh?'' Kit whistled softly to the dog. ''Wimpy name for a dog, you know that?''

Kit went back to his bedroom and Chane stalked into the dark living room. The street leading to the house was quiet, just as it ought to be this time of night. He studied each of the cars parked along the street, recognizing each one.

Even then, he didn't leave his watch by the window until one of the sheriff's cars drove slowly past, turned around, and parked across the street.

Chane went back to the bedroom, where he found Lexi sitting exactly as he had left her. He closed the door and leaned against it.

''I can't stay here,'' she said.

''There's nowhere else to go.''

''But you don't understand.'' She stood up and held a beseeching hand out to him. ''I don't—''

''I know you don't want to be anywhere near me,'' he said roughly. ''Well, that's just too damn bad because tonight I'm what you're stuck with.''

Her eyes locked with his, she swallowed. ''What I was about to say is that he's still after me.''

''El Ladron?''

She nodded.

"And you think he set the fire."

"Yes."

"Hell, Lexi, if the man wanted you dead, why not just shoot you?"

She smiled, an expression so sad, he felt as though his heart were being squeezed in a vise. "If these attempts he's made don't work, sooner or later, it will come to that. You have to understand. He likes fear. It's a power thing with him." Her eyes clouded, and she looked away, fingering the sooty tie of her bathrobe. "It would just about kill me if someone else got hurt because of me."

At last. Her reason for going to New York. She had intended to put several time zones between them, though not for the reasons he'd originally thought. Her concern for his safety surprised him. Slow step by slow step, Chane moved toward her. "I know that."

"I don't want anything to happen to you," she whispered.

"I understand that, too." He took both of her hands in his, pressed them against his lips. "I feel the same way."

Her eyes shimmered with unshed tears. "Don't—"

"I'm sorry I was almost too late tonight," he whispered.

She shook her head. "I don't know why you even came."

"I was worried about you."

A single tear escaped her eye and trickled down her cheek. "Don't say—"

"At a time like this, we have to remind ourselves what is important and what isn't."

She shook her head, repeating, "You don't understand. I can't stay here."

"You can't go anywhere else, honey. Not tonight." He steered her toward the bathroom. "You take a long, hot shower."

She stopped cold. "The last time I took a shower—"

"Some bastard set your house on fire," Chane interrupted, his voice rough. He cleared his throat. "You're safe, Lexi. I won't let anyone hurt you."

She brushed his hand as he stepped past her into the bathroom. Turning to face her, he met her gaze.

"Why are you doing this?" she whispered. "After this afternoon . . ."

"Like I said, you've gotta focus on what's important."

He stepped into the bathroom and turned on the shower to let the water warm. Lexi's eyes were on him, their blue dark as a midnight sky and more beautiful. "Thank God you're okay."

Lexi dropped her eyes to the floor, the swirling marble pattern in the tile matching her chaotic thoughts. *Focus on what's important.* Easy advice. It ought to be easy to take.

She admired him more than just about anyone she had ever met. And she hated what he had done. Despised the thought he was part of the problem that made the selling of babies a lucrative enterprise. Yet, this was Chane, who had been generous beyond belief.

Who had risked his life tonight to save hers.

Focus on what's important. What was important—vital, in fact—was making sure nobody else got hurt because of her. But how in the world did she keep turning aside a man who was there for her every time she needed him. Who had promised her anything. Who had risked everything—his life—for her.

The truth, the awful stark truth, was that she wanted to rely on his strength and his caring. The worse truth was that she didn't want to be alone. Right or wrong. No matter how wrong.

God help her.

She raised her eyes and found him watching her, waiting for some signal from her. It wouldn't take much, she realized, and she would have what she needed as badly as she needed air. His arms around her.

Steam began to flow from the shower stall, reminding Chane that he should leave. He was no gentleman, and what he most wanted was to gather her close and reassure himself that she was alive. And she'd already made it clear, that was the last thing she wanted from him.

His gaze dropped to her mouth. The tip of her tongue appeared, moistened her lips and withdrew. Scant inches lower, his attention fell to the staccato beat of her pulse against her throat.

She swayed toward him, and her arms came around him, drawing him close.

He lowered his head and pressed his lips against her pulse. Her skin was so soft, so warm, so . . . alive.

Chapter 21

A rush of panic flowed over Lexi as Chane's arms came fiercely around her. *He could have died.* The realization—painful, unbearable—shook her to the core. Her hands moved urgently down his back, up again, and across. She trembled with the knowledge, and she grew cold at the thought she might have never been able to hold him this close again.

He was right. Focus on what was important.

Living by the things you believed in.

Feeling loved, if only for a moment.

Standing up and making a difference.

Grabbing hold of the man who made her believe in possibilities. Somehow none of it seemed such a contradiction even though hours ago she had been so sure unsurmountable barriers stood between them.

She opened her eyes to look at him, found all the longings she had reflected there. One night. Surely that wasn't so much to ask. She bit back a cry at the realization a single night might be all she would ever have with him. A single night to fill with memories to last a lifetime.

Having made the decision to make love with him, she consciously closed down her thoughts. There would be plenty of time later for thinking. Just now, feeling—that was what she wanted. The connection she felt with this one man transcended common sense. He had promised her *anything,* and for the moment she wanted to pretend anything was possible.

Her sensitive fingertips skimmed down his arms until her hands reached his. He clasped each of her hands. She arched against him and stood on tiptoe. His stance widened. She leaned into him, letting his body support her weight. On a whisper, she brushed her lips softly across his chin.

He groaned, his grip on her hands tightening. As if she had all the time in the world, she brushed her mouth against his, moved on to his jaw, returned, lingered, then skimmed his other cheek, absorbing the scent, the texture, the warmth of his skin. So long as she lived, she'd never forget this moment.

Even as Chane yielded to her caress, his conscience twisted inside him. Their heightened awareness was a result of shared trauma and the need to reach for the core of life. He didn't care. He wanted the touch of her mouth on his face and anywhere else she wanted to put it.

"I could have lost you before I ever knew you," he whispered against her skin. "Ah, Lexi, do you know what you do to me?"

"Don't talk," she whispered. "Don't say anything."

Her command chimed an alarm against the back of his mind. A warning that was lost when she offered her mouth again without really kissing him. The torture of her soft lips brushing across his jaw and neck made his hands tighten convulsively around hers.

He gave up fighting his internal battle. Maybe this wasn't right. It felt right. It felt *wonderful.*

Their caresses may have been languid, but the beat of his heart thundered in his ears. Once he had prided himself on his discipline, his ability to stay focused, to withstand anything. With restraint he didn't know he had, he stood still and waited. He let her come to him. Nothing had ever been harder.

He opened his eyes and looked deeply into hers. Her need, stripped bare, mirrored his own. Bending to her, he pressed a soft kiss against one eyelid, then other. When her eyes opened again, her expression was awed. His gaze locked with hers, he let go of her hands and tugged at the knotted belt at her waist. Sliding his hands under the robe's collar, he spread the front of the robe apart and pushed it off her shoulders. The robe fell to the floor with a soft thump.

His eyes remained locked with hers, and that, too, was an effort. Last time there had been no light, only consuming sensation. He needed to look at her breasts, her belly, her bared legs more than he needed his next breath. There would be time for that. There would never be another moment like this one.

His fingers skimmed the delicate line of collarbone from her arms to the center. Gently, he wrapped his hands around either side of her neck and eased his hands into her hair. Tipping her head back, he returned each of the soft caresses she had given him, dragging his lips across the line of her jaw to her cheek. He repeated the caress on the other side of her face and was rewarded with the hitch in her breath that indicated he was giving her what she wanted.

She opened the buttons of his shirt one at a time, her eyes once again locked with his. Somehow she managed to undo each one without stepping away from him, without breaking the taut gaze they shared. She spread the shirt wide, and the weight of her breasts burned against his chest. The need to know what her body looked like made him tremble. The moment felt so perfect, though, he wanted to stretch it, take his awareness to another height. He brushed her lips with his, teasing them both.

She tugged the shirt loose from his jeans, pressed her palms between the shirt and his skin, and eased it off him.

Bare torso to bare breast.

His arms came back around her the instant they were free of the shirt sleeves. When her soft lips returned to his mouth, he captured them in a consuming kiss that left him shaking. He caressed the heated interior of her mouth. Her breath became ragged, and she moaned. He withdrew from her mouth and was rocked to his soles when she invaded his, giving him the same consummate caress.

Steam filled the bathroom, making her skin damp beneath his callused fingertips. Her hands found the zipper of his jeans, and his joined hers to push them down his lean hips, taking his briefs as well.

"Shower," he murmured against her mouth.

"Hmm?"

He pressed kisses against her temple, the shell of her ear, the line of her jaw, the vulnerable underside of her chin.

The barest trace of humor filled his voice. "If we're going to shower, we'd better do it before all the hot water is gone."

He swept open the shower curtain, stepped inside, and pulled her in with him. Tugging the shower curtain back across the opening captured the warmth and steam around them. He cupped her head between his hands and kissed her deeply, thoroughly. Water beat down on them. The sensation of her body wetly sliding against him felt perfect. His determination to make this go slow washed away in an onslaught of sensation.

He ran his palms down the front of Lexi's lush body. The line of her collarbone seemed fragile to him. With hands slick from steam and water and soap, he lavished attention on her. A red scratch marred her creamy skin from the side of her neck to the upper curve of her breast. He washed her gently, then kissed the scratch. His glance dropped to her breasts.

They were high, very round, and full—as beautiful as he'd known they would be. Her nipples were pale, barely darker than the surrounding skin. And the exact color of her lips. He cupped his hands around her breasts, savored their weight, tested the firm smooth skin of her belly, skimmed the surface of her secret, slick petals, eliciting a moan from her. One moment he was the master of his control and the next, it was stripped from him.

With sensitive fingertips, he explored her body with more care than he would have given to a slender wedge of rock on a hundred-foot cliff that he expected to support his weight.

She touched him with curiosity and abandonment equal to his own. Her mouth deeply locked with his, she took the soap from him and washed his chest, spreading her fingers to comb through the crinkly mat of hair. The soft patch of hair under his arm deserved her undivided attention as did the swell of muscle on his arm. She looped her hands around his waist and pressed herself closer until, chest to breast, they were close as a heartbeat.

She explored the curve of his buttocks and smiled at his response. He pressed himself against her, leaving no doubt, if there had been any, as to his need or his intent.

The moment of discovery ebbed and flowed. He found she was ticklish when he traced a line from her waist to the base of her spine. Nothing was sexier than her sudden intake of breath when he touched her satin core. Fierce need turned uncontrollable when she ran her fingernails up the inside of his thighs before cupping him intimately.

On a harsh groan, he turned her away from him, exposing her body to the relentless spray of water, sensing its sting sensitized her skin as it had his own. The elegant line of her spine and the feminine flair of her hips were no less alluring than the swell of her breasts and the concave flat of her waist. He rinsed them both, shut the water off, made a cursory attempt at drying them off, and carried her to his bed.

He set her in the middle of the king-size mattress, then covered her body with his own. She held him close, murmuring urgent love words in his ear.

He smoothed her damp hair back from her face. "Beautiful. Do you know how beautiful you are to me?" he praised, exploring her as he had wanted to for weeks.

Sensation swamped Lexi, and engulfed her with the need to touch him and take him inside her. He seemed to have in mind driving her out of her mind, though, his mouth and hands everywhere, but never long enough to satisfy fully. The whisk of his fingers teased. The skim of his lips over her skin eased to life insatiable hunger. He made her ache for him, made her need as she had never in her life needed. She urged him closer, remembering the heat and the completion she'd found within his embrace once before. He touched her everywhere, never lingering long enough to satisfy her at all.

She took his head between her hands and gave him a deep, searching kiss. Fiercely, with strength born of unbearable need, she rolled him to his back and straddled him, parting her legs, seeking the completion she had to have.

The last of Chane's reason gave way to blind need, and in a sole fluid move, he rolled her beneath him, found her legs parted in perfect invitation. Her hands wrapped warmly around him, guiding him toward her sultry, soft core.

He pressed against her, found her soft, wonderfully soft, sweetly . . . soft . . . and not nearly as close to her as he wanted to be. Adjusting, he slid a hand under her spine and tilted her pelvis toward him.

"Open your eyes, sweetheart," he whispered.

Her eyelids lifted, and she gazed at him with those beautiful dark blue eyes.

He rested his brow against her forehead. "Kiss me."

She tipped her head and touched his mouth with her lips. Their softness impressed him, as always. On a sigh, her lips parted, and she opened her mouth to his. Her muscles clinched around him, then relaxed ever so slightly. She sighed and thrust her hips toward him. Watching him, she pushed until they were interlocked as tightly as a man and a woman could be. Then, she smiled.

Bracketing her head with his hands, he bent and kissed her. "You're so beautiful." Timeless rhythm lured them. Her movements were a counterpoint to his own. She wrapped her hands around his biceps, her grip fiercely possessive.

"Nothing has ever felt this good," she whispered against his mouth.

She was right. Nothing had. Ever.

She watched him with a sadness that pierced him to his soul. When he kissed her, deeply buried within her soft body, her eyes remained wide open, branding him in the most intimate moment of his life.

Pressure built. Her hands roved over his face, neck, and chest. She gasped as the first waves of her climax spilled over, tears accompanying her cry. Her pulses against him redoubled his own until he gave himself over to the pressure building within him. The end, when it came, felt more like a cataclysmic beginning, stark and elegant as a bolt of lightning, reverberating and reaching as thunder.

How long he remained slumped against her, he couldn't have

said. Worried about being too heavy for her, he eventually rolled onto his side and curled her against him, sensing she was wide awake.

He pressed a kiss against her nape.

She stirred against him, interlocking her fingers with his as his hand rested against her stomach. Though she was curled within his arms, he felt the subtle tension in her body, a tension that shouldn't have been there after the climax she had experienced.

"Lexi?"

"Go to sleep, Callahan," she whispered.

She had shared her body with him as completely as any woman ever had—and he loved it. And emotionally—he had never felt more distanced from her. She hadn't wanted to talk, though Lord knew, they needed to.

Hauling her closer, he curled his body around hers and pressed a hand against her tummy. Gradually, her breathing quieted and became steadier. Gradually, her skin cooled from the heated flush of making love. He tucked the bedcovers more firmly around her and waited for sleep to come.

On the clock on the nightstand, the minutes passed—too fast. One thing he was sure of—their making love had solved nothing. And if he wasn't smart, tomorrow she would march out of his life just as time marched inexorably forward.

At some point she relaxed more fully against him, and he realized she had fallen asleep. Quietly, he crept from the bed and pulled on a pair of sweatpants. He left the room, and silently moved through the house, checking on his brother and Tessa. As usual, she had kicked off her covers. Chane tucked a blanket around her, watching her sleep a long moment before leaving her room.

Gazing out each of the windows, he heard no movement, saw nothing out of the ordinary but the patrol car he had called for to watch the house. Satisfied all was well—or at least as much as it could be—he returned to his bedroom. Lexi slept in the center of the bed, on her side, just as he had left her.

Stripping, he climbed back into bed with her, once again cuddling her close.

Lexi came more fully awake, at once reassured and saddened when Chane put his arm around her. He was all she had once dreamed of . . . and he represented all she had fought to make right. The people she had hated for buying babies—never once had she imagined a man like Chane being one of them. The one man she could have loved . . .

Laying a hand over his, she pictured just for a moment what it might have been like if things had been different. If El Ladron weren't chasing her. If Chane hadn't bought a black-market baby. If . . . the word that paved the road to hell with good intentions. A word that covered all the might have beens, the should have beens, the could have beens—that simply were not. All she had was what *was*.

And what was . . . was a chasm that could not be breached with simple words or one night of making love, no matter how great it was.

Tomorrow would come soon enough. Tonight, she could fall asleep in his arms and dream about a future that would never be.

Chapter 22

Lexi disentangled her arms and legs from Chane's, propped open one eye, and focused on the bedside clock. Three minutes past six. He murmured sleepily and rolled onto his stomach.

Surprisingly, Lexi felt refreshed. A shock, considering. The first thing she remembered was that her house had burned. The memory was devastating, but somehow not as important or as shocking as the revelations about Tessa's origin.

Lexi's house could be rebuilt, and most of the things in it could be replaced. If she decided that was what she wanted to do. And, she admitted to herself, that decision was a long way from being made.

The señora's granddaughter could not so easily be replaced. And Chane. She suspected rebuilding his life if his daughter were taken from him would be nearly impossible.

Lexi stretched, her attention drifting to Chane. Even in sleep, a frown creased his forehead. The Marine motto, *Semper Fidelis,* fit him. Those two simple words epitomized his approach to life. He'd shown Lexi tantalizing glimpses of what that kind of life could be like. He'd proven it when he took in his brother. As for Tessa, Lexi knew there was nothing in this life more important to him than his daughter.

He loved that little girl. Loved her with a father's boundless love. As a child, it was something Lexi had often imagined and never had experienced. Caring for a child was a sacred trust. One Lexi's father had not honored with her. One that her mother had made only an occasional stab at.

Loud and clear she got the message. Chane took care of the people he loved. He was a man who'd run through fire, if that's what it took, to ensure their safety.

Who had run through fire for her.

Knots of tension churned through Lexi. He could have died last night. And she would have but for his courage. The idea that he had risked everything for her was unbearable. If something had happened to him because of her, she couldn't live with that. Children deserved a caring adult in their lives. Chane being there for Tessa and Kit was more important than anything.

How could she not love a man like that?

She loved him. Her heart pounding, she brushed a kiss over his warm shoulder, letting loose the romantic dreams she hadn't allowed since she was a young girl. To be loved by a man like Chane Callahan was the secret desire she had harbored all her life.

She loved him, even if he had bought a baby.

Loved him despite what he had done.

Remembering her promise to herself when she had left Costa Léon and her promise to Tía Ester, Lexi wondered how long it would be before she hated him for that one act.

Chane had a child who would be four soon.

And so did Tía Ester.

Lexi had given her word to Chane.

And to Tía Ester.

God. What if it was Tessa? What then?

Lexi slipped from the bed, found a clean navy blue T-shirt and a pair of gym shorts in the chest of drawers. Both were huge on her, even after she gathered up the drawstring on the shorts' waistband. With a last look at Chane, Lexi slipped out of the bedroom.

Across the hall, Tessa sat in her bed, quietly sucking her thumb.

"What are you doing, little angel?" Lexi whispered, picking her up.

"Waiting," Tessa said.

"For what?" Lexi headed toward the kitchen, carrying Tessa on her hip.

"The bell on Daddy's clock. I can't get out of bed until it rings."

"Ah." Lexi set the child down on the counter. "Do you know where the coffee is?"

Tessa pointed at a cupboard, which Lexi opened. Sure enough, a can of coffee set inside.

"Did you sleep at my house?" Tessa asked.

"Um-hum."

"And Daisy. Did she sleep here, too?"

"I think she's with Kit."

"Oh." Tessa thought a minute more. "My friend Jenny spent the night with me once. We ate ice cream. And then we whispered like this after Daddy turned off the light."

"That sounds like fun," Lexi responded in a loud whisper that matched Tessa's.

"Did you have fun with Daddy?"

Leave it to a child to get to the heart of things. "Yes."

Within minutes, the coffee was ready. Lexi poured a cup then took Tessa into the living room, where they curled up in a big rocking chair and watched the sun come up. It should have been a moment of contentment. Lexi wanted it to be. Instead, her mind raced, and she planned what she needed to be doing.

Follow through with her plans from last night.

Call Lanatowski and let him know she was on the way to New York.

Get in touch with the bank to get traveling money, replace checks and credit cards.

Buy some clothes.

Fly to New York.

"*Buenas días,*" the señora said from the doorway.

"Tía!" Tessa slid off Lexi's lap and skipped open-armed across the room to Tía Ester.

Tía, Lexi thought, watching Tía Ester hug Tessa. Dear God, what if it was *abuela?* Instead of aunt, grandmother. Lexi averted her glance and gazed out the window.

"¿Qué hace usted aquí?" Tía Ester asked.

"Mi casa se ha quemado." Somehow, relating the fire in Spanish made the fire seem more distant to Lexi. She wasn't sure she could have said the words in English without crying.

"¿Cuando?" Concern filled Tía Ester's voice as she sat down beside Lexi.

"Durante la noche."

She took Lexi's hand, her dark eyes bright with unshed tears. *"¡Qué barbaridad!"*

"Why is Tía sad?" Tessa asked from Lexi's knee.

She lifted the child back onto her lap. "Sometimes grown-ups feel sad."

"But why?"

From the doorway, Kit said, "Because sometimes sad things happen, squirt. You know. Like the time your friend Jenny moved away. Like the time I broke my arm." He sauntered into the living room with Daisy on his heels and knelt in front of the couch, where Lexi sat with Tía Ester and Tessa. "Do you remember the time the fire trucks came to the Smiths' house?"

Tessa nodded and glanced at Lexi. "There was thunder and lightning and ka-boomb right into their house. And the fire trucks came and squirted water on the roof where the lightning was."

"That's what happened to Lexi's house," Kit said. "Right, Lexi?"

"Close enough." She met his gaze, faintly surprised at his tone, as though he really expected she would have told this child that her house had burned down. He was just shy of Chane's height. Maturity would someday give Kit the same breadth. His eyes were the same brown and held a faint challenge.

"Did your house go ka-boomb?" Tessa asked.

Lexi nodded at the unexpected memory of the fireball thrown into the sky above her house.

"And it made her sad," Kit added.

Tessa came back to Lexi and rested her elbows on the chair. "Then it's a good thing you're here," she said solemnly. "My daddy is real good at making you feel better when you're sad."

"I'm sure he is," Lexi whispered, brushing Tessa's hair away from her face.

"My brother has a theory," Kit said, "that secrets foster distrust and generate hurt."

For a man who thought so, he had plenty of his own. "And the truth hurts?"

Kit shrugged. "Sometimes."

Tessa leaned into Lexi and gave her an engaging smile. She whispered, "Sometimes Uncle Kit is a grump in the morning."

"I heard that." He scooped her up and put her over his shoulder. His tone with Lexi may have been aggressive. With his niece, it was pure boyish charm. "Talk like that could get you thrown outside with the dog. C'mon Daisy."

The dog obediently followed him into the kitchen. Lexi watched them go, her own statement echoing through her head. *And the truth hurts.*

"Tía Ester," Lexi said. "I have to leave for New York this morning."

"Why?"

"Business," she answered, hating the lie. Meeting Tía Ester's bottomless eyes, she asked, "When are you returning to Costa Léon?"

"As soon as my granddaughter is found," she said.

"But what if—"

"I do not find her?" Tía Ester shrugged.

"I'm going to make arrangements for you to stay at one of the motels in town."

"I don't stay here? With Señor Chane?"

Lexi shook her head. "Perhaps that is between you and him. But I need to make sure you have a place to stay. All right?"

Tía Ester thought a moment, then patted Lexi's hand. "If this, you need to do. Well, then, I cannot stop you."

Lexi headed for the kitchen. Her phone calls didn't take long. The bank promised she could pick up cash in Granby and assured her she would have replacement credit cards within a couple of days. Lexi requested they be sent to INN headquarters in New York. She spoke with Lanatowski, who said he'd make sure the New York City police got copies of the information that Hank Warner had been accumulating.

Kit came into the kitchen just as Lexi hung up after arranging for a cottage for Tía Ester near the Grand Lake Marina. Pouring a couple of cups of coffee, Kit handed Lexi one of them.

"So. You're Lexi." He sat down in a chair next to the kitchen table.

"So. You're Kit." She took a sip of her coffee and met Kit's gaze over the top of her cup. She pegged his age at about sixteen and wondered if he'd outgrow his cockiness.

He grinned suddenly and she found herself smiling back.

"I didn't know Chane even had a brother until yesterday."

Kit bounced the heel of his hand off the side of his brow. "I've just gotta give that guy hell every day or he forgets I'm here."

"That wasn't exactly the impression he left me with," Lexi responded dryly.

"That I give him hell, or that he forgets about me?"

"I'm sure you keep him on his toes."

The smile slid out of Kit's eyes and his voice grew serious. "Last night, Chane said that, uh, your house . . ."

"You can ask me if my house burned down without worrying I'll fall into a jillion little pieces," Lexi said.

"Well, up to a million or so, I can handle. Your house—"

"Burned," she finished. "To the ground." She made sure her tone was light and didn't reveal a bit of her anger about that. She had survived. And if there was any justice left in this world, El Ladron, whoever he was wherever he was, would be caught.

"I heard fire trucks last night." Tessa came back into the kitchen, wearing teddy-bear slippers. She opened the pantry door and took down a box of cereal. "I'm going to eat while I watch *Sesame Street.*"

"You've gotta eat the cereal in the kitchen, squirt. House rules, remember?"

"Then why do you eat in the living room? she asked.

Lexi suppressed a grin, wondering what Kit's answer to that would be.

"I broke the rules," he said finally.

Tessa leaned against his knee. "Oh." She absorbed that a moment, then turned her eyes on Lexi. "Did the fire trucks come to your house?"

"Yes."

" 'Cause there was a fire?"

"Yes."

"Sometimes the fire trucks make me worry."

Lexi hugged her and stood up, refilling her coffee cup. "I can understand that." To Kit, she said, "You wouldn't have an old pair of jeans I could borrow, would you? And maybe a pair of socks?"

"Sure thing."

Kit left, and he and Tía Ester came back to the kitchen together. She frowned when she saw Tessa's bowl of cereal.

"Azucar," Tía Ester said to Tessa. *"Es no bueno por su desayunarse."*

"That's the American way. Sugar for breakfast," Kit said, dropping a shirt, jeans, and a pair of socks in Lexi's lap. He picked up the box of cereal and sprinkled a handful into his palm. "This stuff is good for you." He pointed to the label. "See? It says so right here." He tipped his head back and poured the cereal into his mouth.

Tía Ester smiled at Kit and shook a finger at him. *"Se bueno."*

"I'm always good," he drawled, winking at Tía Ester. He glanced at Lexi's bare feet. "I'm pretty sure I've got an old pair of canvas and suede hiking boots that might fit you. I had them less than a month before I outgrew them. Let's go see what we can find, squirt."

Like a whirlwind, he left again, this time with both Tessa and Daisy tagging along behind him.

"When are you leaving?" Tía Ester asked in Spanish.

"Soon."

"Do you want breakfast?"

Lexi grinned. "That kinda depends. Are you making oatmeal?"

Tía Ester chuckled. "I think not."

Lexi patted her hand. "You don't have to cook for me. But thank you for offering."

"Found 'm," Kit said, returning to the kitchen.

"Found shoes," Tessa echoed. "See." She held up a pair of lightweight canvas hiking boots.

"Thank you." She took the shoes from Tessa.

She pulled the jeans on over the baggy gym shorts, then sat down to put on the shoes and socks, listening to the ebb and flow of conversation between Tía Ester and Tessa. The shoes were a close enough fit that a pair of socks made them workable. If these belonged to Kit, he had recently been far smaller than he was now.

Lexi found herself adjusting her attitude about Chane again, the knowledge that he was raising his brother revealing a new facet to him. A man who had plenty of responsibilities without adding any more. Knowing what she did this morning, Lexi found it remarkable that Chane had brought Tía Ester home. Most men in his position would have run Tía Ester out of town, not invited her into their home.

"I'm starved," Kit said, draping an arm around Tía Ester's shoulder.

"He likes it when Tía Ester cooks," Tessa informed Lexi. "But Daddy said that's being a show pig."

"A what?" Lexi asked.

Tessa shrugged turning her palms up. "I don't know what it is, but that's what he said."

"Chauvinist pig," Kit explained. "As in male."

Lexi chuckled. "As in cook your own breakfast."

"Cold cereal is sounding better and better." Kit retrieved another box from the pantry.

"You should eat," Tía Ester said.

"In a while," Lexi absently agreed. She put on the flannel shirt Kit had brought for her. It was far too big for her, so she left it unbuttoned, jacket style, over the T-shirt.

Lexi sauntered to the back door and peered outside. Though

early yet, the sun had topped the peaks to the east. She found it hard to reconcile last night's terror with the tranquility outside this morning. A group of birds fluttered around a bird feeder and a squirrel walked cautiously along the fence next to the neighboring house. It made the loss of her home all the more unreal.

That was one more thing to do before she left town, she decided. Go back to see what was left of her house.

Intellectually, she understood that the fire had happened. Last night's remembered terror was harder to acknowledge. Had she really been terrified El Ladron was here? All her memories about him had the heated, musty scents of a tropical climate.

There was a straight line between Joe and the phony FBI agent. There was another straight line between her leaving the hospital and someone trying to run her off the highway. Last night's fire was one more. But damned if she'd sit here cowering. She hadn't lived a bit of her adult life in fear until El Ladron matter-of-factly beat her into submission, using pain and fear as his weapons of destruction.

She turned away from the kitchen window and glanced at Tía Ester and Tessa.

Damned if she'd be responsible for him hurting anyone else. Covertly she studied them both, hating that she was about to lie, hating the idea of leaving, hating more they could be targets simply by being with her.

"If I had keys to Chane's truck, things would be just about perfect," Lexi said. Stealing Chane's truck wasn't the best way to part company, but it was expedient. She could leave it in Granby and from there catch a bus into Denver.

"Here," Tessa said. She climbed onto a chair next to the hook by the back door and pulled down a ring of keys. "This one is for the truck. And this one is for the house."

"You should wait for Señor Chane," Tía Ester said.

"He didn't get much sleep, so I'd like to let him rest awhile longer. And . . . this is something I need to do myself."

Lexi plucked the keys from Tessa's hand, then smoothed a hand over her shiny black hair.

"Tell Chane I'll—"

"*¿Donde salir?*" Tía Ester asked.

"I'm going to my house," Lexi answered in Spanish. That, at least, was the truth. Just not the whole truth. In English, she added, "You tell your daddy not to worry, okay?"

"Okay." Tessa reached toward Lexi.

She knelt and accepted the hug from Chane's daughter.

The sound of the motor on his truck woke Chane from a fitful sleep. He sat up, and in the next breath came wide awake. The sheets beside him were cold, and Lexi was nowhere to be seen. He came out of the bed in a rush. He pulled on the sweatpants lying on the floor, threw open the bedroom door, and trotted down the hall, reaching the front window just in time to see the truck round the corner.

"Damn."

"We're in here, Daddy," Tessa called from the kitchen.

Chane strode into the kitchen, where his daughter and the señora were sitting at the table, eating cold cereal. "Where's Kit?"

Tessa shrugged. "Don't know. He was here."

"Where's Lexi?"

"Alexandra went to her house," Tía Ester said.

"Kit went with her, then."

Tía Ester shook her head. "No. I think she is worried about her house."

"She's upset?"

The señora shook her head, her expression calm. "No."

Chane turned on his heel and went back to the window, hoping the sheriff's car had followed her. The cruiser was still parked down the block. Chane glared at the vehicle as though sheer will could force it to follow. The knucklehead inside didn't have a lick of sense.

Chane ran back to his bedroom, hastily getting dressed. Kit appeared in the doorway seconds later.

"Something wrong, bro?"

"Why didn't you go with her?"

"Who?"

"Lexi, damn it."

"I didn't know she had gone anywhere, damn it," he responded, imitating Chane's tone of voice. "Didn't the deputy follow her?"

"That idiot is waiting for an engraved invitation." Chane sat down and pulled his boots on.

A scant minute later, he ran out the front door without stopping to put on a jacket.

The morning air felt nippy, a fact Chane noticed at the periphery. The driver behind the wheel was a young deputy who had been in one of his classes earlier in the year. Pat something. Or Paul. Pete, maybe. And he was asleep behind the wheel.

Chane rapped on the window, then flung open the door. "Asleep! What the hell do you think you're supposed to be doing?"

The deputy's eyes snapped open and he struggled to sit up. "I must have just dozed off, sir."

"Now why don't I believe that? Unlock the passenger door."

The deputy did as he was told without asking questions, and Chane got in the car.

"A white pickup left here a minute ago."

"No, sir," the deputy responded. "No car—"

"You're digging yourself a real deep one, boy. Drive."

"Where are we going, sir?"

"Did you hear about a fire last night down by the lake?"

"Yes, sir."

Chane snapped his fingers. "Get a move on."

Lexi knew the house was gone, but she was still unprepared for the total devastation that faced her when she rounded the last curve and drove Chane's truck into the driveway. She stopped the vehicle, set the brake, and climbed out of the truck. Unaware of anything but the charred remains of her home, Lexi moved up the driveway where she'd walked a hundred times before.

Only the foundation and stone chimney remained. Scorched

rafters lay crazily across the foundation and on the ground like a child's game of pick-up sticks awaiting collapse.

The incinerated skeleton of her car rested inside what had been the garage. The stale, putrid odor of smoke filled the air. Almost nothing except her car was recognizable.

Lexi closed her eyes. Her hands clenched into fists.

"Let it out, Lexi," came Chane's murmur from behind her.

She whirled around. He stood a pace away, the tips of his fingers caught in his jeans pockets, his stance wide. His eyes were very dark, and within them, she recognized her own pain.

She heard the echo of his voice promising her anything. *Anything.* She hadn't understood *anything* included sharing her pain, wouldn't have dared hope for it if she had understood.

He held out his arms to her. She shook her head.

"Stop being a tough guy," he ordered gruffly, pulling her into his arms. "I keep telling you, you don't have to do this alone."

His embrace was her undoing.

A tear slid from underneath each tightly closed lid. She could no more swallow the sobs that rose in her chest than she could hold back the tears. This hadn't been just a house. It had been a refuge. A place to be safe. A place that turned out not to be safe at all.

Safe.

That single word snagged her attention, and with a shuddering sigh, she tried to push him away. He would have none of it. Oh, how she wanted to rely on his strength, his caring. Oh, how she wanted to believe everything would be okay simply by willing it so. She took a deep shuddering breath and determinedly stepped out of his arms.

"I was stealing your truck," she confessed, meeting his gaze.

Only the momentary tightening of his jaw gave her any indication the statement had surprised him.

"I was going to leave it in Granby," she added.

"And after that?" The carefully neutral tone in his voice did not match the hard glint in his eyes.

"I was going to catch the bus into Denver and from there fly into New York."

"Running?"

She swallowed. "Probably. I figured it might be harder for El Ladron's henchmen to find me in a big city."

Chane nodded once as if confirming something to himself. "Are you coming back?"

She turned away from his penetrating gaze. "I don't know," she finally said.

"Ah, God, Lexi, I thought this was your home."

She faced him and smiled sadly. "More like an ivory tower."

"What's that supposed to mean?"

"That I've spent the last year lying to myself, hiding, wishing my problems would go away. Instead, they followed me. And until I finish it—"

"El Ladron?"

"Yes," she said. "Too many people have been hurt already."

"Are you going back to Costa Léon?" Chane asked.

"If that's what it takes, yes."

"I don't want you to go."

Lexi searched his face. His request tempted her unbearably. Forget what she had suffered at El Ladron's hands. Ignore that Joe had been killed and Tía Ester had been cruelly used. Pretend Chane wasn't one of the beneficiaries of a corrupt system.

She shook her head.

"Why not? What we've got going here, Lexi. It's good." He grasped one of her hands. "Can't you see that?"

She stared at his big hand covering hers. "I promised myself that I'd live by my convictions, Chane." She raised her eyes to his. "Sooner or later, I wouldn't be able to ignore—"

"That Tessa came from The Sisters of Hope?"

"Yes," she admitted, her voice husky.

"You read what was in the envelope on the counter yesterday, didn't you?"

"I didn't mean to. It got mixed up with Tía Ester's papers." Pausing, she cleared her throat. "And, God help me, I wish I had never seen them." Her voice broke, and she added, "Damn you, Chane Callahan. I could have loved you."

His eyes grew very dark, and he let go of her hand. He took

a step backwards. To Lexi that single step put him on the other side of a chasm, one she had created, one she could not bridge and still live with herself.

"Not knowing anything but what you saw there," he said, "and you're ready to throw in the towel, huh?"

"It was enough," she returned.

"So now you're judge and jury. You think you've got all the facts, and I'm guilty, is that right?"

Lexi hated his righteous tone when he was the one who had done something wrong, not her. "I saw the papers, Chane. Tessa wasn't adopted. She was bought—"

"Yeah, she was," he snarled. "And you're sitting up there on your throne, so damn sure you know what's going on. Well, let me tell you something, lady. That little girl is my daughter. Mine. And nobody is taking her away from me." He jerked his thumb toward the truck. "Get in the damn truck. I'll take you to Granby. The sooner you're out of my sight, the better."

Blindly, Lexi turned away from him, casting one last glance at the charred remains of her house, looking like her heart felt.

She trudged toward the truck, noticing for the first time a police car parked next to it. A young deputy leaned against the car, yawning as though he was trying to wake up.

"I'm riding with her," Chane said from behind Lexi.

The deputy brought his fingers to his temple in acknowledgment and got back into his car.

Lexi climbed into the truck on the passenger side. Chane slid in behind the wheel, started the engine, and slammed it into gear.

"You don't have to take me," Lexi said. "I can find some—"

"I said I'd take you," he interrupted, his big hands clinched around the steering wheel.

"Fine," she snapped. She gazed at him a moment, then turned her attention to scenery whizzing by the window.

Suddenly, she heard the quick blare of a siren. The police car raced even with the truck, and the deputy motioned Chane to pull over.

With a muttered curse, he pulled the truck to the side of the graveled road and rolled down the window.

The deputy parked the police car next to Chane's and leaned across the seat to roll down his passenger window.

"A call just came in. There's a disturbance at your house," he said. "Your brother said someone broke in."

Swearing, Chane threw the truck into gear and gunned the engine, spewing gravel behind him as he raced up the road. Its siren wailing, the police car passed them and sped toward town ahead of them.

Hurry, Lexi silently urged. Her heart kept pace as they raced toward town. Ice replaced the blood flowing through her veins, and she grew clammy at a remembered threat. *Hurting people you love is the same as hurting you. Only better.*

Chane downshifted and turned onto the street that led up the hill toward his house. The police car skidded to a halt in front of the house.

Lexi strained to see through the trees. The back door hung open.

"No," she moaned.

"I'll take you to Granby later," he said roughly, turning into the driveway.

Lexi jumped out of the truck before it came to a complete stop. By the back door, the deputy was crouched, his gun drawn.

He grabbed Lexi as she rushed past. "You can't go in there."

She wrenched her arm free. "You can't stop me."

She ran inside. The kitchen was deserted. Chane rushed into the house behind her, roughly pushing the deputy aside when he attempted to block the way.

"Kit, Tessa?" Chane called.

Her heart pounding hard, Lexi went into the living room. Chairs and tables were overturned. The television had a ragged hole smashed into its center. Glass from one of the cabinets lay scattered in jagged shards across the hardwood floor.

"Oh, God," Chane said. "Kit? Tessa? Answer me."

His call echoed through the house.

Chane strode toward the bedrooms, throwing open doors so hard they bounced on their hinges.

Tessa's room was empty.

The guest room the señora used was empty.

His own bedroom was empty.

Kit's bedroom was dark from the drawn curtains . . . empty. And a chaotic mess that matched the one in the living room.

Chane propped a fist against the door jamb, and the most primal fear he'd ever known gripped him.

Where the hell was his family?

"No. No, no, no," Lexi cried as she followed him down the hall. A second later she joined Chane at the doorway to Kit's room and touched his hand. "Oh, God. Look."

Chane dropped his gaze to his hand. The side of his fist touching the doorway was wet and smeared with blood.

Chapter 23

Chane reached inside the room and flicked on the light. Like the living room, furniture was overturned and smashed.

Unlike the living room, spatters of blood covered the wall next to the doorway.

"Chane," someone called from the front of the house.

"Back here."

Lexi groaned. She surveyed the room, her heart pounding wildly, her palms sweaty. Images raced through her mind, layer upon layer. Being beaten. Tía Ester at Lexi's door that first day. Joe hooked to machines keeping him alive. Sweet Tessa's smile. The blood and destruction in Kit's room.

Her fault.

Hurting someone you love. The same as hurting you.

Terrible fear swept through Lexi, and on its tail, fury. If any harm came to Tessa or Kit or—

"Where's Tía Ester?" she asked.

"Gone," Chane muttered, turning away from the door.

He could have been talking about any of them. All of them.

Awful possibilities poured through Lexi's mind as she glanced around the room. So much blood.

El Ladron wanted her. Not Kit. Not Tessa. Lexi was sure of it. Even as she tried to reason what must be done to correct this hideous situation, the blood again caught her attention. All this blood . . . Oh, God, whose was it? Tessa's? Kit's?

Movement at the end of the hallway caught Lexi's attention, and she whirled to face it, ready to do battle if it was El Ladron or one of his thugs.

Hank Warner made his way toward them, peering into each of the bedrooms.

"What happened? he asked.

"You tell me," Chane returned. "You were the one who got the call."

"Don't know anything, except Kit telling the dispatcher someone had broken into the house. There was a kid crying in the background."

"No," Lexi said, shaking her head.

"The call ended as though he had just hung up suddenly."

"It's El Ladron," Lexi whispered. "Oh, dear God, he doesn't want the kids. He wants me."

"And I wish the hell he had you," Chane said.

She agreed with him. She flinched anyway, the words hurting more than any blow. Whatever it took to get the kids back, that's what she would do.

"Chane, look here," Hank called from his bedroom.

Aware Lexi had followed him, Chane joined Hank in the bedroom. A piece of paper was propped up in front of the telephone. Another smear of blood covered the receiver, which was smashed on one end as though it has been used to hit something . . . or someone.

"Goddamn," he breathed. He lifted the receiver and picked up the sheet of paper. The line was dead, which didn't surprise him at all.

At his peripheral vision, Lexi appeared. He didn't have to look at her fully to know she was white, to see the stark lines of tension bracketing her mouth. He dropped his gaze to the scrawled handwriting on the sheet.

Callahan
It's an even trade. Your family for Monroe. No cops. No funny stuff. We'll make the exchange at the old mine up

Stone Gulch. Your brother says you know the place. Be there by 10:30, or your kids are dead. I have a clear view of the road. Anyone else shows besides you and Monroe, and your kids are dead.

"What is it?" Lexi asked, still at the doorway.

Chane extended his arm toward her. She came into the room and took the sheet from him, then began shaking as she read.

"El Ladron," she breathed.

"Damn his soul." Chane set the receiver back in the cradle.

"We don't have much time to meet his deadline," Hank said.

Chane glanced at the bedside clock.

"The silver mine up Stone Gulch," Hank continued, "the only one I know about is the Luckless Love. Is that the one he's talking about?"

"It's gotta be."

"That's every bit of twenty miles, and most of it is over rough road." Hank lifted the portable radio in his hand to his mouth.

Chane grasped the radio. "No cops."

"I agree with Chane," Lexi said. "He wants a trade—"

"No." Hank shook his head. "We're already involved. This is out of your hands."

"The hell it is." Chane grabbed the radio and wrenched it away from Hank.

Hank held up his hands in a placating gesture. "C'mon, man, think."

"There's not one man on the force trained for this kind of thing. You know it and I know it."

"I am," Hank replied calmly. "I didn't spend six years as a Ranger—"

"Okay, so maybe you and a platoon could take this on." Chane tapped the note. "Come alone. And that's the way we're gonna do it."

"A crime has been committed—"

"Screw the crime," Chane said. "This is my family here. I'm not risking them. We'll do it exactly like he says."

"You're being damn stupid. You can't do this alone."

"You guys can fight all you want," Lexi interrupted. "We're wasting time. There is only one way to get the kids back." She paused, waiting for both men to look at her. She swallowed. "Give him what he wants."

"You're serious," Hank said.

Lexi nodded.

"Got any better ideas?" Chane asked.

"We might be able to spring a trap," Hank said. "We could come around up the back side of the mine. If he thought she came alone, it might work."

"The road up the last several miles is open—he'd be able to see if more than one vehicle came," Chane said.

Hank stared at him a moment. "We've both been there, man. The two of us—you and me—we could do this with Lexi. If she's willing to be the bait to get the kids out—"

"I am."

Chane stared at the floor, then raised his glance to Lexi.

She understood that so far as he was concerned, she wasn't just bait. She hated knowing what they felt for one another had come to that, hated more she was to blame for El Ladron having Chane's family. She nodded, silently telling him she understood, she agreed.

"Call off the rest of your guys," Chane said.

Hank spoke into the radio, telling the dispatcher that everything was under control.

"What about the other deputy?" Chane asked.

"I'll send him back to the station," Hank assured Chane.

Chane's attention shifted to Lexi as Hank drew the other deputy outside. She had jumped back a few minutes ago as though he had struck her—and he felt as though he had. He hated the idea of El Ladron having Tessa. And he hated the idea of what El Ladron would do to Lexi.

As Lexi had done the other times Chane had seen her upset, she gathered together some internal discipline similar to his own. He could almost see her thoughts become more clear and more organized. Amazing, considering what she'd been through.

Confirming his speculation, she said, "We're going to need a first-aid kit. And blankets. We have to be able to treat the kind of shock that goes with so much blood loss."

Any other time, he might have praised her transformation from distracted to practical. He blocked her way out of the room.

"I . . . owe you an apology."

She met his gaze, her eyes reflecting her worry. Finally she nodded. "Later, Callahan. When the kids are safe. Now, where's the first-aid kit?"

He told her where it was, then watched her walk away from him. Later. God willing, they would have it.

He retrieved guns and ammunition from a locked cabinet in his bedroom. He didn't have to watch Hank to know the man double-checked the weapons with the same thoroughness that Chane had.

Within minutes they had the truck loaded with the first-aid supplies Lexi had gathered and the basic equipment Hank and Chane figured they might need.

Lexi handed Hank one of Chane's shirts just as they were getting into the truck. "No cops," she said. "Remember?"

He stripped off his uniform shirt and stuffed it behind the seat, and put on Chane's shirt.

"I had some news I was on my way to pass on to you when the call came in," Hank said after they were on their way. He glanced at Lexi. "I went to see Ellen Belsen this morning. You hit it on the nail. The guy you saw her with yesterday afternoon, Chane, is the man who sent Señora Padilla here. George Moody."

"I knew it," Chane said.

"Oh, it gets better." Hank paused dramatically. "She says this guy is El Ladron himself. How the hell did he get the kids?"

"My fault," Lexi said.

"My fault." Chane clinched a fist against the steering wheel and admitted what ate at him. "If I had stayed put. If I hadn't made the deputy take me to Lexi's house. While we were gone—"

"Nobody's fault," Hank said.

"The hell it's not," Chane muttered.

Lexi glanced sideways at him, knowing full well her own actions had set into motion Kit's and Tessa's abduction. Arguing with him, though, didn't get the kids back or solve one other damn thing.

"Tía Ester must be with them," Lexi said.

"Señora Padilla?" Hank asked.

Lexi nodded.

"Anything special we should know about this guy?" Hank asked.

"He's not bluffing." Lexi swallowed. She wasn't about to reveal the man liked hurting people. Chane didn't need any additional demons taunting him.

"I haven't been up Stone Gulch in a while," Hank said. "Remind me what the terrain is like."

"It's a rugged, heavily wooded area." Chane thought a moment, his eyes narrowed. "The mine is in the middle of a clearing. The slope approaching it isn't that steep, but it's built into the face of a ridge behind it."

Hank nodded toward the carry-all behind the cab where Chane kept much of his gear. "I hope the hell we thought of everything."

"Not likely. But it will be enough." The corner of Chane's mouth lifted, but his expression remained stony.

"I figure he's got the kids stashed in the mine."

"Yeah."

"So the trick is getting him to show himself."

"How close can we get with the truck?" Lexi asked.

"There's a hunters' camp just below the mine," Chane said. "We can get within fifty yards of it. And he'll see us coming for a long time before we get there. He's got a clear shot of the road for a long ways except for a couple of switchbacks a mile or so before the mine."

As they drove toward the turnoff to the gulch, they worked out a plan. At the hidden switchbacks, Hank and Chane would get out, and Lexi would drive the rest of the way alone.

"I don't like it," Chane said, hearing the echoes of his own voice in his head, wishing he had never said that Ladron should have Lexi. "There's got to be another way."

"If you've got a better plan," Hank said, "name it. Catching this guy on his blind side is our best shot. And to do that we have to have bait. He wants Lexi."

Chane glanced at Lexi, his gut churning. She'd never looked calmer. Bait. A cold-blooded word for sending a sacrificial lamb to slaughter. And damn her, she knew it. Knew the price for Tessa's life and Kit's was her own.

An unexpected tactile memory of her body sliding over his hit him. She judged him, and he wanted to hate her for that. He couldn't. Firsthand, he had seen what El Ladron had cost her—from the fire last night to her nightmares. He knew the depth of her fear as well as he knew his own.

He shouldn't have to ask this of her. He didn't see any other way.

Calling on the discipline and mental habit of his years in the Marines, he turned his attention back to the mission at hand, trying to remember everything he could about the terrain surrounding the mine.

"The hike is a steep climb, but it's half the distance as the road," Chane said. "We can come in from the uphill side." He slanted Lexi a glance. "Your job is to stay put until Hank and I are in position. We can't get real close. We can sneak in the rest of the way while you keep him occupied."

"It would be better to go ahead and make the exchange. Get the kids to safety before you make your move," Lexi said.

"Agreed." Chane rubbed the back of his neck. "But I didn't mean what I said back there. I don't wish he had you instead of the kids."

"I know." She met his eyes briefly, then looked away. "The kids' safety is first."

"I'm just hoping that he'll show himself when you get out of the car."

"If he does, this will be smooth as greased lightning," Hank said.

"Except, this is life," Chane muttered.

Lexi agreed with that, too, but she remained silent. Chane

and Hank wanted the kids out safely. Lexi had another, equally big concern. That Chane would be around to watch his daughter grow up.

"I suppose it's too much to hope this guy doesn't like guns," Chane muttered.

"He'll be armed to the hilt," Lexi assured them, could have told them earlier had either of them asked.

"That's what we expect," Hank said.

Chane glanced at Lexi. "After you drop us off, I want you to go slow. We need every bit of fifteen minutes. The road is bad, and you'll have every reason to take it slow. Just give Hank and I all the time you can. After you get to the hunters' camp, park and wait until he shows himself before you get out of the truck. Got it?"

She nodded.

Hank cleared his throat. "No hero stuff from you, Lexi. Based on what you told me, I don't think this guy intends for any of you to walk away from here."

Lexi silently agreed, then gave voice to a regret that had haunted her for months. "If I'd had another few weeks in Costa Léon, I could have shut him down. Instead, I got scared and ran."

"And things would have been better until the next greedy son of a bitch came along," Chane said.

"You're right." She couldn't do anything about all the other greedy men and desperate would-be parents she had watched come and go during the long months she had investigated *Las Hermanas de la Esperanza*. But she could do something about El Ladron. This time.

Lexi glanced at Chane. She still hadn't had a chance to photograph him, she thought. She wanted a picture of him with Tessa, his big hands cradling his daughter.

"Lexi?"

"If this costs Tessa her daddy, I can't live with that."

"It won't."

"We'll find a way to signal you," Hank said. "I want you to know where we are. And we need to make sure El Ladron keeps his attention on you."

"That sounds easy enough." Easy, and a thousand things that could go wrong, Lexi thought. "Besides being a trainer for wilderness survival, what did you do in the Marines?"

"If that's a tactful way of asking if I know what I'm doing, yeah, I know," Chane answered. "And so does Hank."

Lexi supposed she should have been reassured. She wasn't. This situation was no military mission, and rescuing people you loved was nothing like calculating anticipated losses in a battle plan. Warriors, Lexi reminded herself, had a nasty tendency to get themselves killed.

Hank had taken out his service revolver and was checking over the gun with the assured movements of a man who had completed the task many times. She supposed the two of them had a chance of pulling this off. Of getting back Tessa, Kit, and Tía Ester without anyone else getting hurt. In her heart, she didn't believe it.

If there was a way to get the job done without risking anyone's life but her own, she had to take it. If anyone else got hurt because of her, she couldn't live with that. She just wished she had a foolproof plan.

Too soon, Chane pulled over to the side of the road and climbed out of the cab. Lexi scooted across the seat to the driver's side.

He reached back in and cupped her head with both of his hands, stared deeply into her eyes a moment, then gave her a hard, seeking kiss.

He tore his lips away from hers. "Remember, Lexi. We need fifteen minutes. Wait here about ten minutes before you go the rest of the way."

Hank got out of the cab on the other side. Chane retrieved a backpack and a coil of rope out of the truck bed. The two of them waved at her, then swiftly climbed the slope, taking advantage of every bit of cover. Seconds later he and Hank disappeared within the timber.

Lexi, her hands shaking as she wrapped them around the steering wheel, made a note of the time on the clock of the dashboard. Against her mouth, she still felt the pressure of his kiss. What it meant, she didn't dare hazard a guess.

She stared at the trees where he had disappeared and debated following his instructions. They didn't know who had been badly hurt. Lexi assumed it was Kit. He needed Chane, an older brother who was the kind of man a boy like Kit could look up to. And Tessa. If a little girl anywhere deserved her daddy, it was Tessa. No matter how Chane had come to be her daddy.

Lexi knew El Ladron had come to Chane's house looking for her. She had put Chane's family in danger, something she could never atone for. El Ladron wanted her. If that's what it took to put Kit and Tessa back with Chane, then so be it.

Lexi put the truck into gear and drove up the road. Necessity forced her to take it slow, but she didn't want to. She wanted to arrive much ahead of Chane. She had survived El Ladron once before. God willing, she'd do so again. Either way, Kit and Tessa and Chane would be a family.

A hundred yards inside the timber, Chane heard his truck slip into gear. He stopped to look back at the road, and a second later the truck appeared and headed toward the curve where it would once again come into view from the mine. Lexi would be at the hunters' camp within another five minutes.

"What the hell is she doing?" Hank asked. "We'll never get there before she does."

Clear as a gunshot, he remembered what he had said in response to her assertion that El Ladron wanted her. *I wish the hell he had you.* And Lexi's voice as she said, *If this costs Tessa her daddy, I couldn't live with that.*

His gut knotted. He understood exactly what Lexi was doing. In her place, he would have made the same choice. Fury flowed through him—at the situation, at El Ladron, at Lexi.

"She's decided to play this out alone," Chane said.

"We'd better pray she's as resourceful as she is stubborn," Hank said, taking off at a ground-eating lope.

Chane overtook Hank, running at a pace that pushed the limits of his endurance, knowing it wasn't fast enough, praying for time he didn't have.

* * *

Lexi rounded a curve. The tailings pile for the mine was above and ahead of her. As Chane had said, the narrow road wound down a steep ridge. Halfway up the other side, she saw the grassy track that led to the hunters' camp. She didn't see anything or anyone move. The charcoal-colored four-by-four that had forced her off the highway on Berthoud Pass was parked just below the mine.

Lexi negotiated the road as fast as she dared. At the bottom, the truck's tires clattered as she crossed an old wooden bridge. The incline to the campsite was steep, and the turn onto the grassy trail was so sharp she had to stop, back up, and pull forward again. The four-by-four was parked at the edge of the trees. Lexi watched it, wondering if El Ladron was hiding inside. The windows were so darkly tinted, she couldn't tell if the vehicle was empty. After a moment's wait, she decided it was abandoned.

She parked the car, killed the engine, and left the keys in the ignition. If Kit was capable of driving back to town, that was the best bet. There was a house back at the turnoff next to the highway where he would call for help. She had to hope that El Ladron wouldn't do anything that kept him from getting what he really wanted—her.

She climbed out of the cab, and used the open door as a shield between her and the mine entrance. Two figures appeared out of the shadows and moved to the edge of the tailings pile.

Darren Burke, bogus FBI agent. He held a gun to Kit's head.

"Kit, are you okay?" she called, ignoring Burke.

"Yes." His T-shirt was ripped and blood caked the side of his face.

"Send Kit and Tessa down," Lexi shouted.

"You come up here first."

"Go back in there and tell El Ladron I'm not that stupid. If he wants me, he's got to let the kids go."

Another man appeared out of the shadows of the mine's opening, the condensation of all her worst nightmares. In his arms, he held Tessa.

"Miss Monroe. At last, we meet again."

Lexi ignored him and focused on the child. From this distance she couldn't know for sure, but Tessa looked unharmed.

"Hi, sweetie," Lexi called. "Are you okay?"

Tessa pushed against the shoulder of the man holding her. "I want to go home."

"Let the kids go," Lexi called. "That was the deal."

"Where's Callahan?" he asked.

"He didn't come. He doesn't even know about this," Lexi lied. "I'm the one who found your note."

"I don't believe you." El Ladron backed up and turned to face the open slope behind the mine. "If he's out there hoping for a bushwack, he's in for a big surprise!"

"He's not here," Lexi called urgently. "It's me you want. Send the kids down and I'll come up." She wondered where Tía Ester was, but knew she had to get the kids out of here first.

"I think you're lying."

"That's a risk you'll have to take." Kit didn't look good to her. She needed him strong enough to drive back to the highway.

"Take off your jacket. Then put your hands on your head."

Lexi did as she was told. Her jacket was nothing more than the flannel shirt Kit had given her earlier. The crisp morning air seeped through her T-shirt, and was a brisk reminder they were no longer in a Central American jungle. She put her hands on her head and stepped away from the vehicle. This had all the potential to be the worst mistake of her life. She hoped it wasn't.

"Come halfway," he ordered.

"Send the kids down," Lexi shouted back.

"A stand-off, Monroe. How much do you want them?"

Warily, Lexi moved away from the truck, coming into the open ground between the camp and the mine entrance.

El Ladron and Darren Burke watched her approach. Halfway she stopped.

"You wouldn't be armed, would you?" he asked, his voice steely. "That would be so much like you. The very rash, the very idealistic Miss Monroe. Pull your shirt up over your head and turn around. If you're armed, Monroe, these kids are dead.''

Once again, Lexi did as she was told. She grasped the bottom of the shirt and pulled it over her head, shook it out so he could see nothing was hidden within it, and turned around, baring her naked back to him. When she faced him again, she put the shirt back on. ''Let the kids go. Your note said, 'No funny stuff.' I'm not stupid enough to double-cross you.''

''You were that stupid once,'' he reminded her.

''Yeah,'' she agreed. ''And I learn from my mistakes. Send the kids down. You've got plenty of range with that rifle to shoot me anytime you want.'' She was betting her life he wouldn't want anything so simple. This man liked inflicting pain, and she felt sure he wouldn't pass up that chance.

He set Tessa down. ''Go on with you.''

Burke let go of Kit, who slumped over like a half-empty sack of flour. He tumbled down the rocky slope of the tailings pile.

Lexi cried out and ran forward.

She knelt beside Kit, and El Ladron pointed the rifle at her. ''Leave the boy alone. Come up here, now.'' A flick of his wrist, and the safety was off.

Lexi ignored him, praying her instincts about this were right. If they weren't, she was about to get them all killed. She put her shoulder under Kit's and hoisted him to his feet. Tessa scrambled down the rocks until she reached them. Lexi briefly touched her hair.

Lexi said softly, ''Tessa, this is very important, so you have to do exactly as I say.''

''I don't like that man,'' Tessa said. ''He's mean. And he hurt Kit.''

''Tessa, listen to me.''

She nodded solemnly.

''I want you to run as fast as you can until you get to the truck. And when you get there, I want you to climb inside and sit on the seat like a good little girl until Kit gets there. Okay?''

''Okay.'' She took off across the clearing and Lexi breathed a sigh of relief. Returning her attention to Kit, she said, "Can you walk?"

A pressure bandage around Kit's thigh was soaked through, and more blood seeped from the bottom of his jeans. One of his eyes was swollen nearly shut, his lip was split, and he had a gash into his hairline that looked as though it would need stitches.

"Get up here, Monroe!" El Ladron ordered.

"When you get to the truck," she whispered in Kit's ear. "Get in and drive. There's a ranch out next to the highway. Go there."

"Where's Ch—"

"Shh," she commanded softly. "Kit, can you do it?"

He nodded. She steadied him as he took the first tentative steps toward the truck. She heard crashing down the tailings pile and turned around just in time to face Darren Burke. He grabbed her by the arm and wrenched it behind her back. He urged her up the tailings pile until she stood face to face with El Ladron.

His eyes were as empty as she remembered. Fighting memories of her beating at this man's hands, she sensed her hunch was right. He wanted to play on her fear. She had just one other worry.

"Where's Señora Padilla?" Lexi asked.

He nodded toward the mine entrance.

"She's in there."

Lexi heard the motor to Chane's truck start up. She prayed Kit had the strength to handle the vehicle over the rough terrain.

"I've waited a long time for this," he said with a flash of teeth. His look was at once savage and satisfied.

"We don't have a lot of time," Darren Burke said, his hold on Lexi tightening. "Let's get this over with and get going."

The pressure on her arm was brutal, but Lexi refused to give either man the satisfaction of so much as a wince. She'd made her choices, and she had no regrets.

"True," El Ladron agreed smoothly. "However, some things do require attention."

He was no taller than Lexi, but she had brutal memories of

just how strong he was. Burke might be the bigger man, but she knew El Ladron was the more dangerous.

"I want to see the señora," she said.

El Ladron stepped away and nodded to Burke. "Then, by all means, you shall see her."

Burke pushed Lexi into the mine. Sudden murky darkness closed around her, and unable to see, she fell. Behind her she heard El Ladron chuckle. He had sounded like this before he had ordered her tied so he could beat her. She had sworn then she would never again be caught in that position.

Never. "Never" turned out to be just a bit more than fourteen months long.

"Alexandra?" Tía Ester sat on the ground next to the wall of the mine. *"Por Dios."*

Lexi got up and went to her. *"¿Está usted bien?"* Tía Ester didn't look as though she had been physically harmed. Yet . . .

"Sí."

"Now isn't this touching?" El Ladron sneered.

In Spanish, Tía Ester said to Lexi, "I'm so sorry, Alexandra. He thanked me for leading him to you. I didn't know. *Por Dios.* I did not know."

Lexi patted her shoulder.

"He told me there were no babies. He bragged that I was so easy to deceive. And then, he pointed at sweet little Tessa and told me that she was my Estella." Her composure began to fracture, and she patted her breast. "Alexandra, how can this be so? I saw the photographs of Señor Chane's wife and Tessa."

"Tell her," El Ladron ordered.

Lexi looked up to meet his gaze.

"Señor Callahan," El Ladron spat. "A paragon of the community. Tell the good señora what kind of people he and his dear departed wife are. Tell how they went to Costa Léon and—"

"No," Tía Ester whispered. Her hands tightened around Lexi's. "This evil man lies."

"Tell her!" he thundered.

"Tessa came from *Las Hermanas de la Esperanza,*" Lexi said. "Tía Ester, I didn't know until yesterday."

"Before I die I must know—"

"You're not going to die!" Lexi said fiercely.

"Tessa. Is she my granddaughter?"

"I don't know, Tía."

Tía Ester closed her eyes and pressed her hands against her face. Tears seeped from between her fingers and her shoulders shook.

Lexi helped Tía Ester stand. "You can let her go, too."

El Ladron smiled, his expression feral and evil. "By all means. She's free to go."

Lexi gave her a push toward the bright entrance.

He sauntered closer as though he had all the time in the world. Lexi fought her instinct to step back.

"You tremble. You remember what it is to be frightened of me?" he asked, his voice suddenly soft, seductive.

God help her, she did.

Chapter 24

"You've got two choices, Monroe," El Ladron said.

"You make it sound like there really is a choice."

He laughed, a sound that made her flinch in spite of her resolve not to react to him in any way.

"Oh, I think you'll like this choice quite a lot." He motioned to the inside of the mine where darkness became utterly black. "I've been back there. A shaft back there drops"—he held his hands wide—"into nothingness." His fingers snapped.

He touched one of the ancient timbers holding back the rock. Lexi's gaze followed the movement. Imbedded within the timber was a stick of dynamite. Its fuse was attached to others, closer to the entrance of the mine.

El Ladron laughed. "Ah, Miss Monroe, if you could only see your face." He took a gun out of his belt with one hand, and a length of rope appeared in the other. "The choice really, is quite simple. Do you want me to shoot you before we dynamite the opening to this old mine?" The uncivilized gleam Lexi remembered too well was back in his eyes. She hadn't seen his face, then, but she remembered the voice, remembered his eyes. "I rather think by then, you'll be quite anxious to have me shoot you."

"I imagine you'll do whatever you think hurts me the most," Lexi returned, surprised her voice sounded steady. "Either way, it doesn't matter. They know who you are, George Moody. I may be dead by then, but at the very least, you'll be in prison."

"At least you won't be leaving this mine." He flipped the revolver's safety off, and motioned with the gun. "Over there."

"Drop the gun!" came Chane's voice from the front of the mine.

He stood silhouetted against the bright light at the opening of the mine, a snub-nosed pistol in his hands. Next to him, Hank stood with his service revolver drawn in one hand, his rifle aimed with the other.

Lexi's glance darted from El Ladron to Burke. He half held out his hands. El Ladron didn't move a muscle. Within that flashing instant, Lexi knew he wouldn't surrender. Knew he would kill first.

"No!" Lexi shouted and rushed forward. She knocked El Ladron's arms up as he fired a shot.

Darren Burke raised his arm the rest of the way and reached for his gun.

Lexi let go of El Ladron and slammed into Burke. She knocked him to the ground. He pushed her away with a backhanded slap to the side of her head. The force knocked her flat.

She heard a volley of shots. Someone screamed with pain.

The ground beneath her trembled. Lexi rolled onto her back. The timbers above her creaked as rock shifted. She scrambled to her feet.

She grabbed Tía Ester and pushed her toward the mine's opening. "Run!"

Darren Burke ran after Tía Ester.

Between Lexi and the opening, El Ladron lay on his side, his leg drawn up against his chest. Blood seeped from a wound in his calf. He still held a pistol, which he turned and aimed at Lexi.

At the mine's entrance, Chane watched, horrified, as El Ladron braced himself on one elbow, the pistol in his hand aimed at Lexi.

"Drop it!" Hank yelled.

El Ladron turned toward him, aiming the pistol.

Chane fired. At the same moment, El Ladron lifted his gun arm toward the ceiling of the mine and fired.

An explosion rocked the mine. Lexi vanished behind a monstrous belch of dust.

''No!'' Chane roared.

His cry was lost beneath the rumble of the blast. Rocks and dirt and timbers shot toward them. From within the belching chaos, the señora appeared. Chane caught her beneath one arm and Hank caught her beneath the other. They ran from the opening, stumbling down the tailings pile. Beneath their feet, the ground heaved like a living, breathing monster.

At the bottom of the tailings pile, Chane let go of the señora and turned around. Dust billowed from the mouth of the mine, like smoke from a dragon.

He climbed back up the talus slope to the mine's entrance. Rock and timbers sealed it. He lifted his arms and roared, ''No! Damn you, no!''

A final slide of gravel and sand and rock tumbled into place. Sound subsided except for his own rasping breath and the wail of a woman faced with inconsolable grief.

Chane clawed at the rock, desperation giving him the strength to toss aside boulders he shouldn't have been able to move. Lexi was trapped in there. She couldn't die! She couldn't! *Damn you, Lexi. Why didn't you wait?* It was a question he knew the answer to. Her way of making sure Tessa and Kit escaped.

Clearly, her husky voice echoed through his head. *If this costs Tessa her daddy, I couldn't live with that. Damn you, Chane Callahan. I could have loved you.* He pushed aside another boulder. . . . *loved you.*

The cold fear inside him expanded, consumed him. She couldn't be dead. She was trapped in there, but she was *not* dead. She had to be alive.

Damn her for not listening to him. For always being a tough

guy. *Lexi, why didn't you wait?* A moan of terrible anguish
filled the air, shocking him when he realized it was his.

Somehow she had gotten the kids out. *Tessa. More precious
than life!* No! Lexi's life couldn't be the price he paid for his
daughter. No.

He and Hank had been high on the hillside when they saw
his pickup drive away. With the binoculars, he'd confirmed
Tessa and Kit were in the pickup. They were going to be
okay. Hank had pulled out his police radio and called in a
report that Kit and Tessa were on the way. An ambulance
and police would meet them before they got back to the
highway.

And Lexi . . . she had to be alive. No other possibility was
acceptable.

Chane tossed aside rock after rock. He loved her, damn
it. He hadn't expected to, hadn't wanted to. That didn't
change the fact one bit. Whatever she wanted, she'd have.
If she could forgive him for being part of it when Rose bought
Tessa, he wanted Lexi in his life. If she couldn't and she
wanted to leave, he'd let her go. Just let her be alive, God.
Alive.

A jean-clad leg appeared within the rubble. Logic told Chane
this had to be El Ladron's partner. Even so, Chane feared this
was Lexi.

At his side, Hank uttered a prayer that echoed his own.

Chane barely heard him. He cleared away more rock, uncov-
ering a hand. A large, masculine hand.

Chane sat back on his heels as tears burned at his eyes. This
wasn't Lexi! Thank God.

If the tunnel inside hadn't collapsed, she might be okay. If
she had survived the blast, she'd be working to find a way out.
If she wasn't unconscious. If she wasn't injured. If El Ladron
had died and wasn't doing something awful to her.

The horror of Lexi buried inside the mine resounded through
Chane, and he renewed his effort digging.

"I'll sure be glad when more help gets here," Hank said.

Chane stopped and looked at his friend. "Help?"

Hank motioned toward the radio sitting on top of the rope and pack and weapons. "The calvary is on the way. We'll get her out."

Chane didn't answer, just kept digging through rubble with Herculean effort he feared was too little, too late.

"I'm not sure you and I could have done any better." Hank squeezed Chane's shoulder. "She accomplished what she set out to do."

"Yeah," Chane agreed, his voice hoarse.

"She's okay." Hank said it with the tone of voice designed to prepare Chane that she wasn't.

"She's not dead," he said flatly.

Lexi coughed and rolled onto her side. Her head hurt, and for a moment she couldn't figure out where she was. She opened her eyes. Absolute darkness met her gaze. Never had she seen anything blacker.

In a flood, the memory of the last few minutes washed over her. El Ladron had fired at the dynamite. In horror, she had watched the opening to the mine vanish. Something had knocked her off her feet, which was the last thing she remembered. There was still dust hanging in the air, so she couldn't have been unconscious for a long time, she decided.

Had El Ladron died, or was he in here somewhere waiting for her?

That thought was the only thing that kept her from crying out. She kept her eyes open. Gradually the darkness took on varying shades of black. She couldn't remember which way was toward the front of the mine.

Realizing that she was gradually able to make out her surroundings, she waited with a photographer's patience for her vision to become clearer.

The glint of something shiny on the floor caught her eye. Within the complete blackness of the mine, distance was nearly impossible to judge, but she decided it was several yards away.

She focused on the object and eventually made out the shape of a gun.

Her heart stopped, then resumed beating double time. As she stared at the gun, she became aware that the impact of the explosion had knocked her farther into the mine. Lexi watched a long time before she became convinced the gun was still held in El Ladron's hand. Silently, she moved toward it. Closer inspection confirmed her hunch.

She couldn't decide what to do. She wanted to take the gun away from him. She wanted to determine whether he was dead or not. She was convinced that if she touched him, he'd grab her.

She stared at the hand and the gun for a long time. Each settling sound of the avalanche unnerved her.

This is ridiculous, she silently scolded herself. Stand up. Step on his wrist and take the gun out of his hand. The idea of his hands clamping around her ankle was almost as real as the actual fact.

Her heart pounding, she finally stood up. Step by slow step she approached him, feeling as though she walked through a void.

She stepped on his wrist and wrenched the gun from his grasp. Shaking, she backed away from him, pointing the gun in his direction.

"I've got the gun," she said aloud.

The words echoed around her, and they sounded totally stupid. She had the urge to giggle. Almost as if to prove to herself she wasn't hysterical, she dropped to her knees, searched for the extended arm that had held the gun.

In her nightmares, El Ladron's cruel eyes had haunted her and his merciless hands had hurt her. Beneath her fingertips, she could find no pulse. She kept expecting his arm to twist suddenly and a hand to grab her. Fear swamping her, her heart galloping, she kept her hand on his wrist until she was positive he was dead. She still expected him to rise from the floor of the cavern like her worst nightmare.

Dead. He was dead.

Relief came with a cold sweat that made her shiver.

"Hello," she called. With the knowledge that El Ladron was dead, her consciousness expanded beyond him. "Hello!"

Her voice echoed around her. She listened carefully, wondering if anyone at all was on the other side of the pile of rock. If she began digging, did she have ten feet to dig through? Or more? She sat on her heels trying to remember how deep inside the mine she'd been when Chane arrived.

God, let him be okay. Had Tía Ester gotten out? The idea that she might have been buried underneath the rock made tears burn at the back of Lexi's eyes.

As she tried to decide what to do next, she kept having the feeling that she smelled fresh air. Probably from a ventilation shaft, she decided. Remembering El Ladron had told her there was a deep shaft, she was reluctant to leave the spot where she stood. At least here, she was safe for the moment.

If El Ladron knew there was a bottomless shaft, she thought, he had explored in the mine deep enough to know.

And that required light.

Touching him again to see if he had a flashlight required almost as much courage as taking away the gun had. A part of her still wasn't convinced he was dead.

She bent over his body and, exploring with her hands, discovered he was half buried under the rock. In his hip pocket she found what she was looking for. A long flashlight. She flipped the switch, and it came on.

The light flooding the interior of the mine was as welcome as daylight. Lexi shone the beam on El Ladron's body. The upper part of his torso and head were buried by the rock slide. Any doubts she had that he wasn't dead were vanquished.

"Hello," she called loudly, wondering if she could be heard on the other side of the slide. She couldn't hear anything except her own breathing. There was no answer. She didn't know whether that meant she couldn't be heard or if no one was there.

She aimed the beam of light down the mine shaft. It fell away at a gradual slope. Lexi wet her finger and held it up. From the inside of the mine, she felt the slightest movement of air over her damp finger. She surveyed the rock slide again. If she had to dig her way out of the mine, there'd be time for that later.

But if there was fresh air, there had to be another way out. She could sit around and wait for a rescue that might be impossible. Maybe digging through the collapsed entrance could make the whole thing cave in. She could wait and hope and drive herself crazy. Or she could do what she had always done. Take care of herself.

Had Tía Ester gotten out, she wondered again. She kept thinking about Kit and hoped he had safely gotten to help. She believed Chane was safe, though she couldn't have said why. If Kit was okay, Lexi had what she had wanted—Chane's family was together.

Her throat tightened as she remembered all the hurtful things they had said to one another yesterday and this morning. Last night he had urged her to focus on what was important. At the time, she thought she had. Only, some things were more important than others. Love. And she had been so sure of her convictions, she had thrown it away.

Chane holding her through her nightmares, Chane giving her the space to be loyal to Joe even when he hated it, Chane running through fire for her. Chane . . . proving again and again that he cared for her. And she hadn't been willing to give him the benefit of a single doubt—had believed an envelope full of old papers rather than the actions of the man.

Focus on what was important.

Squaring her shoulders, she faced the black maw of the mine's interior. Getting out of here came first. And after that . . . that last kiss he gave her tickled to life a thread of hope that maybe he'd forgive her for judging him.

Shining the light ahead of her, she made her way cautiously farther into the mine. Here and there, water seeped through the walls and ceiling of the shaft. The sound of water falling became louder. A few minutes later, she came across El Ladron's bottomless shaft.

She picked up a rock and let it drop into the shaft, counting under her breath, "One one thousand. Two one thousand."

She counted to five before she heard it hit bottom. Unable to remember whether that meant the shaft was fifty or five hundred feet deep, she knew either distance was farther than she wanted to contemplate falling.

She carefully made her way around the edge of it. The scent of fresh air became stronger. The angle of the tunnel changed, and she began walking level instead of down.

She didn't know whether it was fifteen minutes later or an hour later when she found the ventilation shaft. A barely discernible disk of light filtered toward her. Lexi studied the shaft, which was narrow enough to climb. Narrow enough, in fact, that she worried about getting stuck.

Jagged rocks jutted here and there into the shaft, providing footholds and handholds—assuming they would even support her weight. She lifted her eyes toward the narrow beam of light, wishing she could judge how far it was to the top, wondering how big the opening at the top was. If it wasn't big enough to get out, climbing back into the mine would be awful.

Worse, it was a long way to fall.

A cold knot clinched in her stomach as she contemplated climbing out of the mine. Her fear of falling hadn't died with El Ladron. She stood, staring at the faint sliver of light far above her. Who knew where this shaft was in relation to the mine opening? Even if she was sure a rescue was on the way— and she wasn't—no one would be looking for this shaft. She thought about going back to the head of the mine and calling again. Only El Ladron was there. Dead or alive, she didn't want to see him.

Lexi looked up again. Unlike the granite face of a cliff, the shaft had plenty of handholds and footholds. Unlike a cliff, most of these weren't strong enough to hold her weight. She would have to brace herself in the narrow chimney, dependent on her own strength. If she wanted out, this was the way.

Lexi turned off the flashlight and put it into the front of the waist band on her jeans. She remembered thinking the waist was too big when she put the jeans on. That seemed like a million years ago. Because they were too big, the flashlight fit next to her belly, cold and reassuring. She'd have to remember to thank Kit.

Surely by now he had the medical attention he needed. Regardless of what happened, he was safe. As was Tessa. And Tía Ester. Lexi closed her eyes a moment, trying to remember exactly where Tía Ester had been when the mine opening collapsed. "Please let her be safe," Lexi prayed, opening her eyes once again.

She took a deep breath and lifted herself into the chimney. The shaft was narrow enough that she could brace her weight on opposite sides, which made climbing somewhat easier. She took her time with each move. The first time she paused to catch her breath, the light above her didn't seem appreciably closer. She rested for a count of fifty, then began climbing again. The second time she stopped for a rest, the light was much closer, and she knew she had passed the halfway point.

She didn't look down, knowing below her she'd see only the inky blank of the mine's interior and her own fear—urging her to believe that El Ladron waited for her.

She braced herself within the narrow chimney, resting, marshalling her energy for the balance of the climb out. Inevitably, her thoughts returned to Chane. Again, she felt the imprint of that last kiss against her mouth. Would he forgive her, she wondered. Four years ago when she had first heard of El Ladron, she could have never imagined this was how things would turn out. Rumors and innuendo were all she had then, and it had been another eighteen months before she got the first solid lead that babies were being sold.

Four years ago. Odd pieces suddenly clicked into place, and Lexi felt as though she had just brought an image into focus. Four years ago, Joe Robertson had still been in the Middle East. And Chane had been in Mosul. And the airplane ticket to Costa Léon had been for one person—Rose Callahan.

Lexi didn't know what it all meant, but one thing she was sure of. Whether Chane had approved of his wife's actions or not, once Tessa was in his home, she became his daughter.

Being loved and cherished and cared for the way any child should be. And that was what counted.

Lexi looked up at the light above her. God willing, she'd soon have the chance to tell Chane. *Focus on what's important.* She loved him. Nothing was more important than that.

Lexi took a deep breath and began climbing again.

Chapter 25

A crew of people arrived. Where there had been only Hank and Chane to dig through the rock slide at the opening of the mine, there were now men with the equipment to make the job go faster.

At the back of Chane's mind, some important detail just beyond his grasp nagged at him. Frustrated that he couldn't pin it down, he worked harder than anyone, shoveled faster, lifted bigger stones, pushed more intently.

"Pete has your brother on the radio," Hank said to Chane sometime later. Chane couldn't have said whether minutes or hours had passed since the explosion.

He left the mine entrance, his focus still on Lexi. He knew Kit was okay—he'd been assured of that as soon as he had seen Kit drive Tessa away.

A half-dozen vehicles, including a couple of four-by-fours from the sheriff's office, were parked in the hunters' camp.

"Hey, bro," came Kit's voice over the radio when Chane took it from a deputy.

"Hey, yourself," Chane returned. "Are you all right?"

"I'm okay. They're gonna take me down to the clinic in

Granby for some stitches, but it's not a big deal. Really. And Tessa, she's fine, too.''

Chane closed his eyes, reliving the incredible relief he had felt when he had realized his daughter and his brother were safe. Thank God they were okay.

"Lexi," Kit said. "Is she okay? And Tía Ester?"

"The señora is fine," Chane said.

"The paramedics said there was an explosion at the mine." Kit paused. "Chane, what happened to Lexi?"

"She . . . she didn't get out." Chane's voice clogged. "Listen, I'm glad you're okay. Take care of Tessa. I've gotta go."

He pressed the disconnect button and ended the call. All the digging at the shaft opening was going slow. Too slow. She could be in their, injured, bleeding to death in the time it took to get to her.

There had to be another way in, another opening . . . a ventilation shaft. The detail that had been eluding him slipped into place. The mine had a ventilation shaft. And if it wasn't plugged, that was the quickest way into it. Assuming he could find it.

He scaled the slope, his hurry making him clumsy. He began quartering the area, checking each section, measuring his distance from the mine's opening. With any luck, the opening to the ventilation shaft would be in plain sight, not covered with a bush or a fallen tree or any of the dozens of other changes that might have taken place since the Luckless Love was built.

Chane stopped to catch his breath after searching the first quadrant he had visually marked off. There was a momentary lull in the activity at the mine's entrance, and Chane heard another sound. More subtle. More like that of a single rock falling a long ways.

"Lexi!" he shouted.

Again, there was the almost imperceptible sound of rock falling. Chane headed in the direction of its source. He stopped to listen again and heard nothing. He moved, then listened again. His patience was rewarded with the same sound again. Seconds later, he almost stumbled over the hole. No wider than his shoulders, it was black and deep.

"Lexi!"

Below him one of the shades of black shifted.

"Down here."

Chane's heart lodged against his breastbone, then resumed pounding at breakneck speed.

"Lexi!"

"That's my name." Chane knew her well enough to know the trace of humor was a cover for her fear and vulnerability.

Chane dropped to his stomach and peered into the hole. Lexi was many feet below him. "Honey, am I glad to see you!" Sitting up, he called, "Hank!"

Still at the mouth of the mine, helping the others dig, Hank looked up, his face covered with dirt and grit. Fleetingly, Chane realized he looked just as bad.

"Yo!"

"I found her. Bring up my coil of rope!" Lying back down on his stomach, Chane said to Lexi, "Hang tight, honey. Hank's coming."

"A rope will help," she said. "I've been having trouble finding anything stable enough to hold me."

"You weren't hurt in the blast?"

"Nah."

That tough-guy humor again, Chane noticed, his throat tightening. She'd given herself over to El Ladron to save his family, and now she was climbing up a chimney that was probably more unstable than any cliff she'd been on. She had more courage than anyone he'd ever known.

"You don't sound too much worse for the wear, either."

"I'm fine," he assured her, just then noticing the backs of his hands were scraped and his shirt was torn.

"Is Kit—"

"He's fine. He's on his way to the clinic in Granby. He needs some stitches, but he's fine."

"And Tessa?"

"Fine, too."

"Thank God. Did Tía Ester get out?"

Chane heard a tremor in her voice. "Yeah. She made it."

"I'm glad."

The tremor became more pronounced. Chane didn't know

if the source came from relief or fear. She'd made it so far, and he didn't want her thinking about the precarious position she was in. Chane added, "The big guy behind her didn't, though. We found him in the rubble."

"That was Darren Burke. Our phony FBI agent. Is Tía Ester okay?"

"Upset. Physically, though, she's okay." Chane glanced back down the slope where one of the paramedics that had arrived on the scene was examining her. "You can see for yourself in a couple of minutes."

At the sound of approaching footfalls, Chane lifted his head to watch Hank run the last twenty feet up the slope.

"I should have remembered the ventilation shaft," Hank said. "I'm glad you found it."

"I wish I had remembered sooner," Chane replied, taking the coil of rope. He tied a loop on the end of it and fed it down the hole. "Here comes the rope, honey," he called to Lexi. "Let me know when you've got it secured around you and I'll pull you out."

"My kind of guy. Too bad you didn't show up twenty-five feet ago. I wouldn't have been in such a hurry to get out if I'd known a ride was on the way," she said.

Chane couldn't smile at her sass. He imagined her trembling, prayed except for her being frightened that she was unharmed.

Nearly a minute passed before she said, "Ready."

Chane sat up and braced his feet on either side of the opening. Hank stood behind him, the rope threaded behind his shoulders.

"You don't have to do anything but walk up as I pull," Chane told her. He glanced at Hank, and like a well-trained team, they pulled her up the remainder of the shaft, a distance of more than fifty feet, Chane judged.

"I sure hope you've got a candy bar or something," she said, her voice much closer. "I'm starved."

Chane chuckled, the sound a release of tension and an expression of hope.

A second later, her head appeared out of the hole between Chane's legs. Her face was dirty and her hair was a mess. No woman had ever looked more beautiful to him.

"Hi, Callahan." Her smile began bright and became watery. "Oh, Chane. You don't know how glad I am to see you."

"I have a fair idea," he said gruffly. He lifted her into his arms and away from the hole.

She felt so good. Overwhelming relief surfaced, and he shuddered beneath its intensity. Holding her tight, he buried his face in her neck, then lifted his face so he could look at her.

Tears tracked down her face, but she smiled.

"Are you really okay?" he whispered.

"Yeah."

"Do you have any idea how mad I am at you?"

"You don't act mad," she said with a sniff.

"Don't let that fool you," he growled. "I'm furious."

"I know," she whispered. "And you have every reason to be. It's my fault El Ladron came. My fault Tessa and Kit were—"

"Shut up," he ordered. "That's not why I'm mad at you."

She nodded as if understanding. "And I accused you of horrible things—of buying Tessa—"

"Lexi—"

"I don't care about that," she rushed on. "Oh, God, I've been so stupid. While I was climbing out of the mine, I kept thinking this wasn't fair. I'd just met you. I'd just fallen in love for the first time in my life—"

"Are you really?" he asked, his voice husky.

"Yes," she whispered. "I love you."

He cupped his hands around her face. "You're not alone, honey. You'll never have to be alone again."

"Forgive me," she whispered. "I'm so sorry for—"

"There's nothing to forgive," he said. "And I can see there's only one way to shut you up." He kissed her. Hard. Fierce need and overwhelming relief swept through him.

A cheer accompanied by cat calls and whistles made Chane lift his head. He stood up, noticing for the first time that Hank had left them alone. Pulling Lexi to her feet, he faced the rescue workers on the slope below them, and said to Lexi, "Smile. We're on stage."

Tucking her close to him, they walked down the hill. The

one person Lexi hadn't expected to see hovering at the edge of the hunters' camp where the cars were parked was Ellen Belsen.

She met them in the middle of the meadow.

"Chane, where are the kids?" Ellen asked.

"Didn't someone tell you?" he returned. "They're on the way to the clinic in Granby."

"Someone said Kit had been stabbed."

"Yeah," Chane said. "But he's going to be okay."

Ellen's hand crept to her throat. "I'm so sorry Chane." With her other hand, she took one of Lexi's. "And your house. My God." She closed her eyes briefly. "George Moody called me last night and told me to look across the lake. From my house I saw it, and I was terrified that I'd be next."

"He's dead," Lexi told her. Somehow saying the words out loud made the fact more real. "He's dead," she repeated.

Ellen's hand fiddled with her collar, and her gaze darted around the clearing before she met Chane's eyes. "All I wanted," she whispered, "was a baby."

Lexi met Chane's eyes. He shrugged, and they both looked back at Ellen.

"I got interested in adopting a baby because of you, Lexi. And I thought I was being so noble, you know. I had my little boys, but I also thought I was doing a great thing."

"You were," Lexi said. "I don't understand."

"I helped some other couples find babies to adopt. You wouldn't believe the red tape."

"And Rose wanted to avoid the red tape," Chane said.

Ellen nodded. "By that time I knew there were ways to get a baby that weren't quite . . ."

"Legal?" His voice was clipped.

"Yes. I put her in touch with some people." She swallowed. "And they paid me." Her voice dropped to a whisper. "I knew it was wrong. But I did it anyway, and I kept the money."

"I'm not asking you to explain about that," Chane said, then asked the question that had most puzzled him. "Why are there two sets of papers?"

"I tried to talk Rose out of that. She should have told you

the truth." Ellen took a deep breath. "The adoption papers she had you sign are worthless, Chane. She did that to throw you off, knowing you'd expect something. The birth certificate that I gave you is the real one. I don't know what your legal rights are, but according to that certificate, Tessa is yours."

Mine, Chane thought. Was it really that simple? It wasn't right. He knew that without a doubt. But he hoped his attorney would confirm it was just that simple—Tessa was his child.

"I never meant you any harm," Ellen said, briefly touching Chane's arm. "I'm sorry."

She gave him a last long glance, then walked away.

Lexi watched her go. "I would never have imagined my photo essay would have caused all this."

"Ellen got interested. And she helped Rose get Tessa."

"And got all of us involved with El Ladron. I'll regret that for the rest of my life."

Chane tucked a strand of Lexi's hair behind her ear. "It turned out all right." He lifted her face toward him with his cupped palm. "I have a daughter I adore. I have a woman who feels like the other half of my soul. How can I regret that?"

The house was almost back to normal by the time they returned. Hank had called in an investigative unit, which finished its work before they returned to the house. Somewhere he'd found a couple of volunteers to come in and clean things up. They were just finished when Chane and Lexi walked in with the kids. Someone had brought by a casserole, and the aroma wafted from the kitchen.

They had stopped to pick up Tessa and Kit, who were waiting at the clinic. Kit's leg had been stitched up and the cuts and abrasions on his face had been treated. Thankfully, the doctor didn't think he had a concussion.

Tessa squirmed to be put down the minute they came into the house, then she skipped toward the back door. "I have to go find Daisy," she said.

"Okay," Lexi said.

Chane draped an arm around her shoulder. "Are you and the dog a package deal?"

Lexi angled her head to look at him. "Is there one of us you don't want?"

"Nope. I want you both. Tessa, now. She might be a harder sell. Much as she likes you, I think she prefers the dog."

Happiness bubbled up, and Lexi poked him. "Talk like that is going to get you in trouble."

He wrapped a hand around her finger. "I think I can handle it."

"*¿Señor?*"

Chane looked beyond Lexi. Tía Ester stood in the middle of the hallway, her black suit on, her suitcase and satchel in her hand. She looked like the stern matriarch she had been when he first met her.

Letting go of Lexi, he approached her. "What's this?"

She lifted her chin and met his eyes. "It is time for me to leave." Her chin quivered and her dark eyes became very bright. She pressed her lips together, then said, "To return to my home."

Chane took the satchel and suitcase from her. "Why?"

"I led El Ladron here." The shimmer in her eyes became brighter and a single tear spilled down her cheek. "I was a foolish old woman who thought she could find her granddaughter. Instead, I led that evil man here. Señor Robertson is dead. Alexandra's beautiful house is gone, and El Ladron tried to kill her. He violated your home, and he hurt Kit. These things . . ." She paused and swallowed. "These things would not have happened if I—"

"None of this was your fault," Chane said. "I don't blame you."

Tía Ester pursed her lips and shook her head. "You don't understand."

"Then explain it."

"Tessa—"

"Loves you," Chane finished.

Another tear followed the first. "If Tessa is my granddaughter . . . I would sign the paper that makes her your daughter. No child could have a better father.''

Chane took one of the señora's hands in his and glanced at Lexi. "And if I could pick a grandmother for her, it would be you. Please stay.''

Lexi put her arms around Tía Ester. "He wouldn't ask if he didn't mean it.''

"Hey bro,'' Kit called from the back of the house. "Brad and a couple of other guys want to come over after dinner and watch movies. Is that okay?''

"The TV is broken.''

"Oh, yeah. Well, maybe we can do something else. And Tía Ester, maybe you'll make some of that fry bread for us?''

The back door slammed and Tessa ran back into the house. "Guess what, Tía? Daisy likes to play ball. Did you know that?''

Chane glanced back down at Tía Ester. "How can you resist that?'' he asked. "We all need you.''

She glanced at Lexi, who nodded. "He's right. We do.''

A smile lit Tía Ester's face. "And you two,'' she said. "You are getting married. Yes?''

"I don't know,'' Chane drawled. "There's been so much else going on around here, I haven't had time to ask her.''

Tía Ester pointed a finger at him. "These things are important. You take time.'' She picked up her suitcase and satchel and returned to the bedroom. A moment later, she returned wearing an apron, Tessa and Daisy tagging at her heels.

"Strange, isn't it?'' Lexi mused.

Chane lifted an eyebrow.

"I blamed myself for leading El Ladron to your family.''

"And so did Tía and Ellen Belsen.'' Chane took Lexi's hand. "I'm glad the bastard is dead.''

Lexi nodded toward the kitchen, where she heard Tía and Tessa talking. "You're a good man to let her stay.''

"Selfish is more like it,'' Chane answered. "She's good for Tessa and Kit.''

"Ah.'' Lexi put her arms around him. "A practical man.''

"Very."

"So, Callahan, are you going to ask me to marry you?"

Once she never would have been so bold. Once she would have been sure no man could love her the way Chane loved her. He had been there for her, as promised. He had given her *anything*, as promised.

"Depends." His arms came around her, and he kissed her. "I want to make sure the lady will say yes."

Lexi returned his kiss. "Oh, she'll say yes."

"I love you, Alexandra Monroe." He wrapped his arms securely around her and lifted her off her feet.

The feeling was unsettling, delicious, wonderful. She had lost almost everything, and she had discovered what was important. Giving love. Not just to Chane, but to Tessa and Kit. She lifted her face to receive his kiss.

Being loved by this man was better than any of her dreams. She intended to hold on to that for the next eternity or so. They had a sacred trust to fulfill. Not just to Tessa and Kit, but to each other.

Dear Reader,

From the time I first learned to read, I loved knights in shining armor, whether Prince Valiant in the Sunday paper or the prince rescuing Sleeping Beauty from an endless sleep. When I was a little older, Frank Yerby, Zane Gray, and Leon Uris introduced me to contemporary knights, all the more interesting because their armor was tarnished. I loved the adventures of those less-than-perfect knights, but most compelling to me were their romances. As I grew older still, I cherished knights who fell in love with strong, courageous women who deserved the undying love and loyalty bestowed on them. Those knights roamed the pages of romance novels. Within me came alive my own stories of modern-day knights and their ladies. Thus was born Chane Callahan and Lexi Monroe.

I think we each have times in our life when we'd like to lay our problems at someone else's feet, just as Lexi would like to do. A knight would do nicely—a man whose word is his bond, a man who would run through fire for the woman he loves, a man who would face down the devil himself to protect his child. For me, Chane Callahan is such a man.

I hope you enjoyed reading A SACRED TRUST as much as I enjoyed writing it.

> May all life's blessings be yours,
> Sharon Mignerey
> E-Mail Address: Sharon−Mignerey@PRODIGY.COM

P.S. I hope you'll watch for my next knight in tarnished armor. Gray Murdock is a burned-out detective with a single Achilles heel—he cannot resist a woman in trouble. His rescue of Audrey Sussman demands he give the one thing he has sworn to keep—his heart. His story, PUMA'S LAIR, is scheduled for October 1997.